STRANDED

A NOVEL

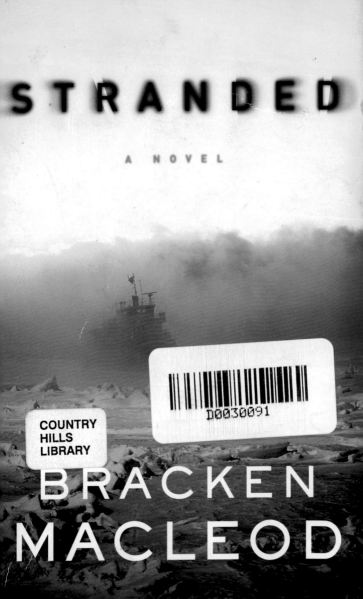

BRACKEN MACLEOD

"As brilliant as it is disturbing. Bracken MacLeod
joins the ranks of today's top horror writers."
—JONATHAN MABERRY, *New York Times* bestselling
author of *Patient Zero*

TOR

$9.99
($13.99 CAN)

ISBN 978-0-7653-8244-3

US $9.99 / CAN $13.99

5 0 9 9 9

Also by Bracken MacLeod

STRANDED

Bracken MacLeod

TOR

A TOM DOHERTY ASSOCIATES BOOK | NEW YORK

STRANDED

Copyright © 2016 by Tom Doherty Associates

All rights reserved.

Based on a concept by Bracken MacLeod and Alexandre Paul Ilic.

A Tor Book
Published by Tom Doherty Associates
175 Fifth Avenue
New York, NY 10010

www.tor-forge.com

Tor® is a registered trademark of Macmillan Publishing Group, LLC.

ISBN 978-0-7653-8244-3

Our books may be purchased in bulk for promotional, educational, or business use. Please contact your local bookseller or the Macmillan Corporate and Premium Sales Department at 1-800-221-7945, extension 5442, or by e-mail at MacmillanSpecialMarkets@macmillan.com.

First Edition: October 2017
First Mass Market Edition: September 2017

Printed in the United States of America

0 9 8 7 6 5 4 3 2 1

for

RICHARD SUENAGA and JILL CHERNISS,

two lights who should have burned longer

than either did

The world will be hard
And the wrong will be great.
The age of the Beard
Of the Sword—shields will shiver—
The age of the Storm and the Wolf are to come.
Before the World falls,
Man shall have no more reverence for man.

—*"Völuspá"* (Henry Morley, translator)

O light! This is the cry of all the characters of ancient drama brought face to face with their fate. This last resort was ours, too, and I knew it now. In the middle of winter I at last discovered that there was in me an invincible summer.

—Albert Camus, *"Return to Tipasa"*

PART ONE

The Invincible Summer

The void churned and swelled, reaching up to pull them down into frigid darkness, clamoring to embrace them, every one. A cold womb inviting them to return to the lightless source of all life, and die, each man alone in its black silence.

The sea battered the ship, waves crashing against the hull as the ship's master tried to quarter—turning the vessel into the waves to lessen their impact. While he struggled at the helm, the crew scrambled to get into their gear. The men grabbed sledgehammers and baseball bats, rushing to the aid of their fellow deckhands like a medieval army mustering to stand against the cavalry that would break them, line and bone. Noah wrestled with his waterproof gear, trying to pull on his pants and jacket, jamming hands into clumsy gloves that would combat frostbite for only so long. The ship pitched and Noah lurched in the passageway, trying not to lose his footing, trying not to be thrown to the deck before he was even out in the storm. He shoved his foot into a boot, staggering away from his locker as gravity and momentum conspired to bash his skull against the bulkhead. He careened into the wall, feeling a pop and a blossom of pain in his shoulder. He gritted his teeth and shoved himself away; he had to get on the cargo deck with the others. He couldn't be defeated before he even got outside.

A pair of deckhands pushed past him, pulling him off balance, slowing his forward momentum. "Out of the way, Cabot!" one shouted. Although the second man had a clear path behind his mate, he shoved at Noah also, cursing him for his idleness. Noah fell in behind the men and ran for the door. He ran to make his stand against the storm.

On the cargo deck, he couldn't tell the difference between the sea horizon and the night sky. Driving wind and rain competed with swells that crashed on the deck. The only break in the blackness was the foam on top of the water and ice building up on the ship, illuminated by the spotlights above him on the forecastle. Water erupted over the sides of the vessel, freezing a new layer to the coat of ice building up as fast as the men could bash away at it. Normally, it would be too dangerous to send men out in weather like this, but the ship was beginning to list, and if more ice built up, it could become top-heavy and roll over. Then, instead of the possibility of some men dying in the storm, they would all die in the sea.

He whipped his head from side to side, taking in what the other deckhands were doing, trying to find a place to lend a hand. An angry voice commanded him to get moving. The bosun, Serge Boucher, loomed over him, his words ripped away by the wind and crashing waves.

"What?" cried Noah.

Serge shoved an orange sledgehammer in his hands, leaned forward, and screamed, "Get aft! Break the ice off the windward side!" He grabbed Noah with a hand the size of a polar bear paw and shoved him away from the bulkhead out onto the free cargo deck. Noah slid and scrambled over the icy surface, struggling to avoid slamming into cargo boxes and shipping crates. The *Arctic Promise* was headed in a bearing for the northeast Chukchi Sea, carrying supplies for the OrbitOil drilling platform Niflheim. The voyage would have been hard under normal circumstances without a hurricane-force storm threatening to capsize their ship.

Noah regained his footing and struggled between containers as he headed for the catwalk along the high gunwale above the deck. He climbed onto the narrow walkway while a wave crashed against the ship, blinding him, choking him, and almost throwing him back over the rail to the cargo deck below. Maybe he wouldn't drown, but would die of a broken neck instead. He swung his hammer. The impact shuddered up his arms, almost making him drop the tool overboard. He held on, and steeling himself, took another swing. And another. And again until the ice began to shatter and fall away, back into the sea.

Another wave crested the ship and he was blind and battered. It pushed and pulled at him. He hung on to the rail as tightly as he could until the wave was gone, and he swung his hammer in defiance of it. As if he could drive the storm away with the force of his rage. He wouldn't allow it to take him. Not while he stood, hammer in hand, ready to fight.

Behind him, a cry rose above the gale. A collective panic sounded that made him more fearful than any choking blast of ice water had already done. He turned to look in time to see the steel cable holding crate six snap and unwind. It whipped wildly, slicing above two of his mates, Henry and Theo, barely sparing them their heads. It lashed back and sparked against the rail to his left. He held up his hands to shield himself from its assault. A wave struck him, pushing him forward into the rail and then snatching his feet out from under him. He fell, head banging on the grate. The only stars in the night were the ones behind his eyes. He felt a hot stinging in his cheek before it went cold and numb again. In his muted ears, he could hear Serge bellowing above the storm. "Secure that shit *now*!"

Noah's eyes stung and his wet eyelashes stuck together with ice. He peeled them open with soaked, gloved fingers and got to his feet. He couldn't help the men below. He could only watch as the crewmen struggled to defend their lives against both the storm and the cargo they'd been charged to deliver. But then, he couldn't watch; he had his own job to do. *Break the ice off the windward side.* He'd been banished to the very edge of their floating world and he knew that if he was lost over it, the crew would not mourn him. When the sea calmed and they reached the Niflheim, the ship's master would write reports and inform the company of another soul lost at sea, before finally finding a good night's sleep. Insurance claims would be made and liability waivers and releases filed before the payout. Noah's death would result in money moving from one pocket to another, and hopefully some finding its way to his daughter. He was worth more dead than alive to most people he knew, but not to her.

He swung his hammer, bashing at the inevitability of

water and ice. He struck until the metal rail was clear and moved up the line, lashing out at the storm, his arms burning with fatigue. Behind him rose up a screech and a howl. He hazarded a glance over his shoulder to see the massive loosened shipping container slide toward a deckhand—yellow rain slicker dull and distant in the maelstrom until it was gone behind the gray behemoth. More hands. They couldn't secure the freight and it wouldn't matter how much ice he defeated if the other men on the deck were crushed. They needed more hands.

He ran for the ladder at the end of the catwalk and climbed down. Rounding the secured cargo, he found the men working to resecure the loose container, straining against winch and chain, wind and rain. Ahead of him, Felix lay on his back, his face red with blood that alternately flowed and washed away. Two men with their hoods up struggled to pull him away from the container. Noah ran to lend a hand.

"What the fuck are you doing off the catwalk?" Serge shouted.

"I thought—"

"I don't give a shit what you *think*!" Serge grabbed Felix's wrist and pulled the man's arm over his shoulders, physically ejecting the other crewman trying to help the deckhand up. He lifted the wounded sailor, spinning him around and away from the others coming to his aid. Felix grimaced with pain, but didn't complain. "Cabot! Here, now!" Serge said.

Noah slipped under Felix's free arm and wrapped an arm around his waist. Serge dropped Felix's other arm and snatched Noah's hammer from his hand. The deckboss towered over him, looking like a furious thunder god, ready to strike him down. Instead of crushing him, he shoved the sledge at another deckhand. The man ran to assault the ice buildup on the port side gunwales without being told. Serge nodded and turned a withering look back to Noah, silently expressing his expectations of how a deckhand should step. As Noah's grandfather used to say, *If I tell you to jump, you ask "how high" on the way up.*

"Get him inside," Serge said. "Get him to Mickle." He grabbed Noah's coat and jerked him forward. Noah struggled to maintain hold of the injured man. "Do this one thing without fucking it up, Cabot. Do it now; do it right! Do *not* let me see you out here again or it won't be the storm that sends you overboard."

Over the PA, the master warned the crew, "We're headed into a big one! Hold on!"

The ship felt like it hit ground. Forward motion seemed to stop all at once, and then the bow rose with the swell, leaving them looking straight down into the seawater rushing over the stern. Noah grabbed blindly for a hand-hold. They were riding low, the ice buildup on the super-structure bringing them down. The sea rose above them on both sides as though the master had parted the wave. But if William Brewster was Moses, the men aft had Ramses' last view before the parted sea collapsed in on itself. Noah gripped a chain with one hand and Felix with his other. Unable to do anything else, he held fast and screamed in terror at the deluge that fell on them from either side as gravity resumed.

Salt water filled his mouth, nose, and eyes. And then his lungs. It froze him inside and out, running through the gaps in his hood into his gear, filling his boots and his gloves. If he didn't drown, frostbite was guaranteed. He spit water, gasping for painfully cold, but welcome, air. The ship leveled out. For a brief moment, he stood on a calm, horizontal surface staring at a mountain of a man instead of a wall of water. Serge stood in front of him, unmoved, staring ahead steely-eyed and fixed like the giant statue of the fisherman in Noah's hometown, Gloucester. The world was right for a second. And then it went right back to hell.

"Get inside," Serge shouted. Noah shoved off the crate, across the slick surface, holding on to Felix as the wounded man hobbled along beside him. If he complained or protested, Noah couldn't hear him. By the time they reached the bulkhead door, Brewster had steered them directly into another monster. They went vertical. Then it fell out from beneath them and crashed to the surface of the water. Noah and Felix were thrown through the door, slamming into the deck. Felix landed on top of him, howling with pain for the first time. Noah's breath was gone; his twisted back ached from the twin impacts as he tried to squirm out from under the injured man.

"Jesus Christ, Cabot!" He felt Felix being lifted away, but no hands returned to help pick him up from the floor. He got to his feet and glanced through the door at the men he'd left behind. "Cabot!" the third officer, Chris Holden, yelled. "What the hell are you looking at? Give me a hand here!" He refocused his attention on Felix and slipped back under the man's arm, assisting him to the first deck and their meager sick bay.

The hospital compartment of the ship was a narrow room with a rolling examination table, a pair of bunks built into the wall opposite a sink, a short counter, and a supply closet. Most of the ship was close quarters, but the hospital—built with the intention of being used rarely, if ever—exemplified the term. Noah helped Holden lift Felix onto the exam table. Felix lay down while Holden grabbed the autodial phone handset from the wall and hailed the wheelhouse. "Pereira's injured. We need Mickle, A.S.A.P." He hung up and turned to Noah. "What happened?"

"A cable broke and a bulk container came loose. It hit him hard."

"You think? Where the hell were you?"

"I was breaking ice off the gunwales."

Holden's eyes narrowed and he gave Noah a withering stare before he turned his attention to the wounded man, wiping blood from his face, searching for the wound. "Where are you hurt, Felix?"

Felix gritted his teeth and said, "Ribs hurt. Hard to breathe."

A moment later, the ship's medical officer appeared in the doorway. Second Officer Sean Mickle shoved past Noah to attend to Felix, asking him more questions while he helped the man out of his weather gear. Felix answered his questions haltingly. He was in pain and short of breath. Lifting his arms looked like agony. "I'm going to give you some tramadol for the pain, okay?" Mickle told him. Felix nodded.

Holden looked at Noah hovering in the doorway and shook his head. "What? Are you waiting for a prize? Shove away. Get back to your cabin."

"My cabin?"

"Yeah, your cabin. Get out of here."

Noah didn't wait around for Holden to repeat the

order. If he did, he knew it would come with twice the force and profanity, as well as an added watch shift. He stalked out of the sick bay, headed from First Deck five levels down to his one-man room on D-Deck. The ship was operating with a small company of sixteen men instead of its full complement. Most were quartered on B- and C-Decks nearer the galley and the day rooms. Noah's cabin was as far below as he could be without setting up a cot between the shaft generators.

He climbed down, careful to hang on to the rails of the steep ladder as the vessel continued to struggle against the waves outside, pitching and falling in the violent sea. If he fell and cracked his skull open, there was no one around to take him back to the sick bay. Again, he doubted it would be a problem for anyone but him.

As he descended, the normal oil and machine smells of the ship grew denser, more acrid. Reaching the D-Deck landing, he opened the door and found the passageway hazy with choking white smoke, creeping out from under the door to the instrument room. Noah grabbed a fire extinguisher hanging on the wall next to a red axe and ran for the door. Yanking it open, he released a noxious cloud of smoke and was driven back. Tearing off his soaked cap, he pressed it over his nose and mouth before diving into the room. Through the haze and stinging eyes he could see one instrument rack orange with flame, not white like the others. He dropped his hat and tried to pull the pin on the powder extinguisher. The zip tie securing the pin so it wouldn't accidentally come loose during shipment hadn't been removed. He couldn't do a thing with the goddamned zip tie on.

Noah bit at his glove, yanking it off. He spit the glove on the floor, cursing as he fumbled at his hip. He couldn't reach his pocket knife through his wet weather gear. "Fucking hell!" He fought at the tie with his teeth. After a few moments of painful gnawing, it finally came free. He pulled the pin, kicking at the cover panel on the front of the burning instrument rack, trying to open it. It didn't budge, and he kicked twice more until the cover shuddered and fell away. The hot metal bounced off his arm, sizzling against the wet rubber. Noah desperately needed a breath. Though much of the smoke had billowed out of the compartment into the passageway, the air was still thick and toxic. He struggled not to choke as he aimed the extinguisher at the base of the electrical blaze and squeezed the trigger. The dry powder stream arced out of the nozzle and the output of smoke and chemical stench doubled. He worried that the single can wouldn't be enough. If he could get the blaze under control, however, he could run and fetch another. Water suppression wasn't an option in the instrument room. He'd short out all of the systems on board the vessel, primary and redundant alike. The orange light diminished, however. He continued to spray down the instrument rack until the can was empty and he felt satisfied the fire was smothered.

Sweating and half blind, he wanted to strip off his clothes and wash out his burning eyes. He had to call the wheelhouse to let them know about the fire. Staggering into the passageway, another lurch of the ship sent him sprawling. He banged his head against a valve and bright blooms appeared behind his eyes. And then he saw nothing.

2

Noah awoke in the top recovery bunk of the sick bay in a panic. He tried to sit up, but disorientation and nausea made the room spin and he flopped back down on his pillow. He breathed, trying to reason with himself. If he was in the hospital bunk, someone had found him and brought him there. That meant the fire was under control and the ship was all right. A slower heart beat would at least lessen the pounding ache in his skull. He lay there listening, feeling for the storm. The ship was calm. He had no idea how long he'd been unconscious, but it was long enough that they'd come out on the other side of the storm. And unless he was dead or dreaming, they'd come out still afloat.

With spots dancing in his vision, he attempted to sit upright again. Propped up on an elbow, he made it halfway. Sitting on a stool bolted to the wall at a tiny table, Mickle turned away from his paperwork and looked at him with an expression halfway between concern and annoyance. "How you feeling, Cabot?"

"Like hammered shit," Noah said. His throat was raw and his voice was little more than a dry croak. He tried clearing it and repeating himself, but his voice was even less intelligible on the second attempt.

"Yeah, you ought to feel that way. You took a pretty good hit belowdecks. At least that's what the cut above your eye tells me."

Noah reached up and pawed at his forehead until his fingers found the wound. He involuntarily jerked away at the pain of his own touch. A little more gently, he explored a raised line of inflamed flesh about three fingers wide, finding it held together with suture glue and tape strips.

"You feel sick to your stomach? Dizzy?" Mickle asked.

Noah nodded, grunting, "Uh-huh."

"You might have a minor concussion. I can't tell for certain, not without a CT scan, but it doesn't take a genius to see you kicked your own ass pretty well. I'm recommending you stay in your cabin for a day or two. If you start vomiting or your headache gets worse and won't go away, we'll reassess your condition."

"What if I fall asleep and don't wake up?"

"I'm calling for a medical evac for Pereira when we get to the Niflheim. You can go home with him."

"That's not what I mean."

Mickle stood and closed the file folder on his paperwork. He shoved it into a plastic wall caddy and said, "You can't work while you recover. And if it's bad, you need a real hospital." He held his arms open as if it needed to be emphasized that the ship's "hospital" was only slightly better appointed than a high school nurse's office. At least he had narcotic painkillers.

Noah carefully swung his legs over the edge of his bunk. "How is everyone else?"

Mickle chuckled under his breath. "Good. Aside

from bruises and a touch of frost nip, you and Pereira are the only casualties of the storm. And despite your best efforts, you're both alive. So that's something."

Noah sighed. Pushing off the bunk as gently as he could, he hopped down, landing hard on his heels. Making contact with the deck sent a wave of pain shooting up his spine and into his skull that made his vision go gray and the room spin. Holding on to the ladder he should have used to climb down, he took a moment to reorient himself. He felt Mickle's hands on his arms, steadying him, but he couldn't see more than a shadowy silhouette of the man. The second officer was professional and occasionally cordial, but they weren't best friends. Noah imagined his concern came from not wanting to have to do the paperwork associated with a shipboard death.

"You all right?"

"I'm fine," Noah said. He stood up straight, holding up his hands to show he was steady on his feet. Mickle let go and stepped back. "I've been hit harder. But you don't want to hear about my love life." Noah winked. Mickle didn't laugh. Although Noah's wife, Abby, had always told him how funny he was, he knew he wasn't. Still, it didn't stop him from trying. *Maybe I ought to,* he thought, looking at Mickle's flat expression.

"Well, Superman, you should get some rest. Let yourself get over the bump and the shit you breathed in putting out that fire. Good job, by the way."

"Thanks. How bad was it?"

Mickle shrugged. "Not my specialty. Martin is looking at it; you'd have to ask him." He turned to leave and hesitated in the doorway. Martin Nevins was the ship's engineer and mechanic. He had a dark sense of humor no one on board seemed to fully appreciate. He was one of Noah's few allies, or at least he had been before Noah filled one of the racks with flame retardant powder.

"I'll drop in on him when I head for my cabin."

"I wouldn't. He's not happy. Anyway, Brewster reassigned you. You're on C-Deck now. D-Deck smells like a refinery took a shit, and he doesn't want anyone sleeping down there. It's a good thing for you he did. You probably smoked the equivalent of ten packs of unfiltereds in the time you spent in that room. You inhale any more and you'll wish you'd chosen coal mining as a career instead of merchant shipping." Noah smiled weakly at the medical officer. This wasn't the career he'd chosen; it was what inertia chose for him.

His father, grandfather, and great-grandfather were all Gloucester fishermen, and he'd practically been raised on board deep sea trawling boats. As soon as he was old enough, he went out with his old man and the old man's old man to work. While other kids were playing baseball and studying for the SATs and going down to Boston for a good time, he was out at sea. But cutbacks and catch restrictions put a hurt on his family's livelihood. Never rich enough to afford more than a couple of small day boats, his father retooled the family business after federal regulators effectively banned cod fishing in the Gulf of Maine. His father refurbished and refitted the boats to take the summer people out for twelve-hour deep sea fishing "adventures." He would smile, his weathered face wrinkling like a man twenty years his senior, and go on for the tourists about how there had been Cabots fishing these waters for as long as these waters had Cabots sailing on them. A bumper sticker was his only admission about how much he hated playing charter tour guide for out-of-towners looking to turn his hard work into recreation. On the rear of his pickup truck, a red rectangle read, "Give a man a fish, he'll eat for a day. Teach a man to fish, he'll starve."

"You used to be able to walk across the harbor, Noah," his dad had told him. *"It's true. There used to be so many boats, you wouldn't get your feet wet going from one end to another. Not now,"* he said, pointing to another new harbor hotel built where an auction house or a packaging plant used to be. Noah had looked at the three or four boats they left behind as they motored out on an "Evening Harbor Cruise." His old man had kept a straight back and square shoulders. But the slouch was in his voice. The defeat of losing the only thing he'd ever known and having to start over. Of having nothing to give his only son.

Noah had been a good, if often absent, student. He didn't have to work hard to get decent grades; he more or less fell into them. So when he applied to the University of Washington, the only one surprised he got in was the guidance counselor who'd told him his options were the military or penitentiary. The only one disappointed was his mother.

"There aren't any schools closer? There aren't any schools in Boston?" she asked.

"It's ranked like fifteenth in the world, Mom. It's a great school. They've got an Aquatic and Fishery Sciences program and . . ." But Annemarie Cabot couldn't hear him extol the virtues of the university. All she heard was *"Seattle."* A continent away.

"Let the boy go," his father said. *"He can't stay here*

and take tourists out fishing. He got in to . . . what'd you call it, Noah?"

"UDub."

"They call it UDub, Annemarie," his father repeated.

"How's he going to pay for it, Ethan? How can we afford 'UDub'?"

"I'll take out student loans, Mom. It's what everybody has to do anyway." He kissed his mother and told her he'd be fine. He told her he'd be home every year for holidays and the summer, and he would call once a week, and it would be like he never left. And then it wasn't.

His first year, he struggled. What had always come easy at Gloucester High wasn't so easy when he was being graded on a bell curve with everyone else for whom learning came easy. He was suddenly average and treading water. He skipped Thanksgiving to study, and that summer he got a job on an Alaskan fishing vessel so he wouldn't have to take out as much in student loans. If he could earn enough in the summer so he wouldn't have to have a part-time job during the year, he'd do better. Every missed trip home made it easier to miss another. The next semester, he met Abby. And the entire world changed. Not all of it for the better.

Noah shook away the memories and glanced back at Felix. He lay in his bunk, his breath a rasp. An occasional look of discomfort passed over his face in his sleep, even with the painkillers. *Broken ribs.* Broken ribs might mean he was a dead man. Especially if he had a punctured lung or some other kind of injury they couldn't see just from looking at him. Why was Mickle waiting until they got to the Niflheim to call for an evac? The seas were calmer. They could call now and get Felix to a hospital sooner than continuing on and making the helicopter fly so much farther to pick him up.

It had to be the ship's master's decision to wait. The Old Man had some bad reason for endangering Felix's life, and Noah wanted to know what it was. He walked out of the sick bay, headed for the wheelhouse.

3

The *Arctic Promise* was a platform supply vessel, a PSV, designed to maximize cargo capabilities for transferring supplies essential to offshore oil drilling platforms. On the way out, it was loaded with pulverized cement, diesel fuel, potable water, and food for the crew. For the return voyage it would haul volatile waste chemicals for disposal. The majority of space on the PSV was dedicated to the long, aft open cargo deck. At the forward end of the ship was a tall superstructure containing operations and a livable area. When Noah saw one for the first time, it looked to him like a boat that had been bred with a semi flatbed truck.

He was conflicted about working in the oil industry. He'd been raised from an early age to have a second nature, gut opposition to Atlantic coast oil rigs. A spill could devastate ocean habitats and the livelihoods that depended upon robust marine life far down the coast from where the drilling was done. His grandfather was politically active and strident. *Fishermen first!* had been Samuel Cabot's hue and cry. Like farmers and ranchers, fishermen fed America, and he was adamant that their livelihood was essential to the health of the nation. He wouldn't hear it when someone said they didn't see any sails on his boat and he needed oil and gas as much as everyone else.

Noah saw what siding with environmentalists against oil drilling one day and then against those same people when they came to protect swordfish and cod populations from overfishing had done to his grandfather, however. Both sides used the middle to get what they wanted, and the fishermen were left with a diminishing fleet, shrinking income, competition from farmed fish, and deteriorating health as they drank to relieve the pressure of being squeezed by twin behemoths. Noah, as a result, learned to just put his head down and work. He wanted no part of politics or activism. He wanted a job he enjoyed, to raise a family, and find a piece of happiness large enough for a single lifetime. Not too much to ask. At least he didn't used to think it was too much. Times changed, circumstances changed, and he needed the work. So, when OrbitOil was hiring, he applied. It was a job, and a safer one than the fishing boats he'd worked in the Bering Sea. At least that's what he'd been told the first time he'd been recruited to work on one. He wasn't sure "safer" was as accurate a description as "differently hazardous." But that was the nature of maritime work. If he wanted a safe job, he should have stayed in school and become a librarian or an architect. Staying in school, however, was not an option available to him. He accepted that his fate was to work ships like the *Arctic Promise*, maybe for the rest of his life.

At the top of the ladder, he pushed through the door into the wheelhouse. It was cast in a dull white glow from the windows ringing the compartment. Sitting at the top of the superstructure, the wheelhouse was designed for a three-hundred-and-sixty-degree view of both the vessel itself and the sea surrounding it. At the moment, the view was a solid wall of fog, reducing visibility to nothing. The ship's master, William Brewster, sat in one of the twin command chairs bolted to the floor, staring at a computer screen installed in the white and gray console in front of him, presumably navigating by instruments. He sipped from a cup of tepid black coffee. The bags under his deeply bloodshot eyes suggested caffeine wouldn't have sufficient effect for much longer. Aside from him, the wheelhouse was unoccupied.

Above the angled windows, a line of computer screens showed instrument performance and views of different areas of the deck; Noah wasn't sure what the instrument screens were displaying. He was a deckhand—a roughneck hired to help load and unload cargo. He knew how to steer and read the controls of a commercial fishing vessel. But in the wheelhouse of the *Arctic Promise*, the bridge equipment was as alien to him as space shuttle controls.

He craned his neck to peer through a window and found he couldn't see a foot past the forecastle. Fog obscured his view of the sea and the ship's prow. His stomach tightened as he had a feeling more like flying than seafaring. Noah would rather spend a month aboard ship than a day on a plane. If something happened, he could get into a survival suit and reach a lifeboat. If something happened on a plane, all he could do was pray. If he'd been a praying kind of man, that is.

"Noah," Brewster said, not looking up from the screen in front of him. "I didn't call for you." He set his cup on the console more or less on top of a brown ring dried between two keyboards.

"Mickle told me you want to wait until we get to the platform to call the med evac for Felix Pereira. He needs a helicopter now. He can't wait until we get to the platform."

Brewster shook his head. "And when did you get your M.D.?"

"William, come on! The guy is hurt bad. It doesn't take a doctor to—"

"I don't have time for this shit, Noah. I think you can see we're in the soup here. I need to focus."

"You do need to focus. You need to focus on the wellbeing of the crew. Felix needs a helicopter ride out of here."

Brewster turned in his chair and pointed a shaky finger at the communication center. Noah couldn't tell if it was fatigue or caffeine that had the Old Man trembling, but whatever it was, he was glad it didn't take a steady hand to steer. "Knock yourself out. Radio plants are all dead. Sat phone isn't working, either. If you can hail anyone, order a fuckin' pizza and a taxi out of here."

"Communication is out? Was that the stack that caught fire?"

"No. According to Nevins, it was a propulsion system. Whatever it was, there's a redundant system for both. I don't know why communication is disabled, but it is. I can only assume it has something to do with this." He jutted his chin toward the window, indicating the fog. "This shit rolled in as soon as the storm calmed down. Never seen anything like it." He turned his head, half-looking at Noah. "Even if I could call in a helo for

Pereira, they couldn't find us in this. Best bet is to get him to the platform as fast as we can. At this point, it's closer than land."

"How can you tell?" Noah leaned closer to a window, struggling to see through the haze and the ambient glow behind it. The fog trailed in wisps over the forward end of the ship, making it hard to see even to the end of the prow.

"I know where we were when the storm started."

"You mean you don't know where we are now?"

Brewster stood. He shoved a gnarled finger in Noah's chest and pushed. Although Noah tried to stand his ground, the pain in his sternum forced him back. A lifetime of hard work had left William Brewster a hard man both in body and mind. He didn't like being challenged or second guessed. And he especially didn't like his son-in-law. Of all the daughters' fathers who'd threatened him with violence if he didn't treat their "little girls" right, Brewster was the only one whose threats had seemed credible. The man did not crack wise and he didn't say things he didn't mean. If he threatened violence, it was on the horizon, if it hadn't already arrived.

"I have a bearing," Brewster said. "And I know what our speed has been since I had us positioned by satellite. I know where we are. You, on the other hand, wouldn't know your ass from your elbow if I grabbed one to help you have a seat on the other. Again, is there a reason you're up here?"

"No. Just Felix. That's all."

"That *is* all. You're relieved. Report to your cabin. You're restricted to quarters and the mess room. I don't want to see you again until we reach the Niflheim.

Once we're there, you can fly home with your pal and I never want to see you again. Period."

"You're firing me? After I saved the ship?"

Brewster snorted with derision. "I'm firing you for disobeying orders. The bosun put you on the ice. You weren't supposed to be anywhere near the deck or any of those shipping containers. And you sure as shit weren't supposed to be in the instrument room."

"It's a good thing I was."

Brewster's face clouded over. His white brows knitted over cornflower blue eyes and the muscles on the sides of his face flexed as he gritted his teeth. Noah tensed, awaiting the swing of a fist. If he could stand the first one, he might be able to hit back. *If* he could stand the first one.

"You don't belong on this boat, Cabot."

"You're the one who approved my application."

"In desperation; I needed hands. Believe me when I tell you I regret it now. Whatever Abby saw in you, I didn't agree with her then and I disagree even more now. If I see you up here or on the cargo deck again, I'll throw you overboard. I wager I'll have half a dozen men fighting each other to help me do it, too. Now get out of here and let me find the way."

"Aye, sir," Noah saluted.

Brewster held up a middle finger in response.

Noah backed out of the compartment, choosing to take the nearest door and descend the exterior ladder. He'd once tried to imagine what it would take for his father-in-law to grow to at least tolerate him, if not outright like him. He'd catalogued all the possibilities: treating Abby with love and faithfulness, getting a good, stable job and providing while she went back for her master's degree, fathering William's only grandchild. None of it had been enough. That he was Noah Cabot and had married Abigail Lynne Brewster was too high a hurdle to overcome. And now they were at logger-heads. No matter what he did, it wasn't good enough. He'd tried to find common ground and even think of the man as family, but Noah didn't crave his approval any longer. It was too late for them both.

The frigid air was strangely humid, and the fog felt like a bed of needles prickling his exposed face and hands. He hurried as much as he could while still being careful not to slip on the ice clinging to the ladder risers and handrail. The bow of the *Arctic Promise* was caked in it and she was still riding low in the water. The good news was they hadn't capsized, somehow, and more ice didn't seem to be accumulating. For the time being, she was seaworthy and the crew was safe. But if they sailed into another storm like they experienced last night, it would be short work for the vessel to grow top heavy and turn over.

On C-Deck he hesitated, giving the starboard fast rescue craft—the FRC—a quick once-over. Serge, the bosun, was also the coxswain and responsible for maintaining the lifeboat. Noah wasn't sure what he was looking for, but he didn't want to run into another problem like he had the night before with the zip tie on the fire extinguisher.

He leaned over the rail to inspect the ropes tied to the vessel in the "securing arrangement" before lifting the cover to look underneath at the craft itself. He didn't know exactly what measures would need to be taken to lower and launch the small craft, but to his eye, it looked good. He breathed a small sigh of relief, even if the feeling he got from his inspection was more confusion than satisfaction. Nothing looked like it would hinder the crew's ability to board and launch the craft. He made a mental note to make it to the port side to have a look at the other FRC as well. There were only sixteen men aboard, and each rescue boat held twenty. Almost all systems on the ship had at least one redundant backup. But if an escape vessel failed, they'd be pulling freezing men out of the ocean. Better if the first one they tried worked as expected.

He turned to head inside and found himself blocked by a crewman. Theo something. Theo Mesires. He was a typical deckhand. Strong and solidly built, the kind of guy who liked working with his hands and liked complaining about work twice as much. "Whatcha doin', Noah? Finding more fires to set?"

"What? Just making sure—"

"Why don't you keep your nose out of shit you shouldn't be messing with?"

Noah shoved past the deckhand, bouncing off his shoulder as he did. "If I kept my nose out of things, you might be swimming tomorrow." He pulled open the door he hadn't heard the man exit and practically ran inside to get away from the chill of both the atmosphere and his coworker. His reputation had preceded him. No matter what, he promised himself, this was his last job for OrbitOil or any other platform outfit. He'd decided. It was time to take Ellie and head home to New England. But first, he had to get back to Seattle in one piece.

4

D-Deck stank like smoke and burnt electronics. Noah was surprised he'd been reassigned to a different cabin, figuring that living in this stench would be just the kind of petty torture the Old Man would subject him to. Then again, Brewster was a company man and would balance potential liability against his personal satisfaction. The crew would make sure he was just as uncomfortable on C-Deck as he was below, and the company wouldn't have to pay worker's comp. Noah came to collect his few private things. Although, smelling the rank passageway, he assumed most of his things were likely ruined. Still, they were his. He was going to need his clothes and the couple of books he'd brought, especially if he was going to be confined to his cabin for a while. He found himself wishing he'd brought more to read. It was going to be a long trip with nothing to do.

He hesitated in the doorway of his cabin, letting his eyes adjust to the dark. The narrow room was wide enough for Noah to walk between the wardrobe and the small desk. At the end of the room was a single bed, barely long enough for him. He wondered how men over six feet, like Boucher, were able to sleep without having to curl up in a ball. The cabin was similar in size to what Noah imagined a prison cell would be, minus a toilet—the head was down the hall. His accommodations were cramped, but he was expected to spend the majority of his time working, in the mess, or in a day room anyway. They even had a gym. The tiny cabin was for intended for sleep, and privacy for those who needed it, definitely not luxury. He didn't even have a porthole window. As a concern, living space was secondary to the company's goal. Space on the ship was dedicated to maximizing area for storage and cargo. The men had to live and work around that. Oil drilling came before everything else.

He opened the closet and grabbed his duffel bag off the floor. Pulling a shirt off a shelf, he sniffed at it and screwed up his face. He couldn't tell if what he smelled was the stink of the fire lingering throughout the level or if it was in his clothes. Either way, it was still in his nose and lungs, and he figured he was going to be smelling that shit for a while, no matter where on the ship he landed. He shoved his clothes into the duffel bag and moved on.

He collected his few things from the desk: a cheap digital music player, a few toiletries, a pair of books, and his electronic Chess Wizard game. Shoving it all into the bag, he moved on to the last things—the most important things—two pictures pinned to a small corkboard above the desk. He took them down and stared for a long moment into the faces of his wife and daughter. He never shipped out without a copy of them. This copy of Abby's picture was the third he'd printed out. The first had grown worn and tattered, and the second was lost somewhere between a different ship and home. He kept the same images on a micro SD card on his phone. No matter what happened, he'd made sure to never be far from them. The images meant more to him than the books and clothes and everything else. He'd rather wear rags and never see another printed word than forget what Abby looked like.

Carefully slipping the pictures into a zippered pocket on the outside of his bag, he scanned the small room for anything he might have forgotten. If there *was* something, it wasn't like he was far. He could always come back. At least until they reached the Niflheim. Pulling the drawstring taut, he slung the bag over his shoulder. It collided with the wall, throwing him off balance for a moment. He steadied himself and stepped out into the passageway to find his new lodgings.

Around the corner, he saw a foot sticking out of the instrument room. He assumed the man owning the limb was Martin Nevins, the ship's engineer and mechanic. Noah walked over, curious to see how things had turned out, since he had no recollection after hitting his head. The last time he saw the room, it was a toxic mess of fire retardant and electrical smoke. Not much had changed.

"Hey Marty. How's it look?"

The engineer sat back and wiped at his forehead with a dirty forearm. He was sweating despite the chill in the room. "Looks like *hell* is what it looks like." He sized Noah up and added, "You don't look any better."

Noah brushed at the cut on his forehead with his fingers and wondered how bad the bruising on his face was. Aside from the hospital and the lockers in the change rooms, there weren't many reflective surfaces on the *Promise*. He hadn't thought to look in the mirror inside his closet. For all he knew, half of his beard might have been singed off in the fire. He ran his hand down his face to reassure himself he didn't resemble a half-man/half-woman sideshow attraction. "I'm sure it looks worse than I feel. Or maybe the other way around. I don't know." He pointed at the instrument stack he'd extinguished. "Fire was in propulsion, huh? Is it salvageable?"

"Yeah. I mean, no way. Yes, the fire hit propulsion, but it's not even a little salvageable. The thing is well and truly fucked; we're running on the backup."

"And if that one goes out?"

Martin huffed a laugh through his nose. "You know what happens then." He didn't have to say it. He pulled a cigarette out of a pack and lit it. Smoking wasn't allowed anywhere on board except the exterior decks. But then, who would be able to pull the smell of a Kamel Red out of the mélange of other noxious scents poisoning the air on D? "What are the chances they both get wrecked, huh?"

Noah shrugged. He didn't want to say it out loud. He didn't believe in jinxes and bad luck, but it still lived in him, like the fear of elevators falling down their shafts and the bus in your blind spot that only appeared once you step off the curb. Then again, you didn't need to believe in bad karma to know that Brewster had been pushing the engines extra hard. If they sailed into another storm, they could have much bigger problems than ice.

Martin took a deep drag of his cigarette and blew a long stream of smoke toward the ceiling. "Speakin' of getting wrecked, I got a bottle of J&B in my cabin. You up for a snort later?"

"Definitely. Come find me; I'm bunking on C now."

"That's a good thing. Down here is no place to be."

Noah held out a fist for Martin to bump. The mechanic knocked his knuckles against Noah's a little too hard and smiled with the half of his mouth not occupied with his coffin nail. The pair had shipped out together in the past, but both of them hailing from New England provided more of a bond than any of their experiences hauling concrete and gas into the Arctic Ocean.

Noah turned to go. "Hey, uh, you know what the deal is with communications or navigation systems?"

"What? You missing your 'stories'?"

Noah laughed. "I was talking to Brewster, and radio and sat phones are both down. I'm guessing that means dynamic positioning, too. I was just wondering if you knew what was going on."

Martin stood and tilted his head to the side as if he was trying to tell what kind of mythical creature was talking to him. "First I'm hearing of it. There isn't a thing built by man I can't fix, but if both radio and satellite have shit the bed at the same time, that ain't mechanical. Not unless we're really getting the smackdown from the gods; they're separate systems. It might be the weather interfering. Or it might be PICNIC."

"Picnic?"

"Problem in chair, not computer." He winked. "The skipper's old enough to remember eight-tracks. I wouldn't be surprised if he doesn't know how to use the 'new-fangled 'puter machines' and took those systems off-line trying to get RedTube to load." He took another deep drag off his smoke, pinched the ember off the end and ground it out underfoot. He stuffed the filter back into the pack. "Still, something must be working if we're in motion. He ain't flying blind."

Noah tried to laugh his fears off. "We're fine. He's steering by stars and charts."

Martin shook his head, saying nothing. Not laughing. He'd looked outside. He knew there were no stars.

"If we needed to shut down propulsion for a while . . . you know, just to make sure it was working properly . . . you know, like to run a diagnostic something or other, you could do that right?"

"Not if it was going to get me charged with mutiny."

Noah held up his free hand. "I didn't say anything about mutiny. If Brewster's headed in a direction based on a best guess and steering us into the Siberian shore, that's his prerogative as ship's master. I shouldn't have said anything. I'm being paranoid; I'm sure Brewster knows what he's doing." Noah felt his headache creeping back in a little, pushing at the edges. He should have grabbed more Tylenol from Mickle in the hospital.

Martin looked like he wanted that drink right now. Instead, he lit another cigarette. Shaking his head, he said, "Let me think about it."

"I'm not asking you to do anything. Just wondering out loud, I guess." He waved his hand dismissively. Noah pointed at Martin's smoke. "You know those things will kill you."

The engineer took a deep drag and held it for a moment before exhaling. "I've never felt better in my life."

Looking at his blanched and sweating face, Noah didn't believe him.

5

Noah stowed his things in his new room. The ship was built to accommodate forty crew members. All the cabins on C-Deck were designed for double occupancy, but with the bare bones complement of sixteen men spread between B and C, none of the crew had to share a room. Moving from his single occupant cabin into the new one meant Noah had twice the space, not that he needed it. Still, it was nice to have walls a little farther apart from each other. If he was going to be confined to quarters, he appreciated being assigned somewhere less confining. Stretching out in the new space, he tried to tamp down his growing feelings of resentment toward Brewster for making him sleep in the single bunk cabin so far belowdecks. He was as successful at that as he was managing his building headache. It had grown stronger since talking to Marty. He dug through his bag trying to find something to beat back at it, but was unsuccessful. He'd forgotten to pack any painkillers.

Peeking out the door, he found the passageway oddly silent. There were thirteen cabins and the gym on this deck, but if anyone was on C with him, they were still sleeping off last night's nightmare.

He left his cabin and climbed to the First Deck, between A and the wheelhouse. He walked past the crew change rooms and the head, to the sick bay. Inside, Mickle was tending to Felix. Without turning to see who'd come to visit him, he said, "All out of aspirin and everything else, so don't even ask. Don't any of you plan ahead for your hangovers?"

"How'd you know I wanted an aspirin?"

Mickle turned and wiped at his brow with a sleeve. Like Marty Nevins, he was sweating despite the ever-present chill on the ship. "I've had maybe a dozen guys come up here looking for analgesics. I ran out an hour ago." He pointed at Noah's wound. "Is it bad?"

Noah shrugged. "Nothing I can't cope with. A dozen, huh?"

Mickle nodded, looking like he might have started rattling off names before thinking better of it. "Yup," he said instead. "And none of 'em with as good an excuse as you or Pereira here. To be honest, I feel a little like shit myself, but I delivered the last of the Tylenol to the skipper a few minutes ago. All I have left is some topical stuff for stitches and whatnot . . . and the tramadol. The first wouldn't knock out a headache and the second will knock you out." His eyes wandered toward Pereira sleeping fitfully in the medical bunk. "You're just going to have to brew up another pot of coffee and hope caffeine can get on top of it."

"You think the fumes from the electrical fire got into the ventilation?"

"Oh, I'm sure of it. But almost everybody was outside dealing with the storm when that was happening.

The fire was out before most of the crew came back in. Vent system had time to cycle that crap through and replace it with clean air. Unless something's wrong with that, too."

"Communications still on the fritz?" Noah asked.

"Yeah. I went up a few minutes ago to follow up on Pereira's ride out of here."

"How'd Brewster respond to that?"

Mickle raised an eyebrow. "As expected. He told me Pereira would get help quicker if people would crawl out of his ass long enough for him to find the Niflheim."

"He has a colorful turn of phrase, doesn't he?"

Mickle smirked. "He uses colorful words to describe you, that's for sure." He pinched the bridge of his nose between thumb and forefinger and squeezed his eyes shut. Noah suspected he was underplaying the severity of his own headache. "He also refused to let me relieve him. He's been at the conn going on twenty hours." Mickle didn't need to say how dangerous lack of sleep could be. A well-rested person attempting to steer the ship in fog as dense as this was dangerous enough. "I stopped here on my way to fetch him a cup of coffee before I try to relieve him again. You have any insights into how to get your father-in-law to listen?"

"The only insight I have is that he doesn't ever listen. It's his way."

Mickle sighed. "If I'm able to scrounge up any aspirin or something, I'll let you know. You do the same?"

Noah held up a three finger salute, regretting the gesture as soon as it bounced off his wound, amplifying the ache behind it. "Promise."

Mickle grinned at the gesture. "I was a scoutmaster

for my kid's troop back in the day. Never saw one who could grow a beard like that."

"It's glandular." He petted his dark pelt and smiled. It was the first time in days he'd felt like he could let his guard down. It was nice . . . and fleeting as he heard footsteps in the passageway behind him. Stepping a pace out of the door, he saw a pair of deckhands rounding the corner, stomping his way like men on a mission. One of them slowed when he caught sight of Noah. He furrowed his brow and missed a step as his eyes darted to follow something behind Noah. Noah turned, wondering if there was someone else in the passageway he'd missed. Empty. He stepped aside as the men shouldered past him into the hospital.

"Hey Doc," one said as he barged in. "We were hoping—"

"Stop right there," Mickle said.

Noah left him to deal with the deckhands and went down to search out the coffee he'd been recommended to take in lieu of a real painkiller.

6

Among the men up and moving aboard the *Arctic Promise,* most were barely moving. In the mess room, a handful of crewmen picked at their food, pushing it around but not eating as vigorously as they had when they first set out. They spoke in hushed tones about the view—or lack of it—out the porthole windows. As Noah passed, he heard one suggest the Old Man was plotting his course using dice. "Mr. Holden, please set a course heading for . . ." The crew member picked up his empty coffee cup, shook it, and slammed it on the tabletop. He tipped the cup back and peeked under the lip. "Yahtzee degrees!" His companions at the table laughed weakly, one, he thought it might be Michael Yeong from Portland, rubbing at his temples like he wanted to touch his fingers together by pushing them through his skull.

A senior deckhand named Henry Gutierrez looked up from his plate. Noah nodded at him. Henry blinked and his head whipped around, following something Noah couldn't see. He wiped a hand down his face and returned to studying his lunch.

Noah stepped in and grabbed a cup from the stack

beside the coffeepot. He held it under the spout and pushed the lever down. Normally, the ship's movement made a task as simple as filling a cup of coffee a test of both aim and endurance, as a pitch of the sea would send hot java spilling over onto Noah's hand. They were moving so slowly after the storm, however, he might as well have been standing in the Starbucks at Pike Place Market. He easily filled the cup and, although he preferred it black, added a creamer so it wouldn't upset his empty stomach. Snapping a lid on top, he slurped at the tepid drink. It tasted as bad as always, yet somehow the act of doing something so ordinary made it better. They were through the storm, and although he had a good cut and a headache, he was more or less no worse for wear. *You can get through this. Just keep your head down and you'll be home before you know it with money in your pocket.* What happened after he set foot on dry land, he had no idea. The simple prospect of being off the ship—and never setting foot on another—was enough to keep going. It had to be.

Noah wandered up the passageway and into one of the day rooms, hoping to find a better-looking group. Instead he found more of the same. A couple of deckhands lay across twin sofas in mirror positions, each with an arm draped over his eyes to block out the light. The ship was normally a noisy place filled with the sounds of men's conversation. They had to shout to be heard over the machinery constantly running on the ship. Aside from the engines, however, the *Promise* was eerily silent. No one spoke. It was as if the fog had penetrated everyone's heads and was filling their skulls with the same kind of stinging cold that he'd felt on the ladder outside.

Andrew something from Olympia—Noah couldn't remember his last name—lifted his arm and peeked at Noah standing in the doorway. He dropped his elbow back over his eyes. The other man jerked as a single growling snore wrested him from tenuous sleep. He turned to his side, facing away from the room. Noah wanted to ask if either man had seen Marty, but thought better of it. Unless these guys had grown eyes in their elbows, they hadn't seen a single thing. All told, he'd run into eight or nine lethargic men throughout the ship. The other half of the complement had to be sleeping it off, awaiting their turn to take a late watch or just trying to recover from the labors of the night before.

He walked out of the room and hesitated at the bulkhead door leading to the port lifeboat. Remembering he wanted to ensure the safety preparations for both FRCs, he pulled down his sleeves and stepped outside.

Setting out, his thick Norwegian wool sweater and work pants had been enough to handle any brief trip outside. The farther north they traveled, however, the more protective gear he needed. Setting his cup on the rail, he zipped his sweater up to his chin. Still, the wind bit at him, making his cheeks sting and his eyes water. Even through his watch cap, his ears were stinging. They'd go numb soon. Without gloves, his fingers instantly ached. He knew, once inside, his ears would sting again when that incongruous heat of supercooled flesh returned to normal temperatures and his knuckles would swell and stiffen. He'd have to sit awhile holding a cup of something hotter than the coffee he'd set on the rail before he could move them well enough to unzip his fly or set up a chessboard. He hesitated, thinking about going inside to gather his jacket and gloves from the change room. No. He was here now, alone with the craft. Any future adventures out of doors were going to require full weather gear, but he could handle this short task. He set to accomplish his inspection as quickly as possible, stuffing his fingers in his armpits until he needed his hands.

The cold reminded him of a friend in Seattle who was a fitness trainer. He seemed to burn calories just breathing. He radiated warmth like a space heater and lived in shorts and, if it was real cold, maybe a long-sleeved shirt. Like Noah's first year at UDub had proved he couldn't coast on his native intelligence, Noah had quickly learned there was no such thing as not minding the cold in the Arctic. Fit or not, you dressed properly. Valuing his fingers and nose, he set to work quickly.

As well as he could tell, the port Fast Rescue Craft was as ready as the starboard one. His ability to tell, however, was limited. The other men were quick to point out his experience deep sea fishing in the Atlantic with his father "meant exactly dick," as they would put it, in Alaska's high seas. They were right, too. He was constantly playing catch-up to the demands of working on a ninety-meter heavy cargo transport as opposed to a seventy-five-foot fishing trawler. The others knew every move required to keep things running smoothly and safely by habit and good instinct. He wasn't green, but he wasn't exactly seasoned, either. Noah existed in a shadow space in between. If he had his druthers, he'd rather spend any day on dry land rather than on board a ship. But he didn't have his druthers. He *had* to work. And finding work that paid the bills was no easy feat in the present economy—not with his skills, anyway.

No more part-time grocery store clerking or university work study jobs.

Finishing his inventory of the lifeboat, he hazarded a peek over the side of the ship hoping to catch a glimpse of the water below. Bending over the rail, he bumped his cup and sent the coffee over the side. It fell into the fog and disappeared without a sound. The thrum of the engines drowned out the splash. "God damn it." He leaned farther over the edge trying to get a look. The fog remained too thick; he could only see halfway down. He strained and thought he could hear the water slapping at the hull. Yep, he could hear it. It splashed. And banged. And scraped. There was ice in the water.

A vision of a giant white and blue cliffside into which they were about to crash loomed in his mind. The mental picture of it made his stomach tighten. He felt the first touch of nausea he'd ever felt at sea in his life. The fear of it clawed at him, ripping at his courage. A gust of wind blew, tightening his skin and making his muscles tremble. It blew the mist swirling below him in an eddy and away from the hull. For a brief moment, he saw the water and what was scraping against the side of the ship. Thousands—or maybe millions, depending on how far what he was seeing extended into the fog—of spiky ice crystals reached up from the water like perfect white stars flaring in space. Each one resembled a small explosion frozen and preserved at the moment when it was most beautiful before revealing blackened crater and scorched death beneath. Frost flowers. He remembered they were called frost flowers. They were pushed away by the ship's wake, pulled under and crushed, broken on the side of the hull tearing through their quiet field of sharp brilliance.

Noah wanted to sprint for the cargo deck and lean over the lower gunwales to get a closer look, but the fog swirled in, obscuring them again. He eased himself back, noticing how badly his exposed hands hurt, even with his stretched sweater sleeves between his palms and the metal rail over which he'd been leaning. He flexed his digits, trying to return sensation and circulation. They barely complied, crackling and hurting. He shoved them back in his armpits and felt icy cold seeping through the wool. It was long past time to go in. He had been bewitched and might have gotten frostbit if it weren't for the fog. The unreality of it snapped him back to reality, stinging his face, telling him this was not his place to be. No matter how lovely and entrancing, he would lose fingers and toes, ears or lips, maybe even die out here if he did something as stupid as linger in the elements without his gear.

He retreated for the interior, mourning the meager warmth of the coffee he'd lost over the side. He needed that and some more rest before the real heavy lifting began when—*if*—they reached the drilling platform. He pulled clumsily at the door, fighting his own dulled and slowed body to find the way in.

Inside, the warmer air hurt and instinct told him to go outdoors again. Noah decided to head to his cabin, hoping a little rest might help clear his head.

Picking his bag up off the bunk where he'd thrown it, he dumped his things out on the mattress. The chill outside had cleared his nose and lungs and he smelled how badly everything stank. He could take his clothes to the laundry on the First Deck, but there was nothing to do about his books and other things. He briefly considered cracking his window, but the residual ache in his stiff fingers convinced him not to. Not enough air would move around the cabin to dispel the odor, and he'd rather deal with the smell of old smoke than suffer more of the cold. Shoving his clothes in a net laundry sack, he threw them toward the door. Shoving his other belongings to the side, he flopped on his bunk.

Stuffing his fingers under his arms to attempt to warm them again, he stared at the ceiling, feeling the motion of the sea. The slower movement was a welcome change from roiling storm waters. He'd had enough of rough seas and dangerous work. But having enough of something didn't mean he could be done with it. He needed the money this job would net him. With it, he hoped to make a change, get a fresh start, and do something different with his life. He hoped to never go to sea again. His instincts up in this part of the world were bad. *Very* bad.

He picked up the book from beside him on the mattress. Noah was on his second attempt reading Yukio Mishima's *The Sailor Who Fell from Grace with the Sea*. It was a slim novel, and while he sympathized with the titular character's desire to begin a new life, he wasn't sure he got what the book was supposed to be about. Or maybe he did. If he'd ever stood in a state of grace with the sea, he'd fallen. He sighed and promised himself he'd give it another shot some other time, and dug the second book he'd brought out of his ruck instead. It was about poisoned beer that made everyone in a college town go crazy and kill each other. He liked that one better. Soon, however, he realized it was hard to keep his attention on anything. His eyes slipped out of focus and he felt heavy. A cat nap, he decided, would help. It was exhaustion from fighting ice and fire. In the back of his mind, he thought it might also be a concussion. Hadn't he heard that concussed people should try to stay awake? That it was dangerous to fall asleep? He assumed it was a myth. If it was dangerous for him to get some rest, Doc Mickle wouldn't have let him return to his cabin; he'd be in the hospital with Pereira. Still, the nagging fear in the back of his mind kept him up, even when he couldn't focus his eyes or even easily keep them open. He lay in his bunk and thought about dying in his sleep.

7

He awoke with a start and a heart beating with panic as his last thought shoved past the disorientation of sleep into clarity. *You will die if you sleep*.

But of course, he hadn't. He'd merely slept. Feeling somewhat better rested but still weary and beaten, Noah pushed himself up onto his elbows and checked his wristwatch. "Figures," he mumbled, tapping at the stopped timepiece with a fingernail. He only wore it when he was working; the rest of the time it sat in a box on his dresser where his preschool daughter coveted it. He couldn't remember the last time he'd had the battery changed. The clock on the desk across the cabin was blank. He tilted his head and saw it was unplugged.

Climbing out of his bunk, he took a moment to orient himself. The cabin was at once familiar and alien. He felt like he'd wandered into the wrong cabin and passed out. He rubbed sleep from his eyes and tried to look out the window, hoping the haze had thinned or even cleared entirely. It hadn't. He stared into a solid field of white that discomfited him. The fog outside mirrored that in his head, solid and impenetrable, while the brightness of it confounded him. He had to have slept at least a couple of hours, but at this time of year, and this far north, a couple of hours should have meant darkness outside. The light through his window, while filtering through fog, was bright. He couldn't have slept until morning. Could he? Noah stood feeling unmoored and adrift. At least the sea was calm. It was too calm, in fact.

He tried to feel the movement of the *Arctic Promise* with his body. He'd become accustomed to the movements of the ship beneath his feet—had his sea legs—and was conscious of the pitch of the ship and roll of waves in the same way he was conscious of his own breathing. If he stopped to think about it, it was there. If he focused on anything else, the feeling receded into the unconscious background where his brain filed the sensation somewhere between the feeling of wearing a shirt and knowing twelve came after eleven. But now, standing still and concentrating on it, he didn't even feel the subtle movements of forward motion in calm waters. He could hear the engines. They were working, but the vessel wasn't moving. He might as well have been standing on dry land.

The view out the porthole window was obscured in a gray haze that showed neither depth nor movement. For a brief moment, he wondered if he was still asleep and dreaming. He tried to reason himself out of uncertainty. The presence of the frost flowers meant that the Old Man would have to slow their progress to avoid damaging the ship as the ice in the water grew thicker. The *Arctic Promise* had a reinforced hull but it wasn't an icebreaker. If they went too fast, the ice would damage the ship. Noah knew they'd have to decrease their speed eventually. And in whiteout fog, moving at all was hazardous. He reminded himself that Brewster had years of experience in these seas with vessels like the *Arctic Promise*. He knew better than Noah how his ship would perform in all conditions. Intellectually, Noah understood that Brewster knew how it would hold together and how to proceed. But experience was a hard teacher, and Noah was certain of one thing: Brewster's clearest thoughts were about what he wanted, and never about what that would cost anyone else.

Noah pulled on his boots and walked out of the cabin hoping to find out where they were—and what time it was. First, however, he needed something warm to drink. Coffee had lost its appeal; he wanted the J&B Martin had offered. He headed down to the lower deck, hoping he'd catch the man in his off-rotation hours. As before, the typically busy ship was abnormally quiet.

The door to the engineer's cabin was open a crack. "Martin? You in there?" Noah knocked. He pushed the door wider and peered inside. The room was dark and he couldn't see much more than what the light from the passageway allowed. He was about to leave and head for the machine room when Martin said, "Come in and shut the door, man."

"You'll never believe it, but I think I just slept like twenty hours. Do you know what time . . . ?" Noah trailed off as he walked in. Martin lay on his bunk in the dark. He'd pulled the curtain over his porthole window and his pillow over his head. Lifting it away from his face, he waved a weak hand at Noah. "Sit anywhere," he joked.

"You all right? You didn't kill that bottle without me, did you?" Noah pulled the chair away from the desk and sat.

"Not hungover. Definitely not all right, either." He tried to stuff his pillow under his head but it hung up on the frame at the top of his bunk. Noah reached over and, lifting Marty's head with a gentle hand, slipped and straightened the cushion beneath him. Marty let out a long sigh. It didn't sound like relief, but rather suffering at the effort of lifting his head. "I've got whatever's going 'round the ship. Fucking killer headache. Kinda want to die. You know. How 'bout you?"

Noah's headache was gone; a dim fuzziness was his only real complaint. Although he was a little achy, he seemed to be getting better. It seemed everyone else on board had caught his concussion . . . or had been poisoned by the same thing. "I'm on my feet," he said. "On the mend, actually. I'm doing better than you and everyone else."

Marty rolled his head to the side, opening his eyes a slit. He squinted and shielded them with a hand. Noah got occasional migraines. He knew what it was like to feel light sensitive, how even dimness felt like staring into the sun. Marty abandoned trying to block the light and instead slapped his hand over his eyes, squeezing.

"Was it something that burned in the fire, Marty? What the fuck have we been breathing that's making everyone sick?"

"What? Nothing, man. It's the same material in every equipment panel. Shit catches fire all the time and nobody gets sick. There was nothing special in that one. At least nothing I know about."

"Then what?" Noah asked.

"I don't know. I don't want to know. I just want to feel better."

Noah leaned forward, wanting to help his friend, but had no idea how. He couldn't make it darker or pull a bottle of Tylenol from the æther. He sat back in his chair feeling frustrated and impotent. Bashing ice off the rails had felt pointless, but it was something. The satisfaction of it breaking under his hammer reinforced the effort and kept him swinging even as the ice built up in front of him. A day or two later, the joints in his fingers and hands were still sore and stiff, but the feeling was earned and had a purpose. By contrast, sitting still, watching someone suffer, struck at the heart of a man whose approach to a problem was to just get down and solve it. He could fix his car, he could repair a thing, he could build something out of useless raw material. But there was nothing in his skill set to help a person overcome suffering. That, too, he'd learned from painful experience.

"You have anything in your cabin?" Martin said. "Ibuprofen or whatnot?"

"I forgot to pack 'em. I saw the doc . . . a while ago and he's tapped, too. All he has left is the hard stuff."

"I'm up for the hard stuff. I could totally Rip Van Winkle the rest of this job," Marty said.

"Is it that bad?"

"I'm seeing things, man. I just wanna go to sleep and wake up on the other end."

"What do you mean, 'seeing things'?"

Marty rolled over on his side, sliding his hand down, covering his eyes. He lay there still and silent for a long while. Noah watched a vein on side of his neck throb. "I don't know," he finally said. "Things. At first I just thought it was the storm messing with me, you know? Lack of sleep with a little seasickness sprinkled on top. But my eyesight got a little blurry, and . . . I started to notice weird shadows and shit moving in the corners of my vision. It's like there's somebody there, but when I turn to see, they're gone. Like ghosts. Except I don't believe in ghosts. I figured I was just catching glimpses of the guys, you know? But I'm still seeing things since I came in here to lie down by myself. I don't know what it is. Hallucinations or whatever."

"Jesus, man."

Marty tried to laugh, but the noise was strangled and weak. It started as a breath, became a cough, and died a hiss. "Whatever I'm seeing, it ain't Jesus. Seriously, I think I'm going crazy."

"You're not crazy." Noah thought back to the crewmen in the hallway and in the day room both seeming to look at something over his shoulder that wasn't there. He wondered if the crew had been poisoned by something other than the fumes from the fire. Noah had breathed more than his share of that shit putting it out and he wasn't seeing things. At the same time, he'd eaten with everyone else and was drinking the same water, breathing the same air. He did everything the other crew members did, and wasn't suffering like they were. He was, relatively speaking, feeling fine.

"Look, I'm going to go find Doc, okay? I'll bring him here."

Marty reached out and grabbed Noah's forearm. "I'm not a horse."

Noah didn't laugh. Everyone knew Sean Mickle only had a minor amount of medical training—enough to care for a cut or rope burn. He wasn't a real doctor or even a nurse. He was a merchant seaman who'd been shown how to glue a laceration together and dole out pain pills. The joke was 'don't break your leg or he might shoot you.' But he was as good as they had, and Noah had to do something to help. Including Marty, he could count the number of friends he had on board the *Arctic Promise* on one hand—with fingers left over. He couldn't spare even one.

"Nobody's getting shot. Don't go anywhere; I'll be right back."

Marty let go of Noah's arm and waved 'bye without opening his eyes. Noah retreated from the room uncertain now whether everyone was covering their eyes because the light hurt, or because they couldn't face the movement in the shadows.

With a full complement, the ship's crew would operate on a three-shift schedule of watchstanders. Noah, before he was relieved, would have been expected to work two four-hour watches, one at eight in the morning and the other at eight p.m. But OrbitOil was in the business of making a profit, and this run to resupply the Niflheim deep sea drilling platform could be accomplished with a skeleton crew. The ship's master had therefore implemented a "sevens and fives" two-team schedule to compensate for the lack of hands. Each team worked one long shift followed by a shorter one after a rest. On a normal day, any merchant sailor's time was filled with whatever job needed done, checking whether the lashing gear holding the cargo in place needed tightening or greasing, sanding away rust and repainting, or cleaning. Workers aboard ship earned money working overtime and most found as much to do on the clock as they could. The salt in both the water and the air was corrosive and an enemy of steel. There wasn't a day when something couldn't be fortified against its constant assault. Today, however, the ship felt deserted. Aside from the few manning their stations, the crew seemed to be down for the count. Not even the deckboss, Serge Boucher, was carrying on the way he usually did. Noah couldn't remember a time when he'd known that man to be sleeping. If he wasn't working, he was playing cards or holding court telling embellished stories of his adventures in ports around the world. Not today.

Noah checked the clock on the wall in the empty day room; it was approaching noon and the change in the watch schedule. Mickle was on the second team with Noah. Under normal circumstances, as an officer, Doc would likely seek out some rest in his cabin or try to pass the time in one of the day rooms. He didn't need the OT. Given Pereira's condition, Noah assumed he'd be working in sick bay until they reached their destination. He hoped he was, and that he'd found something he could take back to Martin.

He returned to the hospital to find Pereira alone, still doped up and sleeping. That hopefully meant the second officer had the conn. He knew better than to look for Doc up there. If he walked in to find Brewster at the wheel, Noah was as likely to be left behind on an ice floe as he was to reach the platform. He glanced at the safe in the far end of the room. If painkillers were in high demand, the second officer might have stashed what little he had left in with the tramadol he'd given

Felix. But if there was anything in the locked compartment, it might as well not exist at all. Noah would have a hard time jimmying open a simple locked cabinet, let alone cracking a digital safe. And if he was caught trying, not only was he out of a job, he'd be arrested once they returned to port and blackballed from work on any other ship. Not that the last part mattered. He intended never to set foot on a ship again as crew or passenger once he returned to Seattle. He desired the life of a landsman, with unmoving, solid ground beneath his feet. Sure footing and steady. Out of grace with the sea.

He heard the engines wind up, working harder, but no sensation followed their vibration. If the ship was moving faster—or at all—he couldn't tell. As he tried to make sense of what he wasn't feeling, heavy footsteps echoed in the passageway outside. Noah leaned out to see Serge Boucher stomping away from the wheelhouse ladder. He had what Noah's wife had referred to as "resting bitch face." In the absence of any other expression, he looked sullen and angry. Upon seeing Noah, however, his normal expression soured and twisted even more.

"Cabot! Where the hell have you been?" he asked, his voice bouncing off the steel walls like buckshot.

"The Old Man told me to stay in my cabin."

"So what the fuck are you doing in sick bay?" The bosun narrowed his bloodshot eyes, sunken above dark bags. He had a sheen of sweat on his pale skin that made him look like sausage left out on the counter.

"I'm looking for Mickle. Have you seen him?"

Boucher's brow furrowed and he ignored the question. "Come with me," he ordered. "I've got a job for you."

"I told you, the Old Man relieved me of duty."

"This comes right *from* Brewster. I'm not telling you twice, Cabot." Boucher's face flashed malevolence and Noah felt himself falling into step behind the man, trailing in his wake. In the change room, the boson opened a locker and began suiting up for the weather. "Get into your gear. Brewster wants you outside."

"What's going on? There's no way we've reached the platform already."

"That's what we're going to find out. You and me, we're going out to have a look."

Noah didn't ask. He didn't want to know. "I've already been outside," he said, zipping up his red insulated jumpsuit.

"Yeah, and? What did you see?"

He debated saying more. He didn't want to have to explain that he'd had the opportunity to see ice in the water because he'd been snooping around, double checking the officers' work. But if he could save himself the duty outside, it might be worth the scolding he'd endure. "I saw ice." Noah had seen frost flowers, not "young" ice or even thin crust "nilas." Neither are a hazard to a ship like the *Promise,* but they can be signs of more treacherous water to come.

"Huh. So when you were strolling along the Promenade Deck, did you think you should tell someone? You try using one of the phones?"

Noah gritted his teeth. "No." Distracted as he was, he hadn't fully comprehended what the combination of fog and small ice in the water meant. It was bad. The presence of small fragments typically meant larger ice ahead. It meant they were headed into dangerous water with a higher concentration of thicker masses in the water. Ice that could damage the ship. Or sink them. He'd gone to sleep assuming if Brewster was moving ahead, he was able to track obstacles in their path using radar. But what if, like the communications systems, that wasn't functioning, either? His guts knotted at the thought of it.

Boucher zipped up his environment suit—big enough for two men to fit inside—and yanked open an equipment locker. He pulled a red and yellow bosun's chair harness out and shoved it at Noah. "You're going to have a closer look." Thrusting his hands into his gloves, Boucher stomped out of the change room and headed for the exterior bulkhead door without waiting to hear Noah protest. Noah scrambled after him, zipping up his gear, the harness clattering and clanking as it trailed on the deck behind him.

Outside, the thick fog drifted over the rails and the decking. Boucher stepped more carefully, leery of ice underfoot, but he still seemed to stomp like an angry giant. He stopped beside the lifeboat and swung a windlass on a boom arm over the rail toward them. Lowering a length of cable from the winch, he beckoned for Noah to come closer. Noah stood frozen. Brewster had actually ordered him overboard? Whether he was thrown unceremoniously or lowered in a bosun's chair, the result was the same: he was going over the side. Boucher straightened his back, growing even larger, and pointed a gloved finger at the deck directly in front of him, like he was ordering a child front and center for a scolding. Noah complied.

Boucher helped him secure the harness belts at his waist and across his chest. A flat board bounced against Noah's ass as he was pulled around so the bosun could attach a hook to the d-rings at the end of the straps by his sides. The latches snapped into place, the last clicking with a finality that sent a shiver of fear through Noah's body. He didn't feel like they were moving, but the engines were humming. He felt a lump grow in his throat as he imagined their seeming stillness was actually an illusion borne of the previously exaggerated and violent movement of the ship in the storm. He banished his dark thoughts and tried to think rationally. *You're not feeling movement, because we're not moving. Even if we were, we're not going to ram anything, because there's nothing out there.* He told himself these things in the hope that somewhere deep down a part of him— the part that controlled fear and irrationality—would hear him and be changed. Clamped to the windlass, his fear remained unchanged.

Once rigged, Boucher fetched up a pair of walkie-talkies and jammed one in Noah's paw. "I'm gonna lower you down real slow. As soon as you can see the surface, I want you to radio up to me and I'll stop the winch. Got that?"

"Aye," Noah said. He tried to swallow, but his mouth and throat were dry and cottony. He sucked on his tongue, trying to produce some kind of moisture, and even sniffed hard, thinking snot would be better than nothing. The frozen Arctic air only hurt his sinus as he did. If he couldn't talk, he hoped at least the squawk of the radio would alert the bosun before he went in the water.

"Out you go," Boucher said. He gestured to the rail gate like a maître d' showing a dinner guest to his seat. Noah stepped into the gap and leaned out from the hull, ready to go down. Starting the windlass motor,

Boucher said, "Remember, as soon as you see water, hit the radio. You copy?"

Noah gave a nod and a thumbs-up. But the combined sounds of the ship's engine, the wind, and the winch motor all meant Boucher wouldn't hear a damn thing when Noah tried to hail him.

Boucher nodded, gave his own thumbs-up, and shoved the winch arm out, swinging Noah past the FRC and into space. He pulled the lever, unspooling the cable, and Noah descended with a sudden jerk into the mist.

He was clear of the ship by a couple of feet, but was careful to keep his legs ready to kick off the hull as the wind blew him around. He clutched the cable to stay upright while doing his best to peer down without unbalancing his seat. He searched for sign of the spiky frost flowers, feeling a little excited to see them again. Keeping the radio close to his face and his thumb on the send switch, he hoped Boucher's reflexes were quick enough. If the surface came in to view with only a foot or two to spare, Noah was certain he was going in. *You wanted a closer look and now you're going to get one,* he chided himself.

The mist remained thick and the mechanical sounds of the ship grew fainter as he moved farther down. He didn't hear water lapping and splashing against the hull as he expected. All the sounds he associated with the sea were absent; it felt like flying through clouds. A small, resigned grin grew on Noah's face as he imagined his father-in-law as a half-mad sky captain clad in leather and copper.

His smile vanished when he fell out of the sky.

8

Abby was resplendent in white. Daylight reflected off the opalescent beadwork stitched around her neckline and over her shoulders; she shone with a radiance that shamed the perfect day. Noah couldn't turn away. Transfixed by the image of her, he wanted to take in every second of her appearance. He longed to conquer time and live in that moment forever, frozen like a traveler in deep space. But time moved with her up the aisle. That perfect vision of a second ago fading into the present as they came together, her closeness obscuring the image of the whole woman.

William Brewster took her hand from the crook of his arm and held it a moment, staring into the veiled face of his only daughter. Finally, he guided her hand to Noah's. Gripping the back of the young groom's neck with a thick, calloused hand, he whispered, "Don't forget." He squeezed, sending a sharp tinge of pain lancing up Noah's neck, and took his seat.

The feeling of Abby's father's fingers remained like a ghost ready to throttle him. The words echoed in his consciousness calling to mind the promise William made at Noah's bachelor party two nights earlier. He'd grabbed his future son-in-law in exactly the same way and said, "If I ever find out you hurt my little girl, I'll break your neck," as casually as he ordered another scotch and soda when he let go.

"What was that about?" Abby whispered.

Noah shook his head and lied, "Beats me." It was the first lie he'd ever told his wife.

Eventually, he'd tell her another.

The bosun's chair was designed to distribute impact forces evenly throughout a person's body in case of a fall. That meant Noah felt like hell from head to toe when he landed on the ice. He lost his grip on the walkie-talkie and it tumbled away across the white surface, squawking and chirping as it bounced. Laying there a moment, heart pounding and nearly hyperventilating with fear, he waited for reality to hit him with blast of the freezing water that would claim him. However, he remained dry. Cold, but dry.

It took some effort to sit up. The plank under his ass pushed his hips forward and prevented him from rolling onto his side. Sitting up sent a spark of pain down his sciatic nerve into his lower back and ass. He had to leverage himself on his elbows and struggle like a turtle before he could sit up. The cable attached to the metal rings of his harness slumped and dangled in front of him. Rising up into the fog, it was presumably still attached to the windlass. The line hadn't broken. That meant either the winch failed . . . or Boucher had hit the release lever, dropping him. The thing should have been able to lower ten times his weight without failure, so that left the second possibility as the more likely one. The way things were going on the ship, however, he couldn't be certain it was malice that had sent him falling. It was equally probable that the machine had been damaged in the storm as it was that the bosun released the catch. If there was a single bit of luck to be had, it was that he'd fallen on a piece of ice instead of in the water. Second stroke of luck: he hadn't broken his neck. It could always be worse. There was always farther down to go.

Noah opened his eyes and tried to see where his radio had gone. He pictured it sliding off the edge of the ice into the frozen depths, but hadn't heard the *splonk* of it entering the water. Ten feet away, a red LED shone dully in the fog. He pushed himself to his feet and stepped carefully, certain that redistributing his weight would unbalance the chunk of ice on which he stood and send him sliding off the edge. It didn't. He felt as sturdy on his feet as he did on board the *Arctic Promise*—as he did on land.

The radio chirped. A faint voice crackled from the speaker. He heard his name, the word "okay," and an expletive. The rest was incomprehensible. He picked up the little yellow device and keyed it. "Boucher! What the fuck happened? Over." He released the button and waited. A second later, another staticky burst of sound erupted, oddly punctuated by the bosun's perfectly clear colorful expressions, as if the fog was blocking all transmissions except profanity.

He looked around, trying to orient himself. The haze afforded a view only a few feet in any direction. He imagined the platform of ice on which he stood had to be huge if it wasn't shifting with his movements. What he'd thought had to be "open drift" ice was more concentrated. This was "very close pack" at least. The kind of solid ice in which ships became trapped—beset.

Taking a few halting steps, he tried to see where the pack ended and the next piece began, but at the end of his cable, he couldn't find a lip or an edge. He couldn't even find a seam. As far as he could see, it looked like old, consolidated ice. But that wasn't possible, was it? Hadn't he seen water and the frost flowers only a few hours ago? Unless the ice had closed in like a living thing to grasp them, it was impossible. They'd have felt the ice hitting the hull, slowing the ship. Brewster would have seen it on the x-band radar. Yet, there he was standing on it. Ice as far as he could see—which admittedly wasn't far—and no sign it would look any different if he walked any deeper into the fog.

He moved to unclip the hook from his harness to do just that, but paused. If he released himself and Boucher got the windlass moving, it'd yank up his only connection to the ship. He'd be lost. Maybe that was the plan. Instead, hanging on to the cable, he moved what the length of it allowed in a wide crescent, looking for any sign of a break under his feet. There was none. He knelt and brushed away the thin layer of snow in a spot, wondering if he could tell how thick the ice pack underfoot actually was. What he uncovered was an opaque surface that gave no hint at its width. He could be kneeling atop ice an inch, a foot, or a yard thick. He fumbled at the pocket on the side of his harness for a tool to pick at it—dig a little and see. The pocket was empty.

The radio crackled and he heard Boucher say, "Got

it!" just before the cable tightened, jerking him off balance. Noah stumbled backward in his crouch across the slick surface, trying to stay on his feet as the winch dragged him toward the hull. His heels skipped and slipped out from under him in a mockery of a Russian dance. Dropping the radio, he grabbed the cable with both hands to try to keep from landing flat on his back again. The cable dragged him to the ship and he held on as it lifted off the surface. He banged painfully into the hull before he was able to orient himself around again with his legs ready to act as shock absorbers against the next impact. His pulse throbbed in his throat and his temples. Blood rushed in his ears, deafening him. As he rose, Noah held his breath waiting for the next drop, this time from a higher point—the height that would cripple or kill him. The machine pulled him up to the deck, however, and Boucher's sizable paw grasped the harness and pulled him in.

"The hell?" Boucher said.

"You dropped me!"

Boucher let out a single barking laugh. "I swear, the release on the winch just gave. It was the damndest thing." The big man looked Noah up and down with an expression of astonishment and confusion. "Why aren't you wet?"

Noah shook his head, unfastening the hook from the harness as quickly as he was able. "I landed on ice."

"Ice?"

"Yeah. When water gets cold enough it becomes solid. They call that 'ice.'" He stabbed his fingers in the air around the word.

Boucher reared up, looking like he was about to knock Noah back over the side. Noah unslung the harness, swinging it back over his shoulder with the seat plank. The straps and rings whipped his back, but he stood his ground, ignoring the pain. "Give me your best shot, Serge. I'll knock your skull all the way to fuckin' Lansdowne Street!" Boucher took a half step forward. "Don't believe me? Finish that step."

The bosun's face grew dark with rage, but he stopped.

"Get out of my god damned way or I'll tell the Old Man the gate just popped open and you fell over the side. 'It was the damndest thing, Brewster, he just lost his balance. Musta been drunk.' " Noah flinched forward with the seat plank. "Move!"

Boucher backed off, hands raised and head lowered. He wasn't cowed; he looked like a boxer with his guard up. Noah was pretty sure if he swung at the man, Boucher would catch the damned chair and fling it over the rail with him following right behind.

"We're not through, Cabot," Boucher said. "This ship ain't big enough for you to disappear in, and you can't hang on to that chair the rest of the trip."

Noah threw the bosun's chair at Boucher's feet. "You want to tussle, I'll be in the wheelhouse."

"And you can't hide behind your father-in-law, you pussy. He'll hold you while I tear your head off."

"I'm not hiding. I'm going to tell Brewster we're beset."

"Beset?"

"Yeah, it's solid ice down there as far as I could see. We're stranded."

Noah turned for the bulkhead door, waiting to feel the blow from one of Boucher's heavy hands or even the bosun's chair plank flat against his already aching back. Instead, what he felt was the man's footsteps falling in step behind him.

9

Mickle watched quietly as Brewster cursed and shouted at the unresponsive vessel. The Second Officer looked like he wanted to take the helm but didn't know how to do it without knocking the ship's master unconscious. Both men's heads whipped around when Noah barged into the wheelhouse. The shift in Mickle's expression suggested he welcomed an ally. Then Boucher followed him in, and that look of hope died under the weight of resignation.

"God damn it, Noah," Brewster shouted. "What do you want? I have bigger problems than you right now." He craned his neck forward as if being two inches closer could help his eyes penetrate the haze. Noah circled around and glanced at the display in front of the Old Man. The order transmission to the engines was "dead slow ahead." Almost a stop, but the propellers were still moving, even if the ship wasn't. Brewster dug his fingertips into his forehead and let out a long exhalation. Ignoring Noah, he said, "Boucher! What did you see?"

The bosun stepped up to the console, but Noah

interrupted him before he had a chance to reply. "He didn't see a damn thing. *I,* on the other hand, got a real close look. We're beset."

Brewster stared at him with a puzzled expression. Noah cast a glance over his shoulder at the deckboss who said, "That's what he says, but—"

"I told *you* to go have a look over the stern, Serge. Noah's not allowed anywhere near the cargo deck."

"I know. I mean, he wasn't," Boucher stammered. "I thought it'd be better to lower someone down over the side and get a good, close look. I ran into him and—"

"He volunteered me as bait to go trawling." Boucher shot him a withering look, but Noah wasn't intimidated. His fury at being dropped on the ice gave him a taste of reckless courage. He might pay for showing spine later, but in the moment, showing meekness or even deference was only going to get all of them in even deeper trouble. He could stand up to Brewster or they could all freeze to death when Brewster burned out the backup engine controls trying to keep forward motion in solid ice.

The Old Man looked Noah up and down. "You don't look like you been swimming to me."

"That's what I'm telling you. He dropped me all the way down and I'm bone dry." As if to emphasize his state, Noah pulled his watch cap off, revealing damp hair plastered to his forehead. He was soaking with perspiration from his excitement and coming out of the cold into the well-warmed bridge, but his gear was dry. He hadn't been swimming in anything but adrenaline and sweat. Brewster raised his eyebrows, silently asking his deckboss for confirmation. Boucher shrugged.

"And?"

"I said, we're beset."

"Bullshit! Boucher, what did—"

"Don't ask him," Noah protested, stepping in front of the bosun. "*I* went over the side. *I* walked around on the consolidated ice pack that's holding us fast. I know what I'm talking about."

Shaking his head at the absurdity of what Noah was saying, Brewster said, "You're fulla shit. We can't be beset; I haven't seen anything on the radar. Hell, I would have seen ice blink out there." He pointed at the white, blank window.

"Yeah? You think you can see the reflection of an ice field ahead when you can't even see the sun?"

Brewster set the throttle to stop, and stood. "Mr. Mickle, take the conn. Keep the engines on standby. I'm going to have a look." Mickle hustled to climb into the seat before the Old Man could change his mind and sit back down. Brewster stomped toward the door, pushing past Noah with an elbow. Noah caught his arm and held.

"Do we even have radar? Communications are down. Do we have *any* instruments or have you been navigating by reading tea leaves?"

The Old Man stood as still as a stuffed bear in a hunter's lodge, looming above a room full of men who knew he looked fierce but couldn't really touch them. "What would your days of experience in the Arctic tell you to do?"

"Keep the engines on standby," Noah said. "Put Nevins on restoring the communications array and, when he gets them back online, call for an icebreaker to come clear the way."

"They're all down at once, genius," Boucher said. "It means it ain't mechanical."

"What is it then?"

Brewster pointed out the window. "It's that shit out there."

Boucher nodded like a kid taking glee in his younger brother being cussed out for something he'd done.

"What? The fog?" Noah said, working to stay focused. He tried to imagine what could cause all the tech on board to go on the blink at once. It wasn't a simple magnetic compass distortion. That wouldn't take down everything. That wouldn't cause hallucinations.

He'd read an article about the Russians dumping old nuclear submarines—complete with their reactors—in the Arctic as late as 1993. What if one of them had broken open, leaking nuclear radiation into the sea? Would it mess with their systems? Would it mess with the men?

He banished the thought as science fiction. Even if they'd somehow steered right into ground zero of some underwater dump site, if it was having these kinds of effects, someone else would have known about it by now. Wouldn't they? Unless the *Arctic Promise* was the first.

"You think it's some kind of signal distortion that's messing with everything?" he said.

"That's the only thing that makes sense. If navigation and communications are both out, it's not a problem with the ship. It's gotta be environmental. We have to get out of this fog if we want to restore systems. And we sure as hell don't want to be sitting here if anything else goes down. We lose the engines and the heating system, they'll be chipping our remains out of a block of ice. Unless you know somewhere on board to build a fire."

Noah opened his mouth to respond but his words caught in his throat when Brewster's eyes darted to the side. It looked like he wanted to jerk his head around to follow whatever it was but forced himself not to. Noah tried to see what it was he was looking at, but there was nothing there. Just Sean Mickle looking pale . . . like he'd seen a ghost as well. Only Boucher looked unaffected by the specter. He looked too ornery to be spooked.

"Come with me," the Old Man barked. He grabbed his coat and hat off the peg beside the door and shoved through. Noah watched Brewster disappear into the mist, with Boucher trotting behind like a pet not wanting to be left out. Noah lingered, letting the door slam behind them, and looked to Mickle for support. The second officer shrugged and said, "I suppose I should thank you for getting him to give up the conn. Although at this point, I don't think I'm any better equipped to be behind the wheel than the Old Man." He pivoted the chair around and ran a hand down his face. "How are you feeling?"

"Me? I'm good, I guess. Hanging in there anyway. My headache's gone. The rest of me feels like shit after being dropped on the ice, but at least my head's stopped hurting."

Mickle laughed weakly. "Keep hanging in, because whatever has gotten its hooks in me and the rest of the crew is bad." He let his mouth hang open as if he wanted to add to his confession but couldn't bring himself to issue another utterance. Noah hadn't known the second officer long, but he didn't seem like the kind of man who complained without good reason or who even let on that he wasn't feeling a hundred percent. He was the kind of stoic sailor his grandfather had been. Mickle wiped at his nose with the back of a finger. It came away red. The man rubbed at the blood with a thumb until his skin was a slightly ruddier shade of pale, but said nothing about it, as if it wasn't anything Noah should feel concerned about.

"Martin told me he's seeing . . . things. Movement in his peripheral vision."

Mickle's eyes widened for a second before his face settled back into its normal inscrutability. "He's not the only one," he said.

The door behind the men slammed open and Boucher stood pointing at Noah. "You think the Old Man was kidding, Cabot? Move your ass!"

The second officer nodded, silently suggesting they'd talk about it later.

"Hang in there, Doc." Noah marched out of the room, brushing past Boucher, who stood like a prison guard leading him to the gladiator yard. The bosun slammed the door as soon as Noah's heel cleared the opening and shoved past, waving a hand for Noah to follow.

Boucher led him to the aft end of the cargo deck where Brewster stood waiting. While they'd battled the ice buildup during the storm, there was still considerable ice on the deck and gunwales. Not so much that the ship was in danger, but enough that they had to step carefully to avoid falling or sliding into or under something solid. The trio climbed the ladder onto the catwalk. Brewster leaned out over the side and tried to see. Although it was a shorter distance to the surface than over by the lifeboats, the swirling mist still obscured everything below. It might have been twenty feet to the surface or twenty thousand. Noah couldn't tell. None of them, experienced seamen all, had seen a fog this thick last this long.

"Listen," Noah said. He nodded his head toward the void. "You hear it?"

Brewster shrugged. "What?"

"Exactly. You don't hear anything because it's frozen solid all around us."

"You walked on it? Did you make it all the way around? Are you sure the ice closed up behind us?"

He shook his head. "I was off the starboard bow. I got a look from there to maybe amidships. But the ice was compact. I didn't even see cracking or breakup beside the hull. It's like we've been sitting still in it for days. And it looks thick, too. Like second-year ice."

"Second-year ice. Impossible!" Brewster said. "You read that in one of your books?"

"There," Boucher shouted, pointing. He grabbed Brewster's sleeve and tugged. The Old Man leaned back over the side and squinted. Like the day before, a short gust of wind peeled back the fog and showed them a glimpse of what it hid. A field of mottled white and cold purple reached to the ship, drifts of snow blowing over the surface. The mist closed in again. The Old Man straightened up, shoving his bare hands in his pockets. The wind pinked his skin and made him blink his watering eyes, but Brewster didn't seem affected by the cold otherwise. He didn't hunch his shoulders, or shiver, standing like there was merely a touch of chill in the air, like the brisk crispness right before a light snowfall.

"I told you, it's consolidated and we aren't breaking through it. We aren't going anywhere without help. We have to call for an icebreaker."

Brewster slowly shook his head and exhaled through

his nose. His breath hung in the air like words frozen before they could be heard, his plan to free the ship taken by the cold before blowing away to disappear in the mist. Shoving Noah out of the way with a stiff arm, Brewster climbed down from the catwalk and stalked off toward the superstructure. Noah followed behind, skidding and slipping on the same ice that didn't seem to affect the Old Man. He called after him, "So what now?"

Brewster spun around. "We can't wait here for someone to come riding up and rescue us. If that ice plate shifts it could capsize us or puncture the hull. I'm not going to sit around and do nothing!"

"I'm not telling you to do nothing, William. Let Martin work on the radio. If he can't get it—"

"Enough! The only say you have on board my god damned ship is 'aye sir.' You understand?"

"Aye sir."

Brewster grabbed the handset from the bulkhead beside the door and pressed the switch for the public address system. He glared while speakers throughout the ship crackled and beeped alerting them to his coming message. "This is the ship's master," he said. "All available hands assemble in the mess room immediately. Repeat, all hands to the mess." He hung up and turned to glower at Noah. "You're going to be our icebreaker."

Noah tried to imagine what Brewster could mean by that. "I thought I was relieved of duty."

"You're reinstated. Now get your ass to the mess room."

10

Slightly over half of the ship's crew assembled at the dining tables in the mess room. Most of the men on watch—excluding Mickle at the helm and Boucher, trailing in Brewster's wake somewhere—had come. Fewer than half of those off duty were accounted for, however. None of them looked like they wanted to be out of bed, let alone awaiting orders.

Noah took a stool at the far end of the room near a couple of guys who were slightly warmer toward him than his other shipmates. Jack Freeman and Kevin Lawless were a couple of deathrock musicians from Seattle who funded their summers playing punk covers in dingy little clubs by working supply vessels in the winter. Noah had met them the day before shipping out. They laughed a lot and talked about preferring to work hung over. "Why waste feeling good on a *job*?" Kevin had said, only half joking. Noah was certain they'd be out on the cargo deck in skinny jeans and Chuck Taylors if the deckboss didn't force them into cold weather gear. Both men were gregarious storytellers, but today they were reserved and quiet. Jack held his hands beside his eyes like blinders. Kevin rested his head on his folded arms atop the table. Both were paler than usual.

Opposite them were a trio of deckhands, Henry Gutierrez, Theo Mesires, and Andrew Puck, sitting in a tight triangle. Noah had worked with them in the past. Henry was a lifer who seemed to actually enjoy the work, not just the money, and Theo was his protégé. The two of them racked up more OT than seemed possible in a twenty-four-hour day. Noah assumed they accumulated their extra hours through a combination of greed and speed. Theo looked like he might be popping pills; he vibrated at a different frequency than any other human Noah had ever met. He wasn't sure about Henry. The guy's engine just always seemed to be in the red. Andrew, by contrast, looked like death. If he didn't occasionally shift on his stool, Noah would have thought the other two had propped his corpse up as a joke.

Brewster stomped into the mess with the bosun bringing up the rear. Boucher normally had to duck his head to pass through the doorways. Today he remained stooped, and walked through without having to bow lower. The Old Man hesitated at the head of the room, counting the men assembled. Leaning over, he whispered something to Boucher. The deckboss shrugged and pointed toward the assembly with a look-at-them gesture before slumping against the far wall. Brewster stood up straight and announced his plan.

"I know this trip has been tough. Tougher than usual, and you can all tell, it's taking longer than it should to get where we're going. Earlier today, I had some recon done to assess our situation and it appears we've . . .

become beset." He paused a moment to let the men vocalize their disbelief. None of them made a sound. He continued. "The ice pack appears to be consolidated and thick. The short version is: we're not going anywhere until we can free the ship."

"How do you suggest we do that?" Theo asked.

Brewster furrowed his brow. "We're going to need to take a closer look. If the ice has closed in all around us, we'll have to break it up by hand."

"If it pays overtime, I'm game," Henry added. While he looked in better shape than most of the crew, it was clearly not a one-man job. No matter how much energy he and his pal could summon, it was going to take more than a couple of men.

Kevin groaned. "I don't know. If it's thick enough to hold us, can a few guys even break it up enough to bust out?"

"You only have to break away enough so I can throttle up the engines," Brewster said. "I'm going to try to chop up what's back there with the propellers."

"Like a blender," Boucher added.

Brewster shot him a let-me-handle-it glance and continued. "The cavitation of the props could break up what you guys loosen. If I can move us astern, we can try to fire the engines harder and plow forward. But I need space ahead to make a run at the ice pack. That means clearing out the ice behind us."

Noah shook his head. "You think the hull fortifications are strong enough to handle that? You're going to damage the ship or even breach the hull. If we're lucky, you'll just burn out the engines trying to get us moving instead of sinking us."

"Stow that shit, Cabot," Boucher snapped. He leaned away from the wall, looking ready to physically silence Noah. Brewster held up a hand.

"Why not call for a breaker?" Kevin said. "Why won't they come help us?"

"We're experiencing interference with the radio."

"It's not just the radio," Noah butted in. "The whole communications array is dead."

"What do you mean, 'dead'?" Theo asked, fidgeting in his seat. The crew seemed to be coming to life—the direness of the situation outside slowly climbing on top of their physical woes. All except Puck, who remained propped against the wall, watching through half-lidded eyes.

Brewster leaned forward, pressing his balled fists onto the table in front of him. His pallid face reddened as he admitted, "We don't know what the problem with communications is. It could be ice built up on the superstructure messing with the antennas, but given that the sat phone is down, too, my guess is the fog."

"You can't know that for certain."

"Nobody asked for your opinion, Cabot. We need to get out of this atmosphere before we can be certain whether we've permanently lost touch."

"My opinion? My opinion is that you've been taking chances with all our lives. You could have skirted that storm. Instead, you steered us right into it and put Felix in the hospital. Now we're in this mess and we can't call for a medevac. We're dead in the ice because you won't admit you're not . . . I don't know. Not thinking clearly about what we should do." Noah felt himself rising from his seat, as though he was being lifted. As soon as he was on his feet, he regretted it.

Brewster's back straightened, his fists still balled up tight and knuckles white. Boucher looked ready to make good on his promise to tan Noah's hide. Noah decided that if he was going to take a leathering for standing up for himself and the crew, he should just lay it all out.

"You want to get out and push, go ahead," he said. "But there are fifteen other men on this ship who want to get home to their families. For fuck's sake, look at Puck." Whatever had gotten into the ship and its crew was affecting them all differently. Brewster was on his feet, but looking pale. Henry was more or less himself, albeit sweatier than normal. Boucher looked like he was on Puck's heels. And Puck, he looked like death. "Working sick men like you're suggesting could kill someone. We need to fix the radio and call for help." Puck groaned and raised a hand to protest his weakened state. It was the first true sign of life Noah had seen in the man. His hand dropped back into his lap like someone cut the string lifting it.

Brewster glared at Noah with a mix of hostility and cool ill intent. He said, "You'd know something about getting people killed, wouldn't you, Noah? Being the only person in this room who's actually done it."

Noah's ears and cheeks went hot with blood, and all the bravado drained from his body. The words hit like a slap in the mouth. He took a step back, looking around the room at the faces of the other men. Jack and Kevin stared down at the table in front of them, leaning away, trying to distance themselves from Noah's shame. Theo's eyes grew wide while Henry's narrowed with contempt. Only Boucher appeared to enjoy the repartee with a sweaty-faced smile. Noah felt perfectly alone, like he'd been left standing on the ice after all and was watching the ship sail away.

"That wasn't my fault," he said, not fully believing it.

"I'm sure Connor MacAllister's gal will love to hear you explain that to her when we get home. Until then, sit down and shut the fuck up. You don't get a say here."

The sting of the dead man's name made Noah's heart pound, and his mind reeled at the memory of standing at his shipmate and best friend's funeral, trying to look his girlfriend, Sheila, in the eye and tell her how sorry he was. Sorry he'd shirked his duty, sorry he'd asked Connor to perform a task *he'd* been ordered to do. He was sorry for a lot of things. Most of all, at that moment, he had been sorry for not being the one in the box they were about to lower into the ground. And not just because of what had happened to Connor.

Noah shook his head, trying to clear away the stress and confusion of the last couple of days. Brewster's condescension wasn't anything new. Neither was his outright hostility and contempt. But his openness about it was. Noah had been pushing him, up in the wheelhouse and now, hard, in front of the crew. He knew he shouldn't be surprised when the Old Man pushed back. Noah wasn't master of the ship, William Brewster was. Then again, Noah hadn't been the one to steer them into an arctic hurricane and almost cripple the vessel by overtaxing the engines. He wasn't the one responsible for a broken man lying in a drugged stupor one deck below, and he sure as shit hadn't driven them into the middle of a field of thick "two-year" sea ice. None of that, however, meant he knew how to get them out of danger. And none of that meant he owned any less responsibility for Connor MacAllister's death a year ago.

Breaking the silence that had fallen over the room, Brewster resumed. "However we got here, we're in a bad way, and we can't sit and wait for things to get worse. I'm the master, and the call to keep going in this shit was mine. I made it, and . . . it was . . . it got us here. I am *not* going to burn out the engines. Even if we did lose one, that's why they built this ship with redundant engines. We got no choice but to try." He looked at Puck, and for a moment, Noah thought he saw the Old Man's self-assurance crack. "On the other hand, this is a special circumstance. I'm not going to ask any of you to put your lives at risk or do anything I wouldn't get down beside you to do. I'm asking for volunteers. If none of you want to chop ice, then I guess that's a vote to focus on the radio and wait for help to come to us."

Theo and Henry leaned in close and whispered to one another. Brewster looked at Kevin and Jack. The rockers shook their heads together like they shared a single consciousness. "This sucks, man," Jack said. "But what choice do we have? If they don't even know we're in trouble, no one's coming to the rescue. By the time we're missed at the Niflheim, we'll be out of food and fuel and we'll be freezing." He raised his hand. "Sorry, Noah. We have to do something."

Kevin raised his arm.

Smiling, Brewster waved his hand to let the volunteers know they could put their arms down. "*This* is how we're going to get home. Everyone in the same boat working together." He glared at his son-in-law as if he could drive the words home by staring them into Noah's skull. "Henry, Theo, Jack, Kevin . . . and you,

Noah, are gonna grab some tools—pickaxes and pole choppers—and meet me at the starboard Rescue Zone in thirty minutes to start clearing ice from the aft. Boucher!" The bosun seemed to feel a shock at hearing his name. He snapped to attention as though he'd been miles away from his body and was suddenly yanked back. "You get Holden and Nevins out of their cabins and on the job. I want them working on troubleshooting and repairing communications."

"Aye, sir." He stood, trying to look ready for the job, but still seemed diminished and tired.

Brewster turned his attention to Puck, slumped against the wall. The deckhand's eyelids fluttered and he let out a low groan. "Jesus, will you two get him back to his bunk before we have to put a stake through his heart." No one laughed at the joke.

The Old Man turned to walk out of the room, but stopped short of the door, looking at Noah a last time. "When we get out of this, Cabot, you're going to owe *all* these men an apology, not just Connor's girlfriend." He disappeared into the passageway, Boucher a step behind.

Noah leaned against a table, drained by the confrontation. Theo and Henry helped Puck to his feet and shuffled him out of the room. Kevin put a hand on Noah's arm and tried to smile. "It's cool, man. I get it'd be hard as shit to work with your father-in-law. Nobody's trying to kill anybody, though. No lie. We'll all get out of this, and then I'm buying the first round. You watch."

The pair walked out, leaving Noah alone in the mess room. Out of the corner of his eye, a shadow seemed to tremble, like the shade of a tree on a breezy day. He tried to focus on his peripheral vision to get a look without turning to face it, remembering what Martin had said. *Like ghosts. Except I don't believe in ghosts.*

The shadow got up and slipped out of the room. Noah stood as frozen as the sea outside.

11

He drove the long-handled chopper into the ice. The flat blade made short scores in the surface resembling hash marks on a prison wall, counting the interminable age it would take to realize freedom, one blow at a time. Noah's knuckles ached and his joints swelled as he thrust the flat spade edge down in front of his feet again and again, hoping the next hit would create the crack showing him he'd reached the point at which the ice would give. But all he did was chip away a half inch at a time at the thick, solid layer. The tool was built to break and scrape ice accumulated on the deck of the ship. It was designed to combat an inch or two of the stuff, not thickly packed floes of sea ice. Still, he was better off than Henry with a blunt sledgehammer, beating against the surface with no effect. Noah could feel the vibrations of the impacts under foot. He thought the sensation should trouble him, make him fear he was standing too near a crack about to open and dump him through. But the surface on which he stood felt as sturdy as downtown asphalt.

The breakup crew was dressed in immersion survival

suits—neon-bright neoprene jumpsuits designed for surviving in frigid water. Unofficially known as "Gumby suits," they were waterproof and warm, with tethered mittens and boots, dye markers, radio beacons, and inflatable bladders to keep the wearer's head above the surface. They weren't formfitting, however, and moving in them was difficult. Working in them was nearly impossible, but Brewster insisted. Noah assumed it was because the Old Man was afraid of going in the water and wanted to wear one himself. He wouldn't want to be the only one looking like a Day-Glo Claymation figure out there. It impeded work, but it was sensible. If they broke through the ice and someone *did* go in, he'd be protected from the frigid temperature of the water. The suit was designed to keep people alive in open water long enough to be rescued. On the other hand, if a person slipped under the ice without a tether to pull him back toward the opening, he'd be dead no matter how warm the suit kept him. Drowning was not at the top of the list of Noah's concerns, however.

The crew had spread out at first, hoping to make headway by each breaking away a section of his own along the length of the ship's aft section. After a couple of hours without success, Brewster ordered them closer together to attack a single spot. He, wielding the only actual pickax, had chipped down farther than anyone else, but after another hour of work and dwindling daylight, they had broken away only a small portion of the ice adhering to the ship. It was thicker than any of them could have imagined, and the pace at which they were breaking it apart meant it would be days, not hours, that they'd have to spend laboring to free the vessel. If it didn't refreeze and reconsolidate when they weren't bashing at it. There weren't enough crew members in healthy condition to run shifts, and Noah imagined the nighttime temperatures would be as big an obstacle as the frozen buildup itself, even with the Gumby suits on.

The Old Man pushed back his hood and stripped off his cap; steam rose from his head in a cloud. His pulse throbbed visibly under the bright red skin of his neck. Noah thought Brewster looked like he might be having a stroke. The Old Man's breath condensed and formed ice in his closely trimmed beard, turning it from salt and pepper to just salt. He threw his pickax at the ice, shouting, "Fuck me!" and stomped in a small circle, kicking impotently at the snow. It dusted up and blew away to settle elsewhere, unperturbed.

The others stopped working and stared, uncertain what to do. Noah stepped forward. "It was worth a try," he said. "We tried, but this is unreal. I mean, you've never seen anything like this, have you?" Brewster stared at Noah, his breath puffing out in quick gusts of mist and blowing away. He said nothing. "I didn't think so," he continued, stepping closer and lowering his voice. "Let's get these men inside before they get sicker. We can see if Marty's had any luck with the radio and try to come up with a Plan C."

"Why the fuck do you think I would ever listen to a word you have to say?"

"I'm just trying to look out for the guys. We're—"

"You think I want to hurt these men? I don't. I want what's best for them and for me. The only person I wish would die already is *you*!" Brewster shoved Noah back. When he kept his feet, Brewster lunged forward and shoved him again. Noah put up his hands to deflect the next assault, the one that would send him sprawling. The last thing he wanted was to get in a fistfight with the Old Man while wearing a Gumby suit. It was as sad as it was comical—like characters on a kid's show brawling. Brewster didn't appear to share Noah's sense of the absurd, however, and seemed more than willing to try to fight in the restrictive suit.

Brewster reared back with a fist. Noah backpedaled to get out of the way of the swing, stumbling over his feet, tripping backward. Henry appeared out of the fog, grabbing the Old Man's arm and holding him. "Hey! Stop!" The Old Man jerked at his trapped limb, but Henry was younger and stronger.

Turning, with teeth bared and eyes wide, he shouted, "Let me go! This doesn't involve you."

The deckhand held Brewster's arm firmly. "Forget about him. You need to see this. Right now."

"See what? There's nothing to see in this shit!"

Henry pointed at the others standing in a group, all staring off in the same direction. At that distance, they should have been lost in the haze. A chill wind gusted up and blew curtains of the fog around, first darkening them, then revealing the men in perfect clarity. Jack, Kevin, and Theo in their rescue-me sunset orange suits, all facing the same way, each man with a hand up by his eyes, as though blocking the diffuse sunlight might improve their vision. "Just come look," he said.

Brewster reluctantly abandoned his assault. The interruption had sapped the worst of his fury, but it was clear it wouldn't take much to rekindle. Maybe as little as a look from Noah would do it. Brewster followed Henry toward the others. Noah got up and trailed along at a safe distance. His steps faltered as he rounded the rear of the ship and saw what his shipmates had stopped work to stare at. He'd been facing the ship, bashing at the crust that held it, not looking away from his work. What was there to see but an impenetrably solid field of white? Except, the fog was indeed lifting. He could see into the distance. The sprawling snow-covered plain was flat and empty as far as the eye could see.

"How?" Brewster whispered. He turned to face the crew as though he needed confirmation they all saw the same thing. "It's impossible."

Noah silently agreed. That they had sailed overnight from open sea into a continental glacier was not possible. He looked behind himself. The fog was lifting all around, revealing the same barren distance spreading away from them in every direction. No fantasy outcroppings of jagged glacial mountains spearing into the sky or even rolling upheavals of ice sheets having collided with one another. Every point on the compass was empty and infinite. He staggered ahead, trying to see farther. But creeping ahead a few feet didn't make any difference. The far horizon was a straight line—white below blue, forever.

"What's that?" Kevin said. He pointed to the right.

"What?" Brewster asked.

"That, there. That . . . *bump* way out there."

"It's just a frost heave," Jack said, his voice filled with defeat and resignation. The view was hard to take in. There was too much expanse, too much nothing to find a focal point. Noah recalled a trip he'd made once with friends to a fishing cabin in Montana. He was used to big skies at sea—the vision of nothing but water for miles and miles. It didn't affect him. He knew that with proper bearings and enough fuel they would reach land. There was always something to find on the other side. There was hope. But standing in a clearing in "Big Sky Country," he'd felt uncomfortably insignificant and despairing. Unlike New England or the Pacific Northwest with dense trees and city valleys rising up around him, bringing the horizon close no matter where he went, the plains were vast. The horizon farther than he could walk, or even drive, in a day or a week probably. Would he ever be able to reach that far distance, and when he did, would it only show him a vision of more emptiness? No. If he wasn't at sea, he wanted to be among close buildings or trees, surrounded by the things that kept him safe, that didn't make him feel so small and insignificant. Even under the big sky in Montana, there were mountains and rivers to break up the look of the land. It was distant, but there was hope in the grasslands under the big sky. Visible shelter and food. On the ice there was no hope. There was nothing.

"It's not a frost heave. Look. It's red."

It was hard to find focus in the white distance, especially with the *Arctic Promise* rising behind them like a red behemoth. "It's just a reflection from the *Promise*," Jack said.

"A reflection? That far out?" Kevin asked. Jack shrugged in reply.

Noah raised a hand to his eyes like the others in the hope it would improve his vision of the distant object. It did little to sharpen what he saw. The remaining fog obscured the distance, the line between land . . . no, ice . . . and sky was a gradient of white to blue. A soft line suggesting the edge of the world. But there it was.

Kevin was right. There *was* something out there. Something not ice maybe a mile or two away.

Brewster turned, his shoes crunching in the snow as he walked quickly away from the men.

"Where are you going?" Henry asked.

"To fetch up my binoculars from the wheelhouse," he replied. A few feet away, he stopped. Letting out a long sigh, he turned and said, "I'm calling it tonight. You guys earned a rest. We'll get an early start tomorrow morning." He stalked off, leaving the men to pluck their tools out of the snow, scrambling to keep up. Henry grabbed his sledge and Brewster's pickax. Noah fell in behind, not wanting to give up trying to see what was in the distance, but also not willing to miss his ride back up to the ship in the FRC. He couldn't afford to be left behind, not the way Brewster had been ready to lay him out only a few minutes before. If he wasn't in the fast rescue craft with the others, the Old Man might "forget" to send it back down for him, leaving him to spend the night outdoors.

As Noah tried to climb aboard the lifeboat with the rest of the crew, Brewster stuck out a stiff arm, holding him back. "You can take the next one."

"What do you mean 'next one'? It's not an elevator."

"You're not riding up with me. I'll send someone to get you."

Noah looked to one of the other men for help. Henry and Theo wouldn't look him in the face. It was hard to tell in the Gumby suit, but Jack might have shrugged again. Brewster slapped the switch and the rescue craft jerked abruptly up. Henry and Jack unwillingly sat while Theo and Kevin reached out for support.

"Wait," Kevin shouted.

"What?" Brewster said, halting their ascent. "What's wrong?"

Kevin awkwardly swung himself over the edge and lowered himself out of the boat. He dropped the few feet they'd risen back down onto the ice. Jack said, "What are you doing?"

"It's cool. I'm gonna keep him company while you guys head up. Nobody should have to wait in this shit by themselves."

Brewster's face turned red again; the vein in the side of his neck visibly pulsed. He didn't say anything, just slammed the lever up again and resumed their ascent. "Don't forget about *us*," Kevin called after them. He waved, but no one saw.

"You probably shouldn't have done that. There's no telling when Brewster is going to send that thing back down."

"Man, he really has it in for you, doesn't he?" Kevin said as he watched them rise. "How'd you even get a berth if he hates you so much?"

"Just lucky, I guess." Noah replaced his hood and zipped the suit up over his chin, settling in for a long wait.

"That's some real shit luck, brother."

"You're telling me." Noah thought about shit luck and how many times, despite trying to avoid doing so, he stepped right in it. When the company had assigned him to Brewster's crew, he'd thought it was a cruel joke. It wasn't. The company wasn't interested in their personal history, if anyone making the decisions even knew about it. He was a cog in the machine, and if he couldn't work with the bigger gears, he was easily replaceable.

The FRC reached the top and disappeared into the gap in the ship where it lived. The winch silenced and Kevin and Noah stood in near silence waiting for the sound of it powering up again, returning to bring them up. The wind whispered in the spaces around Noah's neoprene hood.

Kevin kept looking up, waiting for the boat. Noah knew better than to hold his breath.

12

Doing his best to track the time by watching the path of the pale sun approaching the horizon, Noah guessed it was over an hour before the FRC returned to retrieve the two men. Maybe longer. Without a watch, he couldn't tell for certain. It had been time enough for the warmth of work to have long worn off, leaving both men shivering and numb. What he was certain of was if they didn't come back for the two of them soon, he and Kevin would have fewer fingers and toes to keep track of the hours. Finally, the rumble of the engine sounded in the preternatural quiet.

As the craft descended, he saw Third Officer Holden at the controls. Jack stood behind him holding two cups of coffee. Noah assumed the delay in their retrieval was more a matter of finding someone willing to come get them rather than pouring the drinks. Jack had ditched his survival suit for his regular cold weather gear and danced from foot to foot to keep warm while trying not to spill the coffee. Noah thought about the amount of sweat that had accumulated in his own Gumby suit and figured if he took it off without also changing the clothes underneath he'd be suffering, too. Wind attacked the gaps in deck clothes under normal circumstances. Being wet with perspiration only made things worse.

As the FRC reached the surface, Jack set the drinks on the side of the vessel and leaned out to help the men scramble aboard. Noah climbed in, taking one of the coffees with both hands. He'd drop it if he tried to grip the cup with only one. "Much obliged," he said.

Jack cocked his head and smiled wanly. "We're all in the same boat, right?" Noah almost laughed.

His thick rubber gloves made it hard to hold the drink, but he didn't dare take them off until he was inside. However bad working in the cold had been, standing still in it was worse. An hour had felt like an eternity with the biting wind kicking up snow into his face while his muscles cooled and stiffened. Kevin had started out telling stories of his last time in the port at Juneau, but after only a few minutes he was shivering and his voice trembled. He'd rushed to the end of his tale—the guy begrudgingly paid the bar bet after Kevin showed him the rooster hanging from a noose tattooed on his calf—and zipped his suit up to his eyes.

"I was starting to worry," Kevin said, pulling the zipper down to take a drink.

"You had nothing to worry about, Lawless," Holden said. "Cabot, on the other hand . . ." Holden finished his thought with a half smile and a jerk of the handle that sent the rescue craft lurching upward. Noah staggered a step to get his balance, reaching out with a half-numb hand for a guyline. Steady, he took a noisy slurp of his drink and decided he'd rather interpret the third officer's statement as a joke as well. Holden had come down to get him, after all. Still, if Kevin hadn't bailed out of the first ride, there was no telling how long Noah might have had to wait below.

Noah nodded. He turned to Holden. "You and Martin were working on communications, right? Make any progress?"

Holden's smile disappeared and he shook his head. "Nevins can repair anything, but it has to be broken first before he can fix it." The third officer didn't elaborate. He was as direct a person as Noah had ever met. He said exactly what he meant, and if you didn't get it the first time, you had better have been taking notes; the man didn't repeat himself. Noah thought about asking the follow-up question about environmental interference, but the takeaway from what he'd heard was that nothing was functioning, even if it was in working order.

They rode the rest of the way in silence until Holden docked the FRC and let them back aboard the *Promise*. "Thanks again for the lift," Noah said. He tried his best not to fall out as he climbed from the craft. He could have used two hands, but he would have rather taken a dive on the slick deck than lose the warm drink.

"Next time, ride up with everyone else," Holden said, shutting down the generator engine.

"Believe me, I would've if it had been an option." Holden nodded. He didn't ask for him to elaborate and Noah didn't offer; there was no point telling the story. The third officer already knew it wasn't tardiness that made Noah and Kevin miss the bus. But if Holden had an opinion of what Brewster had done, he wasn't saying. He stayed above the fray in almost every conflict unrelated to chain of command, but his temper was the subject of legend. By the time Holden worked up a cross word, it was too late to take anything back. You weathered him like a storm. He was a good ally to have, but he couldn't be coerced or corralled into taking a side. He'd find the right one when it needed finding. Noah hoped he would, anyway.

Noah started for the door, desperate to get out of the Gumby suit, but more anxious to get to the port side of the ship and have another look at the shape in the distance before the waning daylight was entirely gone. He bent to help secure the rescue boat first. Holden stopped him. "I was told you're to report to the wheelhouse." He waited a beat and added, "Relax. Mickle's on watch. He's the one who wants to see you." He winked.

Perhaps Holden had chosen a side after all.

"Thanks."

"Don't thank me. You don't know what he wants yet." Holden recruited Jack and Kevin to help him secure the FRC while Noah disappeared inside.

Noah stopped in the change room on the way to the wheelhouse to shed his Gumby suit. He secured it in his personal locker instead of with the other suits, but chose to keep his deck gear with him to store in his cabin. His adventure on the ice had him feeling like he should be watching his back. The men would look to Brewster for their cues how to treat him. Between the threatened beating and being left behind, the message was clear: Noah stood alone. Mostly alone, anyway. He seemed to have a small band of allies. Kevin had taken a big chance standing by him and was probably going to suffer for it. Jack would most likely get some on him, too. He suspected Holden would back him if it came down to it. His other friends aboard, Felix and Marty, were in no shape to take anyone's side but their own. Still, there was comfort in his circle of three, maybe four. He wasn't completely alone.

He slammed his locker shut, twisting the dial just to be sure. Any number of tools aboard the vessel would pop the thing open, but if someone had to jimmy the thing with a pry bar, at least he'd know his suit had been tampered with. If any saboteurs wanted to fuck with anything else of his, they'd have to come see him directly.

Now that Brewster had unofficially declared it open season on him, keeping his head down and doing as he was ordered wasn't going to cut it any longer. In that moment, he decided taking the helicopter back to shore with Felix was the best course of action. He'd lose half of his pay for bailing on the return voyage—hell, he'd probably forfeit the whole check for quitting—but however it shook out, he'd have to take the hit and find a way to make it work. It had been bad enough working with a crew who distrusted him, but sailing under the command of a man who openly wanted him dead was more than he could bear. Once home, he thought he could scrounge up enough money from friends to pay for gas and motel rooms on the road back to Gloucester. He'd load up the truck with everything he could and leave the rest for the landlord to sell to cover the unpaid rent. His mom would fall all over herself to make room in her apartment for her son and grandbaby. He could sleep on the sofa and Ellie would make do with an inflatable toddler bed for a little while. She was small, like her mother. They could live like that for at least as long as it took him to get a berth on a trawler or a tourist boat. He'd save a few bucks until he could afford a bigger place for them all. The money would suck, but at least he'd have a continent between him and his father-in-law. Ex-father-in-law. First, however, he had to make it home.

He wanted to call Abby's best friend, Meghan, to see how his daughter was doing. Meg had a girl the same age as Ellie and was more than happy to take her in for a few weeks while he shipped out to work. Meg said she thought it would be good for Ellie to have someone her own age to play with—good for her to just be a kid for a while. He hoped so. Everybody wanted something better for their kids than they had. Ellie needed something good in her life. She deserved better than he had to offer, and he needed to change that. It was her world now.

Leaving the change room, he passed the ladder to the wheelhouse and ducked into the sick bay to check on Felix. The room was empty except for the patient, who was sleeping. The bruises on his face were turning golden and purple, less black and blue, and his breathing was still shallow and labored. Noah imagined he was feeling no pain due to the good opiates. What happened when they ran out? He didn't want to think about it. They had to get out of the trouble they were in before that happened.

"You hang in there, pal," he said. He wanted to stay, to keep watch over his friend, but he'd already taken enough time before reporting to Mickle. He'd sit with Felix for a while afterward, if he could.

Turning off the light, he slipped out into the passageway and climbed the ladder to the wheelhouse deck. Walking into the command room made his stomach knot. At first glance, he could have sworn it was Brewster sitting in the pilot's chair and that Holden had lied. When Mickle turned, the illusion faded, but the sight of him still wasn't reassuring. The best Noah could say about the second officer was that he looked weary. What he really looked like was a man who belonged in the bunk above Felix.

"You wanted to see me?"

"I do. How are you feeling, Cabot?" Mickle coughed and his face went slack as if his mind had to go somewhere else while his body dealt with the pain. Noah waited for him to come back. The light returned to his eyes slowly. While he tried to put on a brave face, Mickle looked like a boxer at the end of the thirteenth round—he might not be beaten yet, but he had taken a beating and there was plenty of time left on the clock for more.

"I'm exhausted," Noah said. "But I'm okay. Aside from the cut over my eye, I feel about as good as I did when we shipped out. You don't look so good. How are *you* doing?"

Mickle waved a hand. He opened his mouth and let out a long sigh, as if whatever he wanted to say died on his tongue and all he could do was let out its last gasp. He collected his thoughts and sat back in the chair. "How was it out there?"

Noah almost laughed. "It's shit. It's cold as a tit in a brass bra and every foot we break up refreezes in the time it takes to get through the next one."

"I wasn't asking about the work."

Noah let out a strangled laugh. He figured word would spread through the ship, but he had no idea how fast it could actually travel. "Oh, you mean that."

"Yeah, *that*. I heard about the stunts Brewster pulled, both on the ice and in the lifeboat. You might think you don't have any friends on this ship, but you do."

"Thanks."

"Don't feel too relaxed. You got one helluva big enemy, and he's got a lot more friends than you, in addition to being the one calling the shots. Whatever it is Brewster's got cooking isn't going to go down easy, if you follow me."

"Believe me, I'm aware. Is that all?"

Mickle looked at his wristwatch and asked, "You know what time it is?"

"No. My watch died yesterday."

"There's a lot of that going around." He pointed to the clock mounted in the back of the wheelhouse. This time of year, this far north, the days were short, but at half past two in the afternoon it should have been a lot brighter outside than it was. "Here, too." The second officer reached over and switched on a control table monitor. The radar display showed an empty circle without even a sweep line tracking around. He turned the screen off. "Holden and Nevins had the whole console over there in pieces and back together like a couple of kids with a Lego set. Nevins said there's nothing wrong with any of it that he can tell. 'All mechanically sound,' is how he put it. Still, we can't even get static on the radios, let alone hail anyone. Both satellites are dead, too."

"Why are you telling me this?"

"I don't think it's a coincidence the ship is shutting

down at the same time the entire crew is sick and getting progressively worse. I know I'm feeling like the same hell that's got into everybody else—a few are pretending it isn't getting to them, but anyone can see it is. The crew is breaking down as fast as the *Promise*, maybe faster. All except you. Why do you think that is?"

Noah took a step back. Mickle was frightening him. His eyes were a little large naturally, but with dark bags beneath sunken cheeks, he looked like he might lurch for Noah's throat to get a drink of whatever was keeping him from getting sick. "It doesn't make any sense to me, either," he said, his voice raspy with sudden dryness.

Mickle pointed out the window. Noah could see a hint of the far shape they'd spied earlier in the distance. In the darkening day, it was little more than a bump on the horizon, and soon wouldn't be anything at all. He'd missed his window to get a better look at it.

"Brewster and Boucher were up here trying to figure out what that thing is. The Old Man's convinced it's the platform. What do you think?"

Noah nodded toward the shape. "Don't know. I suppose it could be. You'd think if it was the oil rig though, the lights would be coming on soon. They can't work in the dark."

Glaring out the window, Mickle nodded. "Same thing I've been thinking. If it's the Niflheim, they should have lights. Unless the same thing that's killing us already got to them."

Mickle's face reflected in the dark window. His eyes narrowed as he squinted to see the increasingly obscure deformity in the distance. His shoulders slumped and Noah could see what the man was thinking. He had the same thing on his mind: it was too much to hope that they'd have a working radio if they didn't even have lights. And it was definitely too much to hope that there was a helicopter already waiting on the pad.

"I still think we need to get over there," Mickle said. "If it *is* the Niflheim, we can see if they can call for a medevac and an icebreaker. If they can't, at the very least we can see if they have more medical supplies. We're all in a bad way, but then there's Felix. Between his injuries and . . . this other thing . . . he's not going to make it if we do nothing. We need help."

"And?"

"And you're the only one fit enough to make the trip, Cabot. You watch yourself. Tomorrow, when you go back out to break up the ice, if you don't already have 'em, you need to grow eyes in the back of your head. Keep a lookout all around, because I have a feeling we're all going to be relying on you sooner rather than later."

Noah nodded. He didn't want to be anything but what he was: a deckhand trying to get home. Instead of saying as much, he backed toward the door. Mickle watched him go. The second officer's face relaxed and his hungry vampire look dissolved, replaced once again by weary resignation. "Keep it together, Cabot. Watch your back."

"Aye, sir."

He didn't want to be anyone's last hope. Because that meant hope was already lost.

13

The mess room was as active as Noah had seen it in days. The ice breaking crew were seated around the tables eating with a somewhat renewed gusto. The encroaching ill ease among the men had soured a lot of appetites, but hard work seemed to revive them a little. Theo and Henry stooped over plates still half full of pasta while Boucher wiped a piece of bread around his, trying to capture every bit of sauce left behind. A few of the men who hadn't been on the breakup crew picked at their food, pushing it around, but not seeming to have much of an appetite.

Meal times were becoming increasingly unreliable since the galley cooks, Michael and David, could barely stand by themselves, let alone prepare food for the entire crew. Fend-for-yourself was the new menu for as long as Noah could foresee. While most had found their appetites waning along with their energy, a couple of the crewmen—Boucher and Henry—seemed to have decided every meal was now a feast. Add labor to that equation and they were determined to eat like they were trying to pack on fat for a long hibernation. If only a couple of them ate like that for few days, it wouldn't be a problem, given how many men, Noah included, had been skipping meals lately. They would likely break even when it came to the larder if they weren't beset for too long. Noah reckoned, however, that if Brewster's plan didn't work, they'd have to start rationing food. The round trip from port in Seattle was typically a clockwork operation, and the company knew exactly how much was necessary to stock to feed the men adequate to their needs and company regulations, while still being the most economical. The company's eye to the bottom line was the crew's worst enemy in dire circumstances.

Even assuming they were on the right bearing when they'd become fixed in the ice, if they got free today they were going to be butting up against the extent of their available supplies. Any more of a delay, and they'd run out of food on the voyage home. Admittedly, there was probably more than enough to eat in one of the shipping crates. Noah hadn't seen the shipping manifest, but the supplies they were delivering to the platform had to include food and drink. Maybe there was enough on board to last weeks or even months. It was stocked and locked away in a shipping crate buried among a half dozen other containers, however. If it was deep in the stack, no matter how much there was, they couldn't get to it.

He had a flash of the earliest days home from the hospital after his daughter was born. Abby hadn't been able to produce enough breast milk and Ellie was losing weight. They went to lactation specialists, bought nursing equipment—suckling tubes and bottles and pumps. Abby ate fenugreek seeds until her sweat smelled like maple syrup. But nothing worked. The baby slept more and ate even less, which made her sleepier still. She'd fall asleep trying to nurse, missing out on even the small quantity of breast milk Abby could provide. Their daughter was starving to death in their arms and everyone was telling them they just weren't trying hard enough, they weren't doing it right. It seemed like an entire industry dedicated to making them feel inadequate as parents was pressing down until they despaired, accepting that they were failures before they'd even had a chance to succeed. Then, one night, full of shame and desperation, Noah went to a drugstore and bought a can of powdered baby formula. When Abby saw what he'd brought home, she cried. Together like a pair of conspirators, they silently mixed it up with the small amount of milk Abby could express and fed their child. Ellie ate more and more and immediately started gaining back the weight she'd lost after they brought her home. She got stronger and more alert, and her parents realized that whatever it took was what they *had* to do. They wouldn't feel guilty about keeping little Ellie healthy and happy, no matter what the "experts" told them. They wouldn't let anyone shame them for keeping the three of them together. Food was her salvation and theirs.

Survival was shameless.

Everyone needed to eat. The crew could bundle up against the cold, wait out whatever was interfering with the instruments, and try to battle illness. But when they ran out of food and drinkable water, they were dead men, no matter what. He imagined, on the other hand, suggesting they ration supplies was going to be met with opposition at the very least, if not outright hostility. It made Noah recall the OTC painkillers. Undersupplied and gone in a day. The crew was irritable and bad-tempered due to the headaches—what Abby called "tetchy" when he got like that at home. When the men ran out of coffee, there would be fistfights. And when they ran out of food it'd be worse. But if he suggested they all take smaller portions to stretch things out . . . he didn't want to imagine it. He had to find a coconspirator. Someone who could back his play, or better yet, be the face of it. He needed an ally the crew would respect and listen to. Someone who could take a suggestion to Brewster and be heard. Chris Holden or Sean Mickle had to be the one to try. He'd start with Mickle. After dinner.

He filled a plastic plate with a half serving and went to sit with Jack and Kevin. When Boucher stood and moved toward the galley window to get seconds—or maybe thirds—he thought about saying something. What was the use? If the food they'd prepared didn't get eaten, it might find its way into the freezer to be reheated later, but given the state of the cooks and the crew, it'd just as likely make it into the trash. This meal was beyond saving. It was the next, and the one after that needed minding.

"What does Brewster got against you, dude?" Jack asked. "He looked like he was ready to take you to the woodshed, for real."

A mental inventory of the reasons for Brewster's hostility marched through Noah's mind in a procession of nightmares. One followed another in a black parade of bad choices and disappointments, sides taken and moments you can never get back, or take back, lost in time, every day adding another regret to a sore and bent conscience. Noah took a breath, filing through his choices, trying to find a way to shrug it off, laugh, and make a joke about "in-laws, you know." Taking advantage of his silence, Boucher turned on his bench and said, "You haven't heard? Shit, Cabot, go ahead and tell him how you got a man killed last year."

"That shit was an accident," Marty said from the corner, holding his head in a hand while he pushed his noodles around with the fork in his other. He sounded like he was already sick of the conversation. Noah definitely was. He wanted out of it before it even began.

"Killed?" Jack said.

"Yeah," Boucher continued. "Your boy here sent a greenhorn named Connor MacAllister out to do something *he'd* been ordered to do. Cabot stayed dry and warm while Connor got crushed to death doing someone else's work."

Noah felt a pull like a hook in his back, dragging him toward the door. Away from the mess to his own cabin where he could lock the door and refuse to talk to anyone. Instead, he swallowed and said, "It wasn't my fault, and Connor wasn't green. He had as much time at sea as me."

"And look at how good you are at the job, professor. Underwater Basketweaving 101 was real good training for you out here, wasn't it?"

"We were en route to a platform called the Nordland I," he said. "On our way we ran into a storm. Not as bad as the one *we* just went through, but still not anything you'd want to be on a weather deck during. It was my turn on watch and I'd been ordered to go check the lashing gear on the cans." He hesitated, searching for the right words. Boucher smirked, knowing why he had to struggle to phrase it correctly. "I had . . . something else that needed doing, so I asked Connor if he could go out and take care of it. It was supposed to just be routine inspection. Walk around, ratchet a strap or two if they looked loose. I'd done the same round the day before and hadn't had to touch a damn thing. Everything was supposed to be secure."

"But it wasn't, was it?" Boucher said, prosecuting the case against him.

Noah's eyes narrowed as he glared at the bosun. He gripped his fork in a tight fist, concentrating on the reassuring feeling of its handle in his palm, pretending it was a railing or a pipe—something he could hold onto to weather the storm of memory. "No, it wasn't. The sea kicked up a big swell and when the ship turned into it . . . a shipping can broke free and killed him."

"Pulped his head you mean. Crushed it like—"

"He's dead! We all know it. Who the fuck wants to hear about the details?" Noah said, standing up. Boucher rose to face him.

"Maybe one of them wants to," he said, swinging his arm toward Theo and Henry. "Everybody oughta know what you did."

Kevin slipped in between the men, holding Noah back with his shoulder. "It sounds like an accident to me," he said. "Sure, he shoulda done what he was told, but who hasn't taken a watch for someone else? Huh? It could've happened to anybody. Way it sounds to me—"

"Way it sounds to *me*," Boucher said, shouting over Kevin's shoulder, "is you might not've put a gun to his head, but you sent him out there and the guy got killed. That's on you. Your job, your responsibility, your risk. You shirked your duty and got someone killed."

"You think I should have died instead?"

Boucher's breath was sweet with spaghetti sauce and whatever was in the flask he kept stashed in his overalls. On top of the combined scents assaulting him, the fight or flight instinct at being confronted yet again made Noah's stomach tighten and sour. He wanted to swing his arm or puke. Maybe both. Boucher said, "Think it? I *know* it. I should be sitting here eating with Connor MacAllister instead of you, motherfucker."

"If I could do it over differently, I would."

"Save it, professor. I'm just waiting for karma to catch up with you and do what it should've a year ago. You're gonna get what's comin' to you, Cabot. And when you do, I'll put on a little skirt and grab my pompoms to cheer it on."

"That's enough!" a voice boomed from behind Noah. Boucher's gaze shot to the door. He took a step back with an expression on his face like a playground bully who spotted the teacher. Noah didn't need to look to know Chris Holden was standing behind him in the doorway. His voice was unmistakable.

"If you two are done pissing on each other's shoes, I suggest you bus up your plates and get your asses in their bunks. The Old Man wants you all out busting ice tomorrow and none of you have the time or energy to waste taking cracks at each other. You copy?"

"Aye sir," Boucher said. His face reddened and his shoulders slumped. Grabbing his plate, he tossed it in the bin in the corner and stalked out of the room, giving Noah a yard stare as he went. Although his face was slick with sweat and his neck bent forward, Noah knew the man would find hidden reserves of strength if it meant finishing the job Brewster had started outside. The bosun slid past Holden, careful not to touch the senior officer, but not masking his contempt for the man's unwanted intervention. Boucher might not have had it out for Holden specifically, but if he'd save Noah from getting at least part of what was coming to him, then he was on the wrong side. No one said anything as they listened to Boucher stomp off down the passageway.

Holden walked up to Noah and said, "What the hell was that about?"

"Ancient history," Jack said.

"A year ain't so ancient." Henry gathered up the debris of his meal and carelessly deposited it with a clatter in the bucket. "Seems like current events to me, knowing what happened to Felix, too."

"I was up doing what Boucher told me to when that happened."

"And if we look at the duty log, are you gonna be the last one responsible for checking the lashing gear before he got smashed?" He didn't wait for an answer, instead following the deck boss out. Noah watched the room divide itself. Theo, Michael, and David stood together and trailed behind the senior deckhand, leaving their plates on the table. Marty, Jack, and Kevin stayed behind, pretending a line hadn't just been drawn down the center of the ship.

Marty rolled his eyes dramatically, and said, "You're never gonna win over that clique, Noah. Those guys are so far up Boucher's ass their breath smells like rum when he takes a pull off his flask. They back him because he hands out extra OT, not because they believe any of his bullshit."

Holden held up a finger to silence the men. "We're in deep enough trouble without the Sharks and the Jets looking to rumble. You with me? I expect you, Noah, to work to keep the peace around here. You're smarter than those guys put together. That means you have brains enough to figure out what you need to do to get by on this boat. You can see as clearly as I do that the answer is not stirring up trouble."

"How about standing up for himself?" Kevin asked. "Is he allowed to do that?"

Holden shot him a poison look and continued. "Speaking of shift assignments, Andrew is on mess duty today, but since he's down with the whateverthefuck, I'm enlisting you three." He pointed to Noah and the twins. "When you're done eating, get to work on those dishes and whatever else needs cleaning in the galley. I want this place spotless for breakfast."

"Why us?" Jack said.

"Why do people climb mountains?" Holden sighed as Jack and Kevin stared at him blankly, awaiting the answer to his rhetorical question. "Just do it. That's an order. When you're done, you're to go get some rest. You all look like warmed-over death. Nevins, you get back on the radios."

Marty groaned. Holden turned to leave.

"Can I have a word, Mr. Holden?" Noah said. Holden waggled a finger at him and walked out into the passageway. Noah followed while the other men groused at each other about being left with the mess.

Holden stalked over to the far wall, checked his watch, and ran a hand down his face. "What is it, Cabot?"

"Stopped?" Noah asked, glancing at the watch.

"Yeah. Like everything else. Still checking it out of

habit, though. But you didn't stop me to talk about my watch."

"No sir. It's . . . the food."

Holden put a pair of fingers to his temple. "You can address all complaints about the quality of the food to the company when we—"

"No sir. It's the quantity, not quality. If we're stuck here much longer, we need to think about rationing and maybe even prioritizing who gets what based on how sick they are."

Holden's eyes widened. He ran his hand over his head. Noah could hear the sound of his palm rubbing over the rough stubble. "You're kidding, right?"

"No sir. If we don't make our supplies last, I think we're going to be in real trouble. You saw how things went in the mess room. I can't be the one to bring it up, but you—"

Holden held up the authoritative finger again, cutting Noah off. He grabbed the deckhand by the arm and dragged him off to a corner, farther from the mess and day rooms. Backing up against the door to the provision room, Holden glanced up and down the passageway for other ears. "Are you nuts?" he whispered. "We've been icebound for a day and you want to tell these guys they have to start going hungry?"

"No. Not that. But we're at least another day out from getting through what's holding the ship, if the Old Man's plan works. If it doesn't work—"

"If the skipper's plan doesn't work, *then* we can have this conversation. But not now. Not when we all need to be working together to get out of this. Stop trying to get these guys to line up against you." Holden put a hand on Noah's shoulder and squeezed. It was meant to be reassuring, but instead it amplified and localized the ache in Noah's shoulders from chopping at the ice all day. "I know you didn't start that bit of business in there just now. But you saw how it ended, right? People are already lacing up their gloves and we've barely been stuck. Suggesting things are worse than they seem isn't going to do anything but ring the bell. I understand why you're talking to me about this, I do. But now's not the time. Even if we don't have enough for the return trip, no one's going to starve if we run low on supplies a couple days out of Seattle. Okay? Let's wait and see. You read me?"

Noah nodded. He hadn't always been a worrier, but repeated experience had taught him to anticipate the worst-case scenario. Even if he hoped for the best outcome for them all, he wanted to plan for the worst that might lie ahead. He'd spent enough of his life reacting to disaster, trying to find the money for school, for rent, for medical bills, only when he was already in arrears. He started educating himself about chemo and surgeries when they had to schedule them. He learned about hospice when the pain was already bad and guaranteed to only get worse. He still had a problem avoiding trouble, but at least he didn't close his eyes to it anymore. He learned that much from experience. Being out of control his entire life had made him want to be the guy with a plan—the one who had a resolution half in play before anyone else even realized there was trouble looming. The problem he couldn't seem to get on top of was that he wasn't in a position to make things better. He loaded ships and unloaded them on the other end. No matter how well he educated himself, on board ship he was muscle, not brains. Born with rough hands, no amount of college was going to get him off the killing floor.

"Okay. Tomorrow then," he said. "I'll come back tomorrow."

"If Brewster doesn't get us out of this by tomorrow night, you won't have to bring it back to me. I'll suggest it on my own."

"Thanks."

"Don't thank me. I haven't done anything yet." Holden let go of Noah's shoulder and walked away, descending through the hatch to B-Deck. Noah returned to the mess to help with the dishes and try to save the leftovers. He was just in time to prevent Kevin from dumping them out.

14

Although they'd gotten an early start, breaking away the ice from around the hull of the ship took longer than anyone anticipated. More men had been recruited to work, but it was still a game of inches, as if the sheet was a living thing opposing them. It started refreezing the minute they moved on to break up another section. For every yard they freed, a man had to return once or twice an hour to keep it loose and away from the ship. They split the work into shifts. Two hours on, an hour off, and an hour on maintenance. Not long into his second working shift, Noah's lungs burned and his breath came in ragged gasps. He wasn't out of shape; at the same time, he wasn't fit for breaking rocks at Leavenworth, either, and especially not in temperatures that stung his lungs with every drawn breath. Still, he pushed through until he could rest again, driving his scraper into the ice. His hands were still swollen and aching from the prior day's labor. He silently wished for a flamethrower. Something he could use at a distance from the edge that would both melt the ice and warm him. But a flamethrower was the last thing the company was going to outfit on a ship manned by bored roughnecks. No matter how useful, it was a greater liability than an asset.

Gripping the haft of the tool was becoming increasingly difficult, and he fumbled it more than once. He feared if he dropped it into the water under the ice, Boucher might send him down to personally fetch it. Although the deckboss looked like death warmed over, he was driving the crew, determined to get the job done in a single day. Even if he didn't like him, Noah agreed, if the job was going to get done, it had to be accomplished as quickly as possible. They didn't have the hands or the gear to pull a twenty-four-hour shift outside. Every successive day meant fewer men fit for duty.

The work, while harder than the day before, was going faster and more efficiently without the Old Man on the team. Men snickered behind Noah's back or cast dirty looks in his direction when they thought he wasn't looking. But for the most part, he was thankful for the passive aggression instead of Brewster's outright hostility. They could distrust him all they wanted as long as they did it quietly and left him alone. Time spent defending himself was time away from coming up with an alternative to get out of this mess if Brewster's plan didn't work. Which he was almost certain it wouldn't.

The men spent their rest shifts looking at the shape in the distance with a pair of binoculars Kevin had brought with him. Although the fog had almost completely dissipated, the distant shape in the ice was frustratingly difficult to see, almost as if it existed in a dream. More so now that the sun was going down. Noah tried refocusing the binoculars, but the little spotters weren't powerful enough to see as far as whatever the shape was. Its size and distance remained elusive. If it was the Niflheim, how long, he wondered, would it take to reach on foot? A few hours? A day or more? He couldn't tell. The white expanse revealed no metric of perspective by which to measure distance. Same as the night before, it was dark and nothing moved except blowing snow and the haze that hid the reality of it. Only its reddish color suggested the shape was a thing apart from the icescape. Even then, no lights shone on it, no plume of smoke suggested labor or even life at all within. Noah wondered if it was possible for a desert mirage to manifest in the Arctic.

Kevin nudged him for another turn with the binoculars. Noah handed them over and shoved his gloved hands into his armpits to warm them. "Where'd you find those anyway?" he asked.

"I always pack 'em. For whale watching and shit."

"Whale watching," Jack said. "Gaaaaaay!"

Kevin dismissed his friend with a wave of his hand. "Whatever, dude. Whales are fuckin' awesome. You need to get over that too-cool-for-school shit." While their cheer was forced and weary, they were doing their best to keep each other's spirits up. They were funhouse mirror reflections of the same person. One tall, one short; one skinny, one stout; one black and one white, but both of a single mind and intention. If Jack farted, Kevin said "excuse me."

Noah tried to ignore their banter while he squinted at the horizon. With or without the binoculars, it looked the same: stuck in the same wintry hell they were. Word was getting around the crew that Brewster thought it might be the Niflheim. The Old Man's theory assumed he'd kept on the right course bearing after the storm had blown them all over creation, the fog settled in, and the instruments had gone tits up. Noah didn't have much faith in Brewster's blind navigating. But it wasn't outside the realm of possibility, either. Nothing seemed impossible anymore. At least nothing bad. If the Niflheim was dead, things were very bad indeed.

"That's it!" Boucher called out. "You got five minutes; everybody get your gear and get on the elevator. One trip is all we're making. You miss the boat, you better hope you brought your sleeping bag!" Boucher picked up a sledgehammer in one hand and the pickax the Old Man had been swinging the day before in his other. He did his best to trot them over to the lifeboat, but he tripped on his own feet halfway there and dropped the sledge, cursing as it bounced away. Pride wouldn't let him admit that he felt as bad as he looked. Merchant sailors loved to complain. They'd bitch about a cash bonus if there was a way to spin it to make it look like they were ever-suffering at the hands of hard work. There seemed to have been a tacit agreement among the men to put an end to grousing for the time being. Complaining ceased being fun the minute the thing being complained about was actually threatening. No one wanted to admit openly that they were frightened of what was happening to them. Even if they had a right to be scared shitless. But right or not, they'd never cop to it.

Noah grabbed his scraper and shuffled toward the FRC, making sure to steer clear of loose ice they'd smashed apart. He followed along after a couple of the guys who hadn't been on the team the day before: Andrew and Heath. Neither looked like they should have been asked to leave their bunks. They staggered and slouched their way to the lifeboat, looking like they'd as likely fall in as climb. More than a couple of times, men had stumbled or slipped, dipping a foot or an entire leg in the water. No one had gone all the way in. If there was a small mercy in the day, it had been that.

Noah climbed into the FRC, seated himself in the back, and waited. Boucher shouted something that sounded like "all in," the wind catching his words and tearing them away. Then the boat jerked as the winch caught and up they went. The same gust that stole Boucher's speech battered them against the side of the ship. The wind chill stung Noah's face and made his eyes water. Tears froze on his eyelashes, threatening to seal his eyes closed when he tried to blink them away. He resisted the urge to wipe at them with the back of a hand or his sleeve. The neoprene suit was covered in flecks of ice that would just make things worse if he ground them into his face.

At the top of the ride, Noah hopped out of the craft first and began helping the others. Most accepted his aid. Henry and Theo didn't. Noah tried not to sweat it. He didn't care what they thought of him anymore. They'd have the same opinion no matter what he did, so why fight it?

When everyone was back on deck, Boucher ordered Jack and Kevin to secure the rescue craft while he trotted up to inform Brewster they were all aboard and ready. He took Henry with him. The senior deckhand had somehow spent more time on light shifts than heavy, taking a supervisory role he hadn't been assigned.

After they finished with the lifeboat, Jack and Kevin devised a plan to climb the aft gunwale and watch the propellers break up the rest of the ice. "You coming?" Jack asked. Noah shook his head. He wanted to lie down and try to warm his hands. His fingers each felt like ten pounds of sausage in five-pound casings, and although he wasn't arthritic before, he feared he would be going forward.

"You two have fun. And be careful," he added. "It's not going to be an easy ride. Just be sure to hang on tight."

Kevin smiled and winked. A touch of blood around one of his nostrils glistened in the late day light. He was either putting up a brave front or in denial. The pair seemed to exist in an alternate world where they were weary from having a drink too many in their favorite bar instead of just coming off a glorified chain gang with a case of frostbite. He wished he was there with them. Whatever it took to get on the other side of their trouble. Noah wanted to believe everything would be all right, too. A drink sounded nice right about now. It might be time to revisit the invitation to share Marty's bottle of J&B—if Marty was conscious. Ignoring the pain in his freezing hands, he fist-bumped the twins and retreated through the door.

After dropping his Gumby suit in the change room, Noah headed for his cabin and a fresh change of clothes. He was soaked with cooling sweat again and he smelled. The survival suit was holding in the funk of his previous labors, adding a history of wretchedness to his present aroma. He could barely stand himself. He resolved to change before heading for the showers, unwilling to put the infected garments on again once he was clean.

If the headway they'd made that afternoon really was an indication of how long it would take to free the whole ship, they could be out there for days breaking up the ice and returning to redo the work undone overnight. Days while the thing that was eating the crew took more, and bigger, bites. Days for the rest of the ship's systems to go black and fail. Eventually, he realized, they'd lose life support. If the radiation or whatever it was didn't shut it down, they'd run out of fuel. When the heat went out, every man on the *Arctic Promise* would freeze to death.

Distracted by their bleak prospects, Noah found himself a deck below his cabin and descending farther. He sighed and tried to work up the resolve to climb instead of let gravity lead him all the way down. He needed a cup—or five—of coffee and something to eat more than he originally thought. His legs were shaky and felt like they might fold beneath him if he unlocked his knees. His arms hung at his sides, the joints in his hands swollen and stiff. The motion of driving the scraper/chopper into the ice for hours had left him unable to lift his arms above his head without resistance and pain, but he had to reach up to climb. Using the steep ladders in the ship hurt in so many ways.

He fished in a pocket for his last nutrition bar. It was squashed and bent from being in his jacket, but it was edible. The gummy brick of oats and frosting smelled better than it tasted, but it was high in protein and had the calories he needed to get him through the next hour, anyway. He'd eaten two already today, taking ribbing from Kevin for even possessing something labeled THE

Bar for Women, let alone ingesting one. He didn't care what was printed on the outside. He liked the lemon frosting. He chewed the dense treat slowly, savoring it instead of powering it down like he had the two outside.

Noah took a deep breath and began to climb, his shoulders and back cramping. He was two decks below where he wanted to be. He'd just have to deal if he wanted to shower, get coffee, and rest.

The whine of the engines spinning up echoed through the stairwell. A dismal howl filled the metal passageways belowdecks. Pipes banged and rattled as the behemoth awakened. The ship's address system pinged and Brewster's voice crackled indecipherably through the speakers. Whatever the Old Man said was lost in the roar of the engine and the faltering PA system. Another thing to add to the list of equipment shutting down like a metastasizing cancer slowly killing all its host's organs.

The ship lurched astern. Noah's grip on the handrail slipped and he slammed forward into the ladder, jamming his chin against the steel nosing. The serrated tread jabbed into his palms as he grabbed blindly to keep from falling. The last of his bar slipped out of his fingers to the deck below.

He heard the sound of ice grinding at the hull. The engines roared in a primal answer. The ship rocked forward before halting abruptly with a peal of sound like rending metal. He scrambled up the stairs before the world could suddenly shift again. The engines shuddered, the steel beneath his feet vibrating, and the air in the passageway took on the familiarly terrifying smell of electrical smoke and burning oil. He had to get to Brewster—had to tell him he was tearing the ship apart.

Lumbering three flights up to the First Deck, he

emerged outside sick bay. Sean Mickle knelt in the doorway holding a glistening red hand to his face. Blood trickled out beneath his palm.

"Christ, Sean! Are you okay?"

Mickle looked at Noah through a squinted eye. "Yeah," he said, groaning through clenched teeth. "Wasn't all the way down the ladder when Brewster goosed the engines. I fell off and banged my head pretty good." He pulled his hand away and asked, "How does it look?"

Noah helped the man up and leaned in for a look. He gently probed at it with his fingers to get a sense of how much was wound and how much was just the excessive gore of a typical face cut. Mickle flinched away, sucking air in through his teeth. Noah grabbed his shoulder instead and led him into the brighter light of the hospital. He helped Mickle have a seat at the desk and tilted his head up to look closer. "Come on. Let me look, Doc." Mickle lowered his hand and a fresh trickle of blood ran down his face, traveling along the deep laugh line in his cheek.

"You must have hit it on a dog," Noah said, referring to the handles on the compartment door. It was a small cut, but deep. Noah grabbed a hand towel off a shelf above him and pressed it into Mickle's hand. He pointed at his own cut. "Looks like we're a matched set." Noah had to shout to hear himself over the sounds of Brewster doing battle with the ice. He jabbed a thumb at the wheelhouse ladder. "It sounds like he's tearing the ship apart, and there's fresh smoke in the companionway."

Mickle peeled the towel away from his face, wincing as the fabric caught at the edges of his wound. He tried to wipe blood from his face, but had little luck with the dry cloth. "The ship isn't built for breaking up consolidated ice, but he won't listen. He's got Boucher and Henry up there with him. They're telling him we're free from amidships back and pretending they can navigate."

"Amidships? We cleared as far forward as the rear quarters, but definitely not as far as that. And only back about twenty feet maybe. Not enough for a running start if the prop cavitation doesn't break up the ice."

Mickle stifled a laugh. "Cavitation? What makes you think that would do anything?"

"Brewster thinks it will."

The second officer pressed the palm of his hand into his eye, trying to push back the pain. "We'll be lucky to be afloat when he's finished, whether or not we break out of what's holding us."

Noah grabbed another towel off the shelf and doused it in the sink, careful to hold on as he moved through the room. He handed the damp cloth to Mickle.

Another lurch of the ship sent Noah grasping for anything to hold on to. Mickle grabbed Noah's forearm to steady him. He dragged himself to the stool bolted to the bulkhead opposite Mickle's desk and sat. Bracing for the next jolt by locking his knees and gripping the edge of the bunk compartment with one hand, he pressed against his lower back with the other. Felix rode out the attempt to free the ship unconscious in his bed. Noah mentally prepared himself to pull the man out of the bunk and carry him to the FRC at the first sound of the collision alarm.

Instead of an emergency Klaxon, the smells of smoke and burning oil intruded into the compartment. Whatever was burning was worse than just a stack in the instrument room. The tinctured air turned Noah's stomach. He tried not to think about what lay ahead of them when the engines finally died.

"I can't sit here and do nothing."

"What do you suggest?" The second officer twisted his head around, stretching the stiffening muscles in his neck. "Anything short of physically dragging him out of that chair won't stop him, and *that* is mutiny."

Noah pushed himself to his feet. "They can arrest me if they want. I'd rather go to jail than die in a shipwreck."

"How are you going to get in there? When William relieved me and ordered me out of the control room, I heard Serge dog down the door and lock it behind me. Unless you can break it down, we have to ride it out."

Noah lurched toward the doorway and looked at the ladder leading to the command room hatch. Even if he could find enough balance and strength to hack at it with a fire axe, he wasn't breaking through. The manufacturer that built the *Arctic Promise* supplied vessels to companies sailing through all parts of the world. They installed breach-proof hatches on all command compartments. If their hatches were strong enough to hold off motivated Somali pirates, he wasn't breaking it down by himself in any state. He returned to his stool and held his breath while the ship bucked and bashed at the ice. Not a combatant, there was no point in riding out the battle on his feet and risking another concussion, or worse.

15

It was an hour before the violent motions of the ship ceased and the wheelhouse door opened. The smell of smoke still lingered, but it wasn't getting stronger. If there had been a fire, it was contained. Or so Noah hoped.

Henry and Boucher lurched past the hospital compartment, lumbering toward the A-Deck ladder. Where they were headed in such a hurry should have worried Noah, but all he could focus on was the hatch above. He pulled himself to his feet. Although the ship was calm again, he felt like he was still struggling against the ghost of the fight. Steadying himself, he realized the ship might be loose in the water—he could feel the slight movements of a free-floating vessel. If the experience of the previous day had any lesson to offer, it was this: free or not, give it a night and they'd be trapped again. He imagined himself back out on the surface chopping away at something with the limitless ability to heal itself. Attacking the ice with hammers and scrapers was futile. It endured.

"Shall we?" Mickle said, pushing himself to his feet.

He'd staunched his bleeding but still looked like the victim in a slasher movie. Gore streaked his face and neck; his hands were red and sticky. He looked at his palms and grimaced.

"Maybe we should wash you up first. Get some glue and butterfly strips on that cut."

Mickle's mouth turned down. "No. If William won't believe what we tell him, I want him to *see* what he's doing to the crew."

The *Arctic Promise* had battered against an insurmountable obstacle for what? Whether Brewster surrendered or the engines did, the casualties of his continued efforts to wage war against the Chukchi Sea were only going to continue to rise. Felix, Noah, Mickle, and who knew who else had been hurt already. Enough was enough. They had to come up with a better plan and convince Brewster to back away from his usual way of dealing with things that didn't do what he wanted. To him, the sound of an object breaking was its compliance.

Noah made way for Mickle, falling into line behind him as soon as he was past. The second officer left crimson handprints on the ladder rails as he ascended. Noah unwittingly stuck his hand in the first one, pulling it away like he'd been burned as soon as he realized what he'd done. He had no compunction getting the man's blood on his hands if he were trying to help clean him up. Sticking a palm on the blood he left behind, however, felt wrong. It felt like a stain that belonged on the ship somehow—a warning to others. Go no further. Beyond lies madness.

They pushed through the door to find the Old Man already facing them, his countenance a mask of impatient fury. "You haven't had time to see Nevins about the engines!" Realization dawned on his face that he wasn't shouting at the men he'd dispatched. His expression shifted from shock to disbelief and back to anger as his eyes traveled from Mickle's grotesque look to Noah's unwelcome face. His gaze settled on Noah and he opened his mouth to begin shouting again. Mickle interrupted him before he could get a syllable out.

"It's time to stop this," he shouted. "Can't you see you're putting us all at risk?" He pointed to his face; the drying blood at the edges of his mouth cracked and flaked away onto his chest where it stuck in the blood staining his shirt.

"What the Christ happened to you?"

"You have to ask?" Mickle stepped forward to give Brewster a closer look, but the ship's master retreated from his second in command.

Shaking his head, he said, "I made the announcement for everyone to—"

"A goddamn *second* before you throttled ahead!"

"And the PA isn't working," Noah added. "It was just a crackle of noise."

Brewster backed into the corner of the console, raising his hands to ward the man off. "If you hadn't noticed, we've got bigger problems than you bumping your head. And you!" He pointed at Noah. "I warned you, if I saw you in the wheelhouse again—"

"Shut up!" Mickle roared. "You've barely been sleeping, and your judgment is impaired. You're making decisions harmful to the ship, its cargo, and crew. I'm relieving you of command."

"The hell you say!"

"If you don't like it, you can take it up with the company when we get back to port. In your present state, you are unfit to steer this boat." Mickle straightened his back, fists balled at his sides, and waited for Brewster's move. Noah had once watched a man in a fight outside of the City Fish Co. counter at Pike Place Market take an elbow to the face. He heard the crack and crunch of breaking bone and cartilage from ten feet away. The man who'd taken the shot landed on his back, but a second after he fell was on his feet again, blood gushing from his flattened nose. He'd raised his hands and said, "I've had worse." Mickle looked like *that*—wild-eyed and ready to give better than he'd just gotten. Brewster dropped his hands and let out a long breath of air.

"This is mutiny. You'll both live to regret this."

"Living is the point. We'll just have to wait and see about regrets," Mickle said.

After a long moment, Brewster stepped to the side and gestured with a sweeping hand to the command chair. "She's all yours. Set a course, Doc."

Noah spun as he heard Henry and Boucher practically fall into the room, stumbling as they caught sight of Mickle. Unlike Brewster, Boucher showed no sign of shock at the man's appearance. His face held only one expression: contempt. He stepped away from Henry, making space between him and his compatriot so Noah and Mickle couldn't keep both men in sight at the same time. Noah had seen this done in a fight, too. He imagined Serge getting ready to signal Henry to rush them. He turned to keep facing the bosun. The second officer was bigger than Noah, and more than a match for Boucher normally, but he'd also hit his head and was sick. All of them were sick. Some more than others. But

Boucher and Henry were doing better than Mickle, despite his attempt to appear formidable.

"That's enough," Mickle said. "Stop right there."

Boucher raised his shoulders like a teenager saying, "I'm not doing anything." They all knew better.

"I've relieved the skipper of command. You can either do as I say, or I'll see that you're all taken into custody when we reach port."

"What? You going to radio ahead?" Boucher plucked the worthless handset off the counter and tossed it toward the man. Mickle didn't flinch. The transmitter reached the end of the coiled cable and sprang back, clattering on the floor.

"Are you finished having your tantrum, Serge?" Mickle didn't follow up his question with a threat or a promise. He waited for the man to either come at him or back off.

Boucher's face flushed red. The muscles in his jaw flexed as he clenched his teeth over and over. Glancing at Brewster, he seemed to silently ask for orders. The Old Man offered him nothing. Finally, he let out a breath and said, "Fine. I'll play along. What are *your* orders?"

"I'm guessing William sent you to get a status report from Nevins about the engines. Am I right?" Boucher nodded. "Well?"

"We found him. He's passed out in the engine room. Guess he breathed too much smoke or something. Holden and a couple of other guys were already helping him out," Henry said. "We came back to report the fire's out, but we don't know nothing about the engines. It's all quiet down there."

Mickle turned to Brewster. The Old Man was expressionless. If he was moved by the news of either Nevins' collapse or the engines' failure, he didn't show it. Red warning lights shone in a row on the console beside him. Noah approached and read them. "Jesus! We have red on the main engines and both auxiliaries."

"We were breaking through," Brewster said. "It was working, but then the board started to light up."

"I told you you were going to burn an engine out," Noah said. "I didn't think you'd burn through all four."

Boucher looked at him with open disrespect. Mickle tensed like he wanted to take a shot at the Old Man. Noah was certain if he swung at Brewster, Boucher and Henry would break free of their collars and come after them both. He stood ready to back Mickle's play, whatever it was. The second officer took a breath and seemed to swallow his frustration, returning to his normal demeanor. "Christ, William. What were you thinking?"

"I dialed down to dead slow as soon as the first beacon lit up. When the second one lit, I slowed to stop, but that didn't keep 'em all from going down. I was hoping it was a malfunction on the board and not in the engine room."

"And now we're dead in the water. What do we do?" Noah asked.

"We need to get the radio working again," Brewster said.

Mickle coughed loudly into the back of his hand. Fresh red shone on top of the drying maroon coating his knuckles. "You put the only man who can fix it on his back. If Nevins dies of smoke inhalation, he's taking the radio with him." He sat down in the command chair and leaned his head against a fist, giving up the illusion of vitality. At that moment, Noah knew wresting command away from the Old Man was Pyrrhic. Command of the ship at this point was worthless.

Boucher and Henry seemed to realize Mickle was done as well, letting the tension out of their shoulders. A trickle of red painted Henry's upper lip and Boucher's eyes flitted around the compartment as if he was trying to keep an eye on more than just Noah and the second officer. None of them were in good shape. And they were getting worse. All but Noah, who seemed immune. At least to the illness that had gotten into the crew. The madness, on the other hand, was catching. He was seeing hints of the visions Martin had described. Even without a headache or weakness, he figured it was an eventuality that whatever was afflicting everyone else would start working on him, too. His hope they could wait this disaster out, wait for the company to notice they were missing and send helicopters to search for them, was as dead as the *Promise*. The idea that they could outlast their dwindling food, heat, and wits would have been laughable if it weren't so frightening. And Noah was frightened. They had officially run out of things to attempt in order to save themselves.

"Noah," Mickle said, without raising his head. The setting sun backlit him, made him look like one of the flitting shadows Noah thought he was glimpsing out of the corners of his eyes. If someone shined a spotlight on him, Mickle would disappear like one of them. "You and Henry round up as much of the crew as you can, right now. Have everyone able to stand with or without help report to the A-deck day room in forty minutes.

"Are you going to get out and push?" Brewster said, pointing to the row of red failure lights glowing on the control panel. "We're not going anywhere."

"Thanks to you. We have to get out if we want to go anywhere," Mickle replied. He pointed at the shape in the distance. "After all, how else are we going to get there?"

16

The day room on A-Deck was as close to cruise ship amenities as things got on the *Arctic Promise*. The room was built in the forward section of the superstructure with windows on three sides overlooking the bow. You could watch the progress of the ship from there if you were inclined. Most of the crew, however, had spent enough time at sea to not care. They preferred the darker day rooms a deck below—the ones with TVs and DVD players. The room was bright and open with tables and comfortable chairs for the crew to play cards or board games. While a couple of the men liked to play checkers or chess, it was too hard to place wagers on Scrabble hands and a fistfight had almost broken out once over a round of Settlers of Catan; they hadn't even gotten past reading the rules before Heath threw the box across the room, tossing insults after it. The Twins were practically in hysterics over his pique, which made him angrier. If it hadn't been bolted to the deck, Heath would have flipped the table. Boucher ended the conflict by threatening to toss the game in the incinerator. No one ever suggested pulling it out again.

The present assembly was less spirited. Noah and Henry had been able to gather seven of the eleven deckhands, including themselves. Felix was still in the hospital with Nevins as his new roommate sleeping it off in the bunk above. John Boduf refused to open his cabin door when they knocked, and Andrew Puck could barely open his eyes, let alone stand. Theo Mesires, Michael Yeong, and David Delgado sat slumped on the sofas against the rear wall, while the rest grabbed chairs. Even without everyone present, there weren't enough seats. Noah stood by the door. He felt better there. He could slip out without being seen if he had to.

At the opposite end of the compartment, Brewster, Holden, and Mickle quietly argued. Mickle was on his feet, but he looked bad. He'd washed his face and hands and taped up his cut, but cleaning away the blood seemed to rob him of the last of his color. He looked as peaked as a squid. He leaned against a window while Chris Holden listened to him and Brewster giving their alternate versions of events on the Command Deck. The third officer, for his part, maintained his neutral look, but as the conversation progressed, he seemed to end up standing closer to Mickle than Brewster. Noah wasn't sure whether that was him taking a side or simply preparing to catch Mickle when his knees buckled and he succumbed to whatever it was infecting him.

While the officers continued to talk, Boucher hovered behind Brewster's shoulder, glaring at the deckhands. No one had the conn. There was no use. The ship wasn't moving and there was no radio to monitor. It felt strangely like they were already to their port of destination and were ready to knock off for drinks before heading home to their families. Except, they were as far from that as they'd ever been. Farther, it seemed, than when they had originally set out. Going home at this moment was no more than a concept, and not one that was in any way a certainty.

Mickle stood, calling on whatever strength remained in the bottom of his tank. Clearing his throat, he tried to attract the attention of the crew. Holden barked for the men to "Listen up!" The low murmur in the room settled down.

"I suppose it's not news to any of you that today's attempt to free the ship was unsuccessful," Mickle began. "Despite your hard work, we're still beset and the radio remains nonfunctional. But there's more you need to know. From communications to navigation, we've gone dark. *All* the instruments are down. We don't know what's causing the systems to fail, but—" The crew voiced their shock and disbelief at once, cutting off the third officer, half of them shouting that they knew this would happen, while the other half fired back that they didn't know a thing. Noah put his back to the wall and kept his mouth shut. He agreed with the men who thought it was a bad idea to try to break the ice, but adding his opinion wouldn't solve anything. At best, it'd be just another voice in the chorus. At worst, his stand would inspire greater opposition from the men who disliked him and disagreed.

Mickle held up his hands trying to get the crew to quiet down. Their incredulity echoed through the compartment drowning him out until Brewster finally stood and ordered them to be quiet. Brewster leaned close and said to him, "How's that command looking now, Sean?"

He stifled a cough and continued. "We have no idea if we're anywhere near where we're supposed to be. It's too early in the season for this kind of ice consolidation in the Chukchi Sea. As a matter of fact, the kind of pack we're bound up in is thick enough to be two-year ice and that just isn't what I've ever seen there. In order to be as icebound as we are, we have to assume we're significantly off course. If we remained more or less on a true bearing, we should be somewhere north of Point Barrow. But between the instruments going down and magnetic compass interference, we have no way of knowing for sure where that is. For all we know, we could be in the East Siberian Sea."

Another murmur grew up from the deckhands. Mickle used the interruption to conceal another cough. But he couldn't hide how glistening red his lips were at the end of it. "We all know that the crew isn't doing any better than the ship. Everyone feels like hell, and whatever it is that's making us feel this way is progressing."

"So what now, Doc?" Michael Yeong asked.

Mickle swayed and Holden put a hand on his shoulder, guiding him back into his seat. The second officer drew a forearm across his brow to wipe away the sweat beading there. "We've discussed our options and believe they are limited."

"No shit!" Theo said. "Why isn't the Old Man telling us this?"

Boucher pointed a thick finger at the man. "That's e-fuckin-nough out of you, Mesires."

Holden turned toward the deckhand, his eyes flashing impatience. "The entire command crew is responsible for the wellbeing of this ship and all aboard. So if you don't like whoever's addressing you at the moment, you can direct your complaints to that wall over there. You copy that?" Cowed by the vigor the man put into telling him to shut up, Theo slumped in his chair stifling a cough.

"We're equally of the mind that waiting for the company to come looking for a lost ship will not only do us no good, but will actually do us harm. We're going to keep working on restoring communications, but we think we need to take further steps to ride this out, starting with rationing our food." The cry from the crew went up again. Holden shook his head slowly and waited for them to quiet down. He turned and pointed toward the darkening horizon. The setting sun illuminated a long straight line of red and orange in the distance, broken by a single shape: the thing everyone had been staring at for the last two days. "Second, we think we need to send a team out to see if that's anything that could help us."

"Is it the rig?" Jack asked.

Holden shook his head. "We don't know. We hope so. If not . . . well, we just don't know. We have to find out though."

"The hell with that!" Henry said. "This shit is above my pay grade. I'm not stepping foot outside this boat again."

"You don't have a choice, Gutierrez." Holden took a step toward the men. While he was pale and sweating, he seemed to grow in the compartment, filling the space with his authority. "We have lights and heat for as long as there's fuel in the generator tank. And after that, we're worse than stranded; we're dead. This ship might be new, but it's insulated as well as those shitty plastic shoes your kids wear. We'll freeze to death within a day or two of the tank going dry."

"We have tons of fuel," Henry countered. "We're delivering it to the platform, right? We can use as much as we need to keep the gens running until they come looking for us."

"Even if you could think of a way to get it from the transfer tank in the hold to the generators, how long will it keep us going? Until we run out of food and water? We're supplied for a four-week voyage, plus a week extra to account for delays."

"The fuck? You're saying we could be stuck here for a month?" Kevin said.

"I'm saying that we're running out of options. We're not exactly beached on a sandbar off of Tahiti. There's nothing here except climate and conditions that will kill us. I for one want to see my wife and kids again, and I'll be damned if I'm going to sit down and wait to freeze or starve to death."

"I am not going," Henry said.

"You either do what we tell you, or I'll personally see to it that you never get a berth on another ship again. You hear me? You'd better make that last check stretch when we get out of here, because I'll shit-talk you to every skipper and shipper from Seattle to Jakarta if you don't pull your weight." Holden's face turned crimson and the veins on the sides of his wide neck plumped and pulsed. He looked like he was less than a minute away from having a stroke. He took a few quick breaths and waited for another retort from the deckhand. When none came, he finished. "As I was saying, we're going to investigate that . . . *shape* for signs of life and functioning technology. Christ, even spare parts would be something. I'd prefer to have volunteers, but if no one steps up, I'll assign men to come with me. Henry, you're first."

"Why don't we draw straws?" Theo said.

"Because this isn't an episode of fucking *Survivor*. Thank you for being second, Mesires. Who else?"

Noah stepped away from the door despite his urge to disappear through it. He raised a hand and said, "I'll volunteer. But I should go alone."

"That's mighty stupid of you, Cabot. We want a *team* on the ice looking out for each other."

"I don't think any of the men are in shape to hike however far that is. You're putting them at risk by asking them to try."

"And you're ready for the Boston Marathon? You're not special," Theo said, seeming to want to defend his selection for a duty he didn't want.

"I'm aware. And thanks for never missing a chance to tell me so."

"Eat me, professor."

Noah sighed and tried to ignore Theo's posturing. "I'm sure I'm not the only one who's noticed that almost everyone aboard is sick and getting sicker. I'm the only one who doesn't have whatever it is that's going around. I can make it."

Mickle's coughing fit silenced the room. Everyone watched him shudder and rattle, knowing he was the prime example of what awaited them all. Holden, pale and sweating, was stage one, while Yeong, limp on the sofa was stage two. Maybe Puck and Boduf, unable to get out of bed, were stage three and ending up like Mickle was the final step before they were wrapped in a shroud. Someone like Henry could try to deny he was sick, but Noah had seen him sweating and wiping blood from his nose. And they were *all* seeing the phantoms. Even Noah.

When Mickle finished hacking, he looked into his hands like he didn't know what to do with them. Instead of wiping them on his clothes, he clasped them together, wiping at his lower lip with a knuckle. With a wet, raspy voice, he said, "Even if you're the only one in shape to do it, I want men out there to help you. It's no use to us for you to go alone and find something you're not strong enough to carry back. Or for you to get hurt and have no one to help. You can't go alone, Noah. Request denied."

Holden nodded. "Anyone else?"

Michael Yeong raised his hand.

Brewster stepped forward and said, "Me and Serge'll go, too." Noah thought Boucher's look of shock probably mirrored his own. The prospect of needing to rely on Brewster for his safety was as frightening to Noah as being told he was going out into sub-freezing temperatures again was to the bosun. Still, Boucher didn't balk. It was one of the man's virtues that he did as ordered, no matter what the order.

"So we have me, Henry, Theo, Mike, Noah, Boucher, and the Old Man. That's good."

"I'll go," Kevin said. "I volunteer."

"Me too," Jack added.

Holden nodded. No one would have expected those two not to want to stick together. "All right," he said. "That's better than we need. We'll go at first light. The last of the crew will stay here and keep the *Promise* lit up and afloat. If we can, we'll get Nevins back on the radio first thing tomorrow, too. And I do not need to remind you that second officer Mickle is in command of this vessel. You *will* do as he says or there will be consequences. Now, get some sleep everyone. There's shit to do. Dismissed."

The men rose and shuffled back to their cabins. Their grumbling about work was as familiar a sound as there ever was on the ship, and it almost felt like nothing at all was wrong when they did it. Of course, everything was wrong and getting worse by the minute.

Noah stopped Jack and Kevin on their way out. "Will you meet me outside with your binoculars in ten minutes?"

Jack huffed through his nose. "Sure. Why?"

"I just want to have another look before we set out in the morning."

17

The shape in the distance was little more than a shadow among shadows by the time Noah met Jack and Kevin on the weather deck. Still, he did his best with the borrowed field glasses to see what, if anything, there was between them and it. He wanted to know before they set out whether they would need to skirt around a deformity in the ice or a break they wouldn't be able to cross. But with the deepening darkness and blowing snow, he couldn't see a thing. It all looked like the same field of unbroken white, indistinct and featureless. It was as close to looking into a void as he had ever seen. And he was about to step into it.

"What now?" Jack said.

Noah lowered the field glasses. Kevin held out a hand to have a turn and Noah passed them on. "Get some rest, like Holden told us to," he said. "Eat and hit the rack. We're going to need our strength."

"No, I mean, like, what do we *do* now? We worked for hours and barely dug out any of the ship. All that accomplished was wrecking the engines. We'd've been better off if we didn't do anything at all. It feels like we'll be stuck doing this shit forever."

"One must imagine Sisyphus happy," Noah mumbled.

"Say what?" Kevin said, lowering the binocs.

Noah shook his head. "I had to read this book in a philosophy class once. It was about how the fundamental question of life is 'why shouldn't we just kill ourselves?' "

Kevin's lip curled up in a sneer. "*That's* fuckin' cheerful, dude. Why would you even take a class like that?"

"My wife was into it. She made me take it so we could talk about philosophy." He remembered how excited Abby got when he'd get home from classes. She'd ask him about what happened, what the professor said, what did he think? Noah loved that last question. No one had ever asked him what he thought about things before. Or since. His smile shrank. He continued, "In the story, Sisyphus was punished by the gods for something—I can't remember what. He had to push this big boulder up a hill, and every time he got it up to the top, it'd roll back down to the bottom and he had to start over. On and on like that forever.

"We're going to be back down there tomorrow and all the work we did today is going to be undone. So what's the point?"

Jack shook his head and frowned. "You're depressing me, dude. What *is* the point if it's all fucked up and meaningless?"

"Living is the point. The guy who wrote the book thought it took more courage to keep on going than it did to just give up. He said something like living in revolt against meaninglessness gives life meaning. 'One must imagine Sisyphus happy.' Then, he died in a car wreck."

Kevin lowered the binoculars and punched Noah in the shoulder. It was weak and he barely felt the hit through his coat. They were all exhausted and apparently weren't going to be getting any better. In fact, some of them were getting worse with each passing hour. Still, Kevin smiled and tried to look like his old self, even if he didn't feel like it. Jack sniffed hard and made a face as what he snorted caught in his throat. He coughed it up and spat a crimson wad of phlegm over the rail. "They're right about you, you know? You're fuckin' weird, man."

The corner of Noah's mouth turned up. "Yeah, I guess so. I didn't really understand it when I read it back then. I suppose, I only thought of it now because of the ice. . . ." He trailed off, staring at the spot in the distance. It wasn't the ice that was making him think of giving up.

"Earth to Noah," Jack said, slapping him on the shoulder in the same spot where Kevin had weakly punched him.

"Huh?"

"You all right, man?"

Noah sighed. He stared up at the subtle pair of silver curves arcing across the sky like a child's ribbons dancing in the wind. Northern lights. He'd seen them before. Those had been more vivid and colorful. These lines were peculiar. Their soft beauty was somehow wrong when viewed from where Noah stood. A place of uncertainty and danger didn't belong under beauty so tender and ethereal. He imagined what it must be like to stand in Hell and look up to Heaven. The distance from it. The alienation it planted in his heart like a seed of despair pushed deep into fertile soil. He wished clouds would roll in, he hoped for a storm to blow the lights away. But they remained above, shining down with false hope.

"Sure. I'm all right. There was this other line by the same guy my wife printed out and hung up on our fridge. It read, 'In the midst of winter, I found there was, within me, an invincible summer.'"

"That's better than that other shit," Kevin said. "I could use some summer right about now."

"Me too," Noah replied. As much as he wanted to believe in the invincible summer within, all he felt was the sting of the wind. His face hurt, and so did his hands. But his heart hurt most of all.

"Let's go in. I'm hungry," Jack said.

Noah agreed it was time to get out of the cold. They'd have more than their share of it in the morning. He took one last look at the northern lights before turning his back to them. He spun on his heel and took a step toward warmth. A dim shape behind him darted forward, disappearing in a blur that blackened his vision and stole his breath like plunging into nighttime water. Noah jumped, and the small of his back slammed against the rail. His feet skidded and slipped on the slick deck. Trying to find purchase, he felt himself pitching backward, about to go over. His center of gravity shifted, climbing up his body and the distant surface below pulled at him like hands on his shoulders. He wished he could just drop to the deck, bend his knees and collapse, but his legs were scuttling with instinctive movement away from the thing that had rushed at him. Equally uncontrollable, his arms struck out, trying to grasp something, anything solid and unmoving. All they found was air.

He felt hands clamp down on his shoulders. He thrust his arms forward to grasp at his friends as they pulled him back from the brink. They held on, their pallid, slick faces distorted with panic.

Noah looked around, trying to see what it was that had almost killed him. But it was gone like a wisp of black smoke, dissipated and spread thin on the wind. All that remained were his friends and the darkness.

"What the fuck is happening, man?" Jack asked. Noah shook his head, trying to get his thoughts straight and his feet beneath him. He'd survived the storm, made it through the fire and the hit on the head. But he almost died jumping at shadows.

"I wish I knew." All he could tell for certain was that he was cold and afraid. His summer had already turned to fall. And winter was howling right behind it, hungry and vicious.

PART TWO

To the Home of Mists

18

"Papa, build me a snowman! Make him as tall as you."
Noah smiled at his daughter, so excited to be looking
out the window at the lightly falling snow. Sometimes
he missed the weather in New England; it wasn't the
same in Seattle. He missed seeing the creative things
people put out to save their excavated parking spots
and watching children climb the tall drifts pushed to
the side of the road by plow trucks while their parents
pushed the blower. Deep snow was a pain to drive in,
it shut down business, and it got old after the second
or third nor'easter piling on an already limping area. But
looking at Ellie, he realized a child's perception of it was
different. He remembered. It was magic falling from the
sky. You could slide on it, jump in it, ball it up and throw
it. Build forts and caves, make snowmen and angels.
Catch it on your tongue. Watch a single flake, crystal-
line and sharp, a thing of delicate beauty unlike any
other while exactly like every other, melt on the window
while you sat inside, warm and safe.

"I can't, honey. There isn't enough."

"Why?"

"You just need a whole lot more to be able to make stuff out of it. If we can't roll it into a big ball, we can't build a snowman."

"But why can't you roll it?"

Abby laid a hand on Noah's back as she leaned over her husband's shoulder. Her scarf slipped back, exposing her high, pale forehead. She tapped their daughter on the shoulder and said, "Do you want some hot Tang, pookie?" The little girl's eyes lit up and she sprang to her feet shouting that she'd love that. Noah had always thought of the drink as something people pretended astronauts drank to justify buying orange-flavored sugar water. His wife treated it as a refuge in cold weather. The sort of thing that not only took the edge off, but was as comfortable as curling up under a favorite blanket in a pair of sweats. It was an indulgence from which she took a kind of sensual enjoyment. She'd passed that simple yet lush pleasure on to their child. He could watch the two of them sit with their steaming cups, cuddling under a fleece throw in front of the television, forever.

Except he couldn't. Not forever. No one gets that.

She straightened her headscarf and held out a hand to lead their child away. "Come with me, pook-kid. Let your papa relax." In the archway to the kitchen, she looked back, wordlessly asking her husband if he was going to come sit with them. He smiled and told her he'd be right behind them.

And then he looked out the window at the snow and wished enough would fall so he could make his girls a snowman.

Noah felt a pit of anxiety in his gut. In the change room, donning his cold weather gear, it felt like business as usual. Another in a string of days where he struck at futility, aiming to break through to hope. Without a tool in hand to do battle with the ice, however, the reality of what he was about to do set in. They were leaving the Gumby suits behind. The *Arctic Promise* wasn't equipped with everyday work suits, but rather "quick don" vessel abandonment dry suits. The baggy, one-size-fits construction made them difficult to walk in under ideal conditions. Standing in place and swinging a chisel, they were restrictive, but not completely inhibiting. Like their namesake, the fixed boots were a straight line from the legs, and not well-fitting. They'd make a walk at least twice as difficult. Noah thought there were as many good reasons to leave them behind as there were to wear them. Ultimately the choice wasn't his. Holden made the decision to leave them behind. Given the thickness of the pack holding the ship, he was willing to take the risk of going without them.

They gathered as many things as they could to make up for the absence of the suits' protection. Extra layers of gloves and socks. Two pair of pants and shirts under latex and rubber weather deck gear. They pulled reflective work harnesses over their coats and jerry-rigged beacons from the survival suits onto them using duct tape. Each man was given a headlamp and a pair of safety goggles. Holden wanted them to be able to see each other no matter what conditions presented themselves. Finally, they brought as long a length of rope as they could find so they could tie themselves together in the event visibility went completely to hell. Differences aside, they had a common goal, and Holden was determined no one would be on his own out on the ice.

The noises of the ship were gone. What had been assaultive and disorienting his first time aboard a ship like the *Promise* had later become understandable and readable. An experienced seaman could tell what the engines were doing by the noise echoing through the ship. Noah knew where he was in the vessel by the clang of pipes and the humming of ducts and vents. Now, it was quiet except for the creaking of the hull being pressed upon by ice. The men dressed in similar silence, all unsettled by the death of the din.

They left the change room and filed out onto the deck where the fast rescue craft awaited. As they climbed aboard, Noah observed that a night's rest hadn't done the men much good, if any. Holden presented the appearance of being more or less ready for their adventure, although he couldn't hide his increasingly frequent cough. Every subtle hitch of his shoulders betrayed what he tried to hide behind closed lips. Henry, Michael, Jack, and Kevin all looked a little more road weary and not one appeared well rested. Noah understood. The anticipation of the day ahead had awoken him every couple of hours. He'd lay in his bunk counting backward from a thousand until he drifted back off into restless sleep. On a tough night of sleep, he'd get as far as eight hundred and fifty, or maybe even seven hundred and ninety before losing count and slipping under. Last night, he'd had to start over once he reached one.

Theo Mesires never showed, and no one bothered to fetch him. Holden insisted they had enough hands mustered for the job. He didn't say it, but all the men knew Theo would pay for his absence when they got back.

Michael Yeong appeared the worst off. Noah thought about suggesting they leave him behind as well. Seven would be enough. But unless someone else brought it up, he assumed no one would listen. Yeong shoved his hand aside when Noah tried to help him into the FRC.

Serge Boucher was doing his deckboss act by the numbers, but his neck remained bent, his head hanging like a weight. And then there was Brewster. If he hadn't known better, Noah would have said he was seventy or more, not a fit fifty-eight. The Old Man climbed in last, closing the gate behind him. It caught with a loud clack.

Holden engaged the crane arm and winch to lower the craft. For a moment, nothing happened. Noah imagined them all having to climb down using the net ladder dropped over the Rescue Zone near the cargo deck. It'd be a quicker way down for the men as individuals, but meant they'd have to find another way to get their gear to the ice. The motor fired to life and the FRC jerked downward. If there was a final thing that functioned for now on board the *Arctic Promise,* it was that.

While he alone among the team seemed to feel like himself physically, mentally he was struggling with pessimism, and emotionally he was swirling the drain. Healthy fear was giving way to terror as the FRC was battered against the side of the ship. The flat-bottomed boat settled on the ice and Noah let out a long breath of relief as Holden killed the motor. The neoprene face mask he wore pushed his breath up into the goggles and steamed the plastic lenses opaque, blinding him. He pushed the eyewear up on his forehead. Clouds had moved in overnight and the day was gray and dim. The northern lights were gone and the sun was a pale circle just above the horizon. It wouldn't rise much higher before it started to descend again.

The crew unloaded the FRC, pulling packs filled with gear out onto the ice. Everyone had a burden to carry. No one had any idea what they might find when they got where they were going, so they'd tried to anticipate all possibilities. Being in the best condition, but also being the crew's whipping boy, Noah's rucksack was stuffed full of heavy tools to scavenge parts or make repairs. John and Kevin carried food and water for the team. Henry grabbed the stick flares and the emergency medical supply pack. Boucher hefted a red hard-shell backpack that could unfold into a sliding stretcher onto his shoulders, pulling the arm straps tight. Holden had assigned himself extra ropes and the hated bosun's chair Noah never wanted to wear again. Michael grabbed a pack filled with LED lights and stands in case they were caught out after dark. And Brewster had his pickax, a flare gun in an orange plastic case hanging from a bright strap over his shoulder, and a black Colt .45 pistol in a leather holster on his hip.

"Is that necessary?" Holden whispered, nodding at the handgun.

The Old Man nodded. "It pays to be prepared."

Noah tried to ignore Brewster. Hefting his pack up on his back, he peered off into the distance. The shape seemed smaller than before. He imagined it as an optical illusion of blowing snow and low light. Without contrast from either the surface below or the sky above, he was uncertain he even saw it. But he was determined not to lose sight of it. Their lives depended on keeping the shape in view.

"All right, men!" Holden shouted to be heard through

cinched hoods and above the wind. "Line up!" The crew took position as the third officer had instructed in the change room. Noah, behind him in the lead, then Jack and Kevin, Michael, Henry, Boucher, and Brewster at the rear. Holden unspooled the lifeline rope. He'd tied a loop every six or seven feet of it; enough space to comfortably move, but not enough to lose sight of the crewmember ahead. Moving back, he handed each man his handhold, lightly pounding a fist on the shoulder of every man for encouragement as he went down the line. When he finished with Brewster, Holden returned to take his place at the head of the line, fitted the lead loop around his left wrist, and shouted, "Let's hit the road!"

Their initial steps were halting and almost comical. Noah nearly dropped his loop twice as the rope went taut and then slack, jerking his arm and once almost tripping him until they found a rhythm and moved together. He tried to imagine a march cadence like he'd heard in the movies, but couldn't think of one. Their steps were oddly timed, speeding up and slowing down without good reason. The weariest among them slowed the line. Both Noah and Holden seemed to want to move faster than they were able, and tugged at the others behind. No matter how much he wanted to break away and jog on ahead, Noah knew it was better to pace himself and conserve energy. Although no one had said as much, the trip was potentially twice as long as it appeared. Once they reached the shape, if it turned out to be nothing more than an irregularity in the ice, they'd have to turn right around and march back; they'd die trying to camp out on the open plain after dark.

Inside the ship, Holden had warned them about the

temperatures as they suited up for the trip. The thermostat aboard the *Promise* read nineteen degrees below zero. That didn't reflect wind chill. And the wind was strong. It was maybe forty below—the intersection where Fahrenheit and Celsius are equal. In this kind of cold, a person could get frostbitten in as little as ten minutes. He told them to leave as little skin as possible exposed. "That goes for your faces, too. Nobody wants to lose a nose."

The wind gusted, pushing them off course. Holden corrected, steering the line true again. A trip in a zigzag pattern was longer than walking a straight line, but as long as he got them oriented again, it'd be better than missing the mark entirely. Where most of the crew kept their heads down, Noah had to keep his up to see. He did his best to help keep an eye out for their destination, although Holden's back dominated much of Noah's field of vision. The old adage about the view never changing for anyone but the lead dog came to mind. At least staring at the back of Holden's coat was better than staring at a husky's asshole, he thought. Squinting against the blowing snow, he tried lowering his goggles again, but the condensation of his breath in the mask fogged the lenses over. Frost formed on the inside of the plastic and he pushed them back up on his forehead. It was either the mask or the goggles. He chose to expose his eyes instead of his nose or lips. He knew his corneas could become frostbitten, but he hoped, if he squinted, not as quickly as the rest of his face. Ski goggles would have solved the problem. But neither the company nor any of the men had anticipated what they were reduced to doing. He carried on. His eyes watered and the tears froze in his eyelashes. Every few minutes, he had to reach up to pry a stuck eyelid open.

The snow around their feet crunched and creaked with every step. It crept up around their shins and tried to get in their boots. It was thick and there was no dragging feet no matter how tired or defeated anyone felt. It was like walking through shallow surf. At this depth, it was difficult but not impossible. Every step forward meant pulling a foot up and out before moving ahead. After maybe a quarter mile, Noah's thighs were burning and his breath was becoming harder to catch. He wasn't out of shape, but this was twice the work of trying to stay upright and balanced on troubled sea. The snow helped to keep him from slipping, but underneath it was slick and treacherous. Every step was uncertain.

Glancing over his shoulder, the *Arctic Promise* was hazy and ethereal-looking in the distance. He wanted another peek through Kevin's binoculars to determine how far their destination was now, but Noah decided it could wait. They'd have to stop to rest somewhere along the way, and when they did, he'd borrow them again.

Trying to distract himself from growing exertion and fear, he pretended the barren stretch ahead of him was actually the Charles River Esplanade. He tried to picture the trees and the joggers and the Harvard rowing crew practicing in their slender boats on the river like fast water-skimming bugs. Then a gust of wind would shake and push him. He would stumble and slip and the line in his left hand would go taut, bringing him right back to the present, the easy paths of the river greenbelt gone.

They walked on. No one had the breath to speak or complain. The wind whipping them fluttered jacket hoods and stole the sound of their feet crunching in the snow. It punished and chilled, and tried to hold them back. Pushing against them, it seemed impossible to move forward without ducking into the blast, trying to cut through it like a swimmer battling the tide. Noah wondered how long they'd been walking. It felt like hours. Time was elongating, becoming meaningless. The sun moved, but he had no idea how to track the hours with its arc. This far north, its trajectory never left the lower half of the sky.

Noah guessed they walked maybe another half mile before the procession stopped. His arm jerked back as the rope snapped taut. Under the howl of the wind, he heard the sounds of coughing. He looked behind to see Michael, doubled over, pulling his scarf down and spitting into the snow between gasps. His red expectorations disappeared into the powder, steaming like tiny souls reaching for Heaven before being blown away to nothing.

Holden set down his end of the rope and walked back to talk to Michael, a hand on his shoulder. The deckhand nodded and replaced his scarf. Behind them, the *Arctic Promise* stuck out of the ice. The sight of it was disheartening. Encrusted and still, it seemed like a wraith. Spectral and thin, it grew more insubstantial with each foot traveled forward. Even if the company sent helicopters to search for them, it might not find the ship once it faded into the white expanse holding it. Soon, it would just be another part of the landscape, nearly indistinguishable from the winter overtaking it . . . like the shape ahead of them.

Noah asked Kevin for the binoculars. Digging them out of his jacket, Kevin passed them over. A strong shudder wracked his body as the wind stole into his clothes in the brief moment he'd unzipped his parka. He zipped up quickly, hugging his arms to his chest in a tight clinch.

Noah looked at the shape. It might be another mile away, or ten. "Do you know how long we've been walking?" he shouted to Holden.

Holden pointed toward the shape and said, "Long enough for that to be closer than it is."

He was right. Their destination looked every bit as far as when they'd departed. If he couldn't see how far they'd made it from their ship, Noah might have thought they hadn't moved at all. And that was trouble. The wind was covering their tracks. Everything in the distance was blurred with kicked up snow and iron-colored clouds darkened the sky. They couldn't see where they'd been. If they couldn't see the *Arctic Promise* well enough to make it back, it wouldn't matter what they found when they reached their goal.

"What do we do?" Jack shouted.

"We have to keep moving ahead," Holden answered. "If we stop, we'll freeze. And if we turn back, we'll be every bit as screwed. There's only one way to go now."

The men nodded their agreement, even while most leaned, hands on knees, trying to catch a breath and mentally prepare for their next steps. For a moment, the wind died down, and in the quiet without the crunching of their boots or the howling gusts, Noah heard the ice speak. A creak and a pop. A groan and a long crack. He'd gone skating as a kid and knew what it sounded like to stand on a frozen lake. He'd skipped stones along the surface to hear the alien chirping of the rock echoing in the water beneath the crust. He'd listened to it as he stepped, a sound of hollow strength underfoot. This was not that. This was the sound of something giving way. Even though they'd stood for hours on the ice the day before, beating and breaking it, they'd never heard it stressing at their weight. The sound of thin ice.

"How is it the wind only blows while we're walking?" Boucher said.

"Maybe the Devil needs a break from beating his wings," Henry said, crossing himself.

"We gotta go," Noah said. "Right now."

Holden held up a hand. "Give it a minute."

"Yeah, not all of us are doing as good as you," Michael said. His words were thin like he couldn't get the air to speak them.

"No. Listen!" Noah held up a gloved hand in hopes of shutting them up. Henry waved dismissively at him, turning to say something to Michael.

"You're imagining shit," Michael said.

A pop. Too loud to dismiss.

"Did I imagine *that*?"

A low groan. And a crack.

Holden's back went straight. He looked at Noah, worry breaking through his stoicism. "He's right. It's time," he announced, composing himself and concealing his worry. It was too late, though; Noah had seen it. The crack in his inscrutability. Abby had always told Noah when they boarded a plane and he started to feel a tinge of panic, *Watch the crew. If the flight attendants aren't worried, you've got nothing to be afraid of.* Holden was visibly concerned. And that made Noah very afraid.

"Grab the line," Holden barked. "Everybody on the move. Now!" He jogged back to his position at the front of the queue, picked his end of the rope out of the snow and gave it a sharp tug to convince those following to step to. He pushed ahead with fresh enthusiasm. Unable to return the binoculars to Kevin, Noah hung them around his neck. They bounced against his chest as he pushed to keep up with Holden.

They marched haltingly for a few steps, the crew having a hard time finding the awkward rhythm it had fallen into previously. He heard more coughing from behind, followed by a crack that sounded like a gunshot. Noah called ahead to Holden, "We're too close together."

Holden turned his head and said, "What do you suggest?" He slipped and staggered a little before regaining his footing.

Noah pointed to the second rope hanging from Holden's shoulder. "Tie the lines together. Put more space between the men." It wasn't as long as the rope they used as a handhold, but it would lengthen the distance, and he hoped spreading their weight out over more surface would make a difference.

Holden opened his mouth to say something about Noah's idea. Another creak and a pop interrupted his meditation. "No. We have to keep going. We'll head up a ways and then try to space out the loops some. You with me?"

"Aye sir." Noah wasn't sure he *was* with him, but he had little choice. They could either move or stand still. Standing still meant their collective weight would keep stressing the ice beneath their feet. Moving would hopefully keep them ahead of whatever weakness they'd wandered into the middle of.

The wind picked up again, muffling any other sounds

the ice might be making. Noah couldn't feel the surface buckling beneath his feet. Without the sound of it, he reckoned he wouldn't know if it was going to break until they were already in the water. No matter how much the surface looked like solid ground, the reality was that they were hiking on ice over sea. Going in would be bad. Getting caught in a current would be worse. There was no coming back once you were away from the open hole unless you were lashed to something or someone.

Holden held a hand up to his face to shield it from the wind as he searched for the shape. While it was finally getting bigger, it was no clearer than it had been from the ship. Still just a shape in the distance. But they were headed toward it, and that was all that mattered at the moment. Not the engines, not the food, not the radio. That their direction was true was everything.

Noah felt the line go tight again and then slack. He heard a shout rise from the rear before it was carried off by the wind. He hazarded a glance back to see Michael on his knees. Boucher and Henry had also let go of the rope to try and help him up.

"Stop!" Noah shouted to Holden. "There are men off the line!"

Holden turned. He pointed at Michael and shouted, "Get him on his feet! Back on the rope!"

Noah rushed over to help. With Boucher and Henry each under an arm, they lifted Michael easily and didn't need him. Yeong nodded and said, "I slipped."

"Get your hands on the fucking rope and let's go!" Holden shouted.

A loud crack and a grinding sound rose up despite the wind assailing their hoods.

Noah slipped the pack off Michael's back, snatched up the loop of the guide rope and helped slip it over his wrist. "Are you going to be okay?"

Michael, said, "I'm fine. I slipped. Watch out for yourself." While he appeared unwilling to accept Noah's help, he didn't ask for his bag back.

Boucher ducked out from under Michael's arm and shoved at Noah's shoulder. "Back to the head of the class, professor." Noah's feet skidded out from under him and he fell, landing hard on his ass. The ice shifted under him like a gymnasium floor, pressing down and springing up. Some long metal tool in his rucksack jabbed into his back and his spine arched involuntarily at the pain. He felt Jack's and Kevin's hands close on his arms and start to haul him up.

"Watch your step," Boucher said. Noah couldn't see his face through the balaclava he wore, but he knew the asshole was smiling. He wanted to fight. And Noah wanted to settle things, too. But he also knew exerting himself out here would make the trip harder and more dangerous. Being beaten and wounded was the same as sitting down and waiting to die. As much as he wanted to stand up and show the deckboss, and *all* the men, that he wouldn't be pushed around, he wanted to get off the god damn ice even more. He shouldered Michael's pack, extended his middle finger, and turned to walk back to his spot to pick up the line that every last one of them had dropped. Everyone but Holden.

Only . . . where was the rope?

Where was Holden?

19

The rope snaked away toward the fissure faster than Noah could run to catch up to it. He dropped his pack and dove for the end of the line knowing that if he missed the loop, he wouldn't be able to get up in time to take another leap before it disappeared over the edge. He had this single chance. Although the snow wasn't too densely packed, the landing was hard. The belly flop and slide on the ice drove his breath in a great wheezing rasp from his body. Snow infiltrated his sleeves as he thrust his arms out to catch the rope. It froze his wrists and dampened the edges of his sweater underneath. He gripped at the spot he last saw the line with fat, padded fingers. He couldn't feel if he had a good grip or not. His gloves were made for warmth and gross movement. Still, he didn't dare open his hands for another try. If he did have a hold of it, letting go would be worse than never having caught it at all.

The tug at his hands surprised him and his fingers almost opened reflexively. Instead, he gripped harder, scrambling to his knees as the rope fought him. It pulled, jerking his body toward the fissure that had opened up in the ice. He leaned back and resisted. The rope stopped sliding away, but he couldn't pull it toward him. Holden was in the water. The ice opened beneath him like a gaping mouth, and he'd fallen in before he could call out. Noah remembered what he'd been told in training before setting out on his first Arctic voyage. Going in frigid water created a "cold shock response." The first thing you do is gasp and begin to hyperventilate. The sudden chill stole your breath, and your body tried to get it back in spades. Which was fine, if your head was above water. But Holden had clearly been caught in Noah's worst nightmare. He'd slipped under the ice, and was being pulled away from the opening by the current.

Noah pulled, leaning back with all his weight. The rope slipped toward him a little and stopped, catching on the edge of the opening. A thump below gave him a terrible perspective. Holden was underneath him. Noah wasn't only pulling against the current, but also against the bend of the line dragging across the ice. He slipped and skidded closer to the edge with every pull. The water was winning. And when Holden ran out of breath, when he ran out of stamina below and let go of the rope, it would win. If Noah went in before that happened, it was doubly a victory for the ice.

"Help me!" he cried. He whipped his head around to see if anyone was rushing to his aid, but the rope yanked at him again and he almost fell forward. Still, he felt no footfalls behind him. Heard no voices raised in alarm. Although he was lucky to have a hold of a loop, he had to get a better angle of attack. Pulling at a man below and now behind him wasn't working.

He struggled to his feet and sprinted as fast as he

could toward the fissure. The ice cracked and roared. He leaped into space. His jump was robbed of power by the ice falling away from his feet as he shoved off from the edge. He landed half on the other side, his legs dangling in the fissure, another lungful of oxygen pushed out of his body by the impact. He clawed at the surface with a hand, the other thrust straight down between his legs, holding on to the rope. Panting to catch his breath, he raised a knee up out of the maw before the slack rope tightened and started to pull him in after Holden. He scrambled out of the fissure and rolled up onto the other side, yanking as much of the line out of the water as he could. He shoved back a few more feet from the edge, trying to make more distance, and the line went taut again, stopping him. Then he pulled as hard as he was capable. And it happened. He felt the rope slide toward him.

It came slowly, but steadily. He reached hand over hand, hauling it in. The rope was wet and frozen. It slipped and his breath caught at the panicked thought of not being able to hold on. But he didn't stop. He gripped tighter and heaved, feeling the weight of it—of Holden—sliding toward him. He pulled until he heard the splash below and a desperate sharp sound in the wind. A gasp.

From the other side of the fissure, he heard a shout go up. He couldn't focus on what the men were shouting. But they weren't on the line. They weren't on his side. He was alone.

He got to his knees and crawled to the edge of the ice, keeping the line taut. Holden was in the water, sputtering and choking. His hood was pushed back and he'd lost both his hat and shemagh scarf. He was blue as sky and looked ready to slip back under. Noah struck a hand out and shouted, "Grab hold!" Holden reached up, blindly batting at the sound of his rescuer's voice. Noah fought to catch his flailing hand, finally catching his parka sleeve instead. Although everything in him screamed not to, he let go of the line to put a second hand on Holden's arm. "Hold on to me!" he screamed against the wind and the water. Holden did.

The fissure was deep, maybe three feet, but they grasped at each other and weren't letting go. Noah fell backward again. Holden kicked up from the water and got as much of himself out as he could. Gravity worked against them, though, and he fell back, unable to keep his upward momentum. Noah fumbled and grabbed at his armpits. Holden wrapped his arms around Noah's neck, and Noah realized that this was where they would both be going in. Like a drowning victim trying to climb on top of his rescuer, Holden would push him down beneath the surface to keep his head out of the water, and then they'd both die.

Noah tried not to imagine a cold end with blue ice above glowing in the light of the dim day, and black below. The chill of it shutting his body down. His limbs instantly numb, he wouldn't be able to swim for the opening. He'd die, suffocating and alone while the men above stood helplessly, never to see him again. The Chukchi Sea, his grave forever.

His guts cramped and he felt a wad of stinging bile at the back of his throat. He panted with effort and fear, and his vision tunneled down to a single point in front of him. Holden. The man he was trying to rescue. The man whose life was now in his hands. He could have chosen to stand by and said later, *There was nothing we could do. One minute we were arguing and the next he was gone—swept away.* But if Holden was lost it would be because of Noah's weakness. His inability to do what had to be done.

The others across the ice bore witness to his imminent failure.

He screamed and arched his back, pulled his arms toward him, dragging Holden out of the water. Holden weakly scrambled up the side, clutching and clawing at both Noah and the snow until he was out and, exhausted, they both lay still on the ice.

"Away from the edge," Noah said, gasping. He shoved with his heels, pushing back from the brink. He never let go of Holden, pulling him along.

First Jack and then Kevin leaped over the fissure. They scrambled toward Noah, babbling and asking questions on top of each other faster than he could process. Holden sputtered and coughed up a lungful of water. He choked and Kevin flipped him over on his stomach, so he could puke up the water he'd swallowed.

"Fuck, dude! That was *amazing*!" Jack said. Michael, Boucher, and Brewster stood on the opposite side of the break, gape mouthed and silent.

Finally, Brewster broke out of his trance and shouted across at Noah. "We have to get him back to the ship. We have to get him into dry clothes!"

Noah looked at where the Old Man stood and couldn't picture them getting Holden back across the gap without dumping him back in the water, maybe even losing one or more of them in it as well. He looked left and right for a narrower portion, or even an end to the opening, but the fissure extended as far as he could see in both directions, as if the plates had become completely separated. How could it have broken apart without them feeling it—without warning? Then he remembered hearing the crack while they argued over Michael. An unbidden image of the ice falling away under Holden's feet intruded in his thoughts and he imagined more of it letting go near the edges or even along another weak line where separate plates had frozen together.

There was no way back.

"We can't. We have to get him to . . . whatever the hell that is!" Noah pointed at the thing looming larger than ever. It was still maybe a mile away. But closer now than the *Arctic Promise*.

"He'll die!"

Boucher shouted, "Tie him to the rope and throw it back across. We'll pull him over."

"I'm—I'm n-not going b-back in the water," Holden said, coughing. Without his scarf, the water on his bright red cheeks had frosted.

Noah was through arguing. The longer they debated what to do, the lower Holden's body temperature dropped. His cheeks were bright red and blistering and the tip of his nose was already turning dark gray. Noah imagined his fingers and toes in wet gloves and boots blackening with frostbite as well. Even if they got Holden out of his wet clothes and into shelter, he still might die from the complications of frostbite instead of hypothermia. Either way, it was time to move. He was guaranteed to die here.

Noah leaned down and pushed Holden onto his back. The man didn't resist. Grabbing an arm, Noah tried to pull him to his feet, but Holden wasn't moving. He shivered and panted, trembling from head to toe. He wasn't getting up on his own. He kept his arms and legs tight against him. "Help me!" Noah shouted at Kevin and Jack. He pulled Holden's arm over his shoulders and ducked under his armpit, getting under his body as far as he could. "Help me lift him."

"What are you doing?"

"Fireman's carry. We have to get him to shelter." Noah pointed. Blurry and mostly white in the blowing snow, in between wind gusts, they could see the red shape. Whatever it was, it wasn't an iceberg; it was manmade, and it was their only hope of getting Holden out of the cold.

Jack and Kevin helped Noah lift him. Noah was thankful Holden wasn't a giant like Boucher or Mickle. They were roughly the same size. Lean too. Good for Noah; bad for Holden. Without a layer of fat to insulate him, he'd freeze to death faster.

Noah took a halting step forward. If it was twice as hard to walk in the snow, it was ten times as difficult with a full-grown man—no matter how thin—on his back. But what choice did he have? He took a step. And then another.

And then he fell.

Turning to the side so Holden wouldn't land on his neck, he crumpled, dropping the man in the snow, his own spine twisting painfully. Holden groaned, his utterance vibrating with the uncontrollable shaking of his body. Jack and Kevin ran to help. "You can't do it," Jack said. "You'll never make it."

"I have to try. Help me get him back up. I can do it."

"No," Kevin said. "You can't."

"Wait a minute," Jack interrupted. He ran back to

the fissure. "Serge, throw me your pack! Noah's going to kill himself trying to carry Holden."

"Let him!" Boucher called back.

"Throw me the pack, motherfucker! I don't give a shit what you think of Cabot. It's for Holden."

Brewster's face darkened as he slipped the rigid red pack off Boucher's back and tossed it almost casually across the fissure. Jack leaned forward to catch it, barely snagging a strap before it fell in the water. He glared at the Old Man with a look of pure poison and spit at all of them on the other side of the line.

Returning to the others, he fumbled the thing open. The two hard-shell sides of the pack became sled treads while he extended and locked the rigid poles and stretcher into place. Noah wished he'd remembered that Boucher was carrying it. Fortunately, he had Jack and Kevin. That it would work was more important than who could lay claim to the idea.

They lifted Holden onto the drag-along stretcher and secured him with restraints so he wouldn't tumble off. Kevin stripped off his watch cap, pulling it over Holden's head, assuring him he'd be all right. They helped Noah fasten the pull straps around his waist.

"Let's go," Jack said.

"You guys get back to the others."

"We need to stay together."

Noah nodded toward the wet, frozen rope lying in the snow. "Take the rope and make sure no one else goes in the water. Make sure Michael gets across okay or that someone takes him to the *Promise*. Either way."

Kevin nodded. His ears were a painful-looking red. He pulled his hood up and cinched the drawstring tight. It would be windproof, even if it wasn't warm. "We'll get them across and be right behind you."

Noah looked at his friend and tried to force a smile before realizing he was still wearing a mask. "Don't be late," he said before he began to trudge off across the snow.

"We're right behind you!" Kevin called as he ran back to help the rest of the team across the fissure.

20

Getting started was harder than Noah thought it would be. The pull-along stretcher was designed for exactly this use, but with a full-grown man strapped into it, it didn't pull along as smoothly as a Flexible Flyer. He leaned forward and dug his feet in as best he could on the slick surface. They began to move slowly. Inches at first. Then a little faster, momentum making up for inertia. It wasn't as difficult as carrying Holden on his shoulders, but still, it was hard. *This way,* he thought, *he won't snap my neck when I fall down dead from a heart attack.*

He pushed on, head down, arms crossed in front of his chest in an attempt to consolidate his effort. His feet slipped and he felt like he was running in place, even though he was moving forward. He was beginning to sweat inside his parka. As soon as he stopped moving, that would be trouble.

Holden was shivering so hard, Noah could feel it through the travois lines. He ducked his head down and called back, "Hang in there. We're almost to shelter." The shape was growing larger; there was maybe a half mile left. Noah could finally see what it was, and his hope of finding the drilling platform and others to help them summon rescue died. It wasn't the Niflheim. It was a platform supply vessel, like their own. But, it was derelict.

Caked in ice and snow, it tilted at an alien angle, suggesting their own eventual fate aboard the *Promise* when the ice clutching the hull shifted and began to crush their ship. Sections of red paint peeked out from under the frost coating the vessel, but for the most part, it was encased. He could make out the words RESCUE ZONE painted on the side. Although the FRCs appeared to be locked in their traveling positions, it was possible they could get aboard. The ship's stern was low in the ice, as though it had been flash-frozen in stormy seas. He hoped that meant a low enough point to climb aboard. Once inside, at the very least he hoped they'd be shielded from the wind. Perhaps he could find blankets and something dry among the crew's belongings for Holden to wear. It was a dead ship, but it was the closest thing they had to salvation.

Behind him, he heard the other crewmen catching up to him. The sound of their footsteps crunching in the snow was barely audible, but it was there and it gave him hope. He was not alone. At the very least, he had the Twins to back him up. He wanted to turn, to hail them, or wait for them to catch up, but his lungs hurt and his legs and back were burning with exertion. If he stopped, he'd be done for good. No amount of effort could get the stretcher sled moving again. Of course, that wasn't true. He'd have others to help him. He could even give the lines to someone who hadn't been bearing the burden.

He stumbled. The sled banged painfully into the backs of his legs, sending him staggering ahead trying not to fall. Holden moaned something Noah couldn't hear. He continued to walk forward, feeling the tug of the line going taut again, desperate to keep them moving. His heart pounded in his chest as his imagination, spurred by exhaustion and desperation, began to fill his head with images of failure at the last moment: another ice collapse opening a fissure beneath *his* feet this time. He saw himself falling off the side, falling through into the cold water and sinking, the thrumming sound of it invading his eardrums, pressing against him until he couldn't feel his body. He almost felt the pressure of deep water enclosing him, holding like a tomb of ice—forever suspended in the water of a dead womb.

He rubbed a hand at his eyes trying to clear away the waking nightmares along with the frozen tears blinding him. The crystals encrusting his eyelashes scratched and hurt when they broke away, tearing at the little hairs. But he pawed at them with nearly the same enthusiasm with which he'd bashed at the ship's rails in the storm. No matter where it built up, the ice was death. He would swing and strike and claw at it for as long as he was able.

As he reached the ship, he stumbled again and fell to his knees. The echo of his fall on the ice and the crack of it beneath him knotted his guts and made him hold his breath. The stretcher slid into his back and he let that breath go in a cry of pain. *All this way. All this way and it's a dead ship.*

He undid the latch at his waist and let the belts fall. Only a few yards from the behemoth, a new despair filled him. One borne of the size and the magnitude of

their problem. In Seattle, he'd stood on the dock looking up at the *Arctic Promise* and thinking how big it
was. But on a dock or a causeway walking aboard, it
seemed like any other tall building. He was impressed
to be on a ship that size, but he'd seen them before. It
was like standing below a skyscraper. No one ever
thinks, "people built that." They just walk through the
revolving door to go to work or transact their business
unaware of the effort of both intention and engineer-
ing it took to create such a structure. Now, kneeling in
the snow at the back of the ship, permanently listing to
starboard and tilted up, it looked like a spacecraft stuck
on a desolate planet, unable to launch, filled with the
cold emptiness and despair of the race of defeated beings
who'd traversed the stars only to die alone on a frozen
sea. He tried to force his thoughts back to his task, saving Holden, but in that minute, in the face of the derelict,
he was nothing, and his efforts to remain something
were meaningless.

He cried out again, not in pain, but frustration. He'd
gotten them there. Now the work began. He had to get
them inside. The sun was on the downward trajectory
of its arc across the sky, and soon it would be dark.
Soon, they'd all die.

"Who's there?"

Noah looked over his shoulder for the speaker. The
rest of the crew was approaching, but they were back on
the line and were only moving as fast as the slowest
one of them: Michael. The trip had taken something out
of them all. Their heads were down, hands up to shield
their faces from the blowing wind. It wasn't one of them.

"What the hell are you doing here?" the voice called
out. Noah looked up. The speaker stood on the ship

above him. No one could have beaten him there. It was impossible.

"We need help," Noah shouted. "He's soaking wet. We've got to get him inside and dry."

"Who is it?"

Noah couldn't understand why anyone would ask. "What? Does it matter? Help me get him inside." The figure disappeared. Noah called out: "Wait! Don't go! His name's Holden!"

Noah fell forward onto his hands. His tired legs tried to refuse, but he forced himself to his feet, staggering the last few yards to the ship. He wanted to bang his fists against the hull like it was a door he could force open, but he knew it would make no difference. He had to find a way up. Holden's only hope was getting inside. Tilted as the ship was, he might be able to jump and reach the bulwark rail around the starboard side of the hull. But once he was up, he had no idea what to do. Holden was still strapped to the sled, and he had no rope to try to lift him. He was certain the man's hands, and probably arms, legs, and feet also were all numb and useless. His body would be fighting to keep his organs warm, and would sacrifice its limbs to save the whole organism. Holden couldn't help himself. They would both have to wait for the rest of the crew.

Or . . . Noah could climb aboard and deal with the other obstacle to Holden's rescue: the man already aboard.

Before his thoughts could grow darker, the man appeared around the side of the vessel. Noah stood paralyzed. At a distance, the man was just a shadow in the late day light, but Noah could see the clear shape of a rifle slung on his back. It was on his back. Not in his hands. Not leveled at him. That was something, at least. He unhooked the travois leads and stumbled toward the man.

As Noah closed the distance, he saw the stranger was dressed for the same kind of outdoor work the *Arctic Promise* crew was. Parka and weather deck pants, waterproof boots and gloves, a face mask, hat and hood. This man, however, had ski goggles.

"Did I hear you right? Did you say Holden?" the stranger said. Although he was shouting, his voice carried a lilt that said Alabama or maybe Georgia. Noah normally had a hard time telling one Southern accent from another, but this one was familiar. He'd heard it before.

"He's our third officer. He fell in the water. He's dying. Will you help me?" Noah could see clearly enough to notice the man's eyes widen with surprise and his brow furrow in confusion. The stranger was trying to work something out. They didn't have time to discuss facts, consider options, and come to conclusions, however. The man seemed to agree with this last unspoken thought of Noah's and hurried over to grab a tow strap.

"There's a net ladder around the side we can use. All of our electronics have failed, but I set up a manual winch we can use to lift him aboard once we're up." The stranger looked to his right; the rest of the crew was almost there. "Let's go," he said with more than a touch of concern in his voice.

Noah grabbed the other end of the harness and together they pulled Holden around to the starboard side of the ship toward the Rescue Zone—a lowered area where a crew would drop a net ladder to help retrieve someone who'd fallen overboard or accept refugees from another boat. Hanging over the side was the net ladder the man had promised. Next to it dangled a hooked line with a net basket attached. And next to that stood an emergency sled stretcher identical to their own, except heaped with boxes and bags full of supplies. The stranger was looting the ship.

"It's going to be uncomfortable, but we don't have a choice. I can't rig up anything else quick enough. Help me get him in it." The stranger dropped his line and dashed ahead, pulling boxes of supplies out of the netting, tossing them in the snow next to the stretcher.

Noah unstrapped Holden and helped him sit up. The semi-conscious man complied, but Noah figured he didn't comprehend much of what was happening. The stranger helped Noah carry Holden from the stretcher to the net. "I'm going to need you on board with me to haul him in. You up to it?"

Noah nodded. "I can help. I'm just tired."

"Well, no rest for the wicked yet."

"Who are you?"

The man turned. "Let's get him aboard and dry and then we'll make our introductions." Hearing his voice, seeing his steely, blue eyes, Noah knew who he was talking to. But it wasn't possible. That man was dead.

Regardless, Noah followed him up the ladder.

21

It was a struggle to get Holden across the tilted cargo deck to the bulkhead door. The surface was predictably slick and at an almost impassable angle. The toppled shipping cans made it even more difficult, forcing them to weave along a maze of debris and wreckage. Eventually, they made it inside and to a crew cabin. The ship had been infiltrated by cold and snow, and the only difference between in and out was shelter from the wind.

Holden's clothes were frozen and stiff. It was hard to peel them off, but Noah got him out of them and wrapped in a blanket stripped off one of the bunks. He had to shake it to get the dust and snow off before using it to dry the third officer as much as he could, but he imagined a cold, dry blanket was better than wet, frozen clothes. Holden's breathing was shallow and ragged. His fingers and toes were swollen with second-degree frostbite blisters. The tip of his nose was turning black and broken blisters wept down his cheeks. Noah had to peel Kevin's cap off of his head; it had adhered with frozen and congealed blister serum. If it hurt, Holden didn't seem to notice. His eyes were stuck shut with the same frost that had plagued Noah. He brushed it off as best he could, hoping the man's corneas hadn't also been frostbitten. Holden didn't open his eyes and he'd stopped trying to ball himself up.

The man from the ship returned with an armload of towels and clothes. "Use these," he said, shoving the things at Noah. Noah looked at the clothes in his hands.

"How do you know they'll fit?"

"They will. They're his."

Noah stripped off the blanket and wiped away the moisture that remained on Holden with the towels before he tried to dress him. Between Holden's limp body and the Dutch angle in the compartment, he wasn't doing well. He fumbled with his thick, gloved fingers, trying to fit a pair of pants over Holden's stiff legs. His grip on the fabric slipped and jerked out of his grasp as the clothing caught on the floor or his damp skin. "Help me, for Christ's sake!"

Holden let out a quiet breath too slight to see in the cold.

The stranger knelt beside Noah. Stripping off a glove, he held his fingers to Holden's neck. His head dropped and he pulled his glove back on. Noah wanted to contradict the answer. But saying it wasn't so wouldn't change a thing. And no one came back from the dead.

The man from the ship pulled his face mask down. He was pale with sharp cheekbones jutting above a reddish-blond beard that twisted in all directions, distorted by his mask. Noah knew him. He looked different—much thinner and bearded. Between his voice and those eyes, Noah knew it couldn't be anyone else. But it couldn't be him, either.

No one came back from the dead.

"Connor," he whispered. "Connor MacAllister?"

"Yep," the man said. "It's me." He pushed back his hood and ran a hand through his unkempt hair. He pointed at the man they'd tried to save. "This is Chris Holden." He took a deep breath and said, "And you. Are you . . . Noah Cabot?"

Noah peeled off his mask and watch cap. "He is. I am."

He shook his head in disbelief. "Can't be. It just can't be." Connor's accent turned "can't" into "cain't," further cementing the reality of this impossible moment in Noah's mind.

"Why not?"

Connor turned to look at Noah. "Because when I left him two hours ago, Chris Holden was asleep in his bunk. And you're dead. Goin' on more'n a year now."

Noah felt like he'd been shoved by some invisible presence. He reached out for the edge of the bunk beside him and barely caught on. "I . . . I'm alive. You're the one . . ."

"Sittin' here next to you. That's the part I'm havin' a problem with. I was a pallbearer at your damn funeral, Noah."

The look on Noah's face went from agitated disbelief to horror. His eyes widened and his mouth dropped open. Unlike in Connor's version of history, Noah hadn't been a pallbearer at Connor's funeral. Since there wasn't anything recognizable of him to put in a box, Connor's girlfriend, Sheila, had him cremated. She set the urn up at the memorial service. He repeated, "Not me. You. You."

Noah heard shouting from the passageway. "Noah! Noah, where the fuck are you?"

"Is that who it sounds like?" Connor said.

The voice in the passageway snapped Noah back to the present. "It's Kevin Lawless."

"I guess that means Jack Freeman is here, too."

Noah took a deep breath and tried to make sense of what was happening. He didn't know whether to run and find Kevin, or stay with this ghost. Wait for him to fade away as Noah came to his senses. But Connor didn't fade. He was as solid as the ship and the body of his friend growing colder beside them.

"Them, Henry Gutierrez, Michael Yeong, Serge Boucher, and . . . William Brewster are all with me." He paused before adding, "And Holden. Was."

"That's quite a roster. That's all?"

"Rest of the crew's back on our ship a couple miles away."

Connor held his face in a hand, squeezing his temples. Noah noticed a small, pink scar above the dead man's right eyebrow. His fingers drifted up to the dressing covering the same spot on his own face.

"Noah! Where are you?" Kevin sounded panicked. He was out of breath and his voice cracked. His footfalls receded. He was headed in the wrong direction.

Noah pushed himself up off the deck, taking a moment to get his partially numb feet solidly beneath him. "I'd better go get him before he gets lost."

Connor got to his feet, too, grabbed a dry blanket off the other bunk and draped Holden's body with it. "Anybody else in as bad a shape as he was?"

Noah shook his head. "Not quite. But everybody's sick. Holden . . . fell in the water."

"I guess we need to go show 'em the way aboard then, if they haven't already found the ladder." Connor reached out to put a hand on Noah's shoulder. Noah flinched. He wondered whether the ghost's hand would pass right through him. He didn't get to find out. Connor dropped his arm to his side, not making contact. "They all gonna be as surprised to see me as you?"

"That would be my guess," Noah said. "Wait a minute. You never shipped out with Jack and Kevin. How do you know them?"

Connor pursed his lips in an expression so familiar Noah felt like he'd traveled through time. Any last doubt he was looking at his friend disappeared. No mistaking it. It made Noah feel at once elated and profoundly sad. It couldn't last, could it? Or maybe, it might last forever. And ever. He pushed the thought out of his head. He couldn't be dead. Not unless they both were. And if they were both dead, that meant this was Hell.

22

Kevin jerked away and let out a small, strangled cry as Noah clapped a hand on his shoulder. "Shit, man! You almost gave me a heart attack." Kevin was pale and sweaty-looking. Frost had formed in his beard and his cheeks were the same bright red Holden's had been. Without his balaclava, he'd be frostbitten before they got halfway back to the *Arctic Promise*. Noah knew he would refuse to take back his hat, however, as soon as he found out about Holden.

"Sorry," he said. He'd followed Kevin's calls up two decks before finally catching up to him. Fortunately, this PSV was similar enough to their own ship that he had no problem following the echoes through the passageways.

"You were really hauling ass out there. Were you expecting there to be finish line tape at the end?" He panted, out of breath. "We could barely keep up. Where's Holden? How'd you get him up that ladder?"

Noah held up a finger to stem the tide of Kevin's questions. "Where are the others?"

Kevin tilted his head toward the ladder. "I left 'em on

the mezzanine deck. They're in the meeting room trying to get warm. Brewster's havin' half a fit since we
couldn't find you. Where's Holden?"

Noah shook his head slightly. "I wasn't fast enough."

"No. You did better than any of us could've." Kevin's
face fell. "I suppose we oughta tell the others." Noah
turned to lay below. Kevin grabbed his elbow, stopping him. "You're the only one he stood a chance with.
You know that, right? It took three of us to get Michael up that ladder and I thought I was going to die
doing it. It's not your fault. I don't even know how you
got Holden aboard."

"I had help," Noah said. "Let's go talk to the others."
He patted Kevin's hand and gently pried it off his arm.
He started toward the Mezzanine Deck.

"Help? Who the hell was here to help?" Kevin fell
into step behind him, continuing to pepper him with
questions, until a coughing fit interrupted his interrogation. He hacked up something wet-sounding and
spit. Noah didn't look to see what had come up. He'd
seen enough of it already.

At D-Deck, he took a turn through a hatch, beckoning
Kevin to follow. They crept up the tilted passageway to
the first state cabin. Through the open door, they saw
Connor sitting in a chair next to the desk. Kevin said,
"Holden?" Connor shook his head and pointed at the
bunk across the room. Connor had finished dressing
the man and lifted him into the bed. A pang of guilt
arced through Noah for not staying to help restore
Holden's dignity. There would be plenty of time to feel
guilt. Perhaps an eternity.

Connor got up from his chair and walked to the door.

His face contorted with both surprise and recognition. "Kevin," he said.

Kevin's brow furrowed. "Who're you?" He turned to Noah. "This is the dude who helped you?"

"Kevin, you really don't know me?" Connor asked. He took a step forward, reaching out. Kevin stepped out of reach. "Why is everybody so afraid of letting me touch them?"

Noah didn't want to tell him why. It had nothing to do with the fact he looked like a shell of the person he'd once been. That should have been apparent from Kevin's response, since the two had never met. But then Connor thought they knew each other. He thought they were on a first-name basis. The moment, as troubling as it was for the other two men, eased Noah's anxiety somewhat. Connor knew Kevin's and Jack's last names despite having never worked with them. He thought Noah was dead when he obviously wasn't. Connor was alive, although he'd died over a year earlier. And the ship. Maybe this wasn't Hell. It wasn't Earth either. At least not the Earth Noah knew.

Noah stepped into the state cabin and pulled the blanket up over Holden's face. "Let's go talk to the others," Noah said.

In the meeting room, Henry and Michael sat slumped in chairs against the wall while Boucher and Jack stood, each man rubbing his arms trying to keep warm. Brewster stopped pacing the length of the compartment when he saw Noah appear in the doorway. "There you are," the Old Man said. "Where the hell is Holden? What've you done with him?"

Noah stopped in mid-step. *Done with?* No matter what he did, nothing would ever redeem him in his father-in-law's eyes. Alive, he was beyond salvation. Dead . . . He looked at Connor standing behind him in the passageway, out of sight of the men. He thought about what he'd said to him only a few minutes ago. *I was a pallbearer at your funeral.* That would have been the happiest day of Brewster's life.

"He's in the engineer's cabin," Noah said. "He didn't make it."

The already dim mood in the room darkened. Boucher shouted and grabbed the arms of an empty chair, looking like he wanted to throw it across the room. Instead, he picked it up and slammed it straight down, driving it into the deck again and again as he cursed with each impact. Jack shook his head in apparent disbelief while Henry and Michael sat, their sallow faces taking on fresh expressions of sick fear. They were in worse shape than the rest of their team and both of them knew it. The rest weren't far behind them. All except Noah.

Brewster looked like he wanted to make accusations, to hold Noah accountable for what had happened. But he'd conceived of the trip along with his officers. On top of that, Noah had volunteered to go alone, trying to avoid this exact outcome. Still, it looked to him like the Old Man wanted to lay it at his feet. Instead, Brewster clenched his teeth and fumed quietly. "Well, we came here for a reason. Let's split up and see if there's anything we can use. I'll check on communications. Boucher, you take the Twins and see if there's anything we can cannibalize from the machine room to—"

"All the electronics on the ship stopped functioning months ago."

Brewster's eyes flashed with anger. "Months, my ass, Cabot! How the fuck would you know this heap has been here for months?"

Connor pushed past Noah. "He didn't say it. *I* did." He brushed a strand of limp, greasy hair out of his face and looked Brewster up and down, taking measure of the Old Man.

Brewster began to ask, "Who the hell . . ." but the question died before it escaped his gaping mouth.

"You look good, William." Connor nodded at Boucher, who almost fell trying to sit in his broken chair. "Henry, Michael, Jack," he said, acknowledging each man. News of Holden's death had upset the crew, but the sight of a dead man standing in the room with them was more than they could process. Only Jack looked more confused than shocked. Brewster walked up to Connor and reached out with a finger. Connor allowed himself to be touched without flinching or backing away. He reached out and squeezed the Old Man's shoulder. "It's good to see you."

"Is it really you?"

"I could ask you the same thing."

Brewster took a step back. "I don't understand."

When Noah knew him, Connor had been an imposing man. He had a build like a college athlete and an easy smile on a full face. He'd been boisterous, happy to do physical work, and got along with everyone. Almost everyone—he didn't like Boucher better than anyone else did. The man reminded him of all those kids who'd picked on him in school, he'd told Noah one evening over drinks—the reason he started going to the gym and lifting weights. Noah had dismissed his misgivings about the bosun, telling him it was an act. *Serge is playing a role for the deck crew,* he'd said, knowing it was bullshit but wanting peace aboard the ship. He had introduced Connor to Mickle and his secret bottles of scotch. And then one night he asked Connor to fill in for him. And he never knew him again.

"I'm not sure how long it's been. We kept track at first—when we thought we could still fix things—but after a few weeks, I lost track. All I can say is we've been here longer than we ever should've. When the *Promise* was first beset—"

"The *Promise*?" Boucher said. "What do you mean, 'the *Promise*'?"

"The *Arctic Promise*." Connor tapped a knuckle against the hull. "You're standing on her." He waited to see if the bosun had more to say before continuing with his explanation. Boucher blinked with mute incomprehension. "Anyway, when we first got stuck, we tried to dig out because we couldn't—"

"You couldn't call for an icebreaker after the communications array went down?" Noah said. "And then digging out didn't work any better because the engines shit the bed when you tried?"

Connor's eyes narrowed. "Yep. Happened just like that."

"So, what about the rest of the crew? Where are they?" Boucher asked. His voice wavered with anxiety and his shoulders hunched as if he was waiting to spring at the man once he heard his answer. In the past, the two would have been evenly matched. But even in Boucher's weakened state, Connor didn't look like he would be able to hold his own. He'd lost too much weight, had aged too much since Noah had seen him last. He was recognizable, but barely. He looked like he might blow away if they went back outside in the wind.

"They're on the platform," Connor said tilting his head toward the door. "When the fog cleared, we caught sight of it. We hiked across to call for an ice-breaker to come plow us out. Except, the Niflheim was abandoned before we even got there—powered down and dark. We turned the lights and heat back on, but we had no idea what happened to the men and women stationed there. Figured maybe the company shipped 'em out in anticipation of the big storm that hit us. If that was it though, they'd've been back by now. That was a couple, maybe two and a half months ago."

"You try calling for a rescue?" Brewster said.

"Aside from lights and life support, ain't nothing working on the rig. Radios, sat phones, radar, nothin'. Just like this wreck. Except it's safer there than here, as you might imagine. This ship is nipped—shifting ice plates are crushin' it. We decamped to the Niflheim as soon as the *Promise* started to list and have been holding out there ever since. We only come back here to collect up more rations as ours over there get thin." He rubbed at the back of his neck. "Everything is getting thin though. Not sure any of us got more weight to lose, and we're almost out of the consumable cargo we had aboard. What we can reach, anyway. Got plenty of concrete and fuel, not so much food. We even tried ice fishing, but nothin'." Connor jerked a thumb toward the rifle slung over his shoulder. "I carry this in case I run into a polar bear or wolf or something. But I haven't seen a living thing other than my crew since we got here. Ain't nothing up here with us.

"And as far as living things go, everyone has started getting sick in the last few days. I'm the only one with enough spunk in me to make the trip anymore. Most of my men are hoverin' about where *they* are," he said, pointing at Henry and Michael. "Some're worse and can't get out of bed."

Noah's stomach tightened at the mention of the other crew falling ill. It hadn't occurred to him that he'd been hoping isolation and starvation were the sum of their problems. Now he realized getting his own crew off the *Promise* wasn't going to be even a partial solution to any of their problems. "Your crew just started getting sick? How long ago?"

Connor tilted his head toward the ceiling, as if he was looking for the answer to come dropping down from it. "Don't know. Three, four days maybe. Started with headaches and bloody noses."

"And then went from nosebleeds to a bad cough and lethargy," Noah finished again. Before he could mention the shadows stalking about, Brewster interrupted them.

"How many people you have over there?"

"Just . . . our crew, like I said. Sixteen souls," Connor said, his mouth stretching in an odd expression, more straight across than upturned, like he was half amused and half struggling to find the right words.

"Who's the ship's master? Do I know him?" Brewster asked.

Connor huffed and shook his head. "I don't even know how to respond to that. Maybe it's better if you see."

"Is it too hard to say a god damned name? I'm not asking for his blood type."

"It's you, William. *You're* the ship's master."

Brewster rolled his eyes and sighed. "I don't know what your game is, but—"

"You're there, too, Serge. Mikey, the Twins . . . and Chris Holden are on the Niflheim along with Theo, Felix, Andrew, Henry—"

"Bullshit!" Henry said. "I'm right here. Ain't another me anywhere else."

Boucher and Michael grunted in agreement with the senior deck hand as if his singularity was a fact that could be established by mutual assent. Whether or not Connor was telling the truth couldn't be determined by a vote. None of them knew firsthand if copies existed, but then, none of them had seen him alive in over a year, either. Some had actually seen the reason why that was so. That he might have somehow recovered was beyond the realm of imagining, let alone actual possibility. Yet, there he stood. Thinner and haggard-looking, but moving around and breathing and claiming that another one of each of them was waiting just a few miles away. Or one of nearly each of them.

Connor shrugged, showing a little of the man he'd been before. Easygoing and unargumentative. "Well, while you're not looking so hot, I'd say the Henry Gutierrez I shipped out with doesn't look as good as you. None of y'all . . . of them are doing good. That's why I'm here by myself. Like I said, I'm the only one up to making the trip these days."

"He just named men we left behind," Boucher said. "How would he know we shipped out with Theo or Felix? Nobody said anything about them."

"Unless Noah told him," Brewster said.

The other men in the cabin were becoming increasingly restless. Boucher had begun to pace while Jack and Kevin both stood slack-jawed and wide eyed. Kevin said, "I can't even deal with this shit right now. What the fuck is this supposed to mean? Him? This ship?"

"What do you mean, 'this ship'?" Henry said.

"Look around, man!" Jack said. "Don't tell me you don't see it."

Brewster held up his hands to quiet the room. It only half worked; the crewmen able to stay on their feet were agitated and half panicked, but they stopped shouting. "If this is the *Arctic Promise,* I'm the Queen of England."

"This *is* the *Arctic Promise,*" Connor said. "And the . . . other you is, frankly, a much easier person to get along with."

Brewster's face flushed. Leaning in, he shoved his finger in Connor's chest, not investigating this time but asserting. "Like I give a squirt of piss what you think of me. I don't know who you really are, but I'm not interested in whatever dogshit fable you're telling. The sun's going down and we need to see if there's anything aboard we can salvage. Ghost or no ghost, I'm going up to check the radio." He turned and staggered across the angled floor toward the door.

"Electronics have all shit the bed, William. Go have a look if you want, though. You know the way."

Noah felt deep in his gut that they were standing in the future of their own ship if they didn't get a handle on things soon. And although he hadn't seen anyone else but Connor, he knew how to get his father-in-law to pay attention. "Connor, you say there's a copy of everyone here on the Niflheim?"

"Nope. Not all of y'all."

Brewster stopped, his head tilted down to glare at the men behind him. "What's that supposed to mean?" he said.

Noah frowned. "There isn't another one of me. In *his* reality, it happened just the way you wanted, William."

Connor opened his mouth to interject, but Brewster let out an explosive single laugh. "Don't I wish!"

"It's true," Connor said quietly. "He died a year ago. Fell overboard in a storm and—"

"Overboard?" Noah said.

Connor nodded. "Yep. You went out to check the lashing gear during a big wet one and got swept off the weather deck." He screwed up his face. "You don't really want to hear this, do you?"

"*I* do," Brewster said.

"Me too!" Boucher added. Noah scowled at the bo-sun. Boucher smiled, his teeth pink with blood and saliva.

"Coast Guard found your body washed up on shore a week or so later." Connor put his hand on Noah's shoulder and squeezed. Noah didn't flinch this time. Although he looked exhausted, there was strength in his grip. Noah hadn't noticed how tense he'd become until his body relaxed a little and his muscles gave up the preparation to fight or flee. "I'm sorry. I truly am."

"Don't be," Brewster said. "As much as I'd love to keep reminiscing about what should have happened, I'm going to have a look in communications. And then we're going." Brewster began checking the fittings on his clothes, making sure they were zipped up and cinched up for the weather outside.

Connor shook his head vigorously and pointed to the porthole window. The light had retreated more since they'd come aboard and the porthole was filled with a dull azure glow. "Take all the time you want. Since we been standing around talkin', we've just about run out of daylight. It's over an hour to the Niflheim from here by foot." He pointed to Michael and Henry. "More, I'm guessing, since they don't look like they can move very fast."

Henry replied with a raised middle finger.

"You thought it was cold on the way here. That's nothing compared to when the sun goes down. Temps drop down to minus forty, not counting the wind chill. Nope. We have to hunker down right here and wait out the night."

"I'm not staying here," Henry said, pushing himself out of his chair. He wobbled and staggered a step to the side before grabbing onto the edge of the table for balance. "It's too god damn cold in here. We'll freeze to death."

"I've done it before. We can gather blankets and stuff from the other cabins."

"I'd rather take my chances on the ice than spend a night spooning Cabot," Boucher said.

"What about *him*?" Connor asked, indicating Michael Yeong. The deckhand could barely open his eyes, even when he heard his name. If he hadn't been shivering, it would have been difficult to tell if he was sleeping or dead. He rocked his head slowly back and forth, but didn't say anything.

Noah sighed. He crossed the room to the window and peered out into the gloaming. In the distance, he saw faint lights like stars hovering just above the ice-pack. He assumed it was the platform. "You have heat at the Niflheim?"

Connor nodded. "It's not the tropics, but it's warm enough."

"There's lights," Noah observed. "We can see it in the dark as long as it stays clear, I guess. But even with the headlamps, we won't be able to see the ice in front of us far enough ahead. If there's another fissure or a break in the ice, none of us will know until it's too late. I vote we stay here, do our best to keep warm with what's on the ship, and take our chances in the morning."

"Vote all you want. I'm not waiting," Brewster said. "I want proof. You can stay here if you want and freeze, but I want to meet this . . . other me. The 'nice' one." His tone was mocking and cruel. He shoved his way out of the compartment and stomped off down the passageway.

Noah didn't want to meet another Brewster, even if he was more agreeable. It would make his experience with the Brewster he had to tolerate all the more bitter. Still, the Old Man had a point. It was cold on this ship and they'd all be better off in a warm, safe, and level structure. *If* they made it there with no more casualties.

"We have the stretcher I used to pull Holden along," he said. "If we take some blankets from this ship and wrap up, I imagine we can weather the wind chill okay."

"You really think this is a good idea?" Connor asked.

"No. Not even a little bit," Noah said. He rubbed at his eyes, remembering the painful frost that had built up on them during the day. He was afraid he'd go blind at night. "But neither is staying here. Plus, the Old Man is going no matter what we do. You want him to show up at the Niflheim without you to make the introduction?"

Connor's eyes widened. "What happened to him?"

Noah didn't answer. He pictured his wife, Abby, lying in bed. The tubes in her arms not feeding her chemo drugs anymore—just saline and the palliative dose of morphine a hospice nurse would inject into the line every few hours. Abby turned down half of what they brought, not wanting to sleep away the last hours of her life. The nurse argued, asking why she was torturing herself. She said she wanted to be able to see her husband. She wanted to hold his hand and hear him speak to her, tell her he'd be all right, that Ellie would be all right. The nurse laid a tender hand on Abby's wrist and gave a light squeeze, telling her not to wait too long. She explained there would come a point at which no nonlethal amount of morphine could get back on top of the pain. Abby smiled and blinked slowly, telling her she'd made her choice.

Abby had asked Noah to put on *Kind of Blue* and read from her favorite book. He wasn't good at reading aloud; he was monotone and missed inflection, but she seemed to like it anyway. Still, after a couple of chapters, she asked him to tell her about their daughter instead. She wanted to hear about all the things Ellie would do someday. Noah told her she'd grow up and go to college. She'd get a degree in biology and go to work . . . he wanted to say, "trying to cure cancer," but instead he said, "helping people." She'd meet a kind man who always smiled and they'd get married. They'd have kids and she'd be an important person who did great things, but still found time to spend with the people who loved her. *And she always remembered her mother, who loved her more than anyone in the world,* he said.

I love you more than anyone in the world, Abby told him. Her voice cracked with the dryness in her throat and the cotton mouth the morphine gave her. *When she gets married . . . promise me you'll be good to the person she loves.*

I promise. He remembered getting up to call William again to tell him he didn't have much time left to say good-bye. His father-in-law never answered the phone.

Noah never told anyone any of that. They were his memories and no one else's. That they were his alone was part of the reason he imagined William Brewster hated him so much.

"Let's get everything we need together. We'll pull Michael along on my stretcher and the supplies on yours."

"This is a bad idea," Connor said.

Noah nodded in agreement. "There are no good ideas left."

23

The sun was a pale yellow disk resting just above the horizon. In maybe thirty minutes it would be half obscured, and in forty-five, merely a burning sliver vanquished by night. Connor assured them that it wasn't much more than a ninety-minute walk to the Niflheim dragging the sled piled with food and extra blankets. Then again, he'd been making the trip by himself for the last day or two. Once his crew started getting sick, he started going with fewer hands until he was the only one and had to make two trips to bring everything they needed back.

Despite his initial objections, Michael had finally agreed to be strapped into the stretcher sled. Noah wasn't pulling him this time. Jack and Kevin volunteered, saying that two men pulling would be faster than one. Noah agreed and handed over the straps. Henry wasn't much better off than Michael, but he was putting up a brave front as he grabbed the loop between Boucher and Brewster's length of rope. Noah wished for a headlamp. Everyone else still had theirs, but somewhere between pulling Holden out of the fissure and running him to the ship, his had fallen off. There were the flares, but they seemed like things they should save. He didn't know exactly what for, but there was no telling what they'd need, or when, to make it through the coming days. Or weeks? It chilled him worse than the wind to think of it. He'd count on the light from the others' lamps to light his way. If it was similar to the trek they'd already made, there was nothing to trip over but his own feet.

Connor pointed to a faint glint in the distance, to the left of the sun, where a small array of lights shone. "That's the Niflheim. If we get separated or lost, follow those lights. It's overcast, like always, and a new moon, so they'll be the only ones you see as it gets darker. And darker it'll get, I assure you. Pitch black. So don't lose sight of 'em." Without waiting for questions or argument, he struck out, bounding through the snow with a practiced gait, pulling his sled behind him.

Hiking up his heavy tool pack, Noah followed suit. Connor—*this* Connor—was much thinner than he'd been when Noah knew him, but he was the same man, ready to attack a task with all his energy and effort. He moved with an experienced stride that kept him going at a good clip, but kept the sled from tilting, catching, or banging into him. It was movement borne of experience and practice. It was something Noah hoped he'd never become proficient at. That thought revealed to him a truth no one had yet acknowledged. They weren't headed to the platform just to satisfy Brewster's curiosity. It was the first visit to their new home. They could stay aboard their ship a while longer, but eventually the ice would shift. It would crumple and crush the hull, tilting and breaking them until they could stay with it no longer. The platform was a safer place to be. Although the ice was moving around it, too, it was bigger, more stable, and had longer legs under the surface to stabilize it.

As they walked along, Noah hazarded a glance up at the prow of the ship. Iced over, cocooned in the thick leavings of freezing rain, it was difficult to see the letters painted on the side. He fell back a step until Jack and Kevin caught up. "Shine a light up there, would you?" he said, pointing.

"Where?" Kevin asked. Noah pointed again and the man turned his head, revealing what the shadows and frost hid, a gap in the ice large enough to see, in three-foot-high letters, white against the red hull:

ARCTIC PROMISE

"Fuckin' hell," Jack whispered.

"I hope not," Noah said. He pushed forward, trying to catch up to his place in the line.

Connor's estimate of the day's remaining light was more or less accurate, but he'd undersold the depth of the darkness that followed. All Noah could see in the distance was the Niflheim's glowing lights. If it weren't for the increasing weight of his pack and his legs, he might have thought he was adrift in some ethereal suspension, wrapped in a shroud of mist. But the snow dragged at his boots like a living thing trying to hold him back. It was work to push forward and stay upright. The combination of ice beneath and heavy pack on his back competed against his balance, trying to topple him. Connor had helped him replace his mask with a cloth wrap around his face so he could wear his goggles and see. It was small comfort. The cold still made his eyes water, but not as much as they had before. His tears froze on his cheeks instead of his eyelashes, and the lenses remained unfogged and clear.

The wrap also blissfully deadened his hearing. He couldn't make out the echo of their footsteps on the ice or its groaning. He heard his own breathing and the wind and the rustle of his arms brushing against his parka. He didn't want to hear anything else. If the ice was going to open beneath him, hearing it crack and break wouldn't help. He could hear the occasional coughing of his shipmates behind him. He was satisfied that if one or more of them called out, he'd hear.

Ahead, Connor shoved on, his red-and-blue back growing smaller as he broke away from them. As badly as Noah wanted to catch up, he had to pace himself. By the look of it, after an hour or more on the trail, there was maybe another hour's walk ahead of them, at least. Time, however, was as much a guessing game as space in this void. The sun's trajectory was alien to him, the stars invisible, and the landscape bereft of marker or point of reference. He could look behind to see where they'd left the . . . other *Promise* . . . but dead as it was, he suspected it was invisible in the distance. His own ship would be lit, but it was even farther away, and he was uncertain they could see it.

What if we can't find it again? he thought. If they couldn't get back to Mickle and Nevins and all the rest they'd left behind with parts to repair the radio or to bring them to the platform, what then? Just abandon them? Leave them to find the Niflheim on their own? No, he told himself. He'd go back tomorrow. Once they got situated on the platform, and he had a little rest and a meal, he'd go back to organize the second team. First, however, they needed to know whether the Niflheim even offered the shelter they needed. If there were enough beds and blankets. And whether what Connor said was true: that there was another one of most of them aboard.

Noah couldn't even conceive of what that meant. The ache in his hands dragged his mind back to reality. He'd been hanging on to his backpack straps, and despite his thick gloves, the dropping temperature was cutting through them, making the backs of his hands hurt and his fingers numb. He shoved them under his armpits, hunching over them as much as he could, trying to conserve his body heat.

"Where is it?" someone shouted from behind him. "I can't see!" Noah slowed and turned to look. Jack and Kevin also looked back, the sled lurching ahead between them. It hit the end of its line and jerked them forward. Behind them, Brewster and Boucher stood on either side of Henry. The senior deckhand had his arms draped over their shoulders, the rope abandoned. His head lolled and he cried out in blind panic. "I can't see!"

Noah trotted toward them. Brewster raised a hand, holding him back. "Don't worry about us, Cabot," he said. "No one here needs you."

He watched them move on without him. Henry howled and the trio trudged on toward the lights. Noah thought perhaps he could just stand there and watch them slip out of view as the night grew darker and the winds blew stronger. He could wait and let them leave him. Eventually, the cold would seep in and drop his body temperature. He'd go numb and lose consciousness. Fall asleep and that would be it.

No. All he needed was the will to take a step ahead. And another. And another until he was in motion again, walking toward the lights. There was warmth in the light. And where there was warmth, he imagined he could find the hope that had left him. Hope did not live in him. But that was the irony of it. To find the will to go on, he had to first take a step forward. The very action that required hope itself.

He lifted a foot. The snow pulled at him, demanding he stop. He swung his leg ahead. He found his footing and leaned forward. His back foot rose and followed, meeting resistance and then coming free. His body moved in spite of his resignation. For the second time in a single day, he fought the infinite ice and snow, stood against the wind and darkness in revolt. He pushed his rock up the hill again.

He fell in behind the crew, keeping his gaze trained down, looking for their tracks. Without a headlamp, he couldn't see them in front of him. Somehow they'd disappeared from sight. And their tracks were blowing over with fresh snow, kicked up by the wind. He felt panic growing in his chest as he looked for them in the sliver of difference splitting the surface from the sky. But in that line of lighter darkness there were no figures ahead. Noah searched for the lights of the Niflheim, the beacon guiding him. If they were still lit, the blowing snow obscured them.

His breathing got faster and his legs heavier. His arms floated up from his sides, ready to do something to aid him. But there was nothing for them to do. They couldn't help him see. They couldn't help him walk. All that was to be done was curse the darkness. Curse his shipmates for leaving him.

In the corner of his vision, he saw it. It separated from the night and darted toward him as it had on the ship. A portion of the darkness that moved. He held up his fists to ward it off. Leaning away, he slipped and the heavy bag slung over his shoulder pulled. The shade whipped itself at him and he fell on the ice. A loud groan went up from the surface, the echo of his impact stretching out through the frigid water beneath. And a crack, loud enough to break through the wrap covering his ears. He squinted his eyes shut and hissed a breath inward through his teeth, waiting for the stabbing pain of the dark thing.

Nothing.

He opened his eyes and looked up. All around him was the void, and he lay in it waiting to die.

The ice groaned and popped underneath him. It sang a low song, urging him to sleep. Unsure if he'd closed his eyes, Noah raised a hand in front of his face. He stared at his red glove. He balled up his numb fingers and made a fist.

In the distance, voices. And dancing distant lights. Head lamps.

"Over here! I see something!"

"Where? I don't see shit."

The ice beneath him vibrated with the approaching footsteps. He drew in a long breath waiting for the shock of cold water enveloping him. Instead, he felt hands gripping him, pulling him up out of the clinging snow and setting him on his feet.

"Noah! Noah! Can you hear me?" Connor shouted.

Noah blinked. He turned his head to see Jack and Kevin standing on either side of him holding an arm, keeping him upright. The men's headlamps made him squint and turn away. He couldn't see their faces. They were like what his grandmother had always said about angels: it hurt to look at them. "Jesus, man. I thought we'd lost you."

"I'm . . . I'm right here," he said. His voice quavered as a fresh shiver rocked his body. One of them stripped the heavy bag off his back. Where it went, he didn't know.

"Come on. Let's get him moving. I'll come back for the supplies."

The men pulled Noah along. He wanted to object, to tell them there were no lights to follow. They had no idea where they were and there was nowhere to go. Then he saw it. Growing in the distance, maybe a half mile away, the drilling platform rising out of the ice like some kind of mad city in miniature. Its single gray spire reached upward like a Brutalist skyscraper, a red light blinking at the top.

"That's it," Connor said. "Home." The word hurt worse than the wind and the cold. Worse than the fall from the side of the ship and the struggle to free Holden from the water. It *wasn't* home. He wouldn't allow that to be true. Noah resolved never to accept it. Home was Seattle. Ellie waited for him there. He had promised he'd come home for her.

He put his head down and pushed forward.

24

Noah was uncertain he could climb the steel rebar "ladder" embedded in the thick pylon leg of the island above him. He'd seen drilling platforms up close before, but never quite like this. Not from this perspective. Not in these conditions. Standing beneath it without a ship to give it some kind of contrast, the edifice was oppressively large. In the dark, even more so. It loomed over him like a hallucinatory beast on building-sized stilts. At its four corners, enclosed lifeboats jutted out like heads. Monstrous things shaped like gargantuan komodo dragon faces waiting to lunge out and bite. Boom arms and platforms, odd cages and spiky protrusions all around robbed the structure of the appearance it had from far away as a miniature city and gave it an otherworldly animal look. It was the astrobiological dream of a madman made real in concrete and steel. And it promised nothing but hardship and pain.

His body shook with stress as he pulled himself up. His arms shuddered, his legs quivering and rubbery from the walk, but he held on as tightly as he'd ever

gripped anything. The island city stood on concrete pylons rising from the ice forty feet up, and descending
who knew how deep into the water beneath the surface.
The ladder was a series of rebar rungs pounded into the
concrete pylon like giant staples, and although none
were actually loose, it wasn't hard to imagine one coming free. There was no safety harness, no ladder cage. If
he fell from higher than a few feet up he wouldn't get
a second try. Not at this, not at anything again, ever.

Connor explained that there was once a more secure
gangway ladder designed for off-loading the crew onto a
rescue ship in the event of a disaster, but that had fallen
away. All that remained of it were the mounts. The rebar
ladder was one of only two ways in, and the second was
only accessible once someone made this climb. Connor
had insisted Noah wait for him to lower the "elevator,"
but waiting with Brewster and his companions was more
daunting than a forty-foot fall, so he opted to climb.
The wind whipped and pulled at him. It bit at the small
exposed pieces of skin that peeked through when he
reached for the next rung. At least he didn't have a rucksack stuffed with heavy tools weighing him down. He'd
left that with the others.

At the top of the ladder, Connor disappeared into an
open hatch. A second later, his hand extended out of
the opening. Noah wanted to take it, but distrusted in
his own ability to maintain his grip on both the last
rung and his friend's hand. He kept ahold of the rebar
and pulled himself up, shoulders shaking with the effort. Connor grabbed the back of his parka instead and
helped haul him through the opening. Inside, Noah collapsed on his back and breathed through his fear. "This
way," Connor said, not waiting. He opened a door

leading to a hall illuminated by hanging work lights in plastic cages strung along the ceiling. The light spilled into the antechamber, illuminating a path away from the hatch. Noah followed, hoping the light would also eventually lead to warmth.

Outside, the Niflheim looked like a city in miniature—a starlit skyline compressed into a single square block. Inside, it felt like a space station. Pipework twisted in all directions, disappearing down hallways, into ceilings, and plunging into the grated and corrugated metal floors. Rubber-coated cables lay everywhere in a tangled, chaotic mess. Blue oil well standpipes and yellow railings separated them from another gap-spaced grate covering some kind of equipment covered in small handwheels and pressure gauges. Connor led the way along a tight hallway into a wider, open room. "Elevator's over here," he said.

The "elevator" was a conical metal basket hanging from a hand-crank winch. It was big enough for three or maybe four men to ride in if they huddled together. Leaning his rifle against the wall, Connor moved a portable guardrail out of the way. He swung the arm of the jib crane over a closed hatch in the floor. "This here used to be attached to an electric winch, but . . . you know. We hooked it up to this hand crank when that died." Connor pulled open the hatch and cupped his hands on either side of his mouth to shout. "Coming down!" Unlocking the catch on the winch, he began cranking the handle, slowly lowering the basket with a noisy clacking. "You ever get the chance to use this, be careful," he said. "You hit that switch right there, it drops the thing. Whatever's in the basket gets a real wild ride and ain't walking out at the bottom."

He kept cranking, peering through the opening into empty space below. The skin on the back of Noah's neck tightened with creeping anxiety at the lack of anything installed to catch a person who happened to fall through. Work on a PSV could be dangerous, but life on a drilling platform seemed downright hazardous. Connor stopped cranking the handle as the basket touched down. He called out, "Two men!" and waited.

"You've been here how long?" Noah asked.

Connor hunched his shoulders while holding onto the steel cable. "Dunno. Two months, give or take. We were stuck in the *Promise* for maybe a week before the fog lifted and we saw this place. It was another week before the ice began to crush the ship and forced us off. Two months after that, I reckon. I didn't think to start counting right away. Thought it wouldn't be a thing, you know? The company would bring everybody back, ship us out, we'd all get settlements or a bonus or something, and I could go back to real life. Instead, I been here long enough for this to grow," he said, pulling at his beard. "How 'bout you? How long has your crew been here?"

"Less than a week. But it's been bad. The way this sickness is tearing through the crew, we'll all be dead in another week. There's no way anyone's making it months, like you have."

"Except you. You're not sick."

Noah shook his head. "No I'm not. You?"

"Aside from losing some weight, I'm healthy I reckon. None of us started feeling all that bad until about a few days ago. You don't think . . . ?"

"I don't think anything anymore. I used to think I could work on a ship with William. I thought I could keep people from getting hurt after we got stranded. Every time I think something, the opposite is what turns out to be true."

Connor grabbed Noah's shoulder and squeezed. "You need to put that idea away, brother. You need to keep your head in the game if we're all going to get out of this." The wire jerked twice in his hand as the men below indicated the elevator was ready to come back up.

"Give me a hand with this?" Connor asked. Noah stepped around to the crank and learned how to set the winch for either upward or downward motion. "It's tough, but one man should be able to haul up two at a time with this. Be careful. You want to keep your footing this close to that opening. Got it?"

Noah nodded and smiled. It was perhaps his first honest smile since setting out from port. "I gotcha," he said. "Switch bad. Crank good."

Connor clapped him on the shoulder. "You get crankin'. I'm gonna go round up a couple of the guys and let 'em know . . . about you and the others. I figure this is the kind of situation where forewarned is forearmed."

"Forearmed against what?"

Connor grabbed the rifle from where he'd set it against the wall and swung it over his shoulder. "I can't imagine anyone is going to like what we're about to tell them. I don't know about you, but I'm still kind of waiting to wake up." Noah nodded even though in his worst dreams he'd never felt the kind of nervous panic in his stomach that he felt at that moment. He felt like he might hyperventilate or vomit at the slightest provocation. He pushed those feelings down, not wanting to give them any better a claw hold than they already had. "I want to head off complete panic, if I can," Connor said.

"What are you going to do with that?"

Connor looked over his shoulder at the barrel of the rifle sticking up behind him. "Lock it up, where it belongs. Any reason I shouldn't?"

From below, Noah heard a faint shout over the gusting wind. "Hurry the fuck up," drifted up to his ears. Noah shook his head. "No. Locked away is exactly where it belongs."

Connor's eyes narrowed and his lips tightened as he seemed to search for the hint of sarcasm in Noah's statement. "Once I let Mickle and Holden in on what's going on, I'll be back. Then we can see about getting some food in y'all and show you where to get some sleep." Connor walked out of the room, leaving Noah alone to lift his crew up. He wondered why Connor would tell Mickle and Holden, but not Brewster. Because, he quickly reasoned, no matter how differently their lives were in separate realities, they were ultimately the same man. That troubled Noah. He had enough difficulty navigating his single father-in-law without doubling up the pressure.

He pulled at the crank, focusing on the work. The wind gusted beneath him, blasting him with frigid air and swaying the elevator the higher it rose off the ground. He leaned into the work, slowly lifting the cage to the platform. Each click of the crank wheel was a small victory against muscles that burned and mental fatigue that told him to sit down, lie down, let go. But he worked as fast as he could, trying to minimize the amount of time anyone had to spend dangling in space at the end of the line. As it rose, he could see Brewster and Boucher had been the first to climb inside, leaving the sickest men below. Noah continued to draw them closer without reaching for the release switch—although he found himself eying it. He pulled the elevator in and allowed the men to step aboard the Niflheim. Before he could object to their decision to leave the others behind, Boucher said, "Go down and help the rest," holding the cage door open for him to step into.

Noah was smarter than to trust himself to a winch with Boucher at the controls a second time. "I'll take the ladder," he said.

"This'll be faster."

"I just bet." He left the two in the winch room and returned to the pylon hatch, hoping his grip would hold. By the time he reached the ice, he knew he'd have to trust them at least once not to drop him. There was no way his fingers would last for another climb up.

Out in the elements again, he felt his muscles tighten and resist his efforts to move. Only a moment of rest was enough for his body to decide on its own that all effort for the day had been expended and no more would be supported. He forced his body into motion, helping Jack load Michael into the elevator first. He and Kevin slipped a few of the supplies in around their feet and closed the door. He called up and watched as the slack in the line drew up and the cage rose.

Next was Kevin and Henry's turn. They disappeared into the dark and Noah stood alone under the platform waiting to hear Brewster call out, "Coming down!" He never did, or if he did, it was lost in the wind. By the time he began contemplating trying to climb the ladder using the crook of his elbow to hold on instead of his hands, they lowered the cage. Staring up, he tried to see if it was still Brewster at the controls. Despite the dim light in the room above, it was too far to tell. All he could see were silhouettes backlit in a golden box hovering in the void above.

When the cage touched down, he shoved the few remaining supplies from the sled they hadn't loaded with the others into the elevator and stepped in after them. He closed the door, shouting, "Ready!" Nothing happened. He remembered the line hanging down from the steel cable above. He reached up and tugged it twice. The cage jerked and started to rise.

He held his breath the entire way up.

25

Although it wasn't anything resembling warm in the elevator room, closing the hatch made a difference. All in and without the wind chill abusing them, Noah felt a last spark of hope ignite. He was exhausted and still suffering the effects of his disorientation on the walk, but they were finally out of the elements into solid shelter. Even Michael appeared to have a renewed energy. He didn't look well, but he had at least enough energy to stand on his own, even if he looked like he might go into shock at the sudden rise in temperature. Relief from the cold and a rest, however short, was what they all needed. If there was warmth, they could survive the night. If they could do that, they could make it another day. And maybe another after that. Their situation had improved, even if they'd taken terrible damage along the way.

Connor beckoned the men up a flight of stairs, leading them deeper into the platform. It grew warmer with every step as they left the working areas of the structure. Despite the habitable conditions, Noah stayed bundled up, daring only to expose his face, pulling down the wrap Connor had helped him tie. He feared what he'd see if he removed his gloves. Fingertips blackened from frostbite and soon to be rotting? He kept his gloves on, letting hope and denial fight in the shadows for a little while longer.

Connor pushed though a single doorway at the end of a long causeway and the industrial spaceship surroundings gave way to the off-duty living quarters. Existing somewhere between a dormitory and an office building, the quarters gave Noah the sensation of stepping across thousands of miles in a single stride into the HUB student union building at UDub. The hallway was lit with flickering fluorescent lights recessed in a sound-dampening drop ceiling. They passed a cafeteria with a long buffet serving area and round dining tables with chairs that were neither bolted to the walls nor the tile floor. He peeked in a rec room with Ping-Pong and pool tables—games you could never play on board a ship. Although the *Promise,* frozen in the ice, had been stable underfoot, the feeling of solidity on the Niflheim gave the illusion of being back on land. For a moment, Noah allowed himself to believe it was true. In his mind, they'd been rescued and he was home again, looking for a place to recharge his mental batteries in between classes. But this was not home. The pernicious lie of the drilling platform concealed the fact that this was only a somewhat slower, but every bit as eventual, death for all of them if they didn't find a way to summon help.

Connor showed the haggard men the way into a large rec room. A flatscreen television was bolted to the far wall opposite a pair of couches. A few soft, padded chairs were placed around the room, a couple near game tables. Jack and Kevin helped Michael over to a sofa while Henry and Boucher took seats near the blank TV. In the corner stood a tabletop chessboard. Not a computer, but an actual board. Noah took a seat behind the white pieces and stared at the rows of soldiers waiting for war.

Connor closed the door behind them. "Rest here a minute and get yourselves warmed up," he said. "I've got . . . someone cooking up a little something to eat, and then I'll show y'all to the sleeping quarters."

Brewster objected to the casual normality of Connor's hospitality. "Who can sleep? I want to see the others now." With his parka open, Brewster's hand rested on the butt of the pistol strapped to his hip. He looked equal parts ridiculous and threatening. Like an old man playing cowboys and Indians with his kids.

If Connor was unnerved by the sight of the firearm, he didn't show it. "Why don't you let me take that and put it in the locker with the other guns?" he said.

"Thanks. I think I'll hang on to it," Brewster said. A shudder ran through his body as he tried to stifle a cough. The sound that came out was thin and wet. His lips glistened red.

"I don't know why you'd want to. What could you be expecting, William?"

"I don't know what I'm expecting, but I want to be prepared for it. And another thing, since when are we on a first name basis?"

Connor scratched at his beard, trying to smooth it back into place. It was untamable, sticking out in all directions. His eyes narrowed and fixed on Brewster's face. "We've been close since I helped you bury your son-in-law. But I guess that wasn't you." He sighed and pulled his hand away from the lost cause of his appearance. "Hey, I understand why you brought it. I take the rifle out with me for all the same reasons, I reckon. But there ain't any wolves or polar bears in here. I'm not bringing a single member of my crew to meet you while you have that on your hip. We're all in this together, William. Let me put it away where it'll be safe and there won't be any accidents."

He held out a hand. Brewster's jaw flexed while he seemed to weigh his options. Finally, he undid the buckle and loosed the holster from around his waist. He held it out by the belt, looking like he might yank it back. Connor took it with both hands, nodding his thanks.

"I expect you'll show me where the gun cabinet is," Brewster said.

"Whatever you want, Will— Sure. I don't even keep it locked. It's just so this sort of thing isn't lying out. Boredom and booze are a bad cocktail. Don't need guns in the mix."

"Booze?" Noah said. "You have something to drink?"

Connor let out a snort of a laugh. "Yeah. We've found a few bottles stashed here and there. Been rationing them like everything else. I s'pose all of us could use a snort, though. It's been a shit-ass hard day. Let me put this away and we'll go get fed. I'll round up something special to take the edge off before bed." Connor left, not inviting Brewster to come see where the gun locker was.

Noah returned to eyeing the chess set. There was comfort within the four corners of the board. Playing would focus him and distract from everything else in the world, even if only for an hour. He touched a piece in the center of the line. Moving it ahead two squares, he made his opening move, starting a King's Pawn

Game with his invisible opponent. If only he had a glass of Scotch to help.

The food was bland and there wasn't much of it. Satisfying his first real appetite since they'd become beset, Noah's plate of plain pasta under a reheated frozen chicken breast tasted like Thanksgiving at his grandmother's table: flavorless and dry. Still, the taste of it distracted from his numb toes and stinging fingers. He gobbled the food down, thankful for the reprieve from hardship. A warm place out of the wind and some hot food—no matter how bland—were welcome respites from the terror of the last few hours. Jack and Kevin wolfed their meals even quicker, cleaning their plates before half the crew had even started. Henry picked at the white slab of meat, teasing it, and Michael didn't touch his at all, the fork and knife sitting clean beside his plate as he stared into the middle distance somewhere not there. Boucher made a move to take Michael's plate and add it to his portion, but Connor stopped him. "We have two rules 'round mealtime. There are no seconds. And whatever doesn't get eaten goes back in the fridge."

Boucher stared at him with a dull menace. "Yeah? You guys saving leftovers for the cat?"

Connor was unmoved. "We only had to institute this rule recently. 'Til a couple of days ago, everyone had a real healthy appetite, and there *weren't* any leftovers." He finished his last forkful and stood, picking up his own plate and Michael's. "You sure you're not hungry?" he asked before taking the food away. Michael snapped back into the present and nodded. Connor took the uneaten meal to the galley window.

"This has been real nice, MacAllister," Brewster said. "But I'm starting to think this talk of others being aboard the ship is bullshit. We've been here over an hour and the only person on this rig I've seen is you. Where's the rest of the crew?"

Connor's lips went narrow and long again. He nodded toward Brewster's plate. "You just met one. How'd you like the second officer?" he asked.

Boucher shoved back from the table with sudden force, his screeching chair echoing in the dead silent room. Jack's and Kevin's mouths hung open in mute disbelief. Noah stared at his friend through slitted eyes searching for the sign it was all a joke. Brewster's expression remained impassive. Connor gave it another beat before allowing a sly smile to creep up his face. "Just kidding. . . . We'd never eat anyone who could pass the officer endorsement exam. Not even if he had feathers." His eyes shifted toward the door. "A few of the men mustered in the rec room while y'all were eating. The ones with the energy to get out of bed, anyway. Y'all are welcome to head over."

Brewster stood and stalked out of the room without saying a word. The rest of the men rose to follow him. Noah hadn't heard anyone moving around in the hall, but then, he and everyone else had been pretty intensely focused on the meal. A New Orleans second line might have marched through the middle of the dining room without him noticing. He scarfed down the last of his pasta and stood up. He took his plate to the galley window, following Connor's lead, and set it on the end of the serving ledge before following them across the hall.

The men waiting in the rec room all had the same shipwrecked look as Connor. Except they all, to a man, looked worse off than he was. Thin and wasted, every one wore an untrimmed beard and their unruly hair was greasy. They were conserving more than food. The *Arctic Promise* had been loaded with supplies intended for the oil workers. Not only drilling material like concrete and fuel, but food and water for their use and consumption. While Connor might have been hauling over supplies a sled load at a time, there was no way to get the water deep in the ship's hold to the platform. It was likely frozen solid in the tank. A person could live without food for much longer than it would take to die of dehydration. Even if they were drinking melted ice, that likely meant no shaving, and limited or no showers.

Noah stared, gape-mouthed, at the unfamiliar yet familiar men looking back at him. Every last one of them had a haunted look in their eyes from months of isolation. Or perhaps it was from seeing the versions of themselves who walked into the room, the same, but a few months younger. A lump grew in Noah's throat at the sight of the crew. Men he barely recognized resolved into familiarity with small postures and gestures particular to each of them.

Even Brewster seemed stunned into paralysis by the sight of the wasted men. If Noah's crew was shocked by what they saw, Connor's looked terrified by what they faced. Each man was staring at a past self, a vision of a lost point in time before abandonment and deprivation. As much as Noah's crew stood as a living reminder of all they'd lost, Connor's men foretold what awaited them. They stared across the room to look lingering death in the face.

Noah wondered how many of Connor's crew were completely unable to get out of bed, like Heath or Andrew. His thoughts turned to Felix and his already dwindling spirit flagged. The Niflheim was their only chance at long-term survival, especially if the *Arctic Promise* got nipped by the ice like Connor's ship had been. But he had no idea how they were going to get Felix from the *Promise* to the rig. The trip was going to kill him . . . if he wasn't dead already. He tucked that unbidden thought away, telling himself he had to assume Felix was alive, until he saw otherwise.

He moved cautiously toward the first man he recognized. The deckhand's resemblance resolved into perfect clarity as he stepped across the gulf between them. "Jack?" he said. Unlike the others, Jack Freeman had never been able to grow a beard. He had a passably devilish Van Dyke and patches of wispy hair peppering his cheeks. As a result, he was the most recognizable of all of them. His black tee overtop a white thermal shirt and skinny jeans were a constant uniform. All that changed was the band on the top layer: Balzac to The Damned to 45 Grave, and repeat. While they had all joked about Kevin being his twin, here was the real thing. Albeit an inexact duplicate, worn by hardship. The man was a vision of Jack's bleak future.

Mirror Jack's forehead wrinkled. "Who're you?" he asked. Noah let out a strangled laugh. This Jack didn't know him. On Noah's side of the mirror, they'd met after Connor died. In their reality, Noah was the one who'd been killed. The mirror Twins knew him in the same way his own Jack and Kevin knew Connor Mac-Allister: as a cautionary tale told to greenhorns standing on the weather deck for the first time. He struggled with the cognitive dissonance. *I can't be dead; I'm standing right here!* He imagined Connor having the exact same thoughts, staring at him as though he was reading his own headstone. Among their respective crews, the two of them were unique. They each lacked a reflection. Instead, they had each other's ghost.

Another man broke away from his crew and crossed the room toward one of Noah's shipmates. Like stepping out of a fog, the resemblance solidified as he came closer to his counterpart. Boucher stood his ground, arms at his sides, fists balled up against the approaching giant as if he was ready for a fight. The mirror man didn't try to touch him, but twisted his head to the side, exposing the nautical star tattoo on the side of his neck partially hidden behind a length of salt-and-pepper beard. Boucher's fingers floated up to his own mark. "How . . . ? The fuck's going on?"

"Beats the shit outta me," the other bosun said.

Kevin moved to confront his reflection, but the man backed away quickly, stumbling over a chair. "Don't touch me! Don't you fuckin' touch me!" The room erupted in a sudden burst of alarm as the men shouted out in confusion and panic, trying to protect one another from the unrealized fear of making contact with a twin.

A reflected crewmate—Henry—shoved Kevin back to his side of the room like a rough game of Red Rover. Noah's crew was not welcome over. Kevin responded with anger, swinging a fist and missing. Noah dragged him away before it devolved into an all-out brawl. The men hurled warnings and threats at one another in a din, invoking the imagined consequences of making contact with a copy of themselves: death, sudden extinction, and misshapen singularities. Noah and Connor tried to restore peace, appealing to the men to keep calm, only to be shouted down by their own crews, demanding answers in a room filled with questions.

Connor backed away as a pair of his shipmates pushed through to take control of the chaos. It took him a moment, but Noah eventually recognized them. Mickle and . . . Holden. A mirror of him anyway. Although wasted like the others, Holden stood straight and moved with more energy than anyone else in the room. With arms wide, he corralled his crew into the corner. Mirror Jack backed into the chess table, knocking it over and obliterating Noah's solitaire opening move.

"Chris?" Noah cried out. "You're alive."

Holden turned, his face turned down in confusion. "Of course I am. What the hell else—" His face paled as he realized who he was speaking to. He shouted for everyone to shut up, quieting the room with his booming voice. Henry and Boucher, unable to completely silence themselves, merely hushed their conversation. Holden shot them both a withering look. He turned to face Noah. His mouth gaped open while he searched for what he wanted to say. Noah had never seen Holden at a loss for words. But then, he'd never seen a dead man walk before. Now, he'd seen two.

"I'm alive," Holden said. "And so are you. I know why I'm surprised to be looking at *you*, but why do you seem so shocked to see me?"

Noah didn't want to vocalize it. Doubt and guilt filled his body as he worried that he hadn't actually left a dead body behind on the other *Arctic Promise*, but a living man. A man suffering and dying in the cold as a result of his negligence. Again. His rational mind told him he knew the truth, that he'd seen Holden die of hypothermia, and confirmed it. But an instinctive part of him only knew what he saw at that exact moment: Chris Holden standing tall. Taller than he had in days, as a matter of fact.

"You . . ." A long hiss of breath escaped his mouth as he tried to explain. Connor stepped in.

"We all have a twin, Chris. Well, most of us do. Me and Noah here don't because it seems we're both dead. Or neither of us is. I don't know. You—your copy—he had an accident on the ice . . . and didn't make it. Like us," he said, pointing to himself and Noah, "There's only one of you."

Chris furrowed his brow and searched Noah's crew with his eyes as if hoping his doppelgänger would stand up from behind a table and shout "April fools!"

"Bullshit. I'm not a copy. *You're* the copy!" Mirror Boucher shouted, stabbing a finger in the direction of his twin.

"That's enough of that," Holden ordered. "We need to be rational while we figure out the explanation for all of this."

Kevin lifted up his shirt, exposing a long, straight scar across the right side of his stomach. "You got one like it?" he asked. From the other side of the invisible line, the other Kevin pulled up the bottom of his tee-shirt, revealing his own long scar, the result of ignoring the symptoms of appendicitis until it was almost too late. "Almost killed me," he said.

"Me too. It adhered to my guts and they had pull them out to scrape it off." Normally Kevin laughed when telling the story of his near-fatal appendectomy, but not today. The mirror version of him appeared to take the close call more seriously.

"So, what is it, professor?" Henry asked Noah. "What's happening?"

Noah shrugged his shoulders. In his philosophy classes they'd talked about the best of all possible realities and "many worlds" theory, but most of what he'd read had gone over his head. The discussions in the classroom were dominated by people smarter and more engaged in the subject than he was. He was more inclined toward biology and ecological studies. Those subjects suited the way his mind worked. Structure and predictability were like a path through the wilderness. If he could learn the relationships between things, he could understand them. But uncertainty was nothing he'd ever been equipped to handle with any kind of proficiency. He'd tried to talk through those subjects with Abby when she offered to help him with the readings, but got frustrated when the idea he thought he had a foothold in collapsed beneath him. He walked out of those graduation requirements with C's and the satisfaction he'd never have to think about them again. Biology, environmental science—those were things you encountered in the real world. Not philosophy. He couldn't explain what was happening any better than he could do a trapeze act with the bosun's chair. Still, he tried.

"Not everything is the same," he said. "It's not a perfectly parallel universe. Some things are different."

"Like what?" Boucher asked.

"Like me and Connor. In his world I died, but since then things are happening to us like we were the same person." He pointed to the butterfly tape holding the cut over his eye closed.

Connor got the idea, pointed to his own scar and said, "I got that cut when William tried to free the ship from the ice. I wasn't holding on and I fell."

"I got mine in the storm. But it happened more or less the same way. Same scar, slightly different cause. Anyone else notice anything different?"

"Who gives a shit what's the same and what's different? What good does it do us?" Brewster said. "We can do your little activity book games and see if the teacher in picture B is holding up three fingers instead of two, but it doesn't help us get out of here, does it? I want to try the phones."

"That's the reason we left the ship," Noah said. "We were hoping to find a working radio we could use to call for a medevac."

"Us too. We tried to call the company first thing when we got here," Connor said. "But the radio and the sat phones are dead as disco."

"You try fixing them?" Boucher asked.

"What do you think? Gear's in fine shape. It just ain't working. At first we didn't think it was a big deal. The company might write off a ship lost at sea, but we thought there'd be no way in hell they'd zero out the books on a drilling platform. A place like this costs something like six hundred million just to build. Between that and the money they're losing every day this beast ain't drilling, you'd think they'd come sniffing around. Our lives might not mean shit to the company, but their dollars do. We thought we'd wait out the weather and when they come back to reopen, grab a ride home. But help ain't comin'." He opened his mouth to say something else but snapped it shut, biting off his next words before he could utter them.

"What about the crew? I mean the original Niflheim crew. What happened to them?" Noah asked.

Connor shook his head. "Gone before we got here. They didn't leave a note."

Noah's shoulders slumped. A vision of the Niflheim crew wandering off across the ice sparked in his mind. He pushed the thought down. There was enough trouble in this world without dreaming up more.

"So what does this mean?" Kevin said. He nodded toward his reflection. "I touch him, are we both going to explode or something?" The mirror Kevin took an involuntary step back.

Noah wished he had a twin he could test the theory with. He knew already that if he reached out and touched any of the men, he'd feel skin and muscle, not the energy of the cosmos or oblivion. He wondered whether, if there was another him standing in the room, he'd have the same confidence. "Anyone up to testing it?" he said. "Somebody want to volunteer?"

"Hell no!" both Jacks shouted out at once. Noah was surprised there wasn't more of that kind of synchrony happening. Like he'd observed earlier, not everything was exactly the same.

The mirror Michael Yeong stepped forward. "I'll do it if he will." He jutted his chin toward his counterpart, slumped on a couch.

Noah's Michael nodded and held out his hand. "What the hell. I can't feel any worse than I already do," he said. Connor's Michael crouched in front of the sofa and reached toward his twin's outstretched hand. He moved to grasp it and both men flinched back suddenly.

"What? What is it?" Connor said.

His Michael smirked and said, "He shocked me."

"I haven't moved. *You* shocked *me*." Yeong smiled, showing the first glimpse of his sense of humor since they'd become stuck. The smile died quickly, and he reached up again. The mirror Michael rubbed his palms on his jeans and tapped his fingers together, testing for a static charge before extending his hand a second time. The men gripped hands and shook.

"Nice to meet you," Yeong said. "You know, you're a hell of a good-looking guy, by the way."

"Likewise," Michael replied. "But you need a shave."

The silent room seemed to let out a collective breath no one knew they were holding. Noah wanted to applaud. It felt like a victory even if it didn't move them toward a solution. At least it put to rest a fear. No matter how small it might be, that was one less obstacle to overcome.

The mirror Michael stood and turned. "Okay. That settles that. The world won't end if we bump into each other in the halls."

"So what now?" Boucher asked. His twin nodded with a solemn look on his face as if he'd just heard someone ask for a vote on the Senate floor.

Connor cleared his throat. "I think we all need to get some rest. These men have been through a lot and it's late. We can rally in the morning and discuss what has to happen next."

"What makes you think anyone can sleep?" Jack said. "I'm ready for that drink."

The corner of Connor's mouth turned up. "I forgot I promised that. I think we could all use a nightcap. Anyone want to go grab some cups out of the galley?"

"I got it," Noah said. As badly as he wanted to lie down and get some rest, he knew Boucher was right. Without a little something to help settle him, he'd lie awake all night thinking about the turn the world had taken. He never gave much thought to what was real and what wasn't, because reality was solid and constant, and the difference between a dream and waking was a bright line, easily seen. Sitting in the Niflheim, however, he had no idea what any of that even meant anymore. The line between original and reflection wasn't just blurred, it was blown away.

"They're in the right bank of cabinets under the serving window," Holden said as Noah headed for the door.

He pushed through the galley door and reached for the lights. It took him a minute to find the switch. Even though light was spilling through the serving window from the mess room, the galley was dark. He found the switch and flicked it up. The overhead fluorescents flickered to life. Noah waited a moment for the dimly burning lights to warm up, orienting himself to the unfamiliar kitchen. He walked around a tall rack stacked with pots and pans to find the serving window. Through it was the mess room where they'd just eaten. The view was both familiar and strangely foreign. Flat and deep at the same time, like looking into something only partially rendered in the real world.

He crouched behind the counter and opened the cabinet below. Milky plastic glasses sat upside down arranged in rows on a steel tray. He slid the tray out and counted fifteen. There were more of Connor's men than his own in the rec room, but not many. He was uncertain of the total count, so he grabbed four more glasses, making it an even twenty. He figured that would cover everyone who would want a drink—which was probably everyone.

A clatter behind him startled him out of his trance and he spun around, toppling cups on the floor. He felt the heat of embarrassment flush his cheeks. Brewster stood half behind the pan rack, his own face flushed red. "You scared the shit out of me, William! You come in here to supervise?" Noah knew the Old Man hadn't come to help with the cups.

"So, we're on a first name basis now, too?"

"We're not on the ship anymore."

"And you think that means I'm not still the one in charge?"

Noah didn't say anything. He knew there was nothing he could say that would please Brewster. Not even "aye sir." Instead, he picked up the spilled cups and restacked them on the tray. Lifting it, he turned to take them to Connor and the others. The Old Man was gone. *Suits me,* Noah thought. As he walked out of the room, he glanced at where he'd caught Brewster hiding behind the rack. On the far wall at the end of the galley hung a magnetic strip holding a row of carving knives. There were no odd gaps between them; it looked like they were all there. He dismissed his dark thoughts and took the glasses to the rec room.

He needed a drink more than ever.

PART THREE

The Promise

26

He sat beside the bed, holding his wife's thin hand. Her skin looked like vellum paper. It was thin and delicately wrinkled, pale to the point of translucence. She had always been pleasantly tan, looking like someone who got her color from the sun on her skin while she hiked or rode a bicycle to just lie in the park and read a book. Hers wasn't color you bought in a salon or sprayed on. And now it was gone. Along with her hair and her childish plumpness. Chemo had desaturated her and left her ethereal, like a photograph left in the light too long, losing its detail. A fading memory of a person.

"Is he coming?" she asked. Her throat was dry and her voice almost inaudible. She couldn't draw a deep enough breath to say more than three or four words at a time. He picked up a salmon-colored plastic cup half full of water and helped aim the straw toward her mouth. With a gentle hand, he tilted her head forward until she could take the straw between cracked lips. He lowered her head after a mouthful and set the cup to the side. He rubbed a little balm on a finger and spread

*it over her lips. She kissed at his fingers and smiled
when he pressed her own kiss to her forehead.*

"I called him again, but he didn't answer." He wanted
to say, "He must be on his way and can't answer his
phone," but he knew better. He knew better than to
lie to his wife. As much as he resented William, Abby
was dying and all she wanted was to see her father.
She needed comfort from the man who'd taught her to
ride a bike and put a worm on a hook and how to tell
the direction from looking at the stars. She needed her
father to hold her hand one last time so she could be
the little girl she'd always be in his heart, the one who
sprinted away from her favorite show on the TV when
she heard the door brush against the carpet in the front
room because that meant her father had come back from
the sea. He smelled like diesel and sweat and brine, but
he smelled like home and love and safety, too. She'd
jump into his arms and breathe in a deep lungful of him
and feel his powerful arms wrap around her in a hug
that could only come from a man who battled the ocean
to return home to his little girl. Noah hoped that in those
moments, passed out from the pain meds—what he liked
to think of as swimming in her dream sea—she was en-
visioning those things. He hoped she got those final
moments with her father, if not beside the bed, at least
in another place where William was able to be everything she needed.

In this world, her father said she was giving up. He
said she was listening to that god damn fool of a man
she married and was throwing her life away. And he
wouldn't have any part in it. In her clear moments in
this world, he was not there.

Abby squeezed Noah's hand and her smile grew a

little wider. Her breath caught and she winced. But the smile didn't falter. He gripped her hand in both of his as tightly as he dared and tried to keep the tears out of his eyes. Not because he didn't want her to see him cry, but because he didn't want his view of her to be marred by anything.

"It's okay," she said. "You're here." She sighed a tiny sigh.

"Can I bring you anything?"

"No. Stay where I . . ." a breath ". . . can see you." He nodded and held on. She tried to shift in the bed, but could hardly move. He tried to get up to help her shift a little, but she shook her head. "Stay."

"I'm not going anywhere," he said.

"Promise me . . ."

"I promise.

Her smile faded and her forehead wrinkled. "No. Promise . . ." a breath ". . . me you'll never go . . ." a gasp ". . . out to sea again."

"I'll never ship out with William again," he said.

"No. Out to sea. Never again." She tried to sit up. Her face contorted with frustration at her weakness. She fell back and breathed, "Promise. Say it."

He was quietly thankful for the tears that filled his eyes now. They made her face blur and fade and he said, "I promise. I'll never ship out again." He wiped his eyes and looked at his beautiful wife. She smiled, and for the first time in days it was the smile he knew. The one she'd had when they first made love, the one on their wedding day, the one as she held their brand-new child to her chest in the hospital bed while the delivery nurse snapped a picture.

"I promise," he said.

Her eyes shifted toward the prescription bottle on the table beside her bed. She nodded. Noah shook his head.

"I'm ready," she said.

"I'm not."

"You promised. Everything's . . . going to be . . . all right."

He let go of her hands to pour more water and open the bottle of what the doctor had given them. He shook a few out into his hand. He put one in her mouth and helped her take a sip of water. And then another.

When they were finished, she lay back, and he held her hands until she slipped away. Like she wanted.

A light but insistent knocking awoke Noah from fitful sleep. He felt unrested and frustrated. He'd been as slow to fall asleep as he'd feared he'd be, and had woken up several times through the night, first needing to find the head in unfamiliar surroundings, and second with the beginnings of a small hangover. Even though he hadn't had much, the combination of exhaustion and hunger made the little bit of whiskey he'd had potent enough. And drink had given him sad dreams.

Although the cabin was similar to his on the ship, it was different enough that he felt lost and disoriented. He'd nearly pissed himself wandering the hallway in the night looking for the head before it dawned on him he wasn't aboard a ship and there was likely a toilet in his room. He found the airplane-sized bathroom in his cabin just in time. He figured he'd get used to the Niflheim after a day or two, and that depressed him more.

He didn't want to get used to it. His hope had been that once they found the drilling rig, they'd spend a day at most waiting for a rescue copter to come. That there was a crew of starved and haggard men aboard meant that hope was gone.

In the early hours of the morning, he finally fell into sound sleep. Still, it wasn't restful; the groan of the ice that had taken Holden and nipped Connor's ship invaded his dreams, threatening to crush the supports beneath the platform and bring them all crashing down into the water below.

The knocking at the door grew a little more forceful. "One minute," he grumbled, swinging his legs out of bed. He could feel his feet again. Examining them in his half-drunken state the night before, he found the tips of his toes were dry and hard with frostnip, the first stage of frostbite. It was unpleasant, but not too painful and he wouldn't lose any of them. Not yet. Going back outside for any length of time, however, likely meant a progression from nip to bite and maybe sacrificing a toe or two—or ten. As much as he wanted to, there was no punting this duty; he and Connor were the only ones well enough to bring everyone back safely, if such a thing was even possible.

He grumbled as he opened the door. Squinting through a single blurry eye, he tried to make out the figure standing in the doorway. Although dim, the light from the hall hurt his eyes. "You look as raw as I feel," Connor said. He stood with his neck bent, massaging at the back of it with a hand. Without asking if he was welcome to enter, he let himself in. He spun the rolling chair by the desk around and sat. The thing protested at the sudden labor of supporting his controlled collapse, but it held together. Noah closed the door behind him and returned to his bunk, flopping down on the mattress. It wasn't the most comfortable bed he'd ever slept on, but it was nicer than the ones on the ship, and he was thankful for it.

"What'd you put in my glass last night?"

Connor chuckled, continuing to knead his neck. "I topped that bottle off with benzene to stretch it out. Was that a bad idea?"

"Whatever was in it, I can't believe we finished the whole thing."

"It seemed worth celebrating, seein' as how you're alive and all."

"You're the one who's alive. I, on the other hand, think I'm dying. My liver hurts."

"I'd offer you a cup of coffee, but we ran out of that maybe a month ago." Connor smoothed his hair away from his face and glanced at his palm before rubbing the oil slicking it on his pants. "The first week without caffeine is the hardest. Jack and Kevin nearly crushed themselves trying to tilt the Coke machine. It never occurred to them to look around for a key to the damn thing." He held up an index finger to preemptively silence Noah. "Before you ask, we're out of that too. It'd be funny if it weren't a sign of how desperate we all are. Life here is better than it was on the *Promise*, but not by much."

"There's coffee on my ship. I'll pack some up when I go after the rest of the crew," Noah said, pushing himself up onto his elbows. It took him a few seconds to fight against the dizziness that made him want to lie down again. He held his breath, a wave of nausea passing through his body. Sweat beaded up on his forehead despite the chill in the room. "I'm starting to believe you about the benzene," he said when he felt like he could risk opening his mouth.

"You're dehydrated. You sweat all your water out yesterday. Get a couple glasses in you and you'll feel better."

"You're not rationing it?"

"Drinking water, we have an endless supply of." He nodded toward the wall. "We bring in snow from outside. Melt it for cooking and washing up, too. We're not getting the laundry and showers back, but whenever you feel like fetching a bucket full, you can have a nice brisk whore's bath. It'll wake you up, and that's no lie."

"I'll take your word for it."

"Give it a week and you'll be begging for a bucket of snow and a bar of soap." Noah imagined him finishing with an unspoken, *if we make it another week.* Connor rose and held out a hand to help Noah to his feet. The nausea had subsided, but the dizziness remained. "Everyone else was headed for the cafeteria. Let's get some food and see who'll head out with us to gather up the rest of your crew. I saw Holden on my way here. He's lookin' better today than he was last night. He might be up for it."

Noah was loath to consider asking the third officer to take even a step outdoors. No matter how good Holden was feeling, he'd watched the man's twin die and didn't want to risk it again, for both of their sakes. It was strange to think of individuals like species; he didn't want to be the one responsible for killing the last of the Holdens. His mind drifted to the crew still aboard the *Promise*. The ones left behind were in the worst shape. The walk outside had been treacherous enough for relatively healthy men—Michael and Henry were definitely worse for wear after having made the trip. He couldn't imagine Mickle and Heath would fare any better, even if the journey was a straight line to the rig with no detours. And then there was Felix. Dragging the broken man across the ice on a stretcher could kill him. If the violence of the ride didn't do it, exposure to the elements would. Noah was out of ideas. Even if all the other men could make it to the Niflheim alive, they couldn't expect Felix to survive the trip. And they couldn't leave him. As difficult as it was to admit, if they weren't rescued soon, Felix was going to die. They were *all* dead men. Felix was just first in line. Still, they couldn't abandon him, and that meant leaving at least one man behind to care for him as long as he could. Noah silently volunteered himself for the duty, figuring the way most of the crew felt about him anyway, they wouldn't mind if he stayed behind for a while.

He hadn't realized he was showing physical signs of the dark thoughts coursing through him until Connor broke his trance and asked if he was all right. The more time Noah spent contemplating their next steps, actually taking them seemed increasingly reckless and an entirely new plan seemed necessary. It was a down-ward spiral of inaction and half steps. The crew couldn't afford more reflection or discussion. They had to do something now if they were going to survive. "Let's go." He took a step and stopped, an idea occurring to him. "I want to stop by the comm room first. Sick bay, too."

Connor chuckled. There wasn't much humor in it, but he seemed to be trying. "Already told you, we ran out of NSAIDs days ago. You're just going to have to push through your hangover."

"But there's a pharmacy with controlled meds, right?"

"I know you ain't hurtin' *that* bad, brother."

"Not me. One of the men aboard our ship got busted up pretty seriously in the storm." Noah skirted around the details. "I'm pretty sure our doc is running low on tramadol if he isn't already out. I want to grab some more before we go."

Connor nodded, accepting his explanation. "Can do. I have no idea where the keys to the pharmacy are though. It's gonna take some time to hunt 'em down if they're even still here. The rig's doc might have taken them with when they left."

"I bet you know where a crowbar or something is."

"One of *those* I can find in about thirty seconds. Sun's up though. That means we're already running out of daylight. We need to hurry if we're going to get out there, packed up, and back before nightfall."

Noah nodded his agreement. "I figure it's a two-day job if we want to get everyone across safely. We get ourselves ready, find a couple of volunteers if we can, and go. Once we're there, we can take our time assessing everybody's condition and ability and make a plan to get them on the move in the morning. All sunlight walking, but with plenty of time to prep and step carefully. I don't want to be caught out after dark again."

"However we do it, we gotta eat first. I don't want to make the trip without at least a little fuel in the tank."

Noah agreed. He was weak enough already. Whatever nutrition he could get before setting out was not only welcome, it was necessary. He turned to find his pack. "We never got the chance to eat it, but we packed up some stuff for yester—"

A glimpse of something dark slipping along the wall in his peripheral vision made the words catch in his throat. He jerked away from it, a revival of the panic he'd felt when the shade on the weather deck nearly knocked him overboard surging through him. Noah was certain Connor could hear his heart pounding in the small compartment.

"You seein' 'em too?" Connor said. Noah nodded. "They worry me almost more'n the sickness. They only started shifting around maybe yesterday or the day before. If you ever asked me before, I would've told you I'm not afraid of ghosts."

"But now?"

"Now, I'm pretty much afraid of everything. I'm most afraid of . . . of whatever it is that makes the shadows run away like that."

"Run away?"

Connor's demeanor darkened. "They don't look like they're trying to get away from something to you?" Noah hadn't thought of it like that, but Connor was right, and the observation unsettled him. With the exception of the one on the weather deck that rushed directly at him, the shapes did seem to be trying to find cover in the other dark spaces into which they vanished. The idea at once made them seem less frightening, and deepened Noah's dread. For the first time, Noah looked harder, trying to see the frightened shades. He looked for what might be after them.

The sight and smell of the cafeteria was familiar enough. But instead of the loud competition between off-color jokes and exaggerated tales of home life, the room softly hummed with hushed conversation and the occasional clinking of flatware against dishes. The men had segregated themselves into twin crews: Connor's along the galley wall, and Noah's opposite them. In the middle was a no-man's-land of empty tables and palpable distrust.

More of Connor's crew had shown up for breakfast than had for the reunion the night before, though several were still missing. Noah assumed the ones unaccounted for weren't getting out of bed much anymore, if at all.

Connor's brow furrowed. "What is it?"

Noah pointed at a man near the back of the room. Although he was as drawn and pale as the others, the smile and strong, pronounced nose were unmistakable. "That's Felix."

Connor grunted. "Yeah. He's been down hard for a few days. Was one of the first to get sick, in fact. He was up bright and early this morning though. Looks like he's feeling better." Connor's mouth hung open like he wanted to add something else to his observation, but all that escaped was a short "Oh," when Holden walked over and laid a hand on Felix's back. The two renewed men told Connor what Noah feared.

"It doesn't mean . . ." Connor tried. Noah knew, however, that it *did* mean the Felix he'd shipped out with was likely dead. Holden had died on the walk across the ice and his copy had apparently started feeling better in short order. Now, Felix was risen after having been the first and worst afflicted of the crew. If Holden's rebound presented a hypothesis they all suspected, but were hesitant to acknowledge, Felix's recovery was confirmation.

Jack and Kevin ate and spoke with each other, putting up a front as though everything was fine. Their frequent side-eyed glances at Connor's shipmates betrayed their concern, however. Brewster, by contrast, openly stared at Felix. Boucher and Henry flanked him, whispering. If their counterparts seemed off-put by the attention, they weren't letting on.

"Come on." Connor guided Noah to the serving line. Behind it in the kitchen, a gaunt John Boduf stood over a steel pot of tepid-looking oatmeal. His signature mutton chops had filled in and he wore a scraggly, uneven beard now instead. He peeled back the encrusted layer on the top of the pot and scooped out a bowl of mush for each of them. "We're gonna run out of food a lot faster with all these extra mouths to feed," John said to Connor. "I hope you have a plan."

"We have some provisions on our ship," Noah said. The cook didn't reply. He plopped a ladle of overcooked yet somehow tepid oatmeal in Noah's bowl and looked away, clearly uncomfortable to be talking to a dead man. Noah sympathized.

"We'll be fine a while longer," Connor said. He lifted

his bowl to his nose and took a deep whiff. "What's the secret ingredient today?" John raised a hand and with a barely maintained serious expression on his face, extended his middle finger. "Mmmm. That's my favorite." John's façade cracked and he smiled.

"Choke on it," he said.

"If it's your cooking, that's a guarantee." John relaxed a bit and even gave Noah an odd half smile as he picked up his bowl.

Connor took a seat at an empty table in the center of the room with his back to Noah's crew. Noah chose a spot across from him. He picked at the contents of his bowl. His appetite wasn't gone, but the unease growing in him threatened to forcibly expel anything he tried to take in. He looked for mold or maggots or something that would give him justification for not eating it without seeming ungrateful or wasteful. He considered taking the bowl back to the cook and asking him to save it for him until later. Refrigeration certainly wasn't something they lacked. At the same time, he didn't anticipate a request like that would be well-received. Everyone was hungry. His assurances that there was more on board his own ship aside, they were about to double the occupancy of the rig. Food would become a concern sooner rather than later for them all.

Lifting a half spoonful, he tasted the pale paste that had once been oats. It was practically flavorless. For that, he was thankful. Less flavor was less for his body to rebel against. He dragged his spoon through the paste, drawing an X. "Everyone else has got a copy, but we're the odd men out," he whispered. "The thing that's making our crews sick hasn't gotten into you, either, has it?"

"We've been through this. No, I'm not sick."

He nodded his chin toward Holden and Felix. "Was Holden in as good of a shape yesterday morning as he is now?"

Connor shook his head. "He was barely able to get out of bed twenty-four hours ago."

"And Felix?"

"Same deal. Worse even."

"What if they're better because their . . . other selves are dead? Everybody else is still feeling like hammered shit because a single . . . life-force, or whatever you want to call it, can't handle the workload of keeping two people alive."

"I didn't think you believed in that stuff," Connor said. "Spirits and whatnot."

"I don't. I don't know. I believe in what I see. You're dead, except you're not. Same goes for me, right? There's only one of each of us and we're the only ones who haven't been sick at all." He nodded his chin toward Holden and Felix. They sat talking animatedly to each another over their gruel. Felix shoveled his meal into his mouth like he'd just woken from hypersleep and needed to restore what he'd lost in the light years between here and home. Holden slid his bowl over and Felix used a finger to wipe out what had stuck to the sides of the bowl. "And now they're on the mend."

"You said your Felix was alive."

"He was when I left." Noah let his silence fill in the rest. "From the look of it, I guess I don't need to go to sick bay anymore."

Connor disagreed. "Nah. You said it: believe in what you see. We don't have any proof your Felix is gone, so we'll get the meds. I'm not writing anybody off on a guess."

Noah glanced up from his bowl and smiled. On the outside, Connor looked like half the man he'd once been. Inside, he hadn't changed at all. He was an optimist and would already be lifting people up and out of trouble before climbing over them to save himself ever entered his mind. "I missed you, brother."

"I'm not asking you out on a date. I'm just promising you drugs." Noah choked and sputtered oats that caught in his beard. He somehow managed to keep hold of his spoon and set it in the bowl quietly, trying not to make a bigger spectacle of himself than he'd already done. Connor handed him a paper napkin and apologized.

"Don't be sorry. It's not you; it's the food."

"I get that all the time. Eat up and we'll go raid the pharmacy."

Noah looked back at Brewster and his companions. They sat nodding as he whispered something. "I think I'm done," he said. "I lost my appetite."

He picked up his bowl and took it over to Boduf. Unlike a true mirror image, there were people on both sides of the reflection. From each side of the glass, the other thought of himself as the original. That couldn't be more the case than seeing how Brewster, Boucher, and Henry carried themselves. "Waste not want not, right?" he said, handing over his dish.

He turned to leave and froze at the sight of the figure standing in the doorway. Unlike the rest of Connor's crew, deprivation had done little to diminish him, as though he was one of those Hindu mystics who lived on only light. When he saw Noah, his eyes narrowed and the reflected William Brewster said, "You're dead."

Noah was unsure whether it was an observation or a promise.

Connor stepped forward. "I'm sure you guys have a lot to talk about, but it'll have to wait. Noah and I were just leaving." He walked toward the door and Noah fell into step behind him. If this Brewster was nicer than the one he knew, it didn't register as Noah pushed past him. The Old Man considered his deceased son-in-law with the same malevolence the other one reserved for the living one.

27

The Niflheim sick bay was considerably larger than the one aboard the *Arctic Promise*. Noah and Connor had room enough to maneuver around without having to brush past each other. Connor rifled the drawers in the room looking for the key to the medicine locker while Noah attempted to inspect its contents through the wire mesh glass. The selection wasn't broad and he didn't know what much of it contained would be used for, but he did recognize a couple of antibiotics and a bottle of phenobarbital—which he knew by name, but couldn't remember what it was used for. He thought it might be a sedative. While he couldn't see any tramadol, a bottle of codeine sulfate grabbed his attention. He thought that might work if there wasn't something else hidden behind the solid portion of the doors below. Either way, he had a narcotic. If Felix was alive, it would keep him out of pain while they attempted to move him.

Connor slammed the last drawer, rattling the tools inside. "Fuck!" He collapsed into in a chair along the wall and began massaging his neck again.

Noah said, "It's okay. We can jimmy it." The cabinet appeared resilient, but he was almost certain the two of them could pry it open with one of the crowbars they'd rounded up on the way. What he was uncertain of was whether they'd set off an alarm when they did, and if they'd be able to shut it off before it drove them all insane.

"I know we can, but all the same, I'd feel better knowing that it's not a temptation goin' forward. We've been lucky however long we been here. No one's gotten injured. But things're goin' south, aren't they. People are gonna be getting desperate." Connor hadn't said much in the hallway on their way to sick bay; seeing Brewster's reaction to Noah seemed to have stolen his happy thoughts and his mood had darkened considerably. Noah was more pragmatic about it. Even if he was dead in the mirror Brewster's world, the Old Man was still likely the kind of guy who'd threatened to break his future son-in-law's neck the night before his daughter's wedding. That he might have softened after Noah's death was merely a consequence of the bastard getting what he wanted.

"Tell me something," Connor said. His chair creaked as he pushed against the armrests, repositioning himself. "How'd I die?"

Noah choked. He'd been pretending their separation was due to the kind of distance that grows between friends in the mundane world. New job, new family, new town. Someone moves and promises they'll keep in touch, but eventually the best you can do is occasionally click a thumbs-up or an emoji on some social media page and keep scrolling.

"Forget I asked," Connor said when Noah didn't reply. "Never mind."

"No. It's okay. It's just . . . weird, you know?"

"Oh, believe me, I know." A touch of humor reappeared in Connor's expression. Not enough to mask his anxiety, but it was something.

"There was a storm and the water was rough, but it wasn't as bad as others we'd been in. Not like the one we went through a couple of days ago." He assumed the storm that had put Felix in sick bay had hit the Niflheim, too, but he didn't know the point at which they'd sailed from one world into another. Perhaps it was the fog that had doomed them and not the storm at all. Either way, he tried to put himself back on track, remembering something one of his professors had said to him: *If you've been shot, what good does it do to ask who sold the bullet? Find a doctor.*

"Boucher ordered me out to recheck the cargo lashing. I was pretty pissed about it because I'd already done that on my watch earlier in the day and didn't see how it'd be any different a few hours later. But, you know, Boucher, right? The guy's always busting my balls. I needed to take care of something else at the same time, so I asked you to cover me and go out to check instead. I figured everything was fine, you'd go eyeball it, I'd do my other thing, and then we'd play some chess and have a drink. That was the last time I ever saw you . . . alive, I guess."

Connor stared at Noah as he recounted the night of the accident. Noah couldn't face the man's gaze, and looked at the floor while he explained the rest. "I must have missed something, or the storm shook it loose, because a shipping can slid across the cargo deck when a big wave hit, and you got pinned. It . . ." Noah tried to swallow, but his throat had gone dry. "How much of this do you want to hear?"

"All of it."

He remembered standing in the master's cabin, his father-in-law screaming at him to get his ass out on the cargo deck as ordered and Noah in the middle of a half-conceived recrimination when the general alarm sounded. He followed the rescue team out onto the deck expecting to hear cries of "man overboard," and having to fish Connor out of the water, frazzled and cold, but alive. Instead, he stood and watched the men fight to move the container away from the wall. It screeched across the deck as the wind howled and rain pounded them. Noah had rushed forward to grab at Connor's survival suit, shake him back to consciousness and help him to sick bay. Instead, despite the merciful dark of the nighttime storm, he could see there was no coming back from what had been done. A pink wash pooled under their feet, rinsed away from the pulped face of his friend.

The memory made his stomach rebel and he coughed, his dry throat stinging with each convulsion. He bent over, holding his stomach while the fit overcame him. When he was able to finally get himself under control, he tried to take a deep breath. His lungs hurt. It didn't bode well for the arduous task ahead of them.

"That bad?" Connor said.

Leaving out the worst of it, he said, "You were crushed. I ID'ed your body for the investigators but they still had to match your dental records for an official identification. Sheila filed for a survivor's payout from the company insurance, but they turned her down because you weren't married."

The last sentence cracked Connor's expression. His eyebrows knitted and he held up his left hand to show the thick tungsten band on his third finger. "We got married right after *your* accident," he said. "I didn't want her to be left with nothing to show if something like what happened to you happened to me."

Noah shook his head. "It should have been me on that deck."

"It *was* you. At least in my experience. I suppose you might owe something to somebody, but it ain't me. There was a storm, just like you said, but you went out to check the lashing yourself. The can broke free, but it knocked you overboard. The Coast Guard found you on the beach at Point Hope, Alaska. They identified you the same way—with dental records. Crabs got a taste of you. If it's any consolation, the company paid out to Abby without a fight."

Noah felt a sudden stab of panic. His legs stiffened as if they were preparing to sprint from the room ahead of his desire. "Wait. What's that again?" he said. His voice was thin and small.

"The insurance company paid. Abby used the money to get through the next year while she looked for a job and got Ellie into preschool, but you know, that money only stretches so far. "

The words punched Noah in the gut and he steadied himself against the medicine cabinet, again struggling for breath. He felt dizzy and the light grew hazy and dim. He squinted his eyes shut and forced his lungs to fill. "Abby's alive?"

"Of course. You trying to tell me she's not?"

"A year and a half ago we got into a car accident, me and Abby. It wasn't bad, but her back and her neck hurt after, so we went to the hospital. They did a bunch of scans and found a tumor. We found out that's why she had headaches all the time and her vision kept getting worse. We thought it was the other way around, you know? The bad eyesight was giving her the headaches.

"After the diagnosis, she tried chemo and radiation, but that didn't kill it. It'd already metastasized or whatever because she'd been ignoring the little aches and pains for months. The doctors told us they could prolong her life for another few months, but that it would eventually get her. No more than a year, they said. She'd already lost sixty pounds, and all of her hair. She couldn't walk to the bathroom on her own and I had to help her down the hall. She hated that she had to hold on to me to get on and off the toilet. Abby said she wanted to die on her own terms, so I brought her home. My mom came out to look after Ellie during those last few weeks." Noah nodded over his shoulder in the direction of the mess room. "William never came to see her. Abby said her mother died from some infection or something in the hospital when she was a kid, and William was still pissed off and bitter about that. He wouldn't accept his daughter was as sick as she was. She tried to get me to leave him alone, but all I could think of was what would I want if it was Ellie? I thought I'd want to be able to say good-bye. He told me he'd be damned if he was going to set foot in our house if she was just going to 'give up.' Like it was a game she could win if she just stuck it out for a few more moves.

"I asked you to check the lashing that night because

I was fighting with my father-in-law over her. I went to his cabin that night to get in another round. I was furious that Boucher was riding me and I knew it was because Brewster told him to. They doubled up my work during the watch and cut back my overtime. That night, I was feeling cagey. I was missing Abby and I wanted to get my licks in. I wanted to make him hurt. I thought you'd be okay. I really did."

Noah tried to control the sob that hitched in his chest and made his shoulders shudder. Growing up in a house full of New England Yankee men who kept their feelings to themselves, meant he held in his tears around his daughter while encouraging her to let her emotions out, only allowing himself a restrained emotional outlet in the deep hours of the night after she was sound asleep and unlikely to rise. Lying in bed, a hand on the cold side of the mattress, he let his tears trail down his face and catch in the graying hair at his temples. He would breathe out his stilled screams in long, shuddering sighs until his breath found the rhythm of sleep. And if he was lucky, he would not dream.

Connor stood and reached out for Noah. Noah reared back and dragged his forearm across his face, wiping away his tears and resetting his expression. There was no one else to see but it didn't matter. Emotional reserve was as much a part of him as the pinup tattoo on his arm. That stoicism had been drilled deep into him until it was a part you couldn't get rid of no matter how much you scrubbed or scratched. "That's the thing, isn't it. You shouldn't be standing there any more than I should be here talking to you now. Looking at you is like looking at . . . I don't know, like the end or something.

Like the way the world is *supposed* to be—without me in it. We should have switched places. She was the better one of us."

Connor wrapped his arms around Noah's shoulders. "This ain't some karmic bar tab comin' due. We're *all* alive here."

"But we're all dying."

"No. Not all of us."

Noah pushed away from his friend. His glistening eyes registering a forming resignation. "We're not sick because the other one of each of us is dead. There's two of everybody else, too, except for Holden and maybe Felix now. And both of them are doing better."

"What are you saying? That one of everybody has to die for the other to make it?"

Noah held up his hands. "I'm saying everyone who's sick has a twin. Everyone who doesn't is either getting better, or never got sick in the first place. What if the tech is like the crew?"

"I don't follow."

"What if to fix the tech in one place, we have to destroy its twin? If we could find a way to scuttle one of the ships, I think there's a chance the other's communications systems might come back online. I don't think it's enough to sink it though. We have to completely ruin it. Blow it up."

Connor stepped back and looked at the ceiling, searching for a flaw in the idea. It wasn't long before he found one. "If that restores one radio. What about the other crew? When yours is rescued, let's say, what happens to mine?"

Noah hadn't considered that possibility, but of course, Connor was right. Just like Holden's rejuvenation came at the cost of his twin, if Noah's idea restored communications to one ship, it would leave the other one utterly beyond repair. And they couldn't all escape to a single time without remaining sick or getting sicker, could they? Noah's shoulders slumped.

"It's not a bad idea. I think it's a start anyway. Better'n any of my guys have come up with."

Noah cursed and drove his elbow into the medicine cabinet. The glass cracked and pieces tinkled on the floor between his feet, but it held together. Noah picked up his crowbar, looking like he wanted to tear the whole thing down. Instead he stood still as a shout that echoed in the hallway carried into the sick bay.

"What was *that*?" he asked.

"I don't know," Connor said.

The men sprinted out of the room, their supply mission forgotten in the heat of a new urgency.

28

They shoved through the door. The cafeteria looked the same as it had when they'd left; the ships' crews remained divided on opposite sides of the room. But instead of quietly gathering in cliques, they stood assembled like soldiers mustering on a battle line. At one end, a table had been overturned, its crossed legs resembling an invasion obstacle on Normandy Beach. Smashed dishes and utensils littered the floor. In no-man's-land, Brewster stood holding a carving knife to his twin's neck. Connor's shipmates implored him to let their skipper go. He pressed the blade harder against his prisoner's white stubbled throat.

Taking advantage of the brief distraction Noah and Connor's return presented, Holden took a cautious step forward, his hands defensively held out in front of him even though he was far from Brewster's reach with the knife. "Calm down, William. No one needs to get hurt."

"No?" Brewster said. He angled the knife back from his twin's windpipe toward his carotid. The third officer halted his advance. "Tell me the exact moment when *you* started to feel on the mend."

"This isn't about me."

"It goddamn well is. It's about you and Pereira and Cabot and MacAllister. They never got sick, and the two of you suddenly have full sails while the rest of us are still dragging ass. I know what happened to you, Holden, and we all know what the spring in Pereira's step over there means for our man."

"So, you're going to murder someone to test a theory? For Christ's sake, William, he's not just anyone; he's *you*."

"*I'm* the only me!" Spit flew from his lips as he sputtered his opposition. The mirror Brewster's hands floated up and down as if he wanted to pull the hand holding the knife to his throat away, but knew also *who* had him in his grip and how serious that person was. "It's self defense. I kill him and if I start feeling better, then we know."

"This is beyond madness!"

Boucher spun and grabbed at John Boduf, who was creeping over the serving counter with his own knife in hand. Catching him by the collar, he punched the cook in the face and pulled him over onto the floor in the middle of the mess in a back flop that drove all the breath from his body in a loud cough and sent the blade sliding away. Henry snatched it up and pointed it at Holden. Boucher scrambled over the low wall into the kitchen. He slipped on the metal rail and nearly toppled over, but caught himself. The big man had never been agile and being sick only made him less so. He flopped over and pulled another knife off the magnetic strip on the wall before anyone could protest. He returned to the mess room, brandishing his serrated weapon in a clenched fist.

Jack and Kevin tried to crawl around to help Boduf, but Henry jabbed at them. "Leave him!" The pair shrank back to cover behind another table.

"What do you think you're doing?" Noah shouted. "Stop, before you do something you can't take back."

Both Brewsters' heads turned. Instead of the resentful glare he'd given Noah before, Connor's Brewster regarded him with silent pleading. Noah's Brewster, however, had taken on the appearance of a Kabuki actor. His face was deep red, and his mouth contorted in a toothy grimace below wild, black-ringed eyes. "Shut your fuckin' mouth, Cabot! I know all about things you can't give or take back. So does he." Brewster dug the knife into his twin's throat. "You really want to save him?"

His twin tried to say something, but Brewster shoved a fist into the small of his back, arching his spine and increasing the pressure on his throat. "You shut up, too. I heard everything I need to know from you."

Connor stepped forward. "You don't have to do this, William. Noah and I think we might've come up with at least part of a solution. We have a way to get everyone back to their own worlds," he lied. "Let him go and we'll discuss it like rational men."

"I'm the only rational one here."

"You're holding a knife to someone's throat, William," Noah said.

"*My* throat. If he's me and I'm him then it isn't murder."

"Don't be stupid," Connor said, letting the crowbar in his hand swing around in front of his leg.

"What are you going to do with that?" Brewster's breathing quickened and he seemed to tighten up like a predator crouched in the brush. "Henry. Boucher. Get the door." Boucher took a step to follow the order but stopped short when Noah tensed and raised his flat crowbar. The bosun's half grin said he was happy to have the chance to settle accounts with Noah. Noah tightened his grip on the tool. Boucher didn't move. His hesitation belied his concern about being outmatched, knife to long steel bar. He coughed and the smile died. His tongue worked behind his lips trying to refuse the metallic taste.

"Get the god damn door, I said."

"I don't want to hurt you," Connor said. "Everyone can live through this. We can all get back to our own—"

"I don't *want* to go back to my own anything. If my daughter's alive in your world, that's the reality I want. I figure I can't have that if he's standing in my way." Noah screamed for him to stop as Brewster pulled the knife across his twin's neck. It didn't drag, but slid with cruel smoothness, an elegant tool honed for the job it was set to do. Blood splashed over Brewster's hand and down his arm. He let go of his captive, whipping his knife hand at the floor, splattering red on the tiles behind him. He absently wiped his other hand on his pants while the man on his knees in front of him retched.

The twin Brewster's eyes were wide with panic as he tried to draw in air, but inhaled his own blood instead. He choked and spit and lurched forward. The sound of William's blood pattering on the floor punctuated the moments in between wet gasps. Holden rushed to catch the man clawing at his slit throat before he hit the floor. Brewster lunged forward, jabbing his long knife deep into Holden's eye.

With a shrill scream, Holden fell back, clawing blindly at the handle sticking out of his face. He fumbled against the sharpened edge of the blade rather than the handle, slicing his fingers open trying to pull it out. He screamed and scuttered backward toward his shipmates. One tried to help him, but Holden shook his head, unable to control his panic, and the crewman couldn't get a grip on the blood-slicked handle.

The room devolved from stunned silence to roaring chaos like an explosion. The crewmen scattered in all directions, desperate for cover ... for escape ... for help. Noah backpedaled as Boucher lunged at him with his knife. Connor swung his crowbar at the back of the bosun's knee, connecting solidly. Noah heard a loud pop as Boucher's knee was whipped apart by the tool. The man crumpled. Connor kicked him in the side as he went down, sending the giant crashing into a table. Noah grabbed Connor before he could take another shot and backed them away toward the door, trying to find enough perspective to make sense of what was happening. The room was a mess of indiscernible movement. Men shoved at one another in the rush to leave, two men fleeing through the serving window pulled at each other, trying to be the first through, slowing both their escapes.

Henry drove his knife up under Andrew Puck's ribs. A long line of drool slipped from Puck's slack mouth as he slumped over the senior deckhand's arm. Henry, unable to handle the sudden dead weight, dropped him to the floor, his knife lost under the fresh corpse. Slipping in the blood spreading over the tile floor, he fell on his hands and knees. He shoved Puck's body over, snarling like an animal, and ripped the butcher knife free, slashing at anyone who moved close enough.

Brewster had his fingers wrapped around David Delgado's throat while Connor's Jack and Kevin tried to pry his hands away. Noah's Twins crawled for the door. Noah helped Jack to his feet while Connor caught Kevin. They shoved the men out into the hall. Connor shouted, "Get to your cabin! Lock the door!" He turned back to the room and yelled, "Felix, Theo, get out of there!" as he dove in after them.

Felix and Theo were trying to drag William's body from where Brewster had dropped it. They pulled him a couple of feet, but Henry came lurching at them. Felix ducked under the swinging knife and tried to run in a shambling crouch toward the exit. Henry bodychecked him, sending them both crashing into a wall. Before Henry could stab him, the deckhand swung the heel of his palm up into his attacker's chin, rocking the man's head back. His neck cracked and popped loudly. Henry's eyes rolled as he swooned on weak knees. Theo drove his knee into the man's crotch and shoved him away as hard as he could. Henry collapsed to the floor, rolling in a pool of gore, cupping his aching balls in his hands and retching up gray oatmeal and bile.

Theo kept trying to drag his skipper's body toward the door, but his feet slipped and he lost his grip. Landing on his ass and elbows, he cried out in frustration. Connor and Noah grabbed him under his armpits and lifted. "Get out of here," Connor shouted. Theo left red footprints as he fled. Felix trailed behind, clutching his midsection as he disappeared through the door in a loping, stooped run.

"Brewster!" Noah shouted. He grabbed a bowl off a table and flung it at the wall behind the Old Man. He wanted to wing it at his head or his feet, but was afraid of hitting one of the others struggling with him. Brewster took the bait and fixed his eyes on his son-in-law. The reflected Jack and Kevin took advantage of the momentary distraction and pried Delgado out of his grip. Kevin shoved Brewster deeper into the room and the trio hobbled toward the door, Connor lending them cover as he followed, backing out of the room.

Noah, transfixed by Brewster's glare, shuddered in the chill of the Old Man's unabashed hatred. The Old Man's face was wild, but his eyes were empty—windows to a soul long gone dark. Malice poured off him like the fog that had transported their ship. The weight of the crowbar in Noah's hands grew and his fingers loosened. He tried to move his legs, but his feet were rooted in place.

Brewster raised his knife and took a step. William wetly groaned as he reached to grab at his twin's leg. Brewster hesitated, looking at a version of himself, half slaughtered at his feet. Then he bent over to finish the job.

Hands clamped down on Noah's shoulders, yanking him out of the fog swirling through his head. "Help me," Connor cried, dragging him toward the hallway. He let go of Noah and ducked under David Delgado's arm. His eyes widened with silent pleading for Noah to help take up the burden. Delgado was pale and choking, the red thumb marks where Brewster had been strangling him already purpling. His eyes rolled as he wheezed, desperate for breath. The man was checked out, focused solely on his throat. Noah slipped under his other arm and together they staggered out of the room. Connor pulled them to the left, toward the crew cabins. "This way."

Halfway to the door at the end of the hall, they found Felix doubled over. He steadied himself against the wall with a glistening red hand, his other arm clutched tightly to his stomach. His back hitched as he gasped for air. Crimson prints on the wall showed where he'd first stumbled and reached out to keep from falling. Whatever burst of energy he'd had in the mess room had scattered like smoke.

"You got David?" Noah asked.

Connor wrapped his free arm around Delgado's waist and pulled him tighter. "Got him. You help Felix."

Noah slipped out from under Delgado's arm to go help his shipmate. He grabbed Felix by the elbow and tried to pull him upright to get under an arm for support. Felix shrieked and pulled his arm away. The front of his jeans was soaked with blood. He kept his arm pressed tightly against his stomach. "Fucking hell!" Noah shouted. He took hold of Felix's free arm, being careful not to open up what the man was trying to hold closed. He guided Felix as fast as he could on the blood-slicked tile. Connor hadn't waited around for them to find their stride. They were only a few feet from danger and had a long way to go yet to find safety—if it was to be found at all. There was no waiting for others to catch up.

Their progress felt painfully slow and Noah waited for the feeling of something stabbing into his back or crashing over his skull as he attempted to make his escape.

Banging through the push bar door, Noah hazarded a glance over his shoulder. They'd left a trail of drizzled blood and smeared red footprints like a wretched Hansel and Gretel. There was no concealing where they fled.

Standing in the middle of the hall, Brewster watched them go with dead eyes. Noah saw him and despaired. He knew there would be no more reasoning with his father-in-law. The Old Man had broken in the worst way.

Connor dragged them through the opening and slammed the door closed behind them. He leaned Delgado against the wall and ducked into the first crew cabin he could find, reappearing a second later with a chair, jamming it up under the handle. It wouldn't hold for more than a few seconds. The chair was short and the legs wouldn't catch at the tile like they would on a carpet. Still, it was something. An extra second or two, maybe.

Through the slender window in the door, Noah saw Brewster walking toward them with a calmness that made his bladder want to loosen. The Old Man was in no hurry. There was nowhere they could run where he couldn't find them. Still, they ran.

They rounded a corner and banged through another door. Noah didn't look back again. The image of the ship's master was seared into his brain like a camera flash. Felix stumbled. Noah pulled him closer and the man cried out, his knees buckling. "Come on. A little farther. Stay with me."

Connor kicked open a door and shouted, "In here." Noah wanted to keep running, put more space between him and the Old Man. But Felix wasn't in any shape to push harder, and Delgado had also reached the limits of how far he could run. Brewster wasn't running to catch up to them because he'd already won. He'd struck first and left them limping. It wouldn't be long before the door opened and Brewster followed to spear the last of the wounded left on the battlefield. They had to find a place to hide and regroup. The drilling platform—at least the inhabitable parts of it—wasn't that big and whether they ducked into a room here or kept going, they couldn't evade him for long.

Noah followed Connor into the cabin and slammed the door shut behind him, throwing the dead bolt. But he knew they would have to put their backs against a wall and fight eventually.

29

The sounds in the hall outside went from loud panic to occasionally broken silence in very little time. Although they hadn't had to convince David to be quiet—he could barely get a breath, let alone make a sound—Felix was another matter. Connor was on his knees putting the finishing touches on a field dressing over the wound in Felix's stomach. Henry's knife had taken a deep bite when he tackled him. Although it tore halfway across his stomach, the cut had sliced through skin only, not muscle. Felix's viscera was contained. He was bleeding badly though, and was growing deathly pale. With the dressing, he might live, but he needed better tending than a torn bedsheet-as-bandage and reassuring words. He needed antiseptic, stitches, sterile dressings, and most of all, painkillers. They all needed better than they had.

Noah had lost his crowbar in the hall. He'd been so focused on getting away, he hadn't even heard it hit the floor. It might be right outside the door or still in the cafeteria for all he knew. Either way, it was out of reach. Aside from a desk lamp and a chair, there was nothing in the room he could use as an improvised weapon.

Checking the dead bolt on the cabin door for a third time, he tried to calm down, to tell himself they were safe. He tried to stop picturing Brewster killing his own reflection . . . killing himself . . . and think of an actual strategy for dealing with a situation he couldn't avoid much longer. The door was the final barrier between him and his father-in-law's rage. There was no walking away from the Old Man, choosing to pretend the hatred wasn't as near as it felt. The cabin door was the last thing standing between Noah and inevitability. And it wasn't built to withstand that kind of assault. The crew rooms were designed for privacy and to protect a few personal effects from casual theft. The door would only slow a motivated person from entering. Crowbars and oversized pipe wrenches were ready at hand nearly everywhere a person turned. Noah tried to remember if he'd seen a fire ax anywhere in the short time he'd been aboard. There had to be one. He tried not to picture it hacking through the door, before slamming into his chest. He tried instead to imagine the weight of it in his hands, reassuring and heavy. Long and deadly. But thinking of having an ax was as helpful as checking the lock again. It changed nothing. He put an ear to the door.

"What d'you hear?" Connor asked.

Noah shook his head. "Nothing." But that wasn't entirely true. In his head, he could hear the shouts and cries of frightened men. He could hear the sound of knife against flesh, and blood falling to the floor. He heard all the sounds of the last hour repeating in his head on a loop, threatening to drive him insane. As much as he wanted to stay silent, to pretend there wasn't a red line leading to their door and that being quiet was the same as being invisible, he needed to banish the sounds in his memory. But they lingered.

Anyone with his eyes open could see how to defeat the sickness. There were four who proved the point. *No. Three,* he thought. The fabled "last of the Holdens" had been stabbed in the face. And that meant Holden didn't prove anything anymore. If he wasn't dead, he was dying, and there was no one to help him. In the rush to save themselves, they'd left him behind. Him and John Boduf. Had he gotten away or did they leave him lying on the floor, too? Noah's gut called him back. The image of Brewster, waiting, pushed him away. Noah imagined his father-in-law returning to the cafeteria to finish what he started.

"How does he know Abby's alive in your world?" he whispered. "We were alone when you told me that."

"Your guess is as good as mine. I imagine everybody was talking about the same things 'round here. William probably said something, comparing notes. I want to know what gave him the idea he could choose my reality instead of yours. What'd make him think that's even possible?"

"I have no idea," Noah lied. From the moment he'd heard Abby was alive, he had imagined living in Connor's world with her and Ellie, having a second chance and being happy, but it was just a pipe dream. He hadn't thought through whether it might actually be possible. But fantasies of reunions and rebuilt lives were a distraction. They had Brewster and his collaborators to focus on. Thinking about being happy wasn't anything they could afford.

The lull in conversation emphasized how bad off they were. The best anyone could say about David Delgado's breathing was that it was labored. He wasn't dying, and they weren't trying to cut open his trachea to shove a pen casing in to help him get air. That said, each gasp was raspy and dry and sounded exhausting. He wasn't going to be doing any sprinting or fighting. He barely had the wind to sit upright.

Felix, who had been spry and on the mend before breakfast, was now on his back in a bunk with a Sharpie marker clenched in his teeth, trying to push through the pain of having been slashed open. He was off the clock as well.

Noah counted out in his head the number of crewmen still alive. Both ships had set out with a complement of sixteen able men. Noah's team left the ship with their eight strongest and arrived at the Niflheim with seven—Holden paying the toll along the way. Among Connor's shipmates, Puck and Brewster were definitely dead, presumably along with Holden ... again. Who knew about Boduf? Assuming he'd gotten away, that left twenty men total on the rig, including three killers. Noah wasn't just afraid that number would shrink; he knew it for a certainty. Brewster hadn't murdered a man only to have a change of heart and stop. He'd made a choice to cross the line. And he hadn't just stepped over it; he'd sprinted past without looking back. And now, he and his monsters stalked the halls. If there was any comfort to be had, it was that Boucher wasn't stalking anywhere—not after what Connor had done to his knee. Even if Brewster and

Henry brought him a crutch and some dope from sick bay, his career as a killer was over for the immediate future. Still, he was free to move around, however clumsily, and scout while the rest of them hid in bedrooms like children afraid of the dark. Regardless of Boucher, Noah and the others were in trouble and in poor shape to get out of it.

Brewster's blitz attack had left them separated and weakened in a matter of only a few minutes. Among the number in their room, Connor and Noah were the only ones who'd escaped without injury. Depending on what the Old Man brought for round two, though, their fitness might not matter at all.

"Where did you say you stored the guns?" Noah asked.

Connor's eyes narrowed. "They're in the rig manager's office."

"And you have the key to the gun locker?"

"There isn't one. A locker, I mean. Or a key."

"I thought you said—"

"I said I put 'em in a cabinet. It's just a regular ol' cabinet behind the desk. It locks, but I have no idea where the key might be. I been using a paper clip to close it up."

"They were storing a rifle like that?"

Connor shook his head. "There wasn't a rifle on the rig until William brought one. It's his."

Noah's inclination to think of the men from Connor's ship as reflections of themselves was more than a little accurate. Brewster had brought a pistol from the *Promise* for his own reasons, whatever they were. In Connor's world, that was a rifle. Like the view through a mirror, their worlds were the same but the perspective was off, flipped around. A gun, a rifle, a death, a life . . . and a living wife.

He shook his head to clear it of distractions. *Focus,* he told himself. Putting his ear to the door again, he held up a finger to ask his roommates for quiet. They obliged him as much as crushed windpipes and barely contained panic would allow. He heard nothing outside the room. Turning to Connor, he said, "I'm going out. I've got to get to those guns first."

"You think he hasn't found them? We been in here at least a half hour."

"I'm hoping he hasn't thought of them yet. I guess that's not likely, since he brought them both, in a way. But I haven't heard any shooting, so maybe there's hope." He wanted to take comfort from the observation, but couldn't. That Brewster hadn't shot anyone didn't mean he wasn't armed with more than a butcher knife. It only meant he hadn't found himself in a position where the firearm was his best weapon. Yet. "I'm going."

Connor stood. "I'm comin' with, brother." Felix tried to get up as well, but Connor held him down with a light hand. "Stay here. Stay quiet," he said. He bent to pick up his crowbar. The tool had never been far from his reach, even after they'd locked themselves in.

Noah smiled. He welcomed the company, even if he feared what it might mean for Connor to leave the room. He wasn't about to ask his friend to once again step in to do work that wasn't his responsibility. Brewster was the way he was, at least a little bit, because of choices Noah and Abby made together. She was gone and he remained. And that meant Brewster was his responsibility. "You got that paper clip?"

Connor pulled the twisted piece of metal out of his pocket. "It'd be irresponsible of me to just leave something like this lying around, wouldn't it?"

Noah unlocked the door.

30

The pair crept along as quietly as they could while still moving with urgency. Each little sound—footfalls, breathing, heartbeats—seemed to echo off the laminate floors and pre-fab walls of the corridor. Everything seemed deafeningly loud. Noah started at every odd creak and clang of the platform as it struggled to stay upright and intact against the assault of the weather outside. Without the sounds of men and machinery at work, the drilling platform groaned softly like a barely sleeping patient due for a dose of morphine.

Crouched and hugging a wall as if there was a shadow to find cover in the brightly lit hall, he was strung tight. His heart beat faster and his breath came quicker, dulling his ears. His skin prickled and his scalp tightened, drawing his focus from the corridor and back to his own body. He felt jittery and weak. His muscles had stiffened up and trembled with the exhaustion of having done nothing despite the adrenaline and lactic acid pumped into them. He felt vulnerable and betrayed by his body. If he didn't find Brewster soon, the effects would grow. His head would ache again and his reaction time and judgment would be dulled.

He felt like kicking himself for hiding as long as they had, letting the Old Man get out in front of them. He tried to rationalize it by telling himself Felix and David needed help before they could do anything else. But that wasn't true. David could have patched up Felix's stomach instead of Connor. Noah could have gone after the guns by himself. In reality, his mind simply refused to accept what had happened. He'd never seen anything as coldly vicious as what Brewster did. Not in person, anyway. Not outside of a movie theater where his unconscious mind could contextualize the unreality of what he was watching. This was reality. And reality crashed the system, shut him down for an hour of his life while he rebooted.

Connor paused in front of a door affixed with a plastic plate that read, MANAGER. Noah put his ear to the door and listened. It was quiet. He wasn't ready to trust his senses, however, and held his breath as he took another listen, trying to ignore his racing heartbeat. Nothing, again.

He pushed down on the handle. He wanted to burst through—kick the door in. If someone was waiting inside, creeping through slowly just gave them time to take aim. If no one was in the room, however, kicking it down and making a loud noise would give away where they were and what they were doing. Now that they were moving without leaving a trail of blood crumbs, there was no sense in crashing around and drawing attention. Unfortunately, he still hadn't found a fire ax. Unarmed, he needed to employ stealth and smarts before balls. Twisting to the side, he slipped through the opening.

"That's it," Connor whispered, pointing above the desk at the far end of the room. The cabinet doors hung wide open. Noah thought of a rhyme his daughter loved: *The cupboard was bare, and so the poor dog had none.* He'd worried about Brewster getting to the weapons before them, but their disadvantage weighed on him heavier now that it was certain. His knuckles popped as he clenched his fists.

"Oh, Jesus Christ!" Connor's face drained of color. He pushed past Noah and ran to the desk only to skid to an awkward stop just short of it. Noah followed more cautiously.

On the floor behind the desk lay Henry. A knife stuck out of his chest and the maroon stain that spread out from the blade covering half of the man's shirt seemed too perfectly formed, like a Halloween novelty. Odors of urine and sweat mingled with the heavy smell of wet pennies. Noah's stomach convulsed. He held in his vomit and backed away. He'd smelled blood and guts hunting with his dad in New Hampshire. That was nothing new to him. But along with those scents came the musk of a deer, the sweetness of pine and fresh air, and the knowledge that they'd cure that venison and save as much as they needed to make their money stretch through the lean winter without having to choose between heating oil and food. They'd even give a little extra to the food bank to help out others. Those were smells of survival. And he was in control of when and where he smelled them.

This was a fresh hell.

This was out of his control, and it threatened to take him offline again. But they couldn't afford another hour of half-catatonic indecision. He had to keep the system running.

It wasn't the smell in his nostrils that made him want to throw up, though. It was the fear. Fear infiltrated every part of him now. Not just his heart and his mind, but his spine and legs and hands. The room began to tunnel and pitch. He forced himself to inhale, taking in the polluted air. Tinctured as it was, it was good to breathe deeply. His vision broadened and he felt his feet firmly under him again.

"I don't get it," Connor said. "I thought Henry was with him."

Noah didn't want to say it. Unspoken, it could still be denied. He shook his head slowly, trying to deny it. But the body at their feet had volumes to say on the subject. He spoke as loudly and clearly as an emergency Klaxon telling them to run, abandon ship.

"He has to kill everybody in his way. First his twin . . . and then everybody from his own reality. When no one's left, he thinks he can pick his world."

Connor dropped his crowbar, chipping a hole in the tile. He growled in frustration through gritted teeth and pressed his fists into his eyes.

Noah's skin tightened at the sound. His head whipped around toward the door, still ajar, waiting to see the barrel of a rifle pushing through. He ran across the room and pushed it shut, throwing the dead bolt. He held a finger to his lips for Connor to be quiet, but his friend didn't see the gesture, still pressing at his eyes as if he could dispel the images assaulting his consciousness with physical pressure. Noah knew that wouldn't work. He'd spent an hour already trying.

"It doesn't . . . make any sense," Connor said. "Why would he think . . . What would make . . ." He doubled over and dry heaved. Noah tried to help him into a chair out of sight of the corpse, but Connor insisted on staying on his feet. Noah moved back to the desk, stepped over Henry's body and opened the drawers in the desk, rifling through papers and office supplies. The drawer on the bottom right was locked, but he popped it open with Connor's crowbar.

"What're you lookin' for?" Connor asked, drawing his sleeve across his mouth. He breathed a heavy sigh and stood up straight, seeming to have expelled what he needed in order to press on.

"I don't know. Something better than this." He set the crowbar on the desk and yanked the hanging file folders out of the drawer, tossing them on the floor. There was nothing under them. He'd hoped for a lockbox with a pistol or even a dangerous-looking letter opener. But there was nothing. If the manager of the rig had secreted away a weapon or even a bottle of whisky, he'd taken it when they abandoned the structure.

He glanced down at Henry. Beside the knife sticking out of his chest were two wounds. It appeared to have taken Brewster a couple of tries before landing the lucky shot that slipped in between Henry's ribs into his heart. What must have been running through the senior deckhand's mind as he was betrayed? *Why me? Why now? Is this all?* Whatever it was, it was too late for his thoughts to matter. Still, Noah wanted to know them. It seemed important for some reason. He might have his own final thoughts soon enough.

Bending over, he grabbed the knife handle. It was cold and tacky. He pulled. It stuck. A fresh sense of nausea bubbled up in his belly at the sensation of pulling at the tool, making him want to let go and give up.

There were other knives in the galley if he wanted a weapon that badly. He didn't need this one. Still, he pulled harder until it came free with a wet, grating sound—metal scraping against gristle and bone. He stood upright and stared at the blade in his hands, knowing what it had done, wondering if it was possible for an object to develop a taste for the uses to which it was put. Noah needed something to help him do the things he wasn't sure he was capable of by himself. A talisman for violence. Still, it felt wrong in his hands, like an artifact from another civilization that had been designed not only for purposes he couldn't conceive, but for an entirely other biology. It felt like something holding him, ready to do wrong, like he was the tool, not it.

He set the knife on the desk and opened his fingers. The tacky blood pulled at his skin as if the thing wanted to stay in his hand. It wanted him to possess it, to put it to its new uses. As much a likelihood it was that he would have to do violence, he decided he didn't want to do it with this tainted thing. It felt too eager for the work.

"You okay?" Connor said. "You still with me?"

"I'm here."

"You were starting to worry me. You had a look on your—"

The lights went out and Connor's thought died on his lips. Noah heard what sounded like the other man tripping over something heavy and hitting the floor hard. He stumbled backward over Henry's feet as he tried to get away from the desk, get away from whatever was in the dark. He sought the reassurance of a solid and unmoving wall at his back. He banged his head on the empty cabinet behind him, barking incoherently at the pain as he ducked underneath.

Something caught around his ankle. He imagined fingers closing around his leg as Henry's corpse pulled itself up, blank eyes fixing him with hungry malevolence. He jerked his foot away and heard a clatter of plastic on the floor. He was caught up in a telephone cord, not a dead man's hand. It was hard to dispel the nightmare image from his mind as he struggled to unwrap the cord from around his ankle. His heart pounded harder as a fresh wave of adrenaline surged through his body. He forced himself to stand still against the wall and wait for his panic to subside. In his conscious mind, he knew he was alone in the room with Connor and Henry's corpse, but his brain screamed that danger had arrived and it was time to fight. He listened for the sounds of someone coming through the door. His ears strained to hear the clack of a rifle bolt being thrown. But all he heard was Connor's quick breathing and his own blood pulsing in his ears. Outside the office door, the faint sounds of crewmen shouting in alarm echoed in the halls. He sympathized. He wanted to yell at them to be quiet. *This is what Brewster wants. He wants us to panic, to leave our hiding places so it's easier to find us. Because he wants to kill us all.*

It still didn't feel like a sane belief to hold, let alone embrace and make decisions using it as a basis. But proof was lying on the floor in the mess hall and on the floor in front of him in the dark and who knew where else. In the space of twenty-four hours, anything had become possible. The worst things imaginable were now probable.

"Why haven't the backup lights come on?" he whispered.

Connor panted. "I don't know. Lights've always worked 'round here. We never set up a detail for anyone to check and see if the emergency gennies were workin'."

Noah untangled his foot from the phone cord and crept away from his hiding spot, following his friend's voice. He gave both the desk and Henry a wide berth. Narrowly avoiding a low black shape he assumed was the overturned guest chair that had tripped Connor, he still turned his ankle, stumbling over something else unseen underfoot. He went to a knee instead of trying to stagger and stay upright, risking a sprain or worse. He knelt still for a moment, trying to manage his frustration. With the lights on, he was outmatched; in the dark, he was utterly impotent.

"I know where we can find some flashlights," Connor said.

"Flashlights seem like a bad idea. Holding one sounds a little like wearing a target."

"What if *he* has a flashlight?"

"If he's got a light, then we'll be able see him coming."

"Yeah? It's not like he's putting himself in any danger carrying one around; we can't shoot back at him, you know."

Connor was right. The dark would put the Old Man on better footing against men who knew how to easily navigate the rig's corridors—find its hidden places.

Another faint scream echoed in the hall.

Maybe it was just meant to increase their panic and

make them run into the trap. Either way, they had to keep it together.

Noah pushed himself up and crept carefully toward the door. Hunched over with his arms out in front of him, he felt his way past the guest chair until he met the wall. He knocked against an empty coat tree, catching it before it could topple. Setting it upright, he moved to the side and brushed his hands over the smooth wood of the door, searching for the door handle. The faint click when he pushed it down made him suck a breath through his teeth that was louder than the sound of the catch releasing. He pulled the door open a crack and tried to peek out into the hall. It was as dark as the office. As dark as he imagined the entire drilling platform was. It was daylight outside, but inside, without windows, it might as well have been midnight. *Hell,* he thought, *midnight outside with the moon and stars would be brighter than this.* More shouts and a crash.

"All the emergency lights are out. You know where the generators are?"

Connor stumbled over to Noah, not wanting to have the conversation across the room. "Well, yeah. I know where everything is," he whispered. "It's dull as dirt living here. I take walks."

"Show me where, then. If the Old Man wants it dark, I want light."

Connor fumbled past him into the hall. Noah followed, holding on to his shoulder.

31

Connor and Noah fumbled along pitch-black corridors for a few minutes, trying to both make forward progress and not give themselves away, until a sound brought them to a halt. From around a corner, they heard something irregular and hollow. Thumping. Each impact accompanied by a breath of exertion. Connor stopped, holding out an arm to hold Noah back. For a moment, they listened while it continued, staccato and arrhythmic. *Thump. Thump. Thumpthump.* "What is it?" Noah whispered. The shape that was his companion shifted in a way he chose to interpret as a shrug. The silent language of shades wasn't something he had the luxury of learning at his leisure. They had to interpret hand signals and body language despite the near total darkness through which they navigated.

He stared ahead, trying to distinguish between hues of black in the hall. He thought a somewhat darker patch to their left suggested another bend in the corridor. Noah's eyes played tricks in the gloom. Gradations of darkness that seemed to suggest obstacles or turns in the path never materialized. He felt worse than blind; he felt deceived by what slight eyesight he did possess.

Another thump echoed. This one was followed by a muffled crack and a long sigh. Noah stiffened as his imagination filled in the blanks his vision couldn't. Connor raised a hand in the dark and pointed in the direction they'd come in an exaggerated pantomime of "go back." Noah shook his head, trying to say he didn't want to find another way. The gesture was too slight to be seen and Connor, reversing direction, bumped into him. Noah grunted and clapped a hand over his mouth.

"Who's there?"

Noah's muscles tightened. Boucher's voice carried around the corner. Running wasn't an option, not unless he wanted to knock himself out again, dashing into a wall or an unseen door.

"God damn it! Who's there, I said?" Heavy, even footsteps moved toward them, as if the bosun could see despite the gloom.

"It's Boucher. *Your* Boucher," he whispered to Connor.

"How do you know that?"

"Listen. He can walk."

Connor stood up and said, "Serge? Is that you, brother? It's Connor."

"Come out where I can see you." His voice was low and his footsteps slowed.

"What are you doing, Serge? What was that sound?"

"Sound? Oh, that. They're right. I feel better already."

The blanks filled in—the thumping, the crack, and the sigh. In his mind, Noah saw an image of Boucher kneeling over his reflection, bashing his head against the floor until it split between his hands. The man at arm's length letting out a final breath as the last of his life was smashed against tile. He imagined he saw the other Serge's hands, dripping wet with the work. All this he gathered from sound. *This is what it's like to be a bat.*

He ducked to the opposite side of the hall and waited, staring into the darkness. The void shifted and a figure emerged, larger than he remembered. It moved like smoke, pulling apart from the blackness and shifting back into it. He felt the weight of Connor's crowbar in his hands. In his excitement to get to the generators, he'd almost left behind both the knife *and* the crowbar. Once he clumsily located the bar, he stopped looking. The knife wasn't anything he wanted to have with him—no matter how much he could have used it. It was tainted.

"Someone with you?"

Connor said, "Just me. What do you mean, 'feel better'?"

The shade stopped. Although all of the men in Connor's crew had lost weight from rationing food and inactivity, the bosun seemed to loom as large as ever. The shadow shifted, seemed to grow slightly thinner. *He turned,* Noah realized. Serge had been tracking his own shadow moving in the darkness until Connor drew his attention away. He waited for the next echo that would bring his form into focus.

"The other one. Get rid of him and it feels better."

"Jesus, man. What did you do?"

Boucher's voice changed from soft to hard. "He came into *my* room. He tried to get me first."

Noah lunged at the sound. He connected hard with what felt like a hip. Something struck him in the back of the head, an elbow maybe, and he saw bright stars. The crowbar slipped from his hands and went clanging down the hall. His momentum carried him forward and he and the big man hit the wall hard. He fell away and heard Boucher collapse with a grunt a few feet to his right. He thought for a second about going after the bar. But he knew he'd never find it in time. The bosun was going to be on top of him in a second. He thought, *one more mistake like that . . .* but looking for the thing would be the mistake that was his end. There would be no others to follow. He had to let it go.

He scrambled in the direction where he thought the mirror Boucher should have been, throwing all his pent up adrenaline and fear into keeping the giant man down, but found only empty floor.

He glimpsed a blur in his peripheral vision right before the bosun's boot connected hard with his ribs, stealing the air from his body and any sense of orientation he'd enjoyed. The room became a gravityless void in which he floated unmoored to anything but the kick that had launched him. He crumpled around the boot. Serge tried to draw back his foot for another blow, but Noah held on despite the breathless agony of the first kick. He heard a solid hit and the bosun let out a groan. Serge tried to step back but Noah clutched at him tighter, until the big man fell. Reminiscent of what had first alerted them to Serge Boucher's presence, the hollow gourd thump of his skull hitting the floor carried up and down the hallway like a shot. The man sighed and lay still. Noah crawled up his leg, ready to repeat the sound by banging his head against the floor. Connor intervened, pulling him away.

"Let me go," he said, taking a ragged breath. All the bottled up history of antagonism and poor treatment at the hands of the deckboss rushed into his head like hot blood. He wanted to take his shots and punish the man. Connor fought to hold him. Although weakened by months of deprivation, he was still strong. By the time Noah broke free, he'd come back to his senses. Mostly.

"Stop, man," Connor said. "He's out."

Shame burned in Noah's chest. He wanted to protect the crew. But he wanted to rescue some of them more than others. Boucher was low on the list of souls to save. However, this wasn't the Serge Boucher who had turned down Noah's OT requests or belittled him in front of his friends. This wasn't the man who had dropped him over the side of the *Arctic Promise* onto the ice or who threatened to beat him up after dragging him back on board. They were the same, but their histories were different. He was a reflection. This man was not responsible for what the other one had done, even if he was his reflection. And based on what they'd heard while creeping up on him, he'd already taken care of the other version of himself.

Noah wrenched his elbow out of Connor's hand. Connor stepped away, his shade fading into the deeper darkness. Noah had a feeling of déjà vu. Seeing the black shapes, watching them out of the corner of his eye as they flitted past was like trying to track Boucher or Connor in the dark hallway. What if *they* were the shapes now? The lights weren't really out, but they were ghosts in someone else's reality. Yet a third world of men struggling to break free of what held them. The darkness was what they were now.

He rubbed at his eyes. "Enough of this shit. I want to get the lights on." Noah felt his way along the wall. His shoes squeaked on the wet floor as he passed what remained of his Boucher.

32

The transition from the accommodations block to the working area of the drilling platform was as dramatic in the dark as it had been in the light. A long, straight hallway bridged the gap between the living quarters and the industrial area of the rig. If they were caught out in a spotlight in that hall, there was nowhere to go. No doorways, no windows, just a straight corridor with a watertight bulkhead door at the end. It was installed to isolate the crew from the hazardous substances beyond, but would serve as a perfect obstacle for a quick escape from danger on this side. It had dog locks like on board ship that would take time to open. Only slamming it shut could be done in a hurry.

When Connor opened the door, Noah felt like someone pressed a rag soaked in gasoline to his face. The stench was thick and the air even tasted bad on his tongue. Although the industrial area smelled of crude oil and sulfur before, the odors had intensified. The day before, he had been on the verge of total exhaustion, his throat and lungs already burning with frozen exertion, and he hadn't been paying attention to how unpleasant it was to breathe on a drilling platform. His mind had been on his toes and fingers and he hadn't taken a full measure of how a place like the Niflheim smelled. And of course, it would, given the nature of the work. He'd just been happy to be inside. A day later and sightless, the powerful stench of what the roughnecks pulled out of the earth was overwhelming.

Noah tugged on Connor's shoulder, asking him to stop. His guide paused and leaned back, the silent language of the unseeing becoming ever more fluent between them. "Is that smell normal?" he whispered into Connor's ear. He tried breathing through his mouth in an attempt to suppress his gag reflex. Still, the tinctured air made him feel sick to his stomach. Crude oil, machine grease, and smoke combined in a potpourri only a native of the most hellish underworld could enjoy. He wondered why it would continue to smell as bad as it did. Shouldn't the smells dissipate with disuse? The answer, of course, was that no one had come to relieve the rig of what it had pulled up from the ocean floor before the crew abandoned it, and Connor's band of refugees weren't drilling roughnecks. Every drop that had been collected had been left neglected, corroding the machines, eating its way out like a demon removing the circle of salt that bound it, one grain at a time.

"Nope. That's nothin' at all like normal. The place stinks, yeah, and you get used to it, even. This, I am *not* used to." Connor led Noah another step down onto a landing before stopping again. He patted Noah's hand. Noah released his shoulder and waited. He listened as Connor moved deeper into the room, his footsteps making wet sounds like walking on a damp sidewalk after a heavy rain. He heard the man sniff and gag. The footsteps moved farther away and Noah tried to rein in his panic. Suppressing the urge to cry out, he knelt down and touched the floor with a pair of fingers. Bringing them up to his nose, he flinched away from the odor. They were covered in a slick film of something horrible. He wiped his fingers on his pants and immediately regretted it. Just standing in the room made him feel filthy down to the roots of his hair.

A few seconds later, he heard wet footsteps returning. In his conscious mind, he knew it was Connor, but instinct told him to get away and hide. Connor's voice emerged from the blackness, easing some of his tension. "Where are you?"

"Same place, over here. Where'd you go?"

Noah felt Connor grip his wrist and press something into his palm. "Look, I know you don't want to use these, but we're out of options. This blind leading the blind shit is slowing us down, and we don't even know what we're walkin' into. We need to *see* if we're going to get the lights back on without killing ourselves. Living quarters are pretty easy to get around in. It's all just halls and doors. But the industrial deck is chock full of dangerous shit goin' in all directions. I don't want to escape being murdered just to fall in a well bay, if you follow me. We don't need to keep 'em on, but I can't find my way by feel any farther than this room right here."

Connor was right. Being right wouldn't keep them from getting shot if Brewster saw them coming, but it would keep him from walking into a low valve and opening a fresh gash in his head or stumbling off the edge of a catwalk into a waste pit. "I'm with you." He felt along the device for the switch. His thumb traced a small rubber circle and, holding his breath, he pressed it, waiting for the gunshot that would follow. A flash of white light shone at his feet. He doused it immediately and traced his fingers along the shape of the tool in his hands, surprised by the bend at the top. "What the hell?"

"Huh?"

"It's bent."

"Oh, it's one of those ninety-degree lights. You stuff it in a work vest pocket or something so you can work with both hands while you use it. They're in boxes all over in case the lights go out, or you just need to get under something, I guess."

His pupils had dilated so much in the complete dark that a light shining away still resulted in large purple circles hovering in the dark after he doused it. Straightening his wrist, he lit the flashlight again, this time shining it ahead of him into the room. The view was still as foreign as before. Man-sized pipes rose out of the floor, extending up and bending away along the high ceiling before disappearing into the walls. Everything was painted autumn colors of yellow, orange, and red in what Noah assumed was a pattern someone somewhere understood. But not him. Maybe red meant something dangerous, but everything else was a mystery. The only answer he had was that this was a drilling station. They pulled raw petroleum out of the ocean floor to ship to be refined elsewhere. Petroleum that was now coating the floors.

"Where are we?" Noah asked.

"This is a pump room. The main generators and switch room are over that way, other side of the well bay. We can cut through that room to get there." Connor pointed to a massive white steel door twice as tall as either of them. While it had likely been designed to facilitate the movement of behemoth machinery, it gave the appearance of a workplace for unknowable cosmic monstrosities like in the pulps his grandfather had given him as a kid. Noah started off toward the doors, holding his free hand around the light lens, trying to focus its shine down to the area exactly in front of him. That he hadn't already been shot or stabbed was good enough evidence they were alone. Still, he felt the need to minimize his visibility.

Noah doused his light and pulled up on the bar locking the door in place. It screeched in its metal guides as he lifted the end out of the floor. Clear of the hole below, the door swung a few inches under its own weight before creaking to a stop. He pulled it open another couple of feet before stopping it. They didn't need more than a narrow space to slip through and Noah didn't want to make any more noise than he had to. There wasn't a single god damn thing on the installation that had been built to be silent.

He tried to angle his body through the opening but the fumes and stench pushed him back. He couldn't stop gagging at the overwhelming rotten egg odor of the room beyond. He shut his eyelids tight and backpedaled away from the assault until a standpipe behind him painfully halted his retreat. Fluid rushed around his feet, splashing onto his shins. The door hadn't swung open because of its weight, but because something behind it had pushed. And it made him want to run, out of the room, right off the rig, and across the ice back to the *Promise*. He didn't know much about the oil drilling business, but he watched the news and had seen videos posted online by environmental activists worried about spills in the Arctic. He knew the shit soaking through his pants legs was highly volatile as well as toxic.

"Jesus Christ!" Connor shouted. He clicked on his flashlight and Noah braced for the explosion. The oil didn't ignite, however. Connor pulled the door open wider and shone his light into the room. He doubled over and vomited into the sea of viscous black shit flooding out around their feet. Noah pushed himself forward despite his instinct to flee, and pulled Connor away from the door.

"We gotta get out of here." The men backtracked toward the stairs to the dormitory. Noah wasn't sure what scared him more, the toxic pool they were splashing through or the darkened hallways of the living quarters they were running toward. Against Brewster, he had a chance. There was nothing to do about the tide of crude oil but run.

They climbed and pushed through the waterproof door, dogging it behind them, sealing off the industrial section of the platform. Noah gasped for fresh air and found none. Although they'd locked off the polluted area behind them, he was soaked below the knees in highly combustible fuel that smelled like Hell. Connor's choking echoed up the hall. Noah felt dizzy and sick. He wanted to stick a finger down his throat to purge the feeling, but the sickness wasn't in his stomach or guts. The poison was in his nose and his throat and lungs. It was on his pants and soaking through his boots into his socks.

"How the hell could that have happened?" he said. His voice was raspy and his words came out in a painful hiss. He shined his light on his legs trying to see how much of his clothes had been stained. How much of him would erupt in flames if he met an errant spark.

"Ruptured tank, maybe."

"Could it have been done from a control room?"

Connor shook his head. "There's no purge button, if that's what you mean—installing something like that would be insane. I don't know exactly how they refine this shit, but I do know the rig is designed to burn off excess natural gas through a vent and crude oil shouldn't ever spill out like that. It's dangerous as all hell. That ain't ever supposed to get out."

"Brewster couldn't have had time to uncouple a pipe fitting and dump a tank, even if he found his way to the room ahead of us. That's heavy work and he's been too busy."

"Shit's been breaking down left and right for a while. My guess is all he had to do was turn off the gennies—or send Henry to do it. That coulda been the last straw. Power to the pumps might've been the only thing keeping those tanks from filling up with pressure and bursting. I don't know. What I know for certain is, we can't turn 'em back on now. Forget about the oil; if even the *vapor* ignites, it could flash back. A single spark would send the whole place up."

Before Noah could ask if it was possible to flush the industrial area, clear out the spilled crude, he heard a shot and squatted low as if he could dodge bullets. The sound had echoed out from another hall, coming from behind at least one closed door, but even muffled it made him want to duck and run. He fumbled to turn off his light and, when it didn't go dark the first time, thought seriously about smashing it against the rail running the length of the wall. A second try darkened it, however, and the men stood in quiet shock waiting for the next shot. A closer shot, followed by the sound of a bullet hitting the wall or the door . . . or a body. What they heard instead was screaming. Screaming followed by another bang from a distance. And then silence.

"If we can't stop him, we've got to get everyone off the fucking rig," Noah said. "Get everyone we can find and get to the *Promise*. From there we can make a plan how to deal with Brewster and flush out the spilled oil. It's not safe to stay here anymore."

"Boucher and Henry are out of the picture. It's us against him."

"There's still the oil. It ignites like you said, the whole place is fucked. If that happens, I want the only person aboard to be the Old Man. We need to fall back to my ship and then come back to clean house after we get everyone else out."

"My ship is closer," Connor said.

Noah shook his head. "You forget your ship is nipped? Plus, half my crew is already on mine. They need to know what's going on. We're going to *my Promise*."

Connor didn't put up any more of an argument. Instead, he fell in behind Noah and they started up the long hall, toward the killing.

33

After the first two cabins, it was clear what finding an open door meant. Staring down at Heath's body, Noah clenched his fists, feeling the nails dig into his rough palms. He told himself that without a universal key, he couldn't have locked in the men too sick to get out of bed to protect them. He had saved two crew members. He hadn't gone around rousing bedridden men trying to get them to lock their doors, though. And now it was too late.

He tried to tell himself he wasn't responsible. While he knew it intellectually, emotionally it still felt like a failure. It felt like finding Connor dead on the cargo deck all over again. Dead because he didn't do something himself that he could have done. *Should* have done.

Shining a flashlight on Heath made him seem unreal. His skin was too waxen, the blood painting his throat and chest, too bright, too vivid.

His eyes open and fixed, throat open and wet, heart stopped, there was nothing to do but cover him.

Theo, in the room they'd first visited, was in the same state—beyond concern.

Noah was almost ready to give up and suggest they head for the *Promise* alone when he heard the faint rustle in the closet. He froze. Brewster was stalking the halls, slitting the throats of every man too weak to rise from his bed, not hiding in closets like some childhood nightmare.

He quietly pulled the door closed and held a finger to his lips. He then pointed to the left of the closet. Connor tiptoed around the side, waiting to follow his friend's lead. Noah took his place squarely in front of the glorified locker and whispered as loudly as he dared, "Who's in there?" He heard shuffling movement and then silence. "It's Noah. You're safe. I'm going to open the door."

"Don't," Jack said from behind the door. "Find your own fuckin' place to hide."

Noah let out a breath he didn't know he was holding. "We're leaving, Jack. It's not safe to stay here. We're heading back to the *Promise* to figure out how to deal with the Old Man. Come out."

More silence. The door cracked open and Jack peeked out, squinting against the light. "No shit it's not safe. What was your first clue?" Noah suppressed a smile at the absurdity of Jack's uncontrollable sarcasm. He wanted to laugh and fully let himself feel the relief that he'd found at least one living crew member, but the threat of the man stalking them weighed too heavily on his conscience. Instead, he pulled open the door and grabbed Jack by the shoulder, giving it a squeeze, assuring him they were in this together as much as convincing himself that the man was real. Jack held a hand up to his eyes. "I don't want to go back out in the cold."

Noah considered telling Jack about the spill. He didn't imagine it would make him any less afraid of another trip across the ice. "You know where anyone else is hiding?" he asked.

Jack tilted his head toward the door. "Kevin's two rooms over, I think. That's where he said he was going. We figured if the Old Man had already been here, he might not come back looking right away."

It was as good a plan as any Noah and Connor had conceived so far. "Anyone else?"

Jack shook his head.

"Okay," Noah said. "Grab Kev and meet us in the gear room where we stowed our stuff yesterday. You copy? We're going to find as many more men as we can and then we're leaving."

"No way. I told you, I'm not going back out there. We can take him out if we all go after him together, right? He's not the fuckin' bogeyman or some shit."

Given what Brewster had accomplished in very little time, Noah wasn't so sure. He didn't believe in supernatural evil, but then again, he hadn't believed in a lot of things earlier this week that he now had seen firsthand. Connor, standing behind him, was his strongest vaccination against blanket denial. For a moment, Noah considered it. The halls were narrow. There wasn't room for more than two or three of them to stand abreast. They were mostly blind and Brewster had guns. Trying to bum rush him would end up a turkey shoot. Someone, likely more than one of them, would die trying and Noah wasn't willing to sacrifice anyone else. All he could think of was getting away to safety.

Afterward, they could come up with some kind of plan. As a strategy, it was only half-formed, but he hadn't had a moment to think of something better. He was reacting to Brewster, not taking his own steps. Just like always.

"You volunteering to be in front for the bum-rush? You bulletproof?" Jack's eyes widened and he shook his head. "Then go get Kevin and meet us where I told you to."

Connor pressed his flashlight in Jack's hand. "Only use this in little bursts, off and on, so you can get an idea what's ahead of you. Don't leave it on. And try not to make any sound." Jack stood frozen in place.

Noah gave him a little push, but the man didn't move. "I'm not dragging you out of here. You've got to move if you're coming with us."

"I'm fuckin' scared, man." Jack and his best friend were slender, wiry goofballs. But they worked hard and had proven themselves on the cargo deck more than once. The Twins weren't the toughest guys he knew, but they weren't weak by any means. In that instant, however, Jack seemed to lose ten years; he looked like a little boy afraid to go on the big ride. It tore at Noah's resolve like sharp claws.

Noah grabbed his wrists and squeezed again, trying to reassure himself as much as motivate Jack. "Good. Stay scared. Stay alive. Get dressed and wait for us. If you hear anyone try to come through the door without . . . knocking three times, brain 'em with a wrench or something. You got that?"

Jack nodded fast and turned for the door. Connor caught him by the arm. "Whatever you do, try not to make a spark."

"The fuck, dude? What do you mean, 'a spark'? Like a *spark* spark?"

"Trust us," Noah assured him. "Fire bad."

Jack slipped through the doorway as if the turn in the conversation scared him more than being caught out. Noah listened for the sounds of him collecting his best friend two cabins down, but he couldn't hear a thing. That was good. Jack was being careful—that was, if he wasn't paralyzed with fear right outside the door. The only way to find out was to get moving.

Connor pulled the stained sheet up over Heath's face. He whispered something under his breath that ended with "Amen." Noah didn't want to stop him praying, but they didn't have time to give every victim his due. They had to take their own advice and go.

In the hall, they found two more doors ajar. Noah didn't have the heart to do more than shine his light in each to confirm what he already knew and move on. One room was mercifully empty. The other, however, was the worst yet. Inside they found the reflected Twins. Brewster had shot them both. The room was a mess. Noah hoped that they'd put up a fight and got a good piece of him before going down. If he was hurt and licking his wounds, it might explain why they hadn't seen him yet. But Noah told himself he couldn't count on it.

Connor didn't repeat his last rites. Instead, he backed out of the room, closing the door. He tried his best to keep an eye behind them, but it was more difficult than before. The light, even in short bursts, undermined the slight adaptation of their eyes to the darkness. They couldn't make out shapes and distance anymore without it.

Around the bend was Connor's room, and hopefully Felix and David. Noah wanted to check other cabins for more survivors hiding in closets and bathrooms, but the rig was too big to do a thorough search for everyone, especially if some had retreated to areas beyond the dormitory. Noah struggled to think of a way to get a message to them.

He clicked his light on and off to get a glimpse of how close they were to the bend in the hallway. A glint of something high up caught his eye. He turned it back on and shined the light on the wall, finding a red fire alarm. "That's it," he said, pointing.

Noah peeked around the corner, tracking his light along the length of the wall looking for the alarm system pull handle. "If it has its own power source—a battery, not a gennie—it might still work, right?"

"Maybe. Who knows what works and what doesn't."

"Our ships are filled with redundant systems. Multiple backups for the engines and controls. Why wouldn't the rig be set up like that, too?" Noah found the alarm pull station halfway down the hall. It looked like the same kind he remembered his friends pulling in high school as a joke. He never thought it was funny, and his gut feeling now was to leave it alone. Respect the reason for it being there. But while it hadn't been installed for this exact situation, this was precisely the reason for its existence: to alert people in an emergency. "It's worth a try. Let's get Felix and David first and then we'll pull it. The strobes will help us see, and if the alarm is loud, maybe it'll deaden the sounds we make getting the hell out of here."

"It'll keep us and everyone else from hearing Brewster, too, you know."

"It's the only way I can think of to get the message to everyone."

Connor waited a beat and then said, "Let's go."

The men crept around the corner toward the room in which they'd first hidden. The door was jimmied open. Noah's head ached. He reached out and held on to the door jamb to ride out the new sensation. He thought he heard Connor ask if he was all right, but he didn't have it in him to answer. He handed the light to his friend and put his back to the wall. Connor let himself into the room. The retching sounds he made inside confirmed Noah's worst fear.

Rage bubbled up inside of him, pushing acid into his esophagus, making his chest burn and a spike of pain lance up his neck. He didn't want to leave the rig anymore. He wanted to find the Old Man. Find him and put him down. Mete out endless punishments for all the Old Man's sins until he couldn't play the Devil anymore.

Connor shook him, shocking him back to their present torment. That other thing—the one he'd felt overtake him back in the manager's office when he held the knife that killed Henry—receded again. Connor nodded toward the gear room. "Let's go."

Noah shoved off the wall. He'd come back. He'd come back and hunt Brewster down.

He reached for the handle on the fire alarm. He feared that it was as dead as the radios and the lights, and they'd have to keep stepping lightly, clicking the light on and off in a signal for *over here, shoot me,* while they cowered like mice trying not to wake the cat.

Connor grabbed his forearm. "It's just you and me. Do we need it now?"

"We haven't accounted for everybody. There are others still hiding." Connor nodded. Noah took a deep breath and pulled the alarm.

The fireworks started.

The strobe flashed a blinding white and a rhythmic Klaxon sounded that made both men wince and cover their ears. They had been in near silence so long with only their whispers and footsteps, the siren was a banshee wail that stunned them. A woman's voice boomed out of the red box.

"ATTENTION! ATTENTION! AN EMERGENCY HAS BEEN REPORTED. ALL OCCUPANTS WALK TO THE NEAREST STAIRWAY AND REPORT TO YOUR ASSIGNED REENTRY STATION."

Then it repeated. But Noah and Connor didn't do as they were told. They ran for the exit.

The flashing beacon light illuminated the hallway, but it also made their own movements feel like slow motion, half of time lost in the dark between pulses. It took precious seconds for them to overcome their disorientation. Noah hoped the unexpected assault on eyes and ears disrupted Brewster longer.

Although he didn't need it anymore, Noah couldn't bring himself to drop the flashlight. He wasn't letting go of this tool, no matter how useless. Gripping it like a relay baton as he ran behind Connor for the door ahead, he knew when he reached the finish line on the Niflheim, the longest leg of the race still lay ahead. And he would have to carry it all the way. But it was a good thing he kept it. The sun would be setting and they'd need a light on the ice.

The flashing beacon made the shadows in every nook and corner seem to shift and jerk along with them as they ran, threatening death and pain. He pushed on, thinking that if Brewster was having as hard a time making out what was real and what was shadow as he was, they might be able to make it at least outdoors. Once on the ice, Brewster was the least of their worries.

The platform shuddered and Noah stumbled. His feet hurt from the crude and chemicals that had soaked into his shoes, but he tried not to let it slow him down. In another second, the blast of heat from the explosion on the other side of the door would take him and his feet would no longer be a problem. The hall to the prep room was cool, though. It wasn't an explosion that had rocked them. Not yet anyway. He pressed on, even though he felt like he might finally be breaking. The culmination of everything that had happened was exerting too much pressure, and he was afraid his mind would give way to the same madness that claimed his father-in-law.

"Here!" Connor shouted, taking a hard right turn and wrenching the wheel on a metal bulkhead door. The bolts screeched as they slid free and he pulled it open. Noah dashed through. He paused, looking around, remembering where he was. One more turn to the left and they'd be at the change room.

Noah saw the shadow separate from the others only a split second before it caught him in the side, shoving him hard into a wall. His head banged against a low pipe. He had no breath and the blitz attack had overwhelmed his ability to react. He leaned against the wall just trying to get his hands up to defend against whatever came next, but they wouldn't respond. He hadn't realized he had more air to lose until the fist slammed into his stomach and he crumpled to the floor in a gasping heap.

"It's us!" Connor yelled, pulling the attacker back. Noah rolled over and kicked away from the figure looming over him. Sean Mickle's mirror reflection struggled with Connor, hands balled into fists and his face a snarl.

"Let me go!"

"Sean, it's us," Connor shouted over the sound of the Klaxon.

Noah rolled away from the wall onto his hands and knees. He fought to get a deep breath of air and failed, choking instead and shallowly panting like a dog in August. The realization that he'd dropped his flashlight alarmed him more than his inability to get enough oxygen. His heart raced as he pawed for it under the low equipment, searching the hidden spaces where it might have slid. His hands came back empty, caked with dirt and grime.

"I see who it is," Mickle said, staring down at him. His tone was pregnant with contempt. "He brought them here. It's *his* fault." He jerked forward, but Connor held on.

"I didn't know," Noah said. Barely able to hear himself under the alarm, he said it again. Abandoning his search for the light, he sat up on his knees, unsure whether to stand or lie down and wait.

"We're leaving," Connor said. "If you want to come with us, then stop and think about who your friends are." He let go of Mickle, shoving him away as he stepped in between the men. Connor extended a hand to help Noah to his feet.

"Those people were my friends," Mickle said, pointing toward the dormitory.

"Mine too," Connor replied. "And we can still save some of them. Do you know where Boduf and Yeong are hiding?"

Mickle hunched his shoulders. "I haven't seen anyone else since we left the quarters. Nevins and I were hiding in a pump room when the Twins ran through—not the real Twins—the ones *he* brought. Nevins went after them."

"*Real* Twins?" Noah said. "Jack and Kevin are as real as you are, asshole."

"Says the ghost."

Connor shoved at Mickle again. "Shut up, Sean. This isn't helping. What do you mean, 'went after'?"

"He's following to see where they go. And stop them if they try something."

Although he was happy to learn Marty—or a version of him—was alive, Mickle's interrogation was keeping them from their goal. Noah wondered what had happened in his world that had made him seem so different from his counterpart on Noah's ship. Where was the point of departure in their lives where the caring man Noah knew became jaded and hostile? Perhaps it was right here. Watching his friends be slaughtered had broken him like it was breaking everyone else. He wasn't the only one fighting whatever was trying to dominate his will.

Whether we live or die, this place will destroy us all.

Noah tried a different tack. "The Twins are going to the change room to get their gear on. The power failure caused a crude spill and we're all in more danger than from just Brewster. We're abandoning the rig."

Mickle's eyes widened as it seemed he got his first

whiff of the odor swirling around Noah and Connor and recognized it. "And how did the power just happen to go out, I wonder."

"We found Serge. *Our* Serge," Connor said. "He killed the other one of him in the hall near the causeway to the power station. It's possible his twin shut down the gennies before he got caught out."

"Good! That's another one *he* brought here out of the picture!"

"Enough!" Connor yelled. "What the hell is wrong with you?"

"I'll be happy to stand trial when we're safe on board the *Promise,*" Noah said. "Until then, I need you with me. Or you can wait here for Brewster and try to explain to him who's real and who's a copy. We're on the same side, Doc. We're friends in my world." But seeing him on his feet and energetic meant that friend was gone. This Mickle was the last. If Noah was going to stay friends with him, he had to win this one over. He held out a hand. Doc didn't take it. He looked afraid to touch him and took a step back. *Of course. In his world, I'm a dead man.*

Holding his hands up in surrender, Mickle took a step to the side. Noah walked past him, hoping the second officer would fall in line behind him and not bash him in the back of the skull. By the time he made it to the door of the change room, he figured Mickle was along for the ride, for a while anyway.

Noah grabbed the handle, and paused. He knocked three times, opened the door and turned to the side, gesturing for Mickle to go first. "I'm not in the mood to get sucker punched again. You set that trap, *you* go defuse Nevins."

Mickle pushed through the door into the room. Inside, the scene wasn't what anyone expected to find. Nevins was helping Jack and Kevin into fitted immersion survival suits. Unlike the Gumby suits on the *Promise,* these were not the loose, bulky emergency-only ones they'd worn to break up the ice. Somewhere between a survival bag and a wetsuit, they would actually be able to hike . . . or run . . . to the ship in these. Nevins looked over his shoulder at the trio standing by the door first with concern and then relief.

"We found these!" Kevin said, like a kid at Christmas, pulling on a pair of boots.

Jack pulled the zipper up to his chin. "Better than our shit. Warm, too. I'm already sweating."

Nevins nodded toward the back of the room. "They're in a closet back there." He hesitated, looking at Noah for a long moment before asking, "You guys find anyone else?" Connor shook his head and Nevins' face fell. *He* was the same as Noah's version. At least he seemed to be at the moment. He didn't look entirely well, either. That was good news for the man left behind on the *Promise,* and bad news for them both. If they lived through Brewster's madness, they still had to figure out how to stop the sickness. Even if that was only a problem for a minority of the men now.

Mickle looked at Nevins and cocked his head, silently asking what had happened to the plan. Nevins shrugged. "It's Jack and Kevin, man. What am I supposed to do, tie 'em up and work 'em over with a phone book?" Mickle pursed his lips and stalked away to find a Gumby suit in his size.

Noah walked over to Nevins and held out the same

hand he'd offered the second officer a moment earlier. "Thanks."

Nevins grabbed his hand and gave it a firm shake. "It's really fuckin' weird to see you, man. But it's *good* to see you. I hope you know what you're doing."

"I have no idea. But I'm working on it. I'm open to suggestions, if you have any."

Nevins tilted his head and half-smiled. "I'm just the mechanic. I follow orders; thinking is for officers."

"I'm glad you know when not to listen to them." He rolled his eyes toward Mickle.

Shaking his head, Nevins whispered, "It's not his fault. I guess you don't know, though. He hasn't been the same since they lost the baby."

Noah didn't even know he was married. That was it. In an infinite number of worlds, there was an infinite amount of suffering, and in each one was that one thing capable of breaking a person wide open.

34

They stood in a circle staring through the hatch at the swirling maelstrom of snow beneath them. Biting wind kicked up and stung their exposed faces. Connor cranked the winch, lifting the "elevator" out of the chaos. It seemed to refuse to come fully into view as it spun and whipped around at the end of its cable. Finally, Connor got it inside with them where it hung like a skeleton in a gibbet. It was dented and smashed. The platform underneath was completely missing. Kevin sat down heavily on a box in the corner of the room while Jack whispered that they were fucked. No one disagreed. Their ride down had been destroyed. Connor and Mickle pulled the cage in to take a closer look at the damage, but it was obvious from even a casual inspection that it wouldn't hold a single one of them. It was useless.

"I don't even know how something like this could happen. I've dropped this thing a half dozen times by accident," Connor said. "It can take the fall."

Mickle held his face in one hand like it was all he could do to keep his head upright. "Well, it didn't take

this fall. Good thing it happened before there was anybody in it and you had another 'accident.'"

"There isn't another one we can use?" Noah asked.

"No. People are meant to either land by helicopter
or board off a ship from the ladder gangways. But the
gangways fell off before we ever got here, so we jerry-
rigged this."

Noah's brow furrowed. "Fell off? I don't remember
seeing them."

Connor locked the winch in place, as if it mattered
whether the cage dropped again. "They're out there.
Snow's covered 'em up. This place . . ." He trailed
off. Noah got the gist: this was a place that consumed
things. It broke them down and made them a part of
itself. Connor's ship was in the process of disappearing
into the ice. The platform would follow it piece by
piece or maybe all at once. And so would his ship if
they didn't get away. There were so many things to run
from and almost nowhere left to run.

"We have to climb down the rebar ladder," Connor
said.

Noah pulled at the chest of his immersion suit. "With
the wind and snow, you sure we can all make it without slipping or being blown off that ladder?" He nodded toward Nevins. "He's in no condition to make that
climb even *without* a storm."

"We're screwed either way. I vote we go back to the
original plan. Find Brewster and take the fight to him."
Mickle slammed the hatch shut. The bang of the door
was louder than both the wind and the alarm, and
everyone in the room flinched as if a shot had been fired
directly at them. He looked like he'd just made his
point.

Noah glared at the second officer, tired of being challenged. "That was never a plan. Remember the spill? This is the only way to be completely safe."

"Safe?" Mickle shouted louder than he needed to be heard over the alarm. If he couldn't go hunting Brewster, he seemed to want to draw the Old Man to them.

"I can climb," Nevins said, cutting off the others before their argument progressed further. "And if I can't, I'd rather die from a fall than be murdered, I guess." No one argued with him. Noah understood; he'd rather die in an accident than at the hands of the man who'd been tormenting him for years for the crime of loving his daughter. Hell, in one version of reality, he'd done exactly that already. He wondered how much happier his life in Connor's world had been. The end coming when it had, sparing him from Brewster's abuse. Sparing him from watching his wife die—which, in Connor's world, she hadn't. She was alive, and now the reflected Brewster was dead, and it felt like a second chance at life. They could all be happy again. He squinted his eyes tightly shut and fought to stay in the present.

"No sense in talking about it anymore. Let's go." Connor snatched the rope from the box next to him and headed for the door to the ladder room.

"Wait!" Noah said. "What about the lifeboats?"

"What?" Mickle said, pausing in mid-stride. "You're fucking insane!"

"No I'm not. Hear me out. If we take the ladder, whoever goes first ends up freezing at the bottom waiting for everyone else. Maybe someone at the top loses his grip and falls and knocks another man off and they both get hurt or die. Or . . . we take the lifeboat. Strap ourselves in and release it. We all go at once like an express elevator."

"That's going to crash nose first into the ice," Mickle said. "It's made for diving into water, genius. You told me to trust you, but it sounds like you're trying to finish Brewster's work for him."

"What if it breaks through the ice and then we're trapped in it under water?" Kevin asked.

Noah sat heavily on a box and rested his head in his hands. "Fine. I'm all out of ideas. I guess we climb down and take our chances one at a time."

"No," Connor said. "I think it's worth a try. We're gonna get whiplash, but it's the fastest way down, not counting that." He pointed at the cage.

Mickle folded his arms and shook his head. "Count me out. I'll take my chances on the ladder."

"I don't think we should split up, but I can't force anyone to do anything," Noah said, pushing himself up off the crates. He wanted to plop right back down again. Stopping felt good. Sitting felt better. He didn't want to run anymore. But he knew if he didn't, it was an inevitability that death would find him in one form or another. If he wasn't shot, and didn't burn, he'd freeze. He had a new reason to live. That kept him standing. And it was the push that made him move to the door. "I'm taking a lifeboat. You go however you want and we'll meet you down there." He opened the door, turned, and said, "If we don't find you in twenty minutes, then just go on by yourselves." He didn't add what he thought should be obvious. If they didn't rendezvous within a few minutes at the bottom, it was because some or all of them didn't make it down alive.

Connor stepped through while Noah held the portal

open. Jack and Kevin followed. He watched Nevins and Mickle, waiting to see which exit they went for. Nevins gave a light pound on Mickle's shoulder with a fist and jogged off to catch up to the others. Noah raised his eyebrows and gave it one more moment. Mickle pushed his hands through his hair and groaned. "You're going to get us all killed," he said, pushing past Noah.

Noah regretted his idea as soon as they were standing outside, preparing to climb into the hard-shelled orange lifeboat. It wasn't hard to imagine what would happen to them inside whether or not the craft withstood the impact of a four-story plummet to the ice below. *We'll be strapped in,* he rationalized. He tried to comfort himself by focusing on structural integrity standards and safeguards designed around gravitational forces on the occupants during free fall. But images of 1980s PSAs featuring raw eggs and frying pans looped in his head. "This is your crew. This is your crew on Noah's Plan. Any questions?"

He climbed down the staircase beside the vehicle and peered over the railing into the void. It should have still been light outside for another couple of hours, but there was no sun. It wasn't behind black storm clouds or setting; it wasn't there at all. It was dark as night and Noah couldn't see the surface below.

Above him, Connor yelled, "Come on! This is your idea!"

Yes it is, he thought. He climbed like a man ascending the scaffold. Swallowing the lump in his throat, he climbed in and chose an empty seat near the center of the craft—the others had filled in the back, presumably farthest from the worst of the impact forces—and strapped himself in. In the aft-facing seat, he tried to find a calm center within himself, but was on the verge of hyperventilating.

Connor closed the hatch and spun the wheel, sealing the vessel. He took his place in the helmsman seat and asked, "Ready?" as he buckled himself in. Shouting to be heard over the two-tone alarm beacon indicating the boat was ready to drop, Connor's voice bounced off the solid walls of the boat, reminding them exactly how enclosed they were. Noah opened his mouth to suggest they trade places. Maybe he should be the one with his hand on the release lever since it was his idea. Before he could utter a sound, the harness holding him tightened, his stomach lifted, and he felt that sick sense of weightlessness before his brain caught up to the fact they were plummeting.

They slammed into the ice like a car hitting a brick wall. The sound of the shell rending in the collision echoed deafeningly inside the molded plastic interior of the vessel. The impact itself sent a jolt of pain up through his back into his neck and down both legs. The boat was normally self-righting . . . in the water. On the ice, it lurched and tumbled once end over end until it slammed onto its side with a massive jolt that wrenched the men's bodies in their harnesses.

The men shouted, unable to hold their voices through the fear and pain. Mickle's voice carried above the others, "God damn you, Cabot!" The escape boat slid across the ice with a grinding sound that blissfully deadened any further prayers for Noah's eternal punishment. At least it had stopped tumbling and was steady at a mostly upright angle. When it finally came to a stop and the grinding died into silence, the shouting started afresh. Noah unhooked himself from his seat and fell across the aisle into the empty chair, cracking his shoulder against the molded steel and plastic. His joint ached and it hurt to lift his arm, but nothing was broken. He set to work helping the others out of their restraints more gently.

Mickle shoved Noah away and rubbed his neck, while Jack and Nevins both pressed their hands against the sides of their heads, squinting against the painful ringing that lingered in everyone's ears. Noah feared something bad had happened to Kevin until he saw the man turn his head to look around. He was stunned, but alive. Jack helped him out of his harness. Connor freed himself from the helmsman's seat. His nose was split across the bridge, blood covering his upper lip and running down his chin. He'd broken it despite his stiff-armed attempt to avoid smashing his face into the steering wheel.

Connor unsealed the door and it fell open. A gust of freezing wind blasted into the compartment, pushing him back before he regained his footing. He pulled down his snow goggles and shambled out of the side-ways opening. Noah stayed behind to help the rest climb out. Connor, on the other side, guided them safely onto the ice. Noah emerged last, and only Connor offered a hand to help him down.

The fall had rattled them all down to bone and marrow, but they were all alive.

Noah looked around, trying to orient himself. The Niflheim was behind them. Large as ever, but dark. No longer like the city he'd first seen, now it was like an ancient structure left behind by another civilization. He found himself happy to be leaving it—perhaps not happy, but unburdened of the oppressive hostility he hadn't realized he was feeling until he was no longer aboard.

He turned and looked for a sign of his ship—a light in the distance or even a dim shape along the straight line of the landscape, the way they'd first noticed Connor's ship. But both vessels were miles away and the snow was blowing in the strong wind, making it hard to see into the distance.

"Which way?" Mickle shouted.

Noah didn't know. "How do you find the way to your ship?" he asked Connor.

"I follow the sun. It rises right over it and tracks back to the Niflheim at the end of the day." He raised his hands to the sky as if Noah hadn't noticed that there was neither sun nor moon to orient them. The wind kicked up snow, but the sky above was clear and dark. A band of the Milky Way shone above, but the stars weren't familiar. There was nothing in the sky he could recognize and use to keep them on the path. They could set out and become irretrievably lost, freezing to death, or stay put and wait to be murdered. There were no good choices left.

Connor pointed to a spot under the platform where a bashed part of the elevator cage still rested. He turned and tracked his finger away from the rig until settling on a point on the horizon to the left of the emergency boat's bow. "When I step out of the elevator, I walk between those two pylons, that way. It's a straight shot right to my ship. I don't know how we'll keep a straight line without something to fix on though."

"It's better than nothing. It was more or less a direct line from the *Promise* . . . my ship to yours. We changed course only a little from there. Let's head toward your ship, and the closer we get, the more likely we'll see my ship's lights. We can adjust our bearing once we do." Before Mickle could break in again and ask a question undermining his reasoning, as simple as it was, Noah started off. The others fell into line behind him.

He pulled up his face mask and set the snow goggles over his eyes. He was better equipped for the walk to the *Promise* than he'd been leaving it. They'd survived the easy part: the first step. Now it was time to run.

35

While Noah was physically tired, his mental and emotional exhaustion were larger threats to their progress as they walked together on the line. As long as he wanted to survive more than he wanted to just be done, he could keep going. "A step at a time," he repeated under his breath as he lifted a foot and dragged it forward. The rope in his hand pulled and tightened periodically as the tired and jangled crew followed. They never found a rhythm together. Another step away from danger. Another toward the unknown. After maybe a mile or more of pushing against wind and snow, they had no better sight of either ship—if either were actually ahead of them and not off to one side or another. For all he knew, they could be passing between them both, never seeing either, blindly marching into nothing. Noah looked over his shoulder from time to time to make sure the rig was in the same position behind them, assuming its presence where he expected it to be meant they were on the same bearing Connor had set. As it grew smaller, his worry increased. When it finally fell out of sight, he knew if they didn't have sight of their destination ahead they would be marching blindly.

He looked again to reassure himself they hadn't strayed since his last check, maybe two minutes ago. He saw a yellow ball of fire grow and had time to say, "No, it can't . . ." before the low thunder rumbled across the plain, stealing his words.

The men stumbled and cried out.

"Jesus Christ!" Connor yelled. "There were still men there!"

"This is your fault," Mickle said, grabbing Noah by the shoulder and rearing back with a fist. Noah ducked the punch, but still stumbled backward as the ice began to tremble. It shuddered under foot and they heard distant cracking coming closer.

"Run!" Kevin shouted. Noah scrambled backward as the Twins hurried past him. Mickle stared, his face hidden behind the balaclava, but his eyes filled with rage. Nevins brushed past his shipmate, breaking the man's trance. Noah turned, and despite his fear, ran ahead of Mickle.

They fled as fast as they could, trying to outrun something that had already outpaced them. A fissure opened beside Noah and he staggered, losing his balance as it tried to swallow him. The ice pitched, time slowed, and he felt that same sense of imminent falling so painfully familiar to him now. Connor grabbed him by the elbow and yanked him away from the lip, shoving him toward the others. Before he'd taken more than a dozen steps, he felt hands on his shoulders again. Mickle yelled in his ear as he whipped him around. "*Your* fault!"

Noah staggered away. He fell, landing on his back,

and slid toward another crack opening behind him. He felt Mickle's stomping on the ice coming closer. Noah shoved with his heels, but didn't move, his boots slipping impotently on the slick surface.

Kevin hit Mickle in the side, knocking him off course. "He got us off there! He saved our lives!"

Mickle pointed at the burning platform. "He brought that down on us! It's his fault the other Brewster was on the rig. His fault the generators got shut off and the oil spilled. It's all his god damn fault my friends are dead. And now I'm going to kill him!" He looked from Noah to Jack and Kevin. "You all did this. Every last one of you!"

Jack grabbed Mickle's arm and twisted him around, trying to draw his focus away from the platform and Noah. Kevin took hold of his other arm, but the second officer broke free of his grip and whipped Jack into him. The Twins fell together in a tangle on the ice. Mickle ran over to them, grabbed Jack by his belt and dragged him over the side of a fissure, dropping the man into the water below.

Kevin screamed, scrambling for the edge. He reached into the fissure for his brother, but Jack was gone. Kevin rolled onto his back and howled at the indifferent sky. The sound was the worst thing Noah had ever heard.

Connor shoved Mickle away a second before he could throw Kevin in after his friend. "What are you doing?" he cried out. Mickle had no answer. He swung wildly at Connor, landing a fist on the side of his neck. Connor staggered back, clutching his neck with a hand as his shoulder cramped up.

"You helped them!"

"You've *lost* it, Sean," Nevins said. "It's *not* their fault." He grabbed Noah's arm and tried to help him up, but let out an explosive whoof of air and fell limp before he could get Noah to his feet. A crack sounded as he crumpled. Nevins collapsed on Noah's legs, pinning him. Noah pulled himself out from under the man and pushed him onto his back. "Marty, what's wrong?" Snow stuck in a clump on the front of his survival suit. A dark spot appeared and grew until all the snow on his chest went dark. Beneath him, a stain of black blood spread like a gently unfolding wing.

"What—" Mickle started to say. Kevin had a hold of him, punching and dragging him toward the edge of the crack in the ice.

"You killed Jack!" Kevin's voice was shrill. He'd come undone.

There was a faint pop and a light bloomed in the sky, hovering above them for a gentle second before beginning to slowly fall. Another distant crack followed.

"It's a flare! He's lighting us up with flares." Noah pointed at the light above, trying to track it down to its source. If there was a launch trail, he couldn't see it in the dark.

"Who?"

"Brewster!" He looked for the Old Man in the distance, but couldn't see anyone beyond their team. Except, they were no longer a team. Jack was gone and Marty lay dead at his feet. Kevin and Mickle fought, and Connor stood paralyzed in the light of the flare. Behind them all, in the distance, the platform burned. Noah moved in to pry Kevin and Mickle apart, but the rig exploded again in an even bigger ball of flame and the thunder that followed was louder and sent more vibrations through the ice. Though it was far off, Noah backed away.

He heard another crack and a cloud of red mist erupted from Kevin's shoulder. He screamed and twisted to get away. His arm hung, bleeding and ruined, but Mickle held on. Connor screamed for them to run; no one but Noah seemed to hear.

Noah turned to flee and saw it. In the light of the flare, he could make out the distant distortion in the icescape. Connor's ship was maybe a half mile away. It had tilted up more than before, and without power, it wouldn't provide them any lasting refuge. It was only good as a landmark, a sign that they hadn't wandered astray. Noah scanned the horizon, searching for his *Promise*. "There!" He pointed.

Connor screamed again. "Don't stand there. Run!" Noah looked back in time to see a flash of white like a pulsing star. A muzzle flash. It was far off, but not as distant as he would have hoped. The crack of the rifle echoed across the night and he felt the bullet tear across his cheek. He flinched and pawed at his mask, fingers searching for where the bullet had grazed him. Although he felt nothing through his gloves, his fingers came away bloody.

Mickle and Kevin disappeared into the fissure.

Connor grabbed Noah and yelled a final time at him to run. Far off, the burning Niflheim tilted and crashed. The world pitched beneath their feet and rumbled again. Along with it, a new sound howled in the dark from another direction. Noah turned to look. Connor's ship shuddered in the distance, pitching upward, its bow pointing increasingly toward the sky as it slipped backward into the ice and the sea below. The rig explosion had freed the ship from the ice that nipped it. He could feel the vibrations of the PSV sinking as the frozen surface beneath his feet rumbled and heaved. The void was claiming it, just as it would claim them all if they didn't run.

He turned and fled into the night behind Connor, moving as quickly as the snow and shifting ice would allow. The flare behind them extinguished and the distant light of his ship seemed a little brighter. "This way," he shouted, redirecting Connor toward their goal. It was more than a mile away. A piece of him felt certain he would fall long before he ever reached the ship. Even if he didn't slip into a fissure or collapse in exhaustion, he couldn't outrun a bullet.

Noah ran, hoping his terror would give him the endurance he needed to outpace Brewster's madness.

36

By the time Noah could read the name painted on the bow of his ship, his legs didn't just burn, they were threatening to crumple beneath him. His hips and back hurt and he tripped and stumbled as often as he stepped surefooted. He could barely take a breath. Despite his protective gear, the frigid air infected every inch of his body, inside and out, with suffering. He had no idea how far they had run, but he knew he wouldn't have made it without Connor. When he fell, his friend stopped and picked him up.

The fast rescue craft that had borne them down the day before had been raised back into place. Noah tried to call out, but the breathless cry died in his throat. He grabbed Connor and dragged him around to the port side of the ship, putting the vessel in between them and their pursuer. Though the shooting had stopped with the bullet that tore a trench in Noah's face, he hadn't counted the shots. Even if he had, Noah had no idea how many rounds the rifle even held. All he knew for certain was if Brewster still had bullets to shoot, they couldn't penetrate the *Promise*.

He pounded on the hull with a fist and tried shouting again. His gloved hand made no more sound than his weak cries. He looked around for something to improvise as a knocker, but there was nothing to pick up. Everything they'd used to break the ice days earlier, they had taken aboard at the end of the work. And everything they'd taken with them to the Niflheim was now gone forever.

His eye came to rest on three dark lumps in the snow near the Rescue Zone. He lumbered toward them, hoping to find a forgotten stash of tools, but stopped short when he saw they were human sized, laid side by side in a row of snow-dusted graves. He dropped to his knees beside one and brushed it off, revealing a body in a canvas shroud. Fallen shipmates wrapped and left outside for the ice to preserve. He counted three, and while he wanted to uncover faces and know their names, doing so wouldn't get him inside and out of danger. He knew Brewster was still behind them, getting closer, if only because it was too much to ask that the Old Man had fallen into the void with Mickle and the others. Noah assumed one of the bodies belonged to Felix Pereira and another, Sean Mickle. The identity of the last dead man would have to wait.

Standing, he approached the Rescue Zone. The bottom rail of the safety gate was perhaps twelve feet above him. It was too high and the side of the ship too smooth to climb. He looked at Connor and said, "I think I have enough energy left to give you a boost. Think you can pull yourself up?"

Connor shook his head and bent over, making a stirrup with his hands. "You're in better shape than I am." Noah looked unconvinced. Connor added, "Plus, those men up there know you." Noah couldn't argue with that. He had no intention of leaving Connor behind for even a few minutes, but it was better his remaining shipmates see a familiar face first.

Lifting a weary leg, he placed his foot in Connor's hands and tried to find the will to put some spring in his standing leg. "You sure?" Connor nodded. He counted three, and pushed off as Connor straightened his back and sent him up. Noah reached for the approaching rail, knowing this was his only shot. If he missed, or his fingers slipped, they would have to find another way. Another way before death closed the distance. Time slowed as he rose, the rail growing closer, his heart seeming to stop. His ascent slowed, and soon would turn to descent and failure. He wrapped his fingers around the steel pole as his body regained its weight. Gravity pulled, the wind pushed, the entire world conspiring against him. He held on.

The single pull-up was harder than anything he'd attempted since setting out. More difficult than loading freight or bashing at the gunwales with a sledge, and definitely harder than running a five-K in the snow, because if he failed at this, there would be no fight left in him, body or mind. And that would be the end of it all.

He swung a leg over the lip of the hull and hooked the inside of his elbow in the rail. He hung there for a second, catching his breath and trying to find the energy to pull the rest of himself aboard. Before he found that inner reserve of strength, a pair of hands grasped his arm. He cried out, afraid they were going to wrench him free of the gate and drop him. But then he heard John Boduf cry out, "They're back. Somebody help me." Boduf leaned over the rail, grabbed a handful of

Noah's immersion suit, and pulled. Once Noah was aboard, he set to unfastening the straps holding the net ladder in place.

Boduf rattled off a series of questions without waiting for answers. "Is that you, Cabot? What the fuck happened to your face? There are only *two* of you?"

Noah said, "Shut up and help me."

The deckhand pulled back the gate while Noah pushed the net over. It rolled down, thumping heavily against the hull. He was afraid he wouldn't have the energy to pull it up again when they were through. And they couldn't leave it down. Connor climbed slowly. The cumulative effects of their flight across the plain and boosting Noah to the rail appeared to have robbed him of the last of his energy. When he was close enough, Boduf and Noah grabbed hold of him and pulled him the rest of the way. He rolled over on his back on the deck, clutching his head. "Permission to come aboard," he said, gasping.

Noah got down and started to pull up the net. "Help me with this," he said.

"What if someone else makes it? There's gotta be more than just you two."

There is, he thought. "You have to trust me. You don't want what's after us getting on the ship."

"After you?"

Having shipped out with Boduf three times, Noah had never seen him move as quickly as he did that minute. Boduf rattled off more questions that passed through Noah's mind, unheard, as they worked. They got the ladder up on the deck, but didn't bother rolling or lashing it, leaving it piled in a heap. Noah slammed the gate shut, figuring that should be enough. Brewster couldn't jump high enough on his own, and had no one to give him a boost. He was stuck outside. That suited Noah perfectly. Once upon a time, he had tried to think of Brewster as family, tried to love him for being the father of the woman who had meant so much to him. He had tried, and every time he had been pushed away. He'd never wanted to kill anyone in his life. Not before. And he wasn't sure, even with the present desire, he could do it. Noah felt sure he could let Brewster die of exposure and hypothermia, however. That seemed easy enough.

He pulled Connor upright. His feet and fingers were numb again and he wondered how many times he could freeze himself to the marrow like this before the cumulative effects left him with stumps. His lungs hurt, and since they'd had a moment to catch a breath, he had a growing headache. He understood too well why Connor held his skull in his hands. "C'mon. Let's get inside." Wrapping Connor's arm around his shoulder, he gestured for Boduf to take the other and help. He asked the deckhand, "Who's in charge now?"

Boduf groaned with the effort of shouldering Connor's weight as they stood together. "If there ain't any officers with you, nobody is."

"Is Mickle down there?" Noah nodded toward the gate.

Boduf grunted an uh huh. "Him, Felix, and Delgado."

"David?" Noah understood what had happened to the first two, or at least he wasn't surprised. He'd already suspected they were dead when he saw their mirror selves on the rig walking around in better shape than he'd seen anyone since the storm. But that final name was a surprise. "How did he die?"

"We better go inside. You can ask Nevins. He's up in the wheelhouse. I guess he's as close as we got to an officer now."

Marty Nevins nearly jumped out of the command chair to greet Noah. Flinging the binoculars hanging on a strap around his neck out of the way, he embraced him tightly. "Good Christ, it's nice to see you." As they parted, he jerked a thumb over his shoulder. "What the holy hell is going on out there, man? What the fuck was that just blew up?"

Noah pulled his gloves and hat off and pushed his greasy hair away from his eyes. Over Nevins' shoulder, he could see the small, flickering smear of orange that was the Niflheim floating in the window like a ghostly flame without a candle. "It's a real long story," he said, knowing he would have to tell it, no matter how much he wanted to push down his recollections of the last two days—even the last several hours. "It was the rig."

Nevins' head whipped around to look and he ran back to the windows, fumbling to get the binoculars off his back and in front of his eyes again. "The Niflheim blew up? Where's everybody else?"

"Some of us made it off, but then . . ." He thought of the reflected Nevins bleeding out on his lap in the snow and the others disappearing into the black water. "Only two of us made it back."

Nevins' head dropped. "Shit. That's it? You and who else?"

"That's the thing," Noah began. He stepped back to

open the door, gesturing for Connor to follow him in. "You have to see for yourself for it to make sense."

Nevins lowered the binocs and looked over his shoulder at Noah. "Don't be cryptic, man. Just tell me who." He looked confused as he tried to suss out the identity of the thin, unkempt man standing in the doorway. A look of astonishment and fear grew on his face. "What the *fuck*," he whispered.

"I'll explain everything, Marty, but everyone should hear it at the same time. I don't want to tell it twice. We need to round up the crew in the forward day room."

"Jesus, man. Not even the Old Man made it?" When Noah didn't say anything in reply, Nevins sighed. Noah hated to tell him it was worse than he was imagining. Nevins pushed up from the chair. "I'll make the announcement, but . . . we've had trouble here, too. Not everyone can meet."

"I saw, outside. Felix, Sean . . ." Saying Mickle's name brought up a mixed bag of emotions. He was still trying to reconcile the Sean Mickle who had been Noah's ally before they left, and the one who'd almost killed him on the way back. "And David Delgado, John tells me. Did he get sick, too?"

Nevins winced. His face flushed red and he gritted his teeth as he backed up to sit in the command chair. "Felix died the same day you guys split. Mickle went in his sleep the next morning. And then . . . motherfuckin' Theo got in a fight with Delgado over some bullshit and shoved him down a ladder. David broke his neck at the bottom. We locked Mesires up in his cabin. Everyone else can muster."

"God damn it!" Noah raised a fist to pound on the communications panel.

Nevins yelled, thrusting his hands out, "Be careful! It's working again."

Noah thought he hadn't heard right and paused a moment with his arm raised, trying to parse the words. "You fixed it?"

"No. It's just working again. When we saw the rig blow, I ran up here to get Brewster's binocs for a better look. The radio was crackling and making noise."

Noah's mind flashed on the other *Arctic Promise* pitching up and sinking into the ice. At that moment, it had filled him with enough panic to run all the way to his own ship, adrenaline and dread providing the fuel. But sinking that ship was what he and Connor had talked about and hoped for. Scuttle one vessel, and hope the other will heal itself, just like the men. Everything here needed its sacrifice—needed to be the only thing like itself. He didn't understand it, but however it worked, it did. There wasn't any more time to ponder it. The time for theorizing and planning had long passed. Now they had to act to secure their rescue.

"Have you tried calling anyone yet?" Noah asked.

Marty looked at him like he was stupid. "I sent out an S.O.S. the minute I saw it working but no one's responded. I've been up here keeping watch, retransmitting the signal."

"I guess you should stay at the conn to answer the call, then."

"Tell me what happened first."

Noah began with the fissure that claimed the first Holden and his race to get him to the other ship. Connor took over, explaining how his ship had become beset and its crew decamped to the rig. Nevins shook his head through the entire story as if he couldn't believe what he was hearing, but had no choice. Looking at Connor standing there, listening to him speak, was a kind of confirmation of every unimaginable thing. Noah kept an eye on the flame in the window. Beyond that, he couldn't see a thing outside.

He started to recount their first meeting with the mirror crew when the outside door of the compartment opened and John Boduf pushed through, a gust of freezing wind and blowing snow intruding behind him. "Guys! Guys! You'll never believe who I found on the weather deck. He climbed up by hims—"

The shot that cut him down was deafening.

37

The room erupted in a muted, incomprehensible mess of muddied shouts and screams. Noah watched John Boduf go down like a felled tree; lock-kneed and stiff, he toppled straight over. Behind him, Brewster stood in a white maelstrom, looking like an elemental force. Gray beard caked with ice and skin paled by frost, nose and cheeks blackened with frostbite, he was the viciousness of winter given flesh. Grimacing, he raised his pistol again.

Noah lurched to make a grab for Nevins, but the mechanic was out of reach, having retreated between the command chair and the curved console table. Noah shouted for him to get away. His warning sounded like it came from someone standing behind him, uttered by a person half hidden in another reality.

The Old Man fired again. A flash of fire and smoke erupted from the end of the gun barrel. Noah felt the round hit the wall behind him more than he heard it and skidded to a stop. Marty made a lunge for Brewster. The Old Man turned. A bullet hit the man squarely in the chest. Marty's body fell next to Boduf's, adding to the growing pool of blood spreading out from the ship's master's feet.

"That wasn't nice of you to leave me out there with no way to get on board, Noah. The other fellas outside were kind enough to give me a boost, though. Even a dead man is more useful than you." Brewster's grimace grew wider into a smile that said all anyone needed to know about madness.

He took steady aim and squeezed the trigger. Connor shoved in front of Noah and Brewster jerked his hand upward, sending the bullet into the overhead. "Out of the way, Connor! I still need you."

"Stop this!" Connor yelled. "Everything is getting better now the other ship is gone. The machines are working again. See?" He pointed to the communication array. "It's working. No one else has to die!"

"No?" he said, pointing a gnarled finger at Noah. "He was supposed to die on that deck a year ago. Not you. I'm setting the world to rights. The way I intended!"

Noah froze, not sure he heard the words through the ringing in his ears, but painfully certain he'd understood them exactly as they'd been uttered. The Old Man set him up a year ago. If Noah hadn't asked Connor to cover for him, he'd have fallen into the trap instead and their separate realities would have turned out the same.

It made sense. The night Connor died, Noah had gone to Brewster's cabin to argue about Abby. He'd wanted to ask one last time for his father-in-law's understanding and for him to forgive his daughter, knowing fully he'd never receive that forgiveness himself. Brewster had been furious and tried to force him to leave. "*Do what I ordered you to. Get out there and check the lashings, god damn it.*" Noah told him the lashings were fine. "*Connor's checking them so we can have this conversation now.*" Brewster wanted out of his cabin, out of that fight, as badly as Noah had ever seen him want anything. But he hadn't let the Old Man loose. He cornered him and said his piece, digging the knife in when it was clear Brewster wasn't ever going to listen to him. He shamed him for not coming to say good-bye to his girl, and if he felt any lasting regret guilt over that, well, he'd earned it.

He *deserved* it.

Noah had misinterpreted the look on Brewster's face in that instant so long ago. What Noah took as regret over Abby's death was actually worry he might have just killed the wrong man. Which he *had* done.

"Out of the way, MacAllister," Brewster said. "Let me kill him so we can go home."

Connor stood still, wide eyes staring into the black bore of the Old Man's gun. He raised his hands, silently imploring him once more to stop. "The radio is *working,*" he repeated. "Nevins called for help and they're already coming for us. We *are* going home."

Brewster's expression softened. He knitted his brow and his blistered lips turned down. They cracked, glistening with blood when he spoke. "No. That's wrong. They can't come for him. They have to come for *you.*" His gun arm dropped a little.

"We can't pick, William. They're already on their way. The choice has been made and we're gonna get whatever we do when they get here."

The Old Man's shoulders rounded as his back slumped and he dropped his gaze into the middle distance, staring somewhere outside the room, but still close, like he was trying to look into the world he wanted to inhabit instead of the one he actually did. "Maybe we can't choose," he said. "But I still want to even the odds." He straightened up, raised his gun, and stepped to the side, taking aim for a better shot. Connor tried to match his step, keeping in between him and his target, but the feint was meant to draw Noah's human shield away. Brewster pivoted quickly in the opposite direction and fired.

The round took a piece of Noah's ear opposite the trench already in his cheek before embedding in the wall behind him. Noah clapped his hand to the side of his head in astonishment at the second close call he'd received from one of Brewster's bullets. It seemed absurd to think his father-in-law's desire to put a bullet in his head was lucky, but it was. Brewster had shot other men in the chest, but something—luck, or more likely, pure hatred—kept his aim on Noah's head instead of a larger target. Noah was thankful for Brewster's impulsivity. It would only be so long before the Old Man would get a real bead on him, though. Once he realized a bullet in the guts would give him a leisurely opportunity to press the gun against Noah's face and really savor the moment, it was all over.

Noah screamed something, but wasn't sure if the words made sense or if he only tried to say them and what came out instead was a terrified babble. He yanked at Connor's coat, pulling him out of the line of fire and shoving him toward the door, hoping as he did that, Connor wouldn't tumble down and break his neck on the landing below like Delgado. Connor came alive at the pull of gravity and half staggered, half leaped down the ladder to land flat-footed on the deck below. His knees buckled and he took a few hard steps, but he stayed on his feet. Noah was right behind him, slamming the wheelhouse door closed as Brewster rushed for the opening. The locks were on the other side and he couldn't dog it down, but Noah spun the wheel, securing the hatch and slowing Brewster's pursuit for a second or two at least.

Though his body had found yet another reserve of temporary energy, Noah felt slower than ever. He was weary of running. Still, he lumbered along the passageway, pushing his friend ahead of him, doing his best to be a moving target, even if he wasn't one that moved very fast. "Lay below," he shouted. "Go!" Connor staggered along the passageway toward the next ladder.

Force of habit made Noah slow as he passed sick bay. He could hear Brewster behind him spinning the hatch wheel and pulling the heavy door open. Even though there might be something useful in the hospital, there was no time to look for whatever that might be. Death was seconds away. He ran on, turning the corner past the change room as footsteps pounded down the steps behind. He skidded around the next bend and leaped down the ladder to A-Deck, pulling another waterproof hatch closed after him.

He was halfway around to the next ladder when he caught a flash of movement out of the corner of his eye. *Not the shades,* he thought. *Not now.* He flinched as one separated itself from the shadows, and despite wanting to press on, turned to confront it, even though he knew the figure would be gone before he could lock eyes on it.

It wasn't a shade, however. Andrew Puck stood in

the doorway to the main passageway, shouting questions. "What's going on? Was that *shooting*?"

Noah told the deckhand to get to his quarters. "Lock yourself in and don't come out."

"The fuck happened to you, Cabot?" Puck looked at Connor. "And who are you? What the hell is going on?"

Noah tried to grab Puck by the arm to pull him along. "There's no time for bullshit. Come on!" Another shade passed in the periphery of his vision, making his step falter. The darkness materialized into Heath running for the ladder Noah had just come down. The shades had been a premonition, the dark movements playing out their last moments out of the corners of their eyes in eternal recurrence—the end in the beginning. They would all suffer the fate of shadows in the dark. Forever.

Puck took advantage of Noah's distraction and slammed him into the wall. "Get your fuckin' hands off me, Cabot." He fell in behind Heath and the two disappeared down the passageway.

Noah started after them but Connor grabbed his arms, holding him back. "They won't listen," he said. Noah watched the pair disappear up the ladder, knowing he couldn't stop them. They would have to see Brewster for themselves. And when they did, they would give Noah and Connor a few seconds more at least. Slowing him down was the best they could hope for.

"Let's get safe. Come up with a plan," Connor said.

"No more plans. There's nowhere left to run." A pair of gunshots echoed in the passageway. Noah ran to the end of the compartment and grabbed the handle of a red fire ax affixed to the wall. He yanked, but the salt and moisture in the air had conspired to rust the metal band holding the head in place and the tool stuck. He shouted in frustration, pulling harder. It gave some, wiggling on the mount, but still wouldn't come free. "God damn it!" He stepped back and kicked at the u-shaped bracket holding the handle in place until it bent far enough out of the way for him to get a surer grip. He pulled it out like a lever. The bolts holding it in place popped and the ax head snapped the wide bracket off the wall. Fumbling with its unexpected weight, the head dropped, clattering on the floor between his feet.

Fixing his grip, he hefted the thing, feeling its weight, its balance. He finally had his ax. Although designed to rescue souls, it would take a life as easily, if put to it. It was power and lethality in his hands. All it needed was intent. And Noah had that. Still, it wouldn't stop bullets.

"Get below," Noah said. "Get somewhere safe. You know the ship."

"You can't."

He bounced the ax in his hands, testing its weight. "Sure I can," he said, and ran to confront his father-in-law.

Noah found Puck and Heath slumped against a wall at the top of the landing, but no sign of his quarry. Heath was panting shallowly, clutching his wet stomach. Puck slumped over, leaking from an eye onto the floor. *He must have run right into Brewster,* Noah thought. He crouched in front of Heath and asked,

"Which way?" Puck pointed toward the far ladder. He coughed, dropping his hand and squinting tightly against the pain. A long line of red saliva slid over his slack lip. Noah caught a hint of a smell from the man's wound that told him no matter what he did to help, Puck was done. Noah left him and ran for the command compartment.

Frigid wind buffeted the room as he pushed through the door. The opposite exit leading outside stood open. Noah gave the cooling bodies in the center of the room as wide a berth as he was able. Still, he found himself stepping in their blood. Trying not to look as he navigated past them, he was unable to help it. He peered down at Nevins and Boduf. Every dead body was another step toward Brewster's goal of being reunited with his daughter. Noah felt a sharp tinge of guilt. A small nagging voice in the back of his mind that accused him of not stopping the Old Man because he wasn't entirely opposed to the plan. Returning to Connor's world instead of his own meant he could have it all. It meant having Abby *and* Ellie. It meant the life he was supposed to have before everything went wrong and he lost the people he loved the most.

The little voice poisoned his mind, telling him he was a collaborator and conspirator in the sacrifice of men with their own lives, their own families and friends who would miss them and mourn. He was complicit in all this wrong. And it was too late to undo any of it.

A blast of wind rocked him, breaking the spell. He crept toward the opening, uncertain if Brewster was hiding behind the door, or had already lay below, rushing to flank him and finish what he started. Noah stalked out of the compartment and into the night.

The wind hit him hard, pushing him off balance and making his descent unsteady on the slick steps. His bare hands instantly hurt in the blast; he gripped the ax tighter, trying to focus on the feeling of the implement in his grasp. He refused to let go of his weapon to use the rail despite his unsure footing. As cold as the handrail was likely to be, he was better off taking his time and possibly falling than using it. At the very least, he'd leave the skin of his palm behind if he grabbed it. He paused, steadying himself before continuing down, careful not to do Brewster's work for him by slipping and impaling himself on the pick end of the ax.

When he reached the first door to A-Deck, he pulled his sleeve down over his hand before trying the handle. The metal still stung. Worse, the door was locked. He glanced at his feet and back the way he had come, searching in the light dusting of snow on the weather deck for footprints other than his own. There were none. The wind was blowing even his tracks away. If Brewster had been this way, he couldn't tell. And he couldn't afford to spend more time trying to guess. He had to get inside before his numbing hands froze entirely and he couldn't fight.

He proceeded on along the length of the deck toward the next door. If that one was locked, he'd have to return to the wheelhouse, leaving him so far behind Brewster, he might as well sit down and wait for the end. He tried the handle. Relief loosened his tense muscles as it clicked and turned freely. He felt the heavy steel door swing free and thought, *I can still get ahead of him.*

A shade burst through the opening at him. No. Not a shade—William Brewster. The man who had slaughtered two dozen others by knife and gun and fire, bellowing with berserk rage, coming to finally kill Noah, too.

The ax handle shoved into Noah's gut as Brewster propelled him backward against the rail. The hard barrier behind him sent all-too familiar pain shooting through his body while the handle pushed the air out of his lungs in a vapory breath. But he didn't let go. Unlike the night he'd fought with the shade, Jack and Kevin weren't here to catch him this time. There was no one to stop him from going over the edge. The ax was all he had to hold on to.

Brewster's breath billowed out of his mouth in a stinking cloud as he howled his inarticulate aggression into the darkness. He shoved and fought with one hand gripping Noah's jacket, the other raising the gun to his face. Its dark hole turned on Noah like a dead third eye about to blossom with the brilliant light of extinction. Noah shoved upward, driving the pick of his weapon into Brewster's elbow. The gun fired. Noah's left ear went dead. It didn't even ring. He felt the heat of the gas flash and burning powder residue searing his face. But the bullet flew into the void instead of shattering his skull.

He jerked the ax up into Brewster's elbow a second time before pushing him away with the handle, trying to create some distance between them. Brewster held on with his left, but his weapon hand sprang open, dropping the pistol over the side. He roared again, baring bloody and crooked teeth, and lunged at Noah's neck. Noah flinched and shrugged his shoulder to protect his jugular. He hit Brewster in the stomach with the ax handle and felt the man's jaws loosen. He shoved as hard as he could, using the rail behind him for leverage. He felt Brewster's jaws open. The Old Man staggered away, his feet slipping on the frozen deck. His eyes rolled and he lurched forward again.

Noah sidestepped and Brewster slammed into the rail. He turned, ready to lash out, but the ax blade stilled him as it buried itself deep into his chest. Noah tried to pry the weapon out for another swing, but Brewster gripped it tightly. His eyes calmed and he looked for an instant like the man Noah had tried so hard to love for his wife's sake. He looked like a man who did the best he could for his family and was protective of his only daughter because she was the star he needed to steer home on unquiet seas. He was the William Brewster who wanted the best for his child and regretted losing her to adulthood, where he could no longer shelter her from all the pains of the world. And all he wanted was to see her a last time.

A long breath drifted from his mouth and was blown away by the wind. Noah let go of the handle and Brewster tipped backward over the side, plummeting to the ice below. Noah heard the fleshy thud and crack of bone with his good ear. He shrank back from the rail. He was a single father of a daughter. How would he behave when she grew up and fell in love and left him to grow old alone while she lived the best years of her life with someone else? Would he be a better man? Would he take Brewster's lesson and be the father she deserved, no matter how painful that would be? Could he do it alone?

Warmth crept down his neck and turned to chilling cold. He staggered toward the door. Toward shelter. He had to get out of the night. At the door, he cast one last glance over his shoulder. The distant candlelight flame of the Niflheim had died and gone dark. The *Arctic Promise* sat in a black void in which not even the stars shone anymore.

He let himself inside and locked the door behind him.

38

Connor stood in the doorway to a crew cabin on B-Deck. Although he'd always been fair-skinned, he had gone ghostly pale. Noah gently pulled him away from the door and peered in. In the far corner, Theo hung from a belt looped around his neck. It was fastened to a bar meant to keep his things from sliding off the high shelf above the desk. A sign pinned to his shirt read in shaky letters, *I'm so sorry.*

"We're all mad here," Noah whispered. He pulled the door closed.

He thought he heard Connor say something in reply, but the man was standing on what Noah was already starting to think of as his "dead side." He neither felt nor heard anything on that side of his body. He turned his good ear—although "good" was an overstatement as it was missing a piece from yet another near miss—to Connor and said, "Come again?"

"Is it over?"

Noah shook his head. "The Old Man's gone. But we're still stranded." He took a step and paused. "Are we the only ones left?"

Connor sighed. "Yeah. We're it."

"We should see about the radio." Noah wandered off.

Although they had a wider range of view from the wheelhouse, Noah and Connor retreated to the forward day room two decks below. They'd moved Nevins' and Boduf's bodies outside where they would be better preserved, but the blood in the command compartment was drying and tacky underfoot and the room smelled like wet copper and gun smoke. Noah couldn't bear to keep watch from there. He hailed the Coast Guard and set the silent beacon. He checked it three more times to make sure it was sending its signal to the satellites or wherever. Then he fled downstairs.

He sat in the day room chair where he'd last seen Sean Mickle talking about plans and risk and getting everyone home safely. His friend, Sean Mickle. Dead. Like all the others. For what? For a madman possessed by regret and guilt and hate to have a second chance? Did it matter why anything had happened? Noah was pretty sure it didn't. No matter how he thought of it, men who should be alive had been sacrificed for nothing.

Connor took the seat opposite and offered to take the first watch. Noah said, "I'm exhausted, but I don't think I can sleep. I'd rather stay up and keep watch, for a while anyway."

Connor nodded his agreement and pulled the chess table near. "Something to make it go faster then."

"I'll drink to that." Noah opened the bottle of J&B

he'd taken from Nevins' room and took a long pull off of it. He offered it to his friend.

Connor took it and tilted the bottle back, closing his eyes as he drank. When he finished, he wiped his mouth with his sleeve and said, "Thirty men died for us to sit here."

"Thirty died, or fifteen men died twice. Which is worse?"

"I don't know."

"Neither do I." Noah stared at the window. A reflection of him and Connor sat in the black glass looking back. The sight of his reflection sent chills up Noah's spine. "Do you think Brewster was right?" he asked.

Connor leaned back, a look of concern on his face. "Fuck no. There was nothing right about that man."

"No, I mean about being able to choose. About the odds of which world we go to being better now that there's only two of us."

"Don't even think about it, brother."

Noah took another drink, then reached over and pulled the photo of his wife and daughter out of his pocket. When he went to get the bottle, he'd gone to pick that up as well. He didn't care about losing the rest of his things, but not this. Not this copy. Never again. "Would it be so wrong to choose your reality or plane or whatever? Abby's alive, we have Ellie, and you're there with Sheila. Everything that's wrong about my world could be right in yours."

"But there's only one of you."

Noah said, "So?"

"So, in my world, Ellie has Abby to take care of her. They miss you, but they're makin' it work, you know? Together. If you decide to be with them, then what happens to *your* Ellie? The one you promised to come home to. She has no one left. It ain't fair to her."

Noah sat and thought about that for a long time. Connor didn't press the issue. Instead, he made a move on the chessboard and had another drink while Noah worked it out.

Connor was right but it took all night and almost all the bottle for Noah to accept it. He'd told his daughter he'd be back. This was his last job out to sea and then the two of them would go home to Massachusetts. He'd find something else to do and never leave her alone again. He'd promised to be there as long as she needed him.

In the distance, a long red line of light appeared behind the horizon. The sunrise. Along with it, a pinprick of white that grew larger as it approached. Their ride home.

The Coast Guard copilot shook her head and shouted over the *whup whup* of the rotor blades as the helicopter idled on the ice. The pilot kept glancing over his shoulder, looking nervous and ready to lift off as soon as he felt any shift, no matter how slight, in the surface beneath him. "No way! This isn't a taxi; it's a rescue. My orders are to pick up *all* survivors and take them back. I can't make two trips unless there are too many crewmen to make it safely in one." She pointed an authoritative finger toward the door to the copter and demanded they board.

"But what about—" Noah tried to argue, but the copilot pointed again, this time with more force.

"Climb aboard yourself or I will *put* you on that bird," she said. She wasn't armed, but he believed she could make him board anyway.

Connor shrugged and climbed in. He extended a hand and helped Noah in after him. Noah held his arms out of the way while the copilot secured his harness like a child in a car seat. He stared out the opening and squinted, trying to see as far as he could in the daylight. He thought maybe he could see the smoke from the Niflheim. Maybe not. It was hard to tell with the rising fog.

As the copilot strapped Connor in, Noah shouted a question at her. She shook her head and tapped the side of her helmet. She plucked a pair of clamshell headsets off a hook and dropped them on the bench beside him. Noah fitted one over his ears while she finished securing Connor's harness. He clicked the switch on the side and a burst of static erupted in his right ear. He thought for a second his left clamshell was malfunctioning before he remembered. Dead side.

"Are we going to fly over the Niflheim on the way?" he asked, adjusting the mic.

"The drilling platform? Are you fuckin' kidding me?"

He shook his head. He wanted to see it. Make sure there was nothing left of either it or the other *Arctic Promise*.

"Even if I wanted to take you to see that environmental garbage heap, it's two hundred miles west of here. A little out of the way for a flyby."

"Two hundred miles? *West?*"

"Yeah! This bird is out of Prudhoe Bay not Barrow. You guys *really* don't know where you are?"

"This isn't the Chukchi Sea?"

The copilot laughed. But there was no humor in it. Only contempt. "Fuckin' oil boys. You ever see ice like this in the Chukchi?"

"We gotta get out of here. Fog's coming in," the pilot announced over the radio.

The copilot said, "Copy that. We're ready." Without another word of instruction or disdain for the PSV crewmen, she jumped out, slammed the door, and hustled to the front of the chopper. Climbing in to take her place beside the pilot, Noah could see her jerking a thumb over her shoulder and saying something animatedly. He couldn't hear them anymore. She'd changed channels.

He got that queasy feeling in his stomach as the blades spun up faster and the copter lifted off the ice. He had never flown in a helicopter before. He soon discovered he hated it worse than flying in a plane. He gritted his teeth and held on to his seat with white knuckles.

They rose into the air, tilting and wavering as the pilot set their course and corrected against the wind. Below them, the fog drifted and he lost sight of the *Arctic Promise* before they'd even traveled a mile. He tried to focus on his photograph and not on the white void surrounding them.

"You know what, Connor?"

"What's that, buddy?"

"It's really hard. I miss her so much. I'd just like to see her healthy again. Have one more kiss."

Connor leaned forward and took the photo from his friend's hand. He looked at it and smiled sadly. He stuffed the picture inside Noah's peacoat, next to his heart, and patted it. "I hear you. But keeping promises is more important than second chances, brother."

ACKNOWLEDGMENTS

First of all, I owe a huge debt of gratitude to Christopher Golden. Without your constant support and confidence in my work, I would not be where I am today. Also, thank you Brendan Deneen, for your enthusiasm and faith in my ability to tell this story. Thank you both so much for believing in me. And thank you Alexandre Ilic for the soul of *Stranded*.

I owe special recognition to Captain Jon C. Bergner, USN (Ret.), and the late Debra Whitehead Bergner, for their technical assistance in better understanding shipboard life and nautical detail. If I got a maritime element right in this book, it is due to their help. All errors herein are mine alone.

To my influences, colleagues, and friends, Chet Williamson, John Dixon, Paul Tremblay, Jonathan Maberry, Brian Keene, Nicholas Kaufmann, Adam Cesare, Thomas Pluck, John Mantooth, James A. Moore, Errick Nunnally, Christopher Irvin, K.L. Pereira, Jan Kozlowski, Adrian Van Young, Brett Savory, Sandra Kasturi, Michael Rowe, Kasey Lansdale, Joe Lansdale, Andrew

Vachss, and Dallas Mayr, you all inspire me to work harder and be better at what I do. Thank you.

Finally, and forever, my abiding love and gratefulness go to my wife, Heather, and my son, Lucien. They fill my sails and are the ever-constant stars guiding me home.

TOR

Award-winning authors
Compelling stories

Please join us at the website
below for more information
about this author and other great
Tor selections, and to sign up for
our monthly newsletter!